The Other Side of the Wire
by Harold Coyle

© Copyright 2019 Master Wings Publishing

ISBN 978-1-63393-827-4

This is a work of fiction. The characters are both actual and fictitious. With the exception of verified historical events and persons, all incidents, descriptions, dialogue and opinions expressed are the products of the author's imagination and are not to be construed as real.

Published by

**MASTER
WINGS**
PUBLISHING

Books by Harold Coyle

Team Yankee

Sword Point

Bright Star

Trial by Fire

The Ten Thousand

Code of Honor

Look Away

Until the End

Savage Wilderness

God's Children

Dead Hand

Against All Enemies

More Than Courage

They Are Soldiers

Cat and Mouse

No Warriors, No Glory

The Eight Day

The Other Side of the Wire

No Small Thing, A Novel of the American Revolution

Novellas

Cyber Nights; Steven Coontes' Combat

Breakthrough at Bloody Ridge; Steven Coontes' Victor

Sedgwick's Charge; Martin H. Greenberg's Alternate Gettysburg

With Barrett Tillman

Pandora's Legion: Harold Coyle's Strategic Solutions, Inc

Prometheus's Child: Harold Coyle's Strategic Solutions, Inc

Vulcan's Fire: Harold Coyle's Strategic Solutions, Inc

With Jennifer K. Ellis

The Legend of Alfhildr

Cyber Knights 1.0

God Save the Queen

By Any Other Name

Ebook Transgender Fiction by H.W. Coyle

Tip

A Different Kind of Courage

Inconvenient Truths

Dance of the Baccha

No Greater Love

A Lion in Waiting

The Gambit

While the Band Played Waltzing Matilda

Grace

The World Turned Upside Down

Caitlin

THE OTHER SIDE OF THE WIRE

A NOVEL

HAROLD COYLE

MASTER WINGS PUBLISHING

TABLE OF CONTENTS

Preface IX

Part One—1935 Blood and Honor

Chapter 1: Herr Koch's Son 1

Chapter 2: Hauptsturmführer Richter 9

Chapter 3: The Bird's Nest .18

Chapter 4: *'Tomorrow Belongs to Us'* 26

Chapter 5: A Female Problem 39

Part Two—1938 'Peace in Our Time'

Chapter 6: The Sturmbannführer's Daughter 55

Chapter 7: Passata-sotto 65

Chapter 8: Mothers and Daughters 75

Chapter 9: Perfection 87

Chapter 10: The Price of Duty 94

Part Three—1940 Deutschland Über Alles

Chapter 11: About a Boy 105

Chapter 12: The Adjutant 113

Chapter 13: To the Victors .122

Part Four—1942 Sonderbehandlung

Chapter 14: The Conference .135

Chapter 15: Adieu 145

Chapter 16: "Welcome to Borkow" 154

Chapter 17: Selection 164

Part Five—1943 Arbeit Macht Frei

Chapter 18: Fräulein Richter 179

Chapter 19: Madame Delome 189

Chapter 20: The Report 196

Chapter 21: The Polish Boy 209

Part Six—1945 Götterdämmerung

Chapter 22: Settling Accounts. 223

Chapter 23: The Forest 234

Chapter 24: Rabbi Asher 244

Chapter 25: The Russians are Coming. 251

Chapter 26: Fifty-seven DPs 260

Epilogue 268

SS Ranks and their US / UK Equivalent 272

Glossary of Terms and Places 273

Historical Notes. 282

Acknowledgments 298

PREFACE

Witnesses of the Nuremberg trials and the trial of Adolph Eichmann in 1961 often remarked how *normal* the men and women charged with Nazi crimes were. Rather than the twisted, pathological beasts all had come to expect, most of the people involved in the planning and execution of the Holocaust who were brought to justice impressed both spectators and those prosecuting them as reasonable, intelligent men and women.

There were of course characters like the sadistic Irma Grese, known as the Beautiful Beast, who by age twenty had become the second highest ranking female guard at Auschwitz; Franz Ziereis, commandant at Mauthausen who is said to have given his ten-year-old son a rifle as a birthday present along with Jews to use as targets, and Karl Otto Koch, camp commandant of Buchenwald from 1937 to 1942. They provided the grist for Allied propaganda and captured the imaginations of Hollywood writers for generations. But most Germans who took up Hitler's call to join him in creating a new Germany were not all like them, at least not when they started down the path that would eventually lead to World War II and the Final Solution.

In 1932 the Nazis were voted into power by people who were still in the grip of a devastating worldwide depression that came on the heels of hyperinflation. Men and women of all classes, angered by the economic and political turmoil tearing their country apart and the harsh measures meted out by the Western Allies at Versailles, were desperate for a leader who would guide them out of the darkness. Hitler appeared to be the leader they prayed for, a man they could believe in. And they did, many until the bitter end.

In depicting the life of a family of a member of the SS Totenkopfverbände, or Death's-Head unit, through the eyes of an adopted child, a Jewish child, I drew upon an observation political theorist Hannah Arendt made at the 1961 trial of Adolf Eichmann while reporting for *The New Yorker.* She coined the phrase *the banality of evil* to describe Eichmann. This concept means the great evils of history are not committed by fanatics or sociopaths, but rather by ordinary people who accept that what they are doing is not only right, it is normal. Edward S. Herman, an American economist, further explained this by pointing out, "Doing terrible things in an organized and systematic way rests on *'normalization.'* This is the process whereby ugly, degrading, murderous, and unspeakable acts become routine and are accepted as the way things are done."

The families of the men who ran the concentration camps played a crucial role in this normalization. Many who made the selections, who oversaw the deaths of thousands in the camps on a daily basis either through direct execution or working them to death, found sanctuary in their families and homes. Home was a place they could go after carrying out their duties and lead a life no different than any other civil servant or soldier. Many, if not most, of the adult members of these families knew or suspected what was going on in the camps. Isle Koch actively participated in the depravities committed at Buchenwald, the camp her husband ran. But it was a topic rarely discussed at home, if at all. Some in the SS went out of their way to shield their families from what they were doing. As difficult as this may be to accept, the ability of the families of the men who perpetrated the Holocaust to delude themselves was stunning.

My story is inspired by the true life of Solomon Perel, an orphaned Jewish-German boy who fled Nazi persecution by becoming a member of the Hitler Youth. It is a story recounted in his book *I Was Hitler Youth* and depicted in the movie *Europa, Europa.* The book *Hansi: The Girl Who Loved the Swastika*, by Mari

Anne Hinschmann, recounts Hinschmann's experience in the early 1940s and provided me with the insight into what life was like for a young girl coming of age under the Nazi regime. As a young Sudeten German, Hinschmann embraced Hitler's new Germany, only to find much of what she was taught to believe in as a member of the Bund Deutscher Madel (BDM) was a lie.

Characterizations, description of events, and language used in my story will offend some. I do not set out to do so simply to be provocative or to glorify, justify, or defend what some Germans and their willing accomplices did. In telling this story, I wish to depict things as they were as best I can, rather than cover them over with an artificial veneer of political correctness. History is what history is. The ease with which the Nazi leadership seduced the German youth is a story we cannot ignore, for it is happening again in various parts of the world today. As Hitler stated in a speech on November 6, 1933, *"When an opponent declares, 'I will not come over to your side,' I calmly say, 'Your child belongs to us already. . . . What are you? You will pass on. Your descendants, however, now stand in the new camp. In a short time, they will know nothing else but this new community.'"*

To pretend otherwise is to condemn future generations to the horrors and suffering our forebears endured. That would be a crime that makes what the Nazis did all the more terrible.

Harold Coyle

PART ONE

1935

BLOOD AND HONOR

CHAPTER ONE

Herr Koch's Son

Easing back, Doctor Koch pulled the binaural tubes of his stethoscope away from his ears and took a moment to assess the girl he had been examining as she ever so gently drifted off to sleep. Only when he was satisfied she was out of danger did he allow himself a small smile before pulling the covers back over the child and turning to the girl's mother. "You've nothing to worry about, Fräu Kruger. With a little rest, your Emma will be up and about in a few days."

Having been convinced her daughter had been standing at death's door, Julia Kruger found herself unable to hold back tears of joy as she profusely thanked the physician. He was the only one she'd been able to find who wasn't at the fairgrounds like her husband Karl, drinking himself blind in one of the beer tents. Not that Julia minded. In fact, for once, she was grateful her husband wasn't there, for she had little doubt he would have never allowed this particular physician to cross the threshold of their modest flat, let alone touch his daughter.

After years of dealing with anxious parents, Koch knew it would be an exercise in futility to play down his role in the girl's recovery from what was nothing more than a minor illness. Instead, he chose to express his gratitude to Fräu Kruger for allowing him to bring his son along. "I'm sure that as a parent, you understand my reluctance to leave Hans on his own, especially at night."

The question of why the physician had felt the need to drag the nine-year-old boy out of bed in the middle of the night and bring him had never entered Julia's mind. She had been overwhelmed by her own concerns. Even if she had asked, Koch wouldn't have told her the truth. Truth was a commodity a person in his position needed to ration carefully these days. So he, like so many of his fellow Germans, had adopted the policy of creating little stories that allowed him to carry on as if all was as it should be.

"It's the housekeeper's day off," he offered by way of explanation, even though Julia had asked for none. "I so hate saddling the poor girl with the responsibility of watching Hans instead of allowing her to enjoy what little free time she has to herself." This was, of course, another lie, for the woman, a gentile like his wife, had left when she had.

None the wiser, Julia Kruger was about to reply she understood perfectly well when the phone in the foyer of the flat began ringing. Excusing herself, she left to answer it while Koch busied himself, carefully packing up his instruments and vials of medicines.

He was still doing so when Julia returned to inform him there was a woman on the phone who was desperate to speak to him. "She says it's important."

Suspecting it was about another patient, Koch excused himself, leaving Julia free to check on her younger sister, who had rushed down to Munich from Berlin that afternoon when she'd heard about Emma's illness. Julia found her in the parlor, seated in a chair across the room from Koch's son, who was engrossed in a book on German history. Stopping in the archway between the foyer and the parlor, Julia could not help but notice the way her sister kept peeking up over the magazine she was pretending to read to where the physician's son was. "He's not going to bite, you know," Julia whispered in a voice she assumed the boy could not hear.

From the moment Lena Richter had laid eyes on the boy, she had been unable to reconcile the disparity between all she'd been led to believe and what she was seeing. Hans Koch no more looked like a Jew than her own beloved husband, an officer who had recently been reassigned from Dachau to the SS Wachverband headquarters in Oranienburg.

Knowing full well what was going through her sister's mind, Julia made her way over to where Lena was seated. "He's the son of the man who saved my Emma," she whispered.

"He's still a Jew," Lena shot back.

"And?" Julia asked in a tone she used whenever she wished to challenge her sister to explain herself.

Knowing there was little point in arguing with her older sister, something she could seldom do successfully, Lena took to muttering under her breath before going back to the article she'd been attempting to read when not keeping an eye on the boy.

For his part, Hans Koch continued with his own reading, pretending as if he hadn't heard the exchange between the two women. Like his father, he'd learned it was best to ignore such comments. Only when his father entered the room did he look up from his book.

Rather than calling over to his son to join him, Koch sidled up to Julia, whom he spoke to in a whisper. "Fräu Kruger, forgiving me for imposing upon you, but would it be possible if I left Hans here with you for an hour or two?"

Before answering, Julia shot a glance at Lena who made no effort to hide her displeasure at the thought of spending any more time with either the Jewish doctor or his son. Ignoring this, Julia turned back to Koch, doing her best to muster up a smile to hide her true feelings, but failing miserably. "That won't be a problem, Herr Koch."

Despite knowing she was lying, Koch returned Julia's smile and thanked her before going over to where his son had been intently watching their exchange. "I've another patient I need to see," Koch declared, doing his best to mask his apprehensions. "While I am gone, you are to remain here with Fräu Kruger. You are to behave and honor any request she asks of you without hesitation or complaint. Do you understand?"

Hans understood. He understood far better than his father suspected. "Yes, Father, I do."

For a long, tense moment Koch stared down in the pale blue eyes of his son, eyes that reminded him of his mother's. Unable to endure the cold, loveless manner with which the boy was returning his gaze any longer, Koch turned and left the room without another word.

When Julia returned after seeing Koch out, Lena came to her feet. "I've a long day ahead of me tomorrow," she announced crisply. "So goodnight."

Not knowing what else to do at the moment, other than pray the doctor returned and took his son home before her husband came staggering in, Julia told the boy to make himself comfortable. Then, without waiting for him to acknowledge her, she too turned and left the room, leaving Hans free to continue his reading, losing himself as he so often did in the myths and legends of a Germany he longed to be a part of.

❋

"Who's the boy?" Erick Kruger groused while looking up from his breakfast to where his wife was doing her best to keep busy.

After waking to find the physician's son curled up and asleep on the sofa in the flat's parlor, Julia had hurriedly fabricated a credible story in her head to explain his presence to her husband. "He's a friend of Emma. He was worried about her."

Not satisfied with his wife's answer, Fritz Kruger grunted. "Doesn't the boy have a home?"

"He does, but no one was there last night." Then, by way of giving her husband a rebuke, Julia glanced over at him out of the corner of her eye. "No doubt they were at the fest like the rest of the city, doing their best to drink the place dry."

Suffering from a hangover and a lack of sleep, Fritz Kruger was no mood to get into a tiff with his wife. "He's to be gone when I get home tonight."

Without missing a beat, Julia raised an eyebrow. "You're coming home tonight?"

Coming to his feet, Fritz gave his wife a withering glare, but said nothing. Instead, he buttoned up the green tunic of his police uniform and took a moment to finish his coffee before heading out for his shift.

Only after she was sure he was gone did Julia tiptoe out into the foyer, pick up the phone, and dial the number Herr Koch had left her to call if there was any change in Emma's condition. When no one answered the first time, she returned to the kitchen where she cleaned up after her husband and began to prepare breakfast for her daughter, her sister, and Herr Koch's son. On her way to rouse Lena and Hans, she stopped in the foyer and again dialed the physician's number. As before, there was no answer.

Julia waited until Lena and Hans were seated at opposite ends of the kitchen table eating their breakfasts in silence before slipping out of the kitchen and trying a third time. When there was again no answer, she began to become concerned.

After hanging up, she snatched a shawl from a coat rack in the foyer and called to her sister without bothering to go back into the kitchen. "I'm going out."

Alarmed, Lena came flying out to where Julia was standing before a mirror on a wall of the foyer putting on her hat. "Where are you going?"

Not wishing to share her concern, she told her sister the first thing that came to mind. "There's medication I need to fetch as soon as the chemist opens his shop." Though that was true, it wasn't the real reason she was headed out.

"You won't be too long, I hope. I've a train to catch if I'm going to make it back to Berlin before Ernst returns home this evening."

"No, I'll not be long," Julia muttered as she turned toward the door, hoping as she did so her concerns were unfounded. "Do look in on Emma for me and see that she finishes her breakfast." Then, without another word, she was gone.

❋

Slowing her pace as she approached the address she'd been given, Julia looked about, wondering as she did so if it would be best to turn around now or continue to where a pair of policemen, one of whom she recognized, were standing about in front of a house that had been vandalized. After checking the scrap of paper upon which Herr Koch had written his address and confirming the number on it matched that of the ransacked house, she did not need to ask anyone what had happened. What she did need to find out was what had become of the doctor.

Pausing, Julia took a minute to compose herself and fashioned what she hoped passed as a smile. Only when she was ready did she boldly march up to the policeman she knew. "Karl, how pleasant to see you."

Caught off guard by seeing his friend's wife advancing toward him, Karl Holtz straightened up and bowed ever so slightly while touching the brim of his helmet. "Fräu Kruger, whatever are you doing in this part of town?"

"The chemist," she offered abruptly while taking in as much of the carnage as she could without making it too obvious that was what she was doing. "I was going to the chemist, for Emma."

Familiar with the neighborhood where the Krugers lived, Holtz suspected Julia was taking a very roundabout way to reach her stated destination. For the moment, though, he set aside his natural curiosity about that. "Ah, yes. I heard she was not feeling well. How is she, if I may ask?"

"She's doing much better, thank you. And yourself? I expect you're looking for the miscreants who did this."

Glance over his shoulder toward the gaping hole where the front door had been kicked in off its hinges, Holtz chuckled. "Oh, we have no need. A rowdy group of Brownshirts returning from the festival decided to pay the Jew who lived here a friendly little visit. They've already turned themselves in."

"Lived?"

"Well yes, I expect you could say he doesn't live here anymore, or anywhere else for that matter." Karl chuckled at his little joke. "The lads, you see, were quite drunk. As is their habit, they got a little carried away. Kicked the man to death right there as he was returning home from somewhere," he added, pointing to the bloodstained steps leading up to the house.

Shaken, Julia drew upon every bit of her willpower to keep her emotions in check. Even so, she failed miserably, for when Holtz looked back at her, he did so in a manner she was quite familiar with, one that told her he was tempted to ask her why she was behaving so. "I must be going," she blurted before turning about and walking away.

She had not gone more than two steps when Holtz called out. "Fräu Kruger."

Stopping dead in her tracks, she slowly faced about, again struggling to keep herself from becoming unglued. "Yes, Karl?"

"The chemist is that way," he stated, thrusting his thumb over his right shoulder.

"Ah, yes, of course. How foolish of me."

Once more Holtz bowed and touched his hat as she hastened past him, wondering if he should mention this to his friend or look into the matter himself. He understood there were times when circumstances required people to turn a blind eye to the laws forbidding the patronization of businesses run by Jews. He also knew it was not in the best interest for family members of government employees to do so, particularly when they were the ones charged with enforcing those laws.

※

Horrified by what her sister was asking of her, Lena didn't even allow her to finish before screeching, "*NO!* Impossible."

"Well he can't stay here," Julia countered sharply.

"And I can't take him with me," Lena shot back. "Dear God, have you gone mad?"

"You don't need to tell Ernst what he is. You only need to keep him until we can arrange to send him off to his uncle."

"A man who emigrated to America with his family in 1932, if the boy is to be believed. What about the boy's mother? Why not ship him off to her?"

"You of all people know that's impossible," Julia declared, drawing herself up and regarding her sister with an accusatory stare. "The precious Nuremberg Laws the Nazis are so proud of and the death of his father have made him an orphan." Julia's accusation was less than subtle, for Lena's husband was not only a dedicated Party member, he was an officer in the SS.

Smarting from her sister's indictment, Lena winced, knowing full well no one with an ounce of sense would take the boy in, not if they had a choice. Instead, she attempted to use logic to defend her refusal to take the boy back to Oranienburg with her until other, more permanent arrangements could be made. "Do you think for one minute that while we're attempting to arrange to send the boy packing, Ernst won't see how he was butchered as a baby by his father's rabbi?"

"We can make the boy promise to be careful when he's dressing or bathing," Julia offered. "I know I don't allow my Emma to go parading about nude."

Planting her fists firmly on her hips, Lena leaned forward, staring intently into her sister's eyes. "Boys are different," she snapped.

"Besides, Ernst is SS," she reminded Julia, though she knew it was unnecessary. "The second I walk into the house, he will want to know everything about the boy, especially since by all outward appearances he is the very personification of the ideal Aryan."

"If it's appearances that concern you, there are ways of hiding his true nature."

Lena folded her arms across her chest. "Oh? And how, exactly, do you propose to do *that*?"

Before answering, Julia walked over to the kitchen door and closed it, lest Hans Koch hear what she was about to propose and flee. While that would have solved her problem, the very idea of betraying the trust of a man who had risked his life to help her when she was in need by allowing harm to come to the man's son violated the Christian ethics Julia stubbornly clung to and, she suspected, her sister did as well, despite her husband's long-standing affiliation with the National Socialists. It was those ethics, and her ability to browbeat her younger sister into just about anything, that Julia was counting on as she began to put forth her idea.

CHAPTER TWO

HAUPTSTURMFÜHRER RICHTER

Going from carriage to carriage, Lena Richter made her way along the train's narrow corridor until she finally found an unoccupied compartment. Sliding the door open, she turned to the child who'd been following on her heels. "In here," she commanded brusquely.

Without a word, Hans Koch made his way into the compartment and took a seat next to the window. Upon entering it, Lena closed the door and locked it, lest someone decide to join them. The trip was going to be difficult as it was. The last thing she wanted was to have a perfect stranger sitting with them the whole way to Berlin, attempting to strike up a conversation with her, or worse, with the half-Jew Julia had all but shamed her into sheltering.

Him, Lena thought as she settled in and took to studying the child across from her. At the moment the boy wasn't much of a "him." Even after watching her sister dress Hans in clothes her daughter had outgrown, Lena was having difficulty seeing anything resembling a boy in the child who had already taken up the same book on German history he'd been reading since she had first laid eyes on him. The longish, scraggly hair Julia had managed to fashion into something resembling a style a girl his age would wear helped disguise his gender.

When Julia had asked why his father had allowed him to go about with such unkempt hair, the boy had answered her with the deadpan expression with which he replied to all their inquiries. "The barber my father would take me to asked that we no longer patronize his shop." Neither woman needed to ask why the man would make such a request. Just as German citizens were being discouraged from visiting establishments owned by Jews, more and more shopkeepers, merchants, and professionals who wished to keep from running afoul of the brown-shirted SA men refused to have any dealings with Jews. In Julia's eyes, this was little more than ideological lunacy, a phrase she used too often for Lena's liking when they were alone. Still, Julia had had to admit the boycott on serving Jewish clients was of benefit in this particular instance, for it gave her more than enough of the boy's blond hair to work with.

Even more than his hair, the boy's lean frame and the sad, almost forlorn expression he hid his thoughts and feelings behind played into the story with which Julia had armed Lena, one Lena would need to explain why she had taken the child in. It centered on a terrible fire that had devastated a row of workers' flats in Munich a few weeks prior. The loss of life had been horrendous, leaving a dozen children orphaned.

"Tell Ernst my Fritz simply could not stand to see him, I mean her, taken away to a church orphanage to be raised by nuns. Tell him we were going to adopt '*her*,' but had to give up on the idea because of Emma's illness."

"Do you think for one moment my Ernst is going to believe such a story? Remember, until Ernst left the force to join the SS, he and Fritz worked out of the same precinct station."

For the moment, Julia avoided pointing out Ernst Richter had not left the Munich police of his own volition. Instead, she did her best to allay her younger sister's concerns. "You worry too much. You always have. I'm sure despite that cold, dispassionate demeanor Ernst wears like a suit of armor, inside he's just as softhearted as Fritz is when it comes to children. Why, you should see the man when he's with our daughter. Fritz positively fawns over her. You would never suspect he was a policeman."

Upon further reflection, Lena could not help but agree her sister had a point. When her Wolfgang had been born, Ernst had all but cried when he saw his son for the first time. Perhaps, she reasoned, he would be mesmerized by the child's unmistakable Nordic appearance and fine, almost delicate features, just as she had been, even though she knew the boy had been hopelessly contaminated by Jewish blood.

Lena was still staring at Hans when the train finally lurched forward and began to pull out of the station. Peeking up from his book, he could not help but notice how the woman across from him was staring. She continued to do so in silence until after the conductor had come by, punched their tickets, and she had once more locked the door.

"I need to make a few things perfectly clear with you before we reach Berlin," Lena finally declared, letting Hans know she wished him to set aside his book and pay attention. "As long as you are with us, you will not say anything unless spoken to. Even then, you are to limit your response to a simple yes or no whenever possible. Is that clear?"

Hans nodded. "Yes, Fräu Richter."

"You must remain fully dressed at all times. You must never bathe when my husband is home. Even when you do, you must lock the door. Likewise, when you are changing you must not only lock the door to your room, you must ensure the shades are pulled down."

Again, Hans nodded. "Yes, Fräu Richter."

"Never, ever leave the house unless I am with you," she continued in a crisp, no-nonsense manner. "If there are introductions to be made or explanations as to who you are, I will do so. Is that clear?"

"Yes, Fräu Richter."

"And never forget your name is Hannah, Hannah Kiefer, a girl whose parents are dead."

Of all the things he would have to remember and rules he would need to abide by, Hans thought this last one would be the easiest. In the boy's eyes, his father's physical passing had been preceded by an emotional death. It had been his father's heritage, after all, that had brought grief to a family that had once been happy and prosperous. It hadn't mattered to anyone of importance that the man had not attended a religious service or observed a Jewish holiday in years. He had been, by birth and lineage, a Jew, and by extension, his son was one as well according to the recently enacted Law for the Protection of German Blood and Honor. And while Hans' mother had stood by her husband for as long as she could, in time, she realized she had no choice but to give into her own family's demands and official dictates and leave him.

Now, Hans told himself as he considered what Fräu Richter was asking of him, the time had come to put all memory of his father and the man's damnedable religion behind him just as one tosses aside a painful pebble removed form a shoe.

Thus resolved, he returned Lena's unflinching stare with one that was just as piercing. "Yes, Fräu Richter. I understand perfectly."

❀

The annoyance Hauptsturmfürher Ernst Richter had felt over his wife's decision to remain in Munich longer then she had promised, exasperated by the need to leave the office early in order to pick her up at Berlin's Hauptbahnhof, evaporated the second he saw her making her way toward him along the crowded platform. So did the scowl he wore whenever he donned the black uniform he had come to cherish, a uniform that inspired fear and respect in equal measure.

It wasn't until after Richter had given his wife a hug and quick kiss that he noticed a waif wearing a forlorn expression and a pleated pinafore dress two sizes too large for her. She was standing next to his Lena, casting fugitive glances his way as if waiting for something. Intrigued by the girl's behavior, and enchanted by her blue eyes, Richter stepped back from his wife and turned toward Hans. "Well, hello, young lady. Is there some way I can be of assistance?"

Shifting his weight from one foot to the next, Hans gave Lena a glance out of the corner of his eye before looking back at the SS officer before him. When he did, two things struck him straight off. The first was the smile on the man's face. He had never seen a member of the SS or SA smile before, especially whenever they had cast their gaze in his direction when he'd been in the company of his father.

Yet as surprising as that was, even more astonishing to Hans was an absence of anything resembling embarrassment or shame. The idea of tromping about in public while dressed in girl's clothing had terrified him at first, for he knew from experience how cruel people could be to those whose mere existence offended them and their sense of propriety. Yet there he was, he thought to himself as he took a quick look about, standing in the middle of a crowded train station's platform with no one giving him a second look. *Well,* he corrected himself, *almost no one,* as he once more peered up into the pale blue eyes of Fräu Richter's husband.

Her husband's sudden distraction came as something of a blessing for Lena, allowing her to recover from a panic attack before hurriedly pitching into the fictitious legend she and her sister had crafted to explain why she had brought the boy with her from Munich. "Ernst, darling, this is Hannah. She's an orphan my sister was looking after."

"An orphan? This girl?" Ernst declared looking back over at his wife.

"Yes," she hastily replied. "Rather than seeing her sent off to an orphanage where she'd be lost in the bureaucratic shuffle, Julia and Fritz were looking after her until they could make arrangements to find her uncle and send her to him. Well, naturally things changed when Emma fell ill."

"So you brought her home with you," Ernst concluded in an even tone that failed to betray his feelings on the matter.

"What would you have me do? Hand her to the nuns and say *Here, she's yours?* You were with the police long enough to know what happens to children in those places."

Recalling his time with the Munich police force, as well as the way the nuns at the school he'd attended dealt with children, Ernst nodded. "Yes, I remember."

Not knowing what else to do while this exchange was taking place, Hans bowed his head and took to intently staring down at a spot on the platform, withdrawing into his own little world as he often did when the one around him became too much for him.

For the longest time, no one said a word as the crowd on the platform began to thin. Eventually realizing they needed to go as well, Ernst looked back to where the forlorn little girl was waiting patiently to find out what would become of her. Unable to stand her downcast expression, he slowly settled down onto his haunches before reaching out and placing a finger under the girl's chin. Ever so gently he tilted her head up until their eyes met.

Fearing the worst, all Lena could do was watch, waiting as she did so for the boy to do or say something stupid, something that would give the game away.

But Hans did no such thing. If anything, he found himself being taken in by the warm, caring gaze with which the SS officer was regarding him.

"Well, little one, we can't very well leave you here all night, now, can we?" Richter murmured reassuringly as his smile returned.

"No, sir, I think not," Hans muttered.

Rising back up, Richter reached out and offered Hans his hand. "Then it's decided. You're to come home with us."

Even before he realized what he was doing, Hans placed his hand into the one the SS officer was holding out to him and allowed himself to be led away to an uncertain future.

❋

During the entire drive from Berlin to Oranienburg in a chauffeured Mercedes-Benz 770, Lena Richter was on pins and needles as her husband bombarded "Hannah" with questions. She had no need to worry, for the child, whose hair and eyes were as near a match to her husband's as anyone but a blood relation could have, took "her" time before answering. When she did so, her responses came out with measured ease that left Ernst Richter none the wiser that everything his wife was telling him was a total fabrication. Eventually, however, he did hit the girl with a question for which she could not supply a ready answer. Unsure as how to respond, Hannah dropped her gaze as she scrambled to come up with something to say, something in line with the legend the two sisters had hastily thrown together.

Richter, of course, did not know this was why Hannah was hesitating. The girl's reaction naturedly caused him to assume he'd touched upon a sensitive subject, one causing her to suddenly recall the recent death of her parents in a tragic fire, one he'd read about in the papers. Hoping to push past this awkward moment, Ernst looked over at his wife, who was just as much at a loss as to how best to answer his question as Hannah was. Gripped by another panic attack, one that left her unable to form a single, coherent thought, much less speak, Lena found herself unable to do anything more than return his stare.

It was while he was nervously glancing about, doing his best to come up with something to say, that Ernst's eyes fell on the book the girl was holding on her lap. When he saw the title, his eyes lit up.

"Do you enjoy the study of history?" he asked tentatively.

Without looking up, Hannah nodded. "Yes, sir, very much."

"What kind of history do you enjoy? Ancient? Medieval? Modern?"

This time, before answering, Hannah peeked up at Richter through her lashes. "German history, sir."

Unable to help himself, Richter beamed. "Excellent! I too love German history. Tell me, what period is your favorite?"

Like the SS officer, Hannah could not help herself as she warmed to the topic, one she could discuss without fear of betraying her true nature. "I love all of it, Hauptsturmführer." Then she paused, tilting her head and furrowing her brow as if thinking. "Well, perhaps not the Thirty Years War. Or the Black Death. Those were sad times for Germany."

"Yes, sad times indeed, but times we must remember if we are to keep ourselves from falling victim to the ravages brought on by our enemies or the plague within our borders infecting our proud cultural heritage," Richter pointed out before continuing. "I myself enjoy reading about our ancient ancestors, the Alamanni, Hermunduri, Marcomanni, Quadi, and Suebi. I find it fascinating to delve into their stories and legends."

Caught up by Richter's enthusiasm for a subject she so loved, Hannah forgot Lena's rule about not speaking unless spoken to. "What about the Cimbri, one of the tribes Caesar fought?"

With a twinkle in his eyes, Richter raised a finger and playfully wagged it at Hannah. "Ah, I see you have been misled, dear girl. It is widely believed the Cimbri were Celts, not Germans, although I can understand your confusion since they were closely aligned with the Teutones when they fought the Roman invaders." Then, looking over at his wife, Richter smiled and gave her a wink. "It would seem as if I have much to do if I am to set this child's understanding of her ancestors straight." It was a task the SS officer wasted no time in pitching into, much to Hannah's delight and Lena's relief.

❋

The lively discussion between Richter and Hannah that had begun on the way to Oranienburg continued throughout dinner that night, where it expanded to take in the full scope of German history. From her place at the far end of the table, Lena watched in utter silence, barely touching her food as she waited for the child she'd brought into their home to say something that would betray her true nature or heritage.

She needn't have worried. Even at the tender age of nine, Hannah had learned to remain ever vigilant lest she fall afoul of those who found her mere existence repugnant. So she listened very carefully to everything the hauptsturmführer was saying and where he was taking their discussions, keenly aware there were pitfalls that needed to be avoided such as the mentioning of historical figures who had fallen out of favor with the newly established party line, subjects best left untouched.

Eventually, when Lena could no longer deal with the stress of sitting there waiting for the girl to make a tragic mistake, she stood up and announced that it was past the time when Hannah needed to be off to bed. "It's late," she declared. "It has been a long and trying day. I imagine the girl is exhausted, as am I."

Though disappointed to see the lively discussion she was enjoying come to an end, Hannah said nothing. Neither did Richter. When it came to domestic matters and children, he was in the habit of keeping out of his wife's way.

※

Not a word passed between Hannah and Lena as they made their way through the house and up a broad set of stairs. For her part, Hannah used this occasion to look about as they went, marveling at the size and opulence of a home owned by a mere hauptsturmführer. This led her to conclude Richter's parents had been wealthy. It also left Hannah wondering about a household staff. After all, one did not live in such luxury without having a suitable staff to maintain it.

Only when they were in one of the spare bedrooms and Lena had closed the door did she turn to where Hannah was standing, tightly clutching the small suitcase stuffed with clothes that had once belonged to Emma Kruger. "Should you need to go to the bathroom, use the one across the hall from this room. When you do, make sure you lock the door and sit down. You are, after all, supposed to be a girl, so behave like one."

"Yes, Fräu Richter."

"In the morning I will begin to look into how best to go about contacting your uncle and seeing what arrangements can be made to send you to him. You understand this may take some time, since your uncle is, well, he isn't a German, which means I must be very careful how I go about this. You understand, of course."

The concept that being a Jew made her and her father less German than her new guardians was a concept Hannah had never been able to comprehend. Of course, she had no need to understand the reason people believed it to be true. All that mattered was that was the way things were in the New Germany, a Germany she longed to be part of. "Yes, Fräu Richter."

"While you are here, you are to stay out from underfoot. Is that clear?"

"Yes, Fräu Richter."

Having said all she intended to, but feeling a bit self-conscious about simply leaving the child without saying goodnight, Lena was about to when Hannah asked about the household staff.

"Since my husband takes his breakfast with the other officers, at present the woman who is serving as a cook only prepares one meal in the evening. As to a housekeeper, I have yet to find a girl who is suitable and possesses the proper credentials. So you will need to look after your own things, make your bed in the morning, and clean up after yourself."

"And your son, Fräu Richter?"

"At present, he is being looked after by a young woman who lives in Sachsenhausen. I'll be fetching him home tomorrow afternoon."

Again there was a strained silence as the two regarded each other, with Hannah waiting for the woman to say something and Lena at a loss as to what to say. Finally lowering her eyes, Lena muttered, "Goodnight," before leaving.

For the longest time, Hannah simply stood in the middle of the room alone, tightly clutching the borrowed suitcase and looking around. Eventually, with a sigh, she went over to the bed where she set the suitcase down and proceeded to prepare for bed.

CHAPTER THREE

THE BIRD'S NEST

ORANIENBURG, SEPTEMBER 1935

I n the morning, Hannah found herself at a loss as to what to do. She wondered as she lay in bed if she should stay where she was and wait until Fräu Richter came for her. Eventually, it dawned upon her the woman might not. And breakfast. What was she to do about breakfast? In her litany of do's and don'ts, the woman had never made any mention of what she was supposed to do about that.

As there was no housekeeper, Hannah decided there would be nothing wrong if she took to exploring the house on her own, so long as she was careful and didn't make any noise. With that in mind, she slipped out of bed and dressed in a skirt and blouse, both of which, like the pinafore, were too large for her. Fortunately, there was a safety pin on the pinafore Fräu Kruger had used to take in the dress' waist. With this, Hannah managed to fold over a portion of the skirt's waistline and pin it so it wouldn't slide down over her hips. Only when she was fully dressed did Hannah dare creep across the hall and into the bathroom, where she went about undressing and washing up at the sink before once more dressing.

Upon emerging from the bathroom, Hannah smelt the faint aroma of coffee. Since Fräu Richter had mentioned her husband took his breakfast elsewhere, and there was no housekeeper, she assumed Fräu Richter was in the kitchen. Pleased the woman was up and about, Hannah followed the aroma of fresh-brewed coffee to its source. This proved to be a mistake.

❊

The second she entered the kitchen, Hannah froze. It was the hauptsturmführer, and not Fräu Richter, sitting at the table.

Looking up from the newspaper he had been reading while drinking coffee he had prepared for himself, Richter could not help but chuckle when he saw the startled expression on Hannah's face. "Ah, I see that unlike my wife, you are an early riser."

Not knowing what to do or say, Hannah simply stood there rooted to the spot, debating if it might be best if she simply retreated to her room.

The look on the girl's face was one with which Richter was quite familiar, for his uniform could be very intimidating, giving pause even to those who were innocent of any crimes against the state. Assuming Hannah was on the verge of fleeing, Richter motioned to a chair across the small table from him with a nod of his head. "Please, join me. There is some fresh milk in the icebox, if you wish to have some."

After nervously glancing back and forth between the SS officer and the icebox, Hannah decided to throw caution to the wind. "May I ask where the glasses are kept, Herr Hauptsturmführer?"

"I do not think we need to bother with formal titles and such here," Richter declared. "We all know who we are. Feel free simply to call me Herr Richter, if you must."

"Yes, Herr Richter. And the glasses?"

"Over there, in the cabinet near the sink."

Though it was a stretch for her, Hannah was able to reach the glasses by rising up on her tippy toes. As she was doing so, Richter noticed the pin holding her skirt up. He was about to ask the girl if she had any clothing that fit her properly, but decided not to since it might embarrass the poor thing. She'd been through enough, he concluded, without making it any worse by reminding her of her past. Instead, he eased back in his chair and watched as she fetched the milk, poured herself a glass, and took a seat.

"I apologize for bothering you like this," Hannah stated after taking a long drink of milk. "Fräu Richter told me you ate your breakfast elsewhere, so when I smelt the coffee, I assumed it was her here in the kitchen and not you."

"I take my breakfast in the officer's mess because, unlike you, my wife does not greet the dawn." For the time being, Richter decided he had no need to tell the girl the reason she slept in was not sloth. Like many children who grew up during the last war, Lena had suffered through long and painful periods of malnutrition thanks to the British blockade, leaving her with a chronically weak heart. It was a condition that had almost killed her while giving birth to their son, another ordeal from which she had never fully recovered, leaving her very often fatigued. "Since I must leave early each morning to tend to the Führer's business, it's either march off to the officer's mess and eat whatever they place before me like a good soldier or starve."

"I could fix you eggs if you wish," Hannah offered without thinking.

"You can cook?" Richter asked incredulously.

Suddenly realizing she had erred, but seeing no graceful way out of following through, Hannah nodded. "Yes, sir. A little."

"Really?"

"Yes, sir."

Deciding to have a little fun with the girl, he challenged her to show him what she could do. It was a dare Hannah took up with delight, for it meant she would be free to fix breakfast for herself without having to wait for Fräu Richter. "How would you like your eggs cooked?"

"Surprise me, Mausi," Richter replied, sporting a cheeky grin and giving Hannah a wink.

Upon hearing the SS officer call her *little mouse*, Hannah beamed. "Very well, sir." With that, she put her glass of milk down, slipped off her chair and began to poke about, searching for all she needed. When she was ready, Hannah cut two slices of bread from a loaf she'd found. In the center of each, she cut a neat, round hole before buttering them and placing them in a heavy cast-iron pan. When the slices of bread were brown on one side, she flipped them over, cracked an egg on the edge of the pan, and carefully dropped the yoke and egg white into the hole she'd made in each slice. "I do not know what the name of this is here, but my mother used to call it a bird's nest, my favorite way of eating eggs," Hannah mused, without looking over to where Richter was watching her every move. "I loved spending time with her in the kitchen," she continued. "Mama was always so happy there. So was I."

Lost in her own fond memories while paying close attention to what she was doing lest she overcook the eggs, Hannah never noticed the expression on Richter's face. It was one that would have brought a smile to Julia Kruger's, for she had been right about Lena's husband. The shell of steel he wore while performing his duties hid a heart easily pierced by a child's chatter.

※

Having finished their breakfast, Ernst Richter took Hannah by the hand and led her to his study, where he sat her in a plush leather chair that all but devoured her before going over to a bookcase that covered an entire wall of the room. After scanning the rows and finding the book he was searching for, he pulled it out, returned to where Hannah was seated, and handed it to her. "This is a rare volume that belonged to my grandfather, published in 1837. It traces the origin of the Siegfried legend all the way back to Hermann, son of Segimerus, tying what many still think of as nothing more than mythology to the very real history of our people. I expect you will find it no less enjoyable and enlightening than I did when my father gave it to me to read when I was about your age."

With eager fingers, Hannah accepted the precious gift of knowledge, wasting not a second as she reverently placed the book in her lap and opened it.

Unable to help himself, Richter smiled to himself before assuming a stern demeanor. "I shall quiz you on what you have read this evening, so take your time and study it well."

Looking up, Hannah regarded the tall SS officer with an expression that reflected her gratitude and joy despite Richter's best efforts to come across as a demanding taskmaster. "I shall do my best."

"We must all do our best in all we do if we are to return Germany to its rightful place and make tomorrow better than today for those with the strength and courage to seize it, Mausi," Richter declared solemnly as he reached out and playfully ran his fingers through Hannah's hair.

Gone were the concerns Hannah had harbored when she'd first laid eyes on the SS officer standing before her. In the past, she had depended on a deadpan expression to hide her emotions, lest she give her tormentors the satisfaction they had fed on. But in place of that now was a shy smile, one she readily shared with Richter as she nodded. "I shall not disappoint you, Herr Richter."

Then, without another word, she enthusiastically dove into reading the book on her lap, leaving Richter to walk away with a grin on his face, one he wiped away with well-measured ease the second he left the house.

❃

The sound of someone lightly tapping the heavy brass doorknocker startled Hannah, causing her to look up from her reading and over to a clock on the desk across the room from her. When she noticed it was well past midmorning, she began to wonder if she had somehow missed hearing Fräu Richter stirring. Another tapping at the front door without any indication someone was rushing to answer it caused Hannah to set aside the book Herr Richter had given her to study, climb out of the leather chair, and head out into the cavernous foyer, looking around as she went in the hope of catching sight of Fräu Richter.

A third tap without any sign of her reluctant guardian left Hannah in something of a dilemma. She expected if she ignored whoever it was at the door long enough they would go away. Ignoring it, therefore, seemed to be the wisest thing she could do. If she answered it, Hannah suspected she would risk invoking Fräu Richter's ire, even though this particular set of circumstances hadn't been addressed by any of the rules she had been given.

Hannah was standing there before the door, engaged in this debate, when the person on the other side tapped once more. After pausing but a second to look over her shoulder without seeing any sign of Fräu Richter, Hannah drew herself up, marched up to the door, and opened it.

Expecting someone else entirely, Anna Diehl was caught off guard when she looked down and saw a pair of striking blue eyes staring up at her. "Well, hello."

Not knowing what else to do or say, Hannah replied in kind. "Hello."

After hefting the child she was holding on her hip about to shift its weight away from the spot it had been resting on for too long, the woman asked if Fräu Richter was about. "No," Hannah replied before giving her head a quick shake as if to clear it. "I mean, she is here, but she is not yet awake."

"Ah, yes. Silly me. I should have called before popping over like this."

Having no idea how to respond to the woman's last remark, Hannah pointed at the child. "Is that Wolfgang?"

"Yes, yes, it is. I was expected to keep him until this afternoon, but I have a very important luncheon meeting with all the BDM leaders in the region I simply cannot miss."

"You're a leader in the League of German Girls?"

"Yes, yes, I am. I am Anna Diehl. And I have been diligently doing my duty, as we all must, by looking after little Wolfgang while Fräu Richter was away."

Ignoring the pretentious hyperbole the woman was tossing about to impress her, Hannah realized she had not introduced herself. "I am Han—Hannah."

"Well, hello, Hannah. It is a pleasure to meet you," the woman beamed in a manner that came across as a bit too ostentatious, given the circumstances.

Once more at a loss as to what to do, Hannah invited the woman in. Fortunately, she refused, claiming she needed to be on her way.

For her part, Anna concluded that given the way the girl was dressed, she must be the daughter of Fräu Richter's new housekeeper and, as such, of no consequence. With that in mind, she handed the small child to Hannah, set a basket containing clothing, diapers, and toys on the doorstep, and left without another word.

Taken aback by the woman's behavior, Hannah simply stood there as she watched Fräulein Diehl climb into a chauffeured car and drive off. The girl's bemusement over this unceremonial dumping of the Richters' son was brought to an end when she felt a tugging of her hair. Turning her head, she gazed into the pale blue eyes of the child she now held on her hip. "Well, what am I going to do with you, little Wolfie?"

Pleased he had the girl's attention, Wolfgang Richter smiled, eliciting one from Hannah in return.

❈

Exhausted from her travels to and from Munich, as well as the unending stress of taking in that pathetic little mischling, Lena didn't awaken until just after twelve noon. Knowing she'd promised to pick up Wolfgang that afternoon, she rose out of bed, washed up, and dressed. On her way toward the stairs, she stopped by the room where Hannah was staying and knocked. When there was no answer, Lena walked on, hoping as she did the child had heeded her warnings and stayed in the house and out of the way.

She was still slowly making her way through the house, checking rooms as she went to see if Hannah was in any of them, when she heard a familiar peal of laughter coming from the kitchen. Concerned, she hastened to its source, bursting into the kitchen to find her Wolfgang in his highchair, merrily slapping his hands on the wooden tray, amused by the way Hannah was going "*choo-choo-choo*" like a steam locomotive while slowly moving a spoon of soup closer and closer to his mouth.

The sudden appearance of his mother distracted Wolfgang from Hannah's effort to feed him which, in turn, caused Hannah to look behind her. Quickly pouring the content of the spoon back into a bowl she had been holding in her left hand, Hannah set the spoon and bowl aside, sprang to her feet, and began to explain what had happened.

Ever so slowly Lena's anger ebbed away, replaced by embarrassment at having assumed the worst of the child she had taken in. Making her way over to the intricately caved highchair, Wolfgang welcomed her by madly kicking his little feet while thrusting his little arms out toward her. With a single, swift motion, his mother hoisted the giggling child out of his seat and up over her head before bringing him down and cradling him snugly in her arms. Only after Lena and Wolfgang had exchanged greetings by rubbing noses did she turn to Hannah.

"I should have known better than to depend on Anna to keep to her word," Lena muttered disparagingly before thanking Hannah for watching after Wolfgang. Even as she did, she cautiously wormed an index finger down between the boy's diaper and thigh to check for wetness, or worse.

Pleased to find there was no mess, Lena withdrew her finger and shifted Wolfgang onto her hip. "How is it you know how to care for babies?" she asked in a tone that told Hannah she was quite surprised by this.

"My uncle's children, Fräu Richter. Before he left Germany, when it became difficult to find someone willing to look after them, I started to."

"Do you enjoy looking after children?"

Before answering, Hannah looked over at Wolfgang and gave the child a wink. In response, the boy giggled. "Only when they are as cute and well behaved as little Wolfie is, Fräu Richter."

Pleased by the girl's compliment and the way her son seemed to have taken to the child, Lena held Wolfgang out in front of her at arm's length. "Well, it would seem you have managed to fool another person, Schnecke." Then, after gathering him back against her bosom, Lena turned to Hannah and asked something that astonished her. "Would you mind terribly if I finished feeding him?"

❋

The balance of that first day passed quietly as Fräu Richter spent an enjoyable afternoon with her son in the yard enjoying the warm, late summer weather while Hannah retreated into the kitchen when Fräu Sander, the woman who cooked for the Richters, showed up to prepare dinner. Even though Lena informed her that the girl was not related to them, the cook treated the child as if she were family, allowing the fetching young girl with penetrating blue eyes to assist her by assigning Hannah simple chores while taking the time to explain what she was doing.

Hannah lapped up the attention, watching everything the cook did while bombarding her with an endless string of questions. Later that evening, as Hannah recounted in great detail what she had a hand in making to Ernst Richter, the hauptsturmführer couldn't help but smile, praising the girl while his wife looked on in silence, concerned by the way Hannah's innocent charms were seducing her husband. Despite what she knew, she too was finding herself being taken in by them. That alone, should have been a warning. It was one she did not heed.

CHAPTER FOUR

"TOMORROW BELONGS TO US"

As a youth, Ernst Richter had been an exceptional student, a boy who showed great promise as evidenced by the academic excellence he achieved while attending gymnasium in Munich. All who knew him then marked him as someone who would achieve great things one day. Unfortunately, his path to greatness would not go through university as his parents had hoped. Instead, his introduction to adulthood came during the bloody street fighting Germans on the left and Germans on the right engaged in when their beloved country fell into chaos in the wake of a war naïve young patriots like Richter thought they had been winning.

Ernst Richter's formal education ended and his first lessons in how to deal with the enemies of the Reich began in April 1919, when the socialists who had declared Bavaria a free state the previous November established a Soviet Republic under a left-wing radical playwright by the name of Ernst Toller. Disgusted by what he saw happening to his beloved country, Ernst Richter set aside his studies and joined a local freikorps company. It was in their ranks, among hardened veterans who had recently returned from the Western Front, that he learned discipline and respect from men who believed in fighting those who sought to bring ruin to Germany. The brutal, uncompromising methods his new comrades used to deal with the Bavarian communists and Munich Soviet Republic anarchists led a young and impressionable Ernst Richter to believe compassion for one's enemies was a weakness. In appreciation of his service during this time of crisis and his unwavering diligence in his duties, Richter was permitted to join a restructured police force in the fall of 1919 despite being underage at the time.

It was in 1923, during the Beer Hall Putsch, that Erich Richter first came to the attention of influential men within the National Socialist German Workers' Party. When their charismatic leader sought to establish Munich as a base from which they could march on Berlin and overthrow the government as Mussolini had in Italy, Richter not only refused to interfere with their efforts, he joined them. Naturally, the failure of the putsch resulted in Richter's dismissal from the police force. It did not, however, spell an end to his association with the Party.

In 1925, when Emil Maurice was charged with reforming the guard detachment responsible for protecting his party's leader, Ernst Richter was invited to join them. Because of his police background, in June 1933, Oberfürhrer Theodor Eicke saw to it that Richer was given a commission in the SS-Wachverband, or Guard Unit, and placed in charge of training SS personnel assigned to a prison Eicke had been ordered to establish at Dachau. Eicke was so impressed by Richter's thoroughness in preparing newly assigned personnel at Dachau that the Oberfürhrer took him along with him when he moved the headquarters of the SS-Wachverband to Oranienburg. There, Richter was given another promotion, responsibility for overseeing all training programs for the Wachverband, and the gift of a house on the Lehnitzsee that had, until recently, belonged to a Jewish banker. It was where Richter intended to begin a family that was, for him, more than a simple longing. For an SS officer and representative of the New Reich, it was a duty.

❀

After exiting the car and walking away without bothering to acknowledge the driver in any way, Ernst Richter began to make his way toward the front door but stopped when he heard his son shriek in delight, followed by a now familiar child's voice.

"No, no, Wolfie. You are not supposed to keep it. You are supposed to roll it back to me. Here, like this."

Ever so gingerly, Richter crept to the side of the house, removing his hat before peeking around the corner toward the sound of children's voices and laughter.

Aggravation and annoyance over the incompetence of the dunces in Berlin Richter had to deal with had been building up in him all day. But in the twinkling of an eye, his cares disappeared when he saw his son sitting in the grass across from Hannah, who was seated in front of the one-year-old boy. Holding a ball up, Hannah gave it a shake. "I roll it to you like this," she declared while doing so. "Now, roll it back to me."

Naturally, Wolfgang did no such thing. Instead, he picked up the ball in his two hands and clutched it tightly against his chest. When Hannah ordered him to return it, the boy simply laughed, leaving her no choice but to reach over and wrestle it away from him before trying once more to instruct him in the rules of their little game.

Rather than disturb the two children enjoying themselves in the late afternoon sunshine, Richter backed away and went into the house, where he quietly searched for his wife. He found her in a chair set in front of the window overlooking the part of the yard where Hannah and Wolfgang were playing. Making as little noise as possible, Richter crept up behind her, bent over the back of the chair, and planted a gentle kiss on top of Lena's head.

Roused from her nap, she stirred. Her eyes fluttered ever so slightly. "Ah, I didn't hear you come in."

"I dare say you wouldn't have heard a thing even if a horde of Huns came sweeping through the house," Richter replied, straight-faced.

Drawing in a deep breath, Lena sat up, glancing out the window as she did so to ensure the children were still in the side yard and playing as peacefully as they had been when she'd drifted off. Satisfied all was in order, she looked back up at her husband. "It seems I've become quite the layabout since returning from Munich." She was about to add she was glad Hannah was there to watch over Wolfgang and keep him occupied, but didn't.

Once more looking out the window, Lena found it necessary to remind herself Hannah was not a *she,* something she was finding more and more difficult with each passing day. That the girl was also a mischling was even more difficult to fathom, for everything about Hannah went against what Lena had come to accept as true about a race who arrogantly thought of themselves as God's chosen people. It was this growing confusion over the beliefs she shared with her husband that reminded her the sooner the girl was gone, the better. It wasn't to anyone's benefit, she told herself, if either of them became emotionally attached to the other. To keep herself from dwelling on it further, she asked her husband how his day had been.

Settling down on the arm of Lena's chair and draping an arm about his wife's shoulder, he sighed. "Berlin is pushing hard to expand our operations, too hard in my opinion. To accommodate the influx of undesirables as well as provide us with a convenient place to train new personnel in the proper administration of camps, they're talking about establishing one in Sachsenhausen."

Upon hearing this, Lena made a face. Though she didn't know any details of what had gone on at Dachau, where Ernst had earned something of a reputation, she knew conditions there hadn't been pleasant, thanks to stories her brother-in-law freely shared with her when Ernst wasn't around. The idea there would be another like it so close did not sit well with her.

Ignoring her sour expression, Richter continued as he gazed out into the yard where Hannah had given up trying to teach Wolfgang to roll the ball to her and instead, was in the process of giving the boy a piggyback ride. "There is a delegation from Berlin coming up here to discuss the matter. While they're here, the HJ and BDM will be putting on a program of entertainment for them as well as the officers and their families stationed in the area."

"I suppose I will be expected to make an appearance," Lena groused.

"But of course, my dear," Richter replied smoothly, as he bent over her and planted another kiss on top of her head while looking out at the window, noticing as he did so Hannah was now on the ground, crawling about in a circle on all fours. For his part, Wolfgang was laughing so hard his face was turning red as he chased his new playmate as fast as he could make his little arms and legs go. "We should take Hannah with us, introduce her to some of the girls her age and the local BDM leader, what's her name?"

"Fräulein Diehl," Lena sniffed, still peeved by the way the pompous young woman had dropped her son off after she had returned from Munich. "I do not think that would be a good idea, Ernst."

"And why not?"

"Hannah isn't going to be here that long. I, for one, think it would be best for everyone concerned if we kept her from becoming too attached to people here since she'll be leaving for America once I've had an opportunity to make the necessary arrangements."

A grin tugged at the corner's of Richter's lips as he glanced over at his wife. "Speaking of those, have you made any progress in locating Hannah's uncle?"

After visibly wincing, Lena attempted to explain away her failure to pursue the matter by informing her husband she hadn't yet found the time.

Knowing her better than she often gave him credit for, Richter listened attentively, but did not believe anything she was saying as he once more looked out into the yard where Hannah, laying on her back, was holding Wolfgang at arm's length above her. Hannah, Ernst realized, wasn't the one his wife needed to worry about growing too fond of. Whether his wife wished to admit it or not, the forlorn little girl who had swept into their lives like a Hunnish horde had already conquered their hearts.

❋

Even before stepping across the threshold of the assembly hall, Hannah could feel her heart racing. The mere sight of a entire room full of SS officers, Hitler Youth in full regalia, girls uniformly attired in the white blouse and dark blue skirt that marked them as BDM, and red banners emblazoned with the Party's distinctive swastika set upon a field of white hung all about the room sent a shiver down her spine. Not even the new red dress Lena had bought for her to wear to this gathering bothered her nearly as much as the presence of so many SS men. For her, this was akin to being tossed into a bear pit.

Feeling the grip the girl at his side had on his hand tighten, Richter correctly guessed she was nervous, though he incorrectly assumed it was due to nothing more than shyness and not the real reason. Reaching across his body with his other hand, he took to patting the hand he was holding. "You've nothing to be afraid of, Mausi. I assure you, everyone here will be as taken by you as we have been."

Giving her husband a glance, Lena was tempted to say something but didn't. This was neither the time nor place to once more debate the wisdom of bringing the girl to this event. Ernst was the kind of person for whom no amount of guile, cunning, or persuasion could change his mind once he had made it up. As infuriating as this could be at times, it was one of the traits Lena so loved about him.

From across the room, Hannah caught sight of a senior SS officer motioning for them to join him. And while she had no idea who the gruppenführer inviting them over was, the man who was standing with him, also a gruppenführer, had the sort of face one did not easily forget, even if you only saw it in the newspapers. Fading back behind Richter as much as she could without letting go of his hand, Hannah followed along, tightening her grip even more as they went.

"Ernst, I'm glad to see you and your lovely wife could make it to our little gathering today," Gruppenführer Theodor Eiche proclaimed broadly before turning to the other officer, the one Hannah recognized. "Gruppenführer Heydrich, I believe you know Hauptsturmführer Ernst Richter."

With a smile that struck Hannah as neither warm nor friendly, Reinhard Heydrich nodded in Richter's direction. "We chatted once at a party rally in Nuremberg, when he was still with the Leibstandarte."

It was obvious to Hannah that for some reason, Richter was not at all pleased the man remembered him. She was trying to figure out why this would be, given the high position Heydrich held within the SS, when the man's eyes lit upon her. "I wasn't aware you had a daughter," he declared, giving Hannah a smile no more inviting than the one with which he had greeted Richter.

"I am afraid she isn't my daughter, Herr Gruppenführer. She's only staying with us until we can discover how best to go about contacting her relatives and making the necessary arrangements to send her off to them."

This revelation seemed to pique Heydrich's curiosity. "If there is a problem with finding the girl's relatives, perhaps my office could help."

"They live in America now," Lena blurted hastily, an act that caused her husband to cringe. "Hannah has been orphaned recently due to a terrible fire in Munich. She's no one left here in Germany to take her in."

Ignoring the way Lena had interupted their conversation, Heydrich pulled back ever so slightly, looked at Richter, then over at Eiche, before once more casting his gaze down at Hannah. "Surely you can't be serious. I mean, who in their right mind would send such a lovely child to a savage place like America? You know as well as I do they're nothing but gangsters, mongrels, and malcontents. Why this girl is the personification of the kind of children we will be relying on to build a new Reich when you and I are too old to carry on."

In the wake of that statement Richter, Lena, and Eiche took to exchanging nervous glances amongst themselves while Heydrich leaned over ever so slightly toward Hannah. "Tell me truthfully, child, do you really wish to leave Germany just when the Fatherland needs you?"

Unable, and more to the point, unwilling to look to either of people who had taken her into their home with the understanding it was temporary for guidance about how best to answer, Hannah returned Heydrich's penetrating gaze. "We all have our duties to perform, Herr Gruppenführer," Hannah answered, choosing her words with great care. "They are burdens we must not turn away from. Mine is to my family, wherever they may be."

Pleased with the girl's answer, Heydrich stood up and looked about the small gathering. "You see! Just as I said. Even at her age, this girl understands her responsibilities and duties. She is *exactly* the sort of youth Germany will need in the difficult days ahead."

Wishing to whisk Hannah away as quickly as possible before she said something they'd regret, Lena took the girl's free hand and gave it a tug. "If you gentlemen would excuse us, I would like to take Hannah around and introduce her to some of the girls here."

Heydrich bowed ever so slightly. "Yes, of course, Fräu Richter. But before you go, you must promise me you will reconsider your decision to send this lovely child away."

Clearing his throat, Richter caught Heydrich's eye. "Perhaps that is something we can discuss at a later time, Herr Gruppenführer."

Again the blond SS man flashed a smile of which Hannah was wary. "Oh, rest assured, Hauptsturmführer, we will," Heydrich replied with a smoothness that caused Lena to shiver visibly.

❁

Ever alert to who was talking to people she considered important enough for her to bother with or who could further her interests, Anna Diehl had been watching the Richters and the girl in the red dress who struck her as vaguely familiar. Wishing to find out who the girl was and, more importantly, why Heydrich had taken such an interest in her, Anna maneuvered herself about the crowded assembly hall until she could chart a course that would allow her to cross paths with Lena.

Seeing the leader of the local BDM group approaching her out of the corner of her eye, and knowing it would be useless to attempt evading the ambitious young woman, Lena slowed her pace. As Anna drew near, Lena mustered up the best smile she could and greeted the BDM leader, taking the initiative and setting the tone of a conversation she had no chance of dodging. "Fräulein Diehl, I was hoping to run into you here. I must apologize for not thanking you sooner for the way you looked after Wolfgang the way you did," Lena proclaimed in an overly saccharine tone only a fool would take as sincere.

Anna, however, was such a fool. Not seeing Lena's demeanor or left-handed compliment for what they were, she returned her smile while doing her best to glance over at Hannah without making it seem as if she was doing so. "Your little Wolfgang is an absolute delight, Fräu Richter. A real joy."

"I understand you and Hannah are already acquainted," Lena continued, knowing the only reason the BDM leader had bothered with her was to find out who the girl was.

It was only then that Anna realized the ragamuffin whom she had pegged as nothing more than the daughter of Lena's hired help was the same girl standing there before her. Naturally, she assumed Hannah was related to the Richters and, even more important to her, was someone in whom Gruppenführer Heydrich himself had taken an interest, which meant it was in her best interest to become better acquainted with the girl. In double-quick time, the BDM leader's attitude did a complete one-eighty. "Yes, we have met. I am so sorry we didn't have an opportunity to be properly introduced the other day," Anna declared while looking down at Hannah. "I can tell by those blue eyes of yours you are Hauptsturmführer Richter's niece."

"No," Hannah replied crisply, making no effort to add an appropriate honorific at the end of her curt response.

"Ah! Then you must be Fräu Richter's niece."

"No."

"How is it you are related to the Richters?"

Without answering, Hannah looked up at Lena, who took up the question, but not before telling Hannah to run along and introduce herself to some of the other girls.

Anxious to put as much distance between herself and the adults involved in personal politics of which she had no understanding and no wish to be a part, Hannah wasted no time in fleeing to a table piled high with treats and refreshments she had spied.

❈

With no idea what was permissible or thought to be acceptable behavior in this setting, and seeing no one who seemed to be in charge of passing out the biscuits, fancy petit fours, and sweets on the table, Hannah slowed her pace as she approached it, then stopped. From behind her a girl's voice called out, "Go ahead. Help yourself."

Looking over her shoulder, Hannah saw the voice belonged to a girl with raven black hair neatly arranged in a pair of long braids draped over her shoulders. She looked not much older than Hannah. She was, of course, since she was wearing a BDM uniform. "You're new here, aren't you?" the girl asked as she came up to Hannah.

Hannah nodded. "Yes. I've only been here a couple of weeks."

With a knowing twinkle in her eye, the raven-haired girl thrust out her hand. "Your accent, it's Bairisch, isn't it?"

"Yes. I was born and raised in Munich."

"Frisian," the girl declared proudly. "I'm Sophie, Sophie Fromm."

Taken in by the girl's quick smile and unabashed straightforwardness, Hannah took the girl's hand. "I'm Hannah, Hannah . . ."

She stopped, panicking when she found herself unable to recall the full name she was supposed to be using. Not that this seemed to bother Sophie. Hanging onto Hannah's hand, Sophie dragged her up to the table. "Come on, Hannah. Let's gather up as much of the good stuff before it's gone and we're stuck with nothing but the hindquarters."

Amused by Sophie's brashness, Hannah took an instant liking to the girl, merrily following her lead. "Once we've gathered up all we want, I'll introduce you to the other girls. The fun ones, not the prudes who think they're better than the rest of us simply because their father is an ober this or a haupt that. I can't stand those girls. Can you?"

Not knowing how to answer, particularly since Herr Richter was a hauptsturmführer, Hannah merely shrugged. "I don't know. I haven't met anyone here, girls, that is, other than you."

"Well, I'm sure you'll find out soon enough for yourself. Now, what looks good to you, Hannah?"

"Chocolate," Hannah declared without hesitation. "I love anything with chocolate."

"Me too," Sophie squealed as the two dashed to where the plates were. Each of them snatched one before pushing their way through to where chocolate cakes and confections were and took to collecting their booty, laughing and giggling as they did.

From across the hall, Lena caught sight of Hannah. It was not all that difficult, as she was one of the few girls not wearing a BDM uniform. For a moment she was tempted to go over to the table where Hannah was in the process of piling a plate high with sweets and rein her in, but stopped when she realized Hannah had managed to latch onto another girl who had taken her under her wing.

It struck Lena as more than a little odd that Hannah seemed to be fitting in as well as she was, far better than she had initially expected given the child's background. Not that she minded. If anything, it was something of a relief, for it allowed her to relax for the first time since entering the hall. The girl would be all right for the time being, Lena concluded, never once appreciating how her attitude toward the child was changing.

With no need to worry about her, Lena set about looking for the small clutch of women she preferred to associate with during events such as this, wives who felt no need to go about lording over those whose husbands held a lesser rank. Like Sophie, she despised them, making a point to avoid their kind whenever she could.

❈

Even before the applause for what everyone thought was the final performance of the day's formal program had died away, Fräulein

Diehl was up and out of her seat, making her way to where the trio of Hitler Youth who'd just finished performing was taking their bows. Raising her hand, the ambitious young BDM group leader quieted the gathered families and visiting officials as if they were schoolchildren.

"Though I know she's not one of us yet, I would like to invite a new member of our little community to join in today's program." Then, turning to where Hannah was sitting between the Richters, Fräulein Diehl smiled at her. "Hannah, would you care to sing for us?"

Stunned, Hannah sat there staring wide-eyed at her, not knowing how to say no. She never had a chance to do so, as Richter leaned over and whispered in her ear. "I would love to hear you sing."

Slowly turning her head, she looked up into Richter's eyes, eyes imploring her to honor his request. Deciding there was no graceful way of refusing without embarrassing a man she'd come to respect, Hannah slipped off her chair and mechanically made her way to where Fräulein Diehl was standing. Beaming, the woman motioned to Hannah that the floor was hers before stepping back to enjoy the girl's performance.

For several long seconds Hannah scanned the sea of faces, all focused on her. Unable to stand the way they were staring, she closed her eyes and concentrated on what she would sing. A rapid-fire succession of songs her mother used to sing to her flashed through Hannah's mind until she hit upon one, a melody she loved and expected this gathering would enjoy.

Taking a moment to draw herself up and catch her breath, Hannah did her best to recall exactly how her mother had sung it. It was a folk song, one that started out softly, almost as a whisper, but ended in a rousing, celebratory fashion. Whether she could acquit herself as beautifully as her mother had was something Hannah doubted. Still, she had no choice but to try.

Ernst Richter watched the girl as she stood there in the middle of the room with her eyes screwed shut and head slightly bowed, taking deep, measured breaths to calm herself. He suddenly realized it had been a mistake to push her as he had. He was about to stand up and go over to where she was standing when she began to sing.

The sun on the meadow is summery warm,
The stag in the forest runs free.
But gathered together to greet the storm,
Tomorrow belongs to me.

Throughout the hall, there was total silence. Every ear strained to enjoy Hannah's clear, high-pitched voice.

Having made it through the first verse, Hannah opened her eyes and looked over to where Herr Richter was positively beaming.

When he realized she was waiting for some kind of sign from him, he gave her an encouraging nod. With that, Hannah began the second verse, raising her voice ever so delicately as she did so, just as she remembered how her mother had.

The branch on the linden is leafy and green,
The Rhine gives its gold to the sea.
But somewhere a glory awaits unseen,
Tomorrow belongs to me

Enthralled by the girl's performance, Richter reached over, grabbed his wife's hand, and gave it a joyous squeeze without ever taking his eyes off the enchanting waif who had managed to capture the undivided attention of every SS officer in the hall.

This time, as she prepared to pitch into the next verse, Hannah took to looking around the room, making eye contact with all the visiting guests from Berlin and Herr Richter's superior as she continued to sing with greater confidence and force.

The babe in his cradle is closing his eyes,
The blossom embraces the bee.
But soon says the whisper, arise, arise,
Tomorrow belongs to me

By the time she was ready to start the last verse she could recall, Hannah realized she was thoroughly enjoying herself, which allowed her to give it the powerful emphasis it so rightly deserved. As she did so, she lifted her eyes, gazing out over the heads of the audience at the blood-red banner of a new and vibrant Germany hanging over the hall's entrance.

> *Now Fatherland, Fatherland, show us the sign*
> *Your children have waited to see.*
> *The morning will come*
> *When the world is mine,*
> *Tomorrow belongs,*
> *Tomorrow belongs,*
> *Tomorrow belongs to me.*

Upon completing the last stanza, Hannah once more closed her eyes and ever so slowly bowed her head, anxious to hear the verdict of her audience. She did not have long to wait, for the room erupted into a standing ovation. When she did open her eyes and look about, she could not help but feel proud of what she had been able to achieve. She had managed to earn the admiration of men who were the leaders of a Germany she longed to be part. She also took pride in her ability to be accepted as a part of such a select and highly respected community. But most of all, for the first time in her life, Hannah found she was proud of who she was.

CHAPTER FIVE

A FEMALE PROBLEM

ORANIENBURG, NOVEMBER 1935

S tanding in the open doorway, it took the unterscharführer who served as Ernst Richter's secretary several seconds to catch his superior's eye. When Richter finally did look away from the officer newly assigned to his section, a young man who was doing everything to impress Richter with his knowledge but failing miserably, the unterscharführer raised his hand to his ear, mimicking the way one held a telephone's receiver. With nothing more than a nod, Richter acknowledged his secretary's nonverbal message before turning to the enthusiastic young officer seated in front of his desk. "If you would excuse me, I have a phone call I need to take."

"Yes, of course, sir," Untersturmführer Horst Fischer replied crisply.

Reaching out, Richter placed his hand on the telephone's receiver, but did not pick it up. Instead, he glared at Fischer, who was making no effort to leave. "I would like to take this call in private," Richter growled menacingly.

Suddenly realizing his error, Fischer jumped to his feet, snapped to attention, and thrust his right arm out with great gusto. "My apologies, Hauptsturmführer. Heil Hitler!"

In response to the officer's smart salute, Richter quickly lifted his right hand and muttered "Heil Hitler" in return before taking up the phone's receiver. "Richter here."

"Ernst! How are you, you slovenly sod?" a familiar voice replied.

"Oh, doing my best to beat the children you people in Berlin insist on assigning to our growing fiefdom."

"Funny you should mention children. That's exactly what I need to talk to you about, specifically that girl your wife brought back with her from Munich, a Hannah Kiefer."

Suddenly the friendly, easygoing tone was gone as Richter sat up and took to leaning over his desk. The realization that Otto Havermann, an old friend of his and part of Heydrich's SS's counterintelligence division, was making inquiries about Hannah alerted him to the fact the conversation he'd had with Heydrich the previous month about the girl had not been forgotten. Doing his best to sound as nonchalant as he could, Richter asked what this was all about. "It seems Heydrich is not at all pleased with the idea of seeing a child like your Hannah sent away to an American family. He asked me to look into the child's ancestral background to see if she's a suitable candidate for adoption."

"Adoption by who?"

"Well, if her bloodline is impeccable, I would imagine one of our own."

Unable to help himself, Richter rebuked his willingness to give into his wife's insistence that they drop any thought of keeping Hannah and instead look into contacting the girl's uncle in America. That, quite naturally, was going nowhere, since Richter was looking for someone with the last name of Kiefer who had emigrated from Munich to the United States. Lena, unbeknownst to him, had left it to her sister to quietly seek Hannah's uncle using the man's correct name. It was an effort that needed to be handled with great care lest someone begin to ask why she was interested in the whereabouts of a Jew. As a result, Julia had had little success.

"Ernst, are you still there?"

Richter gave his head a shake. "Yes, yes. I'm here."

"I'm calling you in the hope you can help me. I can't seem to find anything on this girl."

Suddenly seeing an opportunity too good to pass up, Richter smiled, reminding his friend who he was talking to and what he did.

"Listen, why don't you let me see what I can find. My brother-in-law is still with the Munich police."

Havermann grunted, "Yes, I know."

"Tell me, when do you need to wrap up this investigation?"

"I wasn't given a deadline, but you know how Heydrich is. He's not happy until he has a nice, complete dossier on whoever it is he's taken an interest in."

Yes, Richter thought, he knew *exactly* how Heydrich was when it came to collecting information on people of interest. Everyone in the SS did. "Right, then, I'll get back to you as soon as I can."

"Excellent," Havermann beamed. "I owe you one."

Though he suspected it was he who was indebted to his old friend, Richter knew better than to pass up an opportunity such as the one Havermann had just handed him since he had no idea what he would find once he started digging into Hannah's past. "I'll remember that, Otto. Now, if you'll excuse me, I need to get back to the young fool your office recommended to me as my adjutant."

"Do go easy on him, Ernst. Finding good men with blood as pure as his and brains to go with it is becoming harder and harder."

❅

A sudden sharp rapping of a wooden spoon on the side of a metal pot and a crisp "Stop that!" caused Hannah to jump.

Feigning innocence, she stepped back away from the table and spun about, quickly hiding her hands behind her back even as she was looking over to the stove where Fräu Sander was standing. "Stop what?"

Not at all taken in by Hannah's antics, the cook regarded her with narrowed eyes while waving her wooden spoon in the girl's direction. "Your little tricks will not work with me, young lady. Keep your fingers out of the cake batter, or I will have no choice but to show you this spoon has other uses."

Though tempted to be cheeky and ask what they could be, Hannah knew better. She had felt the sting of her mother's wooden spoon more than she cared to remember. It was a memory that left her wondering if all mothers were instructed on the use of wooden spoons as paddles in some secret class women attended when they were preparing to have children. "Is there something else I can do to help you, Fräu Sander?"

"You can start by cleaning the batter off those little fingers of yours before setting the table."

"I was hoping to help you cook," Hannah whined.

"Your kind of help isn't help," Fräu Sander groused before softening her expression. "Perhaps tomorrow, if you are in a mood to behave, I will show you how to make spätzle."

Only the promise of being allowed to help, as well as learn something new, kept Hannah's tongue in check. Instead, she set about dragging a chair to the cabinet where the dishes were kept, climbing up on it, and collecting what she would need to set the table for that evening's meal.

Hannah was in the midst of arranging the place settings on the dining room table, carefully aligning the knives, forks, and spoons with the same military precision with which she had noticed Ernst Richter kept everything in his study when she heard an automobile pull around to the front of the house. Anxious to see who it could be, Hannah called out to the cook she'd answer the door even before that woman had a chance to ask her if she would do so. Once she was in the foyer, Hannah threw the door open.

The second she saw it was Ernst Richter, her face lit up. The idea of having an opportunity to spend time with him in the study before dinner, going over the section of the book he had assigned her to study that morning, thrilled her. Though he was uncompromising when he quizzed her on what she had read, Herr Richter was fair and, even more important to Hannah, quick to praise her when she had acquitted herself well. To a child deprived of affection for as long as she had been, the gift of adoration was more precious than anything she could imagine.

The sight of the young girl who had stormed into his life standing in the open door waiting for him almost brought a smile to Ernst Richter's face. Almost, but not quite, as the implications of his conversation with his longtime comrade overrode any joy the mere sight of her was able to evoke. It was the thought of losing her, not a fear of what he might discover about her background, that worried Richter. In his mind, any thought the girl's blood was not as pure as his was foolish. One only needed to look at her to see she was as

Aryan as he was. Determined to keep his concerns from showing, Richter walked up to Hannah and patted the girl's head. "Have you been staying out of trouble?"

"Of course, Herr Richter."

"Good, good," he muttered distractedly as he took the hand Hannah held up to him and followed her into the house.

Hannah wasn't fooled in the least by Richter's efforts to pretend nothing was wrong. His expression alone was enough to tell her he had something troubling him. That she might be the cause of his concern could not be discounted. A morning did not pass without her wondering if this would be the day when the marvelous dream she'd been enjoying would come to an end.

After pausing in the foyer where he tossed his hat onto a side table, Richter looked about as if distracted. "My wife, is she about?"

"Both Fräu Richter and Wolfgang are upstairs enjoying a quiet midafternoon nap together."

"Hannah, do be a dear and ask her if she would join me in the study."

"Yes, of course."

With that, Hannah made her way up the stairs. Pausing before the door of the master bedroom, she knocked softly. When there was no answer, she slowly opened the door and slipped into the room. Tiptoeing over to the bed, Hannah found Fräu Richter lying on her side with an arm draped over her son, who was snuggled up against her. Both were sound asleep. Before waking them, she took a moment to reflect how peaceful mother and child looked, cuddled together in a loving embrace she wished she could share.

With a quick shake of her head, Hannah set aside such a silly notion, knowing full well she would never be able to find the kind of happiness she so desperately craved. Reaching out, she gave Fräu Richter a gentle nudge. "Herr Richter wishes to see you."

Befuddled, Lena was slow to stir. "Where? Here?" she asked as she pushed herself up, disturbing Wolfgang as she did so and causing him to whimper.

"Yes, ma'am. He is downstairs in his study waiting for you."

Knowing full well her husband would never leave his office in the middle of the day and return home unless it was important, Lena slipped off the bed and dashed over to her vanity where she took a brush to her hair. She had no need to wonder why he was there. Like Hannah, Lena had been expecting this day to come. That things would be ugly once Ernst discovered just how badly she had deceived him was a given, leaving Lena praying she would be able to find some way of making him understand why she had done what she had while begging him to forgive her foolishness. "Hannah, take Wolfgang to his room and stay there."

Scooping up the cranky child in her arms, Hannah headed out of the room without another word, leaving Lena to gather up the courage she would need for the coming ordeal.

❋

Richter didn't turn away from the window of his study and face his wife when she entered. Instead, with his hands thrust deep into the pockets of his trousers, he continued to gaze out over the Lehnitzsee. "I spoke with Otto earlier this afternoon," he announced in a tone that betrayed nothing.

Lena dismissed out of hand the idea of playing coy with her husband. She had little doubt the topic of their conversation had been Hannah. Instead, she drew herself up, clasping her hands before her as she waited for Ernst to continue.

"He was ordered to look into Hannah's background. It seems Heydrich was quite serious about not letting the girl leave Germany."

When she heard the word "girl," Lena wondered what else Heydrich knew or, more precisely, didn't know. "May I ask what it is he intends to do?" she asked tentatively.

Turning around, Richter looked over at his wife. "If Hannah passes muster, I expect she'll be offered up for adoption to someone, an SS officer if her bloodline is sufficiently pure. A child like her is exactly the kind the Party cherishes, for they are our future."

While she was relieved no one had yet to discover Hannah's true nature, Lena knew this was only a stay of execution. A thorough investigation, the kind men like Otto Havermann conducted on behalf of his superior, would surely discover Hannah not only was a mischling, but wasn't female. The consequences of that revelation for her and her husband were simply too terrible to contemplate.

Averting her eyes, Lena scrambled for a solution, one that would allow her to keep anyone associated with the SS from digging into

Hannah's past. "Perhaps I can help," she offered. "I can ask my sister's husband to look into the girl's background."

Having already considered that possibility, Richter nodded. "I expect that would be the quickest way to sort this mess out since he was the one who initially took the girl in and has access to all the records and files I need to look at. I'll give him a call later tonight, after dinner."

Unable to help herself, Lena blurted. *"No!"*

"No?"

Lena blinked. "What I mean is perhaps it would be best if I called him. The two of you don't exactly get along."

Pulling a hand out of his pocket, Richter bowed his head and scratched the side of his nose. What had once been an amiable friendship when they had been on the same police force had soured when he had joined the SS. Whereas Ernst saw the National Socialist movement as the answer to their nation's many woes, Fritz considered the whole lot to be little better than thugs, opportunists, and miscreants. He'd had great fun at Ernst's expense when word got around that Ernst Röhm, leader of the SA, had been caught by Hitler himself in bed with another man on what came to be known as the Night of the Long Knives. Since then, the two men could not exchange more than two words before their conversation degenerated into an argument.

"Perhaps you're right," he concluded sadly before turning to another subject, one more pressing. Once more jamming his hand in his pocket, he looked over at his wife. "If things do turn out the way I expect them to, we are going to adopt Hannah."

Stunned, Lena stared slack-jawed at her husband. "We can't do that," she declared without hesitation.

Ordinarily, this was the kind of thing Richter would have discussed with Lena, much as he had when he had suggested she become pregnant even though all the physicians she had gone to had advised against it. In truth, the idea of giving birth to a child despite the dangers was one idea Lena herself readily embraced, for she wanted to be a good wife to a man she dearly loved. Hannah's adoption was an entirely different matter.

Unfortunately for Lena, it was something her husband had no wish to debate, with her or anyone else. In the short time he had known

Hannah, Richter had convinced himself the girl was everything a father could wish for in a daughter. To lose her to another would be intolerable. Besides, he candidly admitted to himself, to give a girl like her away might make his superiors question his judgment. At a time when so many opportunities were opening up to him, the last thing he wished was to have a black mark placed next to his name in the little book Heydrich kept on everyone, even the Führer himself if rumors were to be believed.

With an expression he ordinarily reserved for dealing with subordinates, Richter regarded his wife. "Unless something untoward turns up in the girl's background, we *will* adopt her." With that, he walked past her and out of the room.

❈

Using the excuse that she needed to go into town and pick up a few things for Hannah, Lena went to the post office in Oranienburg, believing it would be best to discuss this matter with her sister from there rather than doing so over the phone in her husband's study.

Julia was stunned to hear Lena was even considering adopting the Jewish boy. "We had agreed you would see to it he was sent off to America."

"Julia, remember who I am married to. Even more than you, I can't go casting about trying to find the whereabouts of someone in a foreign country named Solomon Koch. Besides, things have changed. Hannah has come to the attention of some very high-ranking people. Sending her away is no longer possible."

Julia ignored the way her sister continued to refer to the boy as a *she*. Instead, she asked who was looking into the matter.

Even though she was in a private booth at the post office, Lena couldn't keep from looking out through the glass to see if someone was watching her. "The kind of people who can cause us all a great deal of trouble if they discover the truth," she whispered.

Sensing she wasn't going to get a straight answer out of her sister, Julia asked the obvious. "What do you expect me to do about this?"

"Fritz must know people, people who can provide the necessary documentation that will prove Hannah is free of Jewish blood."

"You do know what you're asking of me," Julia asked cautiously.

"Yes, I do."

"You also know documents alone will not suffice. At some point, the boy will need to be thoroughly examined or wish to participate in some sort of athletic activity in which he will not be able to conceal his true nature."

Lena winced. "I know. But what can I do, Julia? I'm in a corner with nowhere to go other than to you."

In the silence that followed, Julia considered her options. To say no to her sister was ruled out right off. To offer to take the boy back was also no longer possible. It seemed as if the only way out of this mess was to appeal to her husband. While she had no doubt he'd be able to use his leverage as a policeman to have the documentation they needed fabricated, the child's sex wasn't something one could change with the mere stroke of a pen or a forged birth certificate. "I'll get back to you after I've talked this over with Fritz," Julia finally affirmed.

"For heaven's sake, don't take too long."

"I'll take as long as I need to," Julia shot back. Then, realizing what they were discussing over the phone, she instructed Lena not to call her at her home or even discuss this matter over the phone again. "The SS aren't the only people with big ears."

With that, Julia hung up without telling Lena how she would contact her when she had something. Instead, she immediately set her mind to figuring out how best to broach this extremely delicate matter with her husband.

Most of Fritz's friends on the force dealt with known criminals without a second thought when they needed to help a friend or circumvent a silly law the Nazis had implemented. But Julia suspected her husband wouldn't do what she was about to ask of him out of any sense of family loyalty or love for her. While he was a good man and did love her after his fashion, the same post-war chaos that had led Ernst Richter to put his faith in the National Socialist movement had made Fritz Kruger a pragmatist. He wouldn't stick his neck out for anyone unless he had to or there was the promise of something of value to him in return. That he just might do what she was about to ask him for nothing more than the chance to have some fun at Ernst Richter's expense, even if he could never tell another soul the daughter of a rising star in the SS was actually a Jewish boy, was a possibility Julia was counting on.

With that thought in mind, she made her way into the kitchen and set about preparing Fritz his favorite meal. That would be the approach she would use, one even she found deliciously evil and fun.

❋

It was close to a week after her call to her sister that Lena was surprised to answer the front door and find Julia standing there, suitcase in hand. When Lena asked why her sister had come in person without notifying her, Julia suggested the two go over the matter they'd discussed on the phone while taking a walk along the shore of the lake. Agreeing without hesitation, Lena called out to Hannah.

Preceded by a chorus of giggles, Hannah came loping down the stairs with Wolfgang clinging to her back in a manner that caused Lena to grimace. It was the sight of Julia, not the expression of displeasure on Fräu Richter's face, that caused Hannah to slow her pace, then stop. Without having to be told, she knew Julia Kruger's presence somehow related to whatever it had been that was causing both Lena and Ernst Richter to go about behaving as they had of late.

For her part, Julia found it difficult to believe what she was seeing. The young girl wearing a dark green skirt and a yellow rollneck sweater bore little resemblance to the child she had packed off with her sister little more than a month before. Perhaps, she thought as she watched Hannah approach, what she had planned would be far easier than she had thought. It was obvious the boy had more than taken to his role.

After instructing Hannah to carry Julia's suitcase up to the guest bedroom and watch after Wolfgang, Lena pulled on a coat and led her sister to a path she, Ernst, Hannah, and Wolfgang strolled along on Sunday afternoons when the weather allowed. Only after they were well away from the house did Julia explain her sudden appearance. "What I am about to say is something I didn't feel comfortable discussing over the phone or putting in a letter."

"Go on," Lena replied without looking up from the path ahead of her as the two women slowly made their way along it arm in arm.

"Several years ago, there was a clinic in Berlin that dealt with sexual deviants, run by a man named Hirschfeld."

Lena nodded. "I recall hearing about him when his clinic was closed and his books burned. At the time, Ernst joked the only reason the SA did so was that too many high-ranking Brownshirts had been clients of his."

"The place was gutted, and all who worked there fled the country," Julia sniffed. "One of them was a physician by the name of Ludwig Levy-Lenz who has recently returned to Germany from Paris, where he fled to when the clinic was closed down. Fritz learned he's opened a private clinic in Berlin, on the Kurfürstendamm of all places."

Anxious to cut to the chase, Lena glanced over at her sister out of the corner of her eye. "And how does this help? If I recall correctly, that lot dealt with homosexuals."

"Not all of their patients were homosexuals. Levy-Lenz specialized in helping men who wish to become women achieve that goal."

Dumbfounded, Lena stopped dead in her tracks. For the longest time, she was unable to do anything more than stare at her sister. "How is that possible?" she finally managed to ask.

Stepping back, Julia grabbed her sister's arm and began dragging her along. "I do not know exactly, but if you really want to see this through, if you wish to adopt the boy without anyone knowing what he is, or was, it is the only way."

For the longest time, the two women walked in silence. Eventually, Lena turned to her sister. "Even if what you say is true, and even if Hannah agrees, I can't take her there. You do appreciate everything that goes on at a place like that always finds its way to Heydrich's office sooner or later, one way or another."

"You worry about talking Hannah into going. I'll handle the rest," Julia volunteered. "After all, I was the one who managed to get you into this mess. Besides," she added, "if we don't find a way out of this, you and Ernst won't be the only ones paying a visit to Dachau."

"Ernst!" Lena declared. "What do I tell Ernst?"

"He's the least of our problems at the moment."

Lena regarded her sister as if she were barking mad.

Julia rolled her eyes. "All you need to tell your precious Ernst is that Hannah has a female problem, one he doesn't wish to know about," she offered. "Tell him if it's not looked after now, Hannah will have difficulties later on in life, which at this point is quite true."

"And what if he insists on knowing more or, worse, going to the clinic to visit Hannah while she's there?"

Julia gave her sister a dismissive look. "He won't. Men don't ask about such things. When it comes to women, all they're interested in is that we're not menstruating when they're in the mood to rut and whether they can keep it up long enough to enjoy themselves."

"You don't know Ernst."

"Trust me, Lena, he won't ask."

✻

To Lena's great surprise and considerable relief, her sister's prediction proved accurate. Ernst made it abundantly clear he had no wish to delve into the details. All he wished to know was whether Hannah would be all right after whatever she needed to be done had been taken care of. Though she was still skeptical, Lena assured him she would be.

As astonishing as her husband's attitude had been to Lena, more so was the way Hannah dealt with Julia's proposal. When Lena asked her why she so readily agreed to something so radical, Hannah told a half-truth, saying she wished to stay with the Richters and that if an operation to create something resembling a female's genitals was necessary to keep her from developing into a normal boy, she would gladly do so.

Though this statement was true, the real reason Hannah looked forward to the operation was that the removal of her genitals would eradicate the part of her that marked her as a Jew. Once that was gone, she would be free of her past, a past that had brought her nothing but misery and pain. While Julia Kruger explained the result would be far from perfect, and that she could never have babies, Hannah hoped the result would be adequate enough to become the daughter of an important man whom she had come to admire. And while she knew women would never be permitted to play prominent roles in the new Reich outside of the traditional ones Germans had always revered, at least she would be able to be part of the new and exciting Germany, her Germany.

PART TWO

1938

"PEACE IN OUR TIME"

CHAPTER SIX

THE STURMBANNFÜHRER'S DAUGHTER

ORANIENBURG, MAY 1938

Scrambling out of the classroom like a herd of stampeding gazelles, the gaggle of girls crowded into the hall, eager to rush home and gather up things they would need for the weekend field trip Fräulein Diehl had just sprung on them. Desperate to make good her escape from a woman she loathed, Sophie Fromm elbowed her way through the press and into the lead. Once clear of the jabbering crowd of excited girls, all uniformly dressed in the crisp white blouses and dark blue skirts of the BDM, Sophie spun about and pressed herself up against a wall. Rising up on her tippy toes, she peered out of the heads of the milling mass making its way down the corridor toward the exit.

Upon seeing one of her friends, Sophie bellowed out in a most unladylike manner. "Gretchen!"

Ignoring the scathing glare from the girl whose ear she had just screamed into, Sophie again called out to her friend, who was on the other side of the corridor. "Over here."

Cutting across the flow of young girls, Gretchen Bauer, a tall, gangly, bespectacled girl with mousy, brown hair, made her way over to Sophie.

"Have you seen Hannah?" Sophie asked as Gretchen joined her.

"Fräulein Diehl asked her to stay behind," Gretchen replied, as she did her best to press herself up against the wall next to Sophie so as to keep from being swept away by the other girls.

Making a sour face, Sophie grunted. "I'll bet she's trying to talk her into joining choir again."

"I hope she does and Hannah agrees," Gretchen opined wistfully.

"As much as I'd love to have Hannah join us, I doubt she'll agree," Sophie countered without having to give the matter any thought. "You know how she detests the Blond Cow."

Gretchen attempted to hush her friend, fearing one of the girls passing in front of them would overhear Sophie refer to Anna Diehl with the nickname some of them used behind the pretentious BDM leader's back.

Sophie, being Sophie, was having none of it. "I don't care if anyone hears me."

"Well, I do," countered Gretchen.

"That's because you're no better than Hannah when it comes to sucking up to *Fräulein Diehl*," Sophie declared, making a point of exaggerating their BDM leader's name as she did so.

"We don't suck up to that woman. We simply conduct ourselves in a manner that is expected."

"Oh please," Sophie responded derisively.

Gretchen's efforts to defend her friend was cut her short by Sophie. "Well, speak of the devil."

Turning, Gretchen caught sight of Hannah coming toward them down the now-empty corridor. When she was close enough, Gretchen asked what Diehl had wanted.

Shooting a glance over her shoulder and back toward the open door of the classroom she'd just left, Hannah grunted. "Not here."

Falling in on either side of her and cradling their books in their arms, Sophie and Gretchen made their way down the deserted corridor with Hannah and out of the school building. Only when she was sure no one would overhear their conversation did Hannah speak, groaning and rolling her eyes as she did so. "When will that woman get it through her thick skull I have no intention of joining her precious choir."

Grinning, Sophie leaned forward, looking past Hannah and over toward Gretchen. "See. I told you the cow wanted Hannah to join."

Paying no heed to Sophie, Gretchen looked at the ground as the three girls sauntered along. "I wish you *would* join. We three could have such great fun together."

"*You* might have fun on the trips she drags us on," Sophie countered. "I don't."

"That's because you always manage to get yourself in trouble by making faces during our performances," Hannah stated matter-of-factly.

Feigning shock, Sophie pulled away from the other two. "I do not make faces! I merely allow myself to express my feelings as we sing."

"You make faces," Gretchen muttered under her breath, before asking Hannah what excuse she'd used this time.

"I informed her I would not have the time to devote to choir practice."

"Because you're doing what, if I may ask?" Sophie said incredulously. "Perfecting that cute little act of yours you use to charm all the teachers?"

"I do not put on an act," Hannah sniffed.

While Sophie howled at this, Gretchen glanced over at her friend out of the corner of her eye. "You do too. Everyone knows you do."

"Just because I behave appropriately, conducting myself in a manner expected of the daughter of an SS officer by respecting my elders, as we all should, does not make me a prig."

"Oh, please," Sophie snorted. "Spare us. You're a toffee-nosed little suck-up if ever there was one."

Tiring of defending her behavior, Hannah turned to Sophie and made a face while sticking her tongue out at her. "You're just jealous because you can't get away with pretending to be a proper little lady."

"Who wants to be? All you have to do is look at Eva Wenders. She's so worried someone will think she's not perfect that she never has any fun."

Annoyed by Sophie's mockery, and eager to learn what excuse Hannah had used to frustrate Fraulein Diehl this time, Gretchen asked Hannah what it was she'd be doing that precluded her from spending time practicing with the girl's choir.

A broad grin flashed across Hannah's face as she leaped out in front of her two friends, spun about, and thrust her right arm out at them as if she were holding a sword. "Fencing lessons."

Sophie stopped short. Her eyes lit up. "Really?"

"*No!* You're kidding?" Gretchen squealed as her jaw dropped.

Beaming, Hannah jerked her head to one side, making her tightly braided hair swing wildly about as she drew herself up. "I've already started," she declared crisply. "Father has been teaching me some of the basics at home."

"And your mother is allowing you to do so?" Gretchen asked, still astonished by Hannah's good fortune.

Before answering, Hannah fell in with her friends again as they continued to stroll along. "It goes without saying Mama was not at all pleased when Father informed her of his decision to give in to my pleas and allow me to take up fencing, particularly since he did so on the condition I take up the saber instead of the foil. He says foils are for children and sissies. When using foils, you only score a hit if you strike your foe's torso. With sabers, any strike above the waist is permissible, except for hands and the back of the head."

Hannah was about to pitch into a detailed discussion of the sport when the sight of a new Mercedes Grosser pulling up to the curb brought their conversation to an end. Turning around, Hannah began to walk backward toward the automobile. "I must be going."

Unable to help herself, Sophie sighed. "You are so lucky, Hannah."

Hannah winked mischievously. "Oh, trust me, luck has nothing to do with this or anything else I do." Then, without explaining any further, she twirled about and ducked through the open door being held for her by a uniformed SS driver.

❀

Without waiting for the auto's door to be opened for her, Hannah slid across the seat and hopped out, taking a moment to give the driver a friendly wave and bid him goodbye using the familiar *"tschüss"* she preferred whenever her parents weren't about and she felt she could get away with it.

Even before she had a chance to put her books down, Wolfgang came thundering out of the kitchen calling her name. *"HANNAH!"*

The girl barely had enough time to toss her books aside and brace for impact before Wolfgang charged her. *"Oooppff!"* Hannah grunted as she absorbed the force of the collision, wrapping her arms about the precocious four-year-old and swinging him around before hoisting him up and onto a hip.

Once she was sure she had a firm grip on him, Hannah thrust her face toward the giggling little boy who did likewise. After rubbing noses, each pulled their heads away. "Where's Mama?" Hannah asked.

"She's resting."

"And Clara?"

"In town, on an errand."

"And she didn't take you with her?" Hannah asked as she did her best to hide her anger over this. It did not surprise Hannah the housekeeper failed to look after Wolfgang whenever she thought she could get away with it, even though that was part of her responsibility.

"I don't think she likes me," Wolfgang muttered, as if confused by the very idea there was someone in the world who did not.

Not wishing to make an issue of Clara's behavior, at least not in front of Wolfgang, Hannah changed the subject. "You're getting too big for me to pick up, Wolfie," she proclaimed as she set the boy down.

"Not big enough to be a panzer commander," the boy replied, pouting.

"A panzer commander? I thought you wanted to go to Spain and be a Stuka pilot like we saw in the newsreels?"

Looking up, the four-year-old crossed his arms, taking up a stance he had often seen his father assume whenever he was in no mood to argue. "I have changed my mind."

Knowing better, Hannah cocked her head to one side as she also crossed her arms while looking down at the stern-faced boy. "What happened?" she asked flatly.

Having learned the hard way there was no getting around telling the truth when it came to his sister, Wolfgang dropped his arms to his side as well as his gaze. "I broke the Stuka Papa gave me."

Doing her best to keep from laughing, Hannah maintained her stance, asking the boy how he had managed to do that.

"I sat on it," Wolfgang muttered dejectedly.

"You what?"

"I forgot I put it in Papa's big chair," Wolfgang replied sheepishly as he looked up at Hannah with a pair of big, blue eyes that never failed to undo what their father had come to call her "Stare of Doom." It was a demeanor Hannah had found she had needed to adopt since she often found herself having to care for her little brother. And though she knew she should have admonished the boy for going into their father's study without permission, especially when no one was around to keep an eye on him while he was there, she didn't have the heart to do so at the moment.

"Well, perhaps it's best if you do become a panzer commander," Hannah concluded as she reached out and took Wolfgang's hand before leading him to the kitchen. "Panzers don't break as easily as airplanes."

❁

Hannah and Wolfgang were seated at the kitchen table, drinking milk, nibbling on Honiglebkuchen, and listening to Fräu Sander hum as she hustled about preparing dinner when Clara came in through the back door. All Hannah's thoughts of admonishing the young housekeeper for not taking Wolfgang along with her were forgotten the second the housekeeper placed a box on the table next to Hannah's plate.

Wide-eyed with excitement, Hannah set aside her half-eaten biscuit, slipped off her chair, and snatched up the box emblazoned with the gold lettering of a noted fencing clothier. She was about to dash out of the kitchen when the sound of Fräu Sander clearing her throat caused her to stop and slowly turn around.

From where she stood, the cook regarded Hannah questioningly. "I seem to recall a certain young girl's pledge to help me with dinner after she'd finished her snack," the cook mused as if to herself.

Tilting her head to one side, Hannah pleaded with Fräu Sander with her eyes, raising the wondrous gift she held ever so slightly.

Although she would never admit it to anyone, the cook could not resist the bright-eyed girl when she used her well-honed charms to get her way. "Oh, go ahead, child," Fräu Sander harrumphed. "Let me see what you look like with it on."

Beaming, Hannah spun about and stormed out of the kitchen and into the foyer, where she took the stairs two at a time. Once in her room, she closed the door, locked it, and pulled down the shades before turning to the box she'd placed on her bed. With great reverence, she ever so carefully slipped the satin ribbon off the corners of the box and removed the lid. Pausing, she took a moment to savor the sight of the pristine white fencing jacket neatly folded on top of the other items so that its sleeves were folded over, revealing the diamond-shaped Hitler Youth patch sewn on the upper portion of the left sleeve.

It took every bit of self-discipline Richter had instilled in his daughter to keep her from snatching up the jacket. Instead, she gingerly took the cotton garment by its shoulders and slowly lifted it from the box, holding it out at arm's length to admire it. In doing so, she noticed it had a croissard, a groin strap designed to keep it from riding up during a match. Though she would have preferred a short jacket in the style favored by those who fenced with sabers, it did not matter much to Hannah. Perhaps later, she told herself as she set her new jacket aside, when she outgrew this one, her father would see to it she had a proper short jacket.

The white, formfitting kickers brought a smile to Hannah's face. Not since she'd left Munich had she worn trousers. Mother would not hear of her even owning a pair. If truth be known, Hannah didn't much mind skirts and dresses, except of course when it was bitter cold outside and the wind was whipping along the ground. In Hannah's mind, enduring days like that was all part of being female, no different than the painful procedures she had been subjected to shortly after being taken in by the Richters. She had come to believe it was her willingness to meet challenges such as that without reservation, and not luck as Sophie assumed, that allowed her to achieve what she once had thought was an unobtainable dream.

Piece by piece, Hannah reverently laid every item in the box neatly upon her bed. To Hannah, this custom-made fencing outfit, like the saber engraved with her name her father had given her on the day he informed her he would allow her to take up fencing, was more than part of a sports ensemble. Unlike the collection of dolls neatly arranged on a shelf set aside for them in her room, gifts her mother gave her on every birthday and Yuletide, it was a passport to adulthood. It allowed her to stand before her father, not as his child, but as close to his equal as a young German girl could ever hope to be. And while his face would be hidden behind the tight metal mesh of his fencing mask, she knew when he looked out from behind it he would do so with an expression that told Hannah she was more than merely loved. She was adored.

※

With focused determination, Hannah dueled with the imaginary foe before her, doing her best to execute the steps, parries, and lunges her father drilled her in each afternoon when he returned home. She tried to move with the same seamless precision with which he did. She still had to pause and consider her next move when afforded the opportunity to attack, but once she pitched into it, she did so smoothly and with an élan that impressed him.

She was in the midst of a series of quick thrusts and a parry before retreating ever so briefly and lunging forward again when Ernst Richter slipped in the room he had set aside for their practices together. When he saw his daughter had not noticed him, he hung back, taking this opportunity to watch her.

Hannah was good, he told himself. Better than good. He only needed to show her something once. And while she was not able to demonstrate complete mastery of each new technique the first time through, Richter marveled at the alacrity with which she took to his instruction. It did not matter to him that Hannah's adeptness when it came to mimicking proper behavior was borne out of a desperate need to conform to a society she wished to embrace fully. To him, Hannah was more than a pleasant diversion from the grim but necessary tasks he dealt with every day at the Sachsenhausen facility where he oversaw the training of personnel destined for the growing number of camps the Totenkopfverbände was responsible for administering. The girl was a gleaming source of pride, proof to all who met her that he was more than an efficient officer. To those who mattered or wished to emulate his success in all things, Hannah was the last bit of evidence they needed to view Ernst Richter as the personification of Aryan manhood, every bit the perfect soldier, husband, and father.

With a high-pitched cry so out of character with the enchanting singing voice Richter never tired of hearing, Hannah executed an appel as she advanced from the en grade position, thrusting her saber straight into the heart of her imaginary foe.

Drawing himself up, Richter wiped the smile off his face with well-measured ease. "You're overextending again," he barked brusquely. "With your arm stretched out like that you're leaving yourself open to a quick-witted opponent willing to risk countering with a Passata-sotto."

Though started by her father's voice, Hannah was able to recover from her surprise without much effort. Rather than greeting him as she ordinarily would have with a squeal of delight, beaming smile, and a heartfelt hug, she assumed the First Position, placing her leading foot toward her approaching father with her rear foot at a right angle, so that her heels were touching. Drawing herself up to her full height with legs together, she deviated slightly from what Richter had shown her by giving her head a quick shake, one that caused her hair, worn in a high ponytail, to flop about from side to side over her shoulders. It was a feminine conceit Richter made no effort to correct since he enjoyed it, though he did his best to keep Hannah from realizing this.

Once she had assumed the proper stance, Hannah lowered her saber until the guard was slightly below the belt line of her new jacket, with the weapon's blade on a downward diagonal and toward the rear as though it were in a scabbard. With that, she placed her left hand on the rear hip and watched as her father approached in a leisurely, almost nonchalant manner meant to convey to his opponent he had no fear of him.

In truth, Ernst Richter had little to fear from those who crossed sabers with him, whether while fencing or in the performance of their duties. The crop of officers now entering the ranks of the SS were men drawn from the best and brightest the universities had to offer or who had abandoned the practice of law and other professions. But unlike them, Ernst Richter had learned his trade in the bloody streets of Munich under the tutelage of battle-hardened trench fighters. His approach to his duties was not grounded in the ideological drivel young bucks like Horst Fischer relied upon to justify their decision to join the SS. No, the newly promoted Sturmbannführer carried out his tasks with cold efficiency, for he knew there was only one way to deal with the enemies of the state. His unflinching commitment to his duties and dispassionate demeanor while doing so made him both a credit to his superiors and an invaluable asset to the Reich.

When he had finally given into Hannah's pleas to teach her how to fence, Richter had resolved that he would use the same unsentimental approach he applied to his duties. "Your opponents will show you no mercy," he had warned the girl in a manner that served notice he was deadly serious. "So expect none from me."

Rather than being intimidated by this, Hannah embraced the challenge. In her eyes, her father was honoring her with respect few of her friends enjoyed. He wasn't treating her as if her only value was to produce children, a duty to the Reich she would never be able to fulfill. No, Hannah told herself as she waited to cross sabers with a man she admired with all her soul. The man who had adopted her and taken her into his heart was affording her the opportunity to become the kind of woman their New Germany would need; strong, capable, and unafraid.

Ever so slowly, Hannah pivoted her head about, following every movement her father made as he took up his position at the far end of the piste. When he began to don his leather gauntlet and take his fencing mask out from under his arm where he'd been cradling it, Hannah did likewise. "We shall start where we left off yesterday," Richter announced crisply. "You *do* recall what we were doing when we finished?" he asked mockingly.

Having no intention of falling for her father's effort to pique her ire and cause her to lash out at him, Hannah countered with a smirk. "But of course, Father. Do you?"

Richter found he could not help but chuckle to himself as he donned his mask. When ready, he too assumed the first position across from his daughter. *"EN GARDE!"*

CHAPTER SEVEN

PASSATA-SOTTO

Sophie emerged from a dark forest bereft of even the slightest breeze into a grassy opening bathed in blinding sunlight. It took a moment for her eyes to adjust before she was able to spot Hannah and Gretchen lazing about on the grass with the other girls. Trudging up to where they were, the raven-haired girl, covered in sweat, threw herself on the ground in the space they'd saved for her between them. *"Ugh!* Is that woman trying to kill us by marching us to death?"

Lying on her back with her fingers knitted together behind her head and legs crossed at the ankles, Hannah didn't bother looking away from the white, puffy clouds she was watching drift lazily across the sky as she repeated the oath they'd all taken the day each of them had joined the League of German Girls. "In the presence of this blood-banner which represents our Führer, I swear to devote all my energies and my strength to the savior of our country, Adolf Hitler. I am willing and ready to give up my life for him, so help me God. One people, one Reich, one Führer."

"Oh, shut up, you," Sophie muttered as she pushed herself up off the ground into a seated position, brought her canteen around, and unscrewed its cap.

"I thought you enjoyed our outings?" Hannah mused. "Why just two weeks ago, I recall a certain someone I know complaining how we never went anywhere."

After taking a mouthful of warm water from her canteen and swishing it about in her mouth before swallowing, Sophie looked around at the small, featureless clearing in the forest. "This *isn't* anywhere. This is *nowhere.*"

Gretchen took a moment to look about as well. "I rather like it here. It's so peaceful, and . . ." After closing her eyes and drawing in a deep breath, she added, "So clean and fresh."

Giving her mousy-haired friend a filthy look, Sophie groaned. "You're as bad as Hannah."

Hannah, Gretchen, and some other girls who had been listening in on this exchange were enjoying a good laugh at Sophie's expense when Anna Diehl came to her feet and clapped her hands. "All right, girls. Our little break is over. Everyone, up, up, up."

"But I just got here!" Sophie exclaimed.

Their leader showed no sympathy for the exhausted girl, choosing instead to humiliate Sophie in the hope of spurring her to do better in the future. "And whose fault is that, Fräulein Fromm?" she snipped. "If you were more like your friend Hannah and kept up with the rest of us, you would have had plenty of time to enjoy this lovely field filled with wonderful spring flowers."

Turning her head away from where Fräulein Diehl was and looking over to Hannah, who was already on her feet adjusting her bread bag and canteen, Sophie mimicked their leader under her breath. *"If you were more like your friend Hannah, if you were more like your friend Hannah.* If I were more like Hannah, I'd shoot myself."

Hannah made a face and stuck her tongue out at Sophie as soon as she saw Fräulein Diehl wasn't looking in their direction. "Oh, hush. You're just jealous."

"Of you?" Sophie retorted. "You bet. You don't have to stay out here tonight with the Blond Cow. You get to go home."

"I can't help it if Father is having some important people from Berlin over for dinner tonight and he's expecting me to be there," Hannah explained.

"Lucky cow," Sophie groused.

"Come on, slowpoke," Gretchen called out as she and Hannah each offered their friend a hand. "At least *try* to keep up with us for a while."

With a sigh, Sophie reached up and took their hands. "Yes, yes. I know," she muttered dejectedly as the two girls pulled their friend up off the ground. "I need to be more like Hannah."

❋

Dining with the adults when her father was entertaining important guests was a treat to which Hannah always looked forward. Lena Richter would try to point out that allowing a child as young as Hannah to do so was inappropriate. But her husband casually brushed her concerns aside. "Ordinarily I would agree," he would counter. "Our Hannah, however, is a very special girl." Mercifully, Ernst Richter did not know just how special she was.

One of the more intriguing aspects of the tight-knit community in which Hannah lived, at least in her eyes, was the opportunity to meet and associate with people from all over Germany. Sophie was Frisian, born and raised on a windswept island in the eastern edge of the North Sea. She was fond of saying it was a nice place to live, but only if you enjoyed having sand in your shoes all the time. Gretchen was a Rheinlander whose parents came from a small town not far from the Lorelei Rock. "According to Mother, that is where I get my singing voice," the tall, mousy-haired girl informed Hannah.

Through her friends and the guests her father frequently brought home when they were visiting the headquarters of the Totenkopfverbände or the camp at Sachsenhausen, Hannah became aware of things about Germany and its people she could never have learned from a book. Most of what she learned was fascinating.

The down side of this was now and then, something was said that allowed the families of the men who ran the growing number of camps a glimpse behind the thick curtain they used to protect their loved ones from the truth of what they were doing.

The guests that evening were of particular interest to Hannah as they were Austrian, or had been until the Anschluss. According to her father, the real work that stunning diplomatic coup demanded of men like him was just beginning. Folding all the functions once handled by an independent Austrian government into the greater

German Reich was no easy matter, Ernst Richter opined when explaining to Hannah why he had been spending so much time with the Austrian SS men.

"In addition to combining two systems into one, procedures, policies, and organizations that are now well established here need grafting onto Austrian society and institutions. Even those organizations that had been working closely with their German counterpart before the Anschluss such as the Austrian SS and Hitler Youth have to make adjustments to fit into the overall scheme of things."

What he didn't tell his daughter was this included the establishment of new camps such as those at Dachau and Sachsenhausen in what was now being called Ostmark.

Things did not start out well that evening, at least as far as Hannah was concerned. When she came down to assist in setting the table and helping Fräu Sander in the kitchen, Hannah was wearing a clean BDM uniform she'd changed into after returning from her hike. Lena took one look at the girl before sending her marching back up the stairs to change. "That is not proper attire for a young lady when entertaining at home," Lena informed Hannah.

"But everyone else will be in uniform," Hannah countered.

"I won't be."

"That's because you don't have one," Hannah snipped.

Canting her head to one side, Lena glared at her adopted daughter. "You *will* go upstairs right this minute and change, or you will find yourself spending the evening alone in your room nursing a very sore bottom."

Realizing she'd pushed her mother to the brink, and not wishing to miss dinner with the Austrians, Hannah tromped off to change with her head hung low and bottom lip stuck out. She was tempted to dress in something totally inappropriate as a way of getting back at her mother. But Fräu Sander wasn't the only woman in the house who knew wooden spoons could be used for more than cooking.

❊

The conversation at the table was all Hannah had hoped for, at least in the beginning. In addition to the Austrians, Horst Fischer, who was serving as Ernst's adjutant, was seated to Hannah's right and kitty-corner to her mother. When not otherwise occupied with her responsibilities as the spouse of a distinguished officer and mother to her children, Lena had been trying to find Fischer a proper wife with all the enthusiasm of a knight in search of the Holy Grail. Unfortunately for Hannah, the woman her mother had settled on to fill that role was none other than Anna Diehl. That meant Hannah's BDM leader was often invited to join them as Fischer's partner at dinner parties and other social events. Naturally, Sophie used Fräulein Diehl's frequent visits to tease Hannah, calling her nothing more than a bootlicking little prat, in a friendly sort of way. Only the camping trip the other girls were "enjoying" with the Blond Cow spared Hannah from having to spend the evening listening to the obnoxious woman as she blathered on about this or that.

It wasn't long before another guest, Hauptsturmführer Albert Sauer, who was seated across from Hannah, picked up those traces of her Austro-Bavarian accent she had not been able to purge. Curious how this was possible since neither of her parents betrayed any hint of it, Sauer engaged Hannah in conversation whenever the opportunity arose. Not knowing what was afoot, Hannah eagerly played along, bombarding the Austrian with questions about his people, the history of his country, and Austrian folklore, while he did likewise with Hannah. When she mentioned she would love to travel to places she'd heard and read about, Sauer pointed over to the SS officer seated to Hannah's left with his knife. "If you're interested in hearing about travel, there's the young man you should be talking to. Eichmann's been all over. He's even been to Palestine to discuss the possibility of shipping our Jews there rather than dealing with them here." Pausing, Saur glanced over at Richter. "He even met with Jews in a ragtag militia they call the Haganah. Can you imagine that? There are Jews who actually believe they can fight."

Drawing in a deep breath, Ernst Richter took a moment to temper the anger welling up within him over Sauer's indiscretion. As much as he shared with his wife and daughter, there were specific topics he avoided in their presence. Their handling of undesirables, especially of Jews, was one of them.

The look on Richter's face, and the way he was drawing himself up was enough to tell Sauer he had erred. For the longest time, the two men stared at each other in utter silence, which was fortunate for Hannah, as the mere mention of Jews or anything related to them made her tense up. Lena was also unable to keep her expression from clouding over, as an underlying fear she was never quite able to put behind her once more leaped to the fore.

Obersturmführer Adolf Eichmann took note of the curious way mother and daughter were behaving. As an officer who worked for Reinhardt Heydrich, he had learned people very often betrayed more than they wished to by the way they reacted in certain situations or during the course of a conversation. He could not help but think that unlike the mask people uncomfortable with the topic of the Jews often hid behind, the expression he saw on the faces of the two females was more akin to fear, or perhaps guilt over a shared secret. Such a secret clearly had something to do with Jews.

As much as he would have liked to root about to determine just what that secret was, Eichmann appreciated this was neither the time nor place for that. Instead, he turned his attention to defusing the standoff between his fellow Austrian and their host. "I've also been to Cairo," he announced casually, taking up his wine glass. "I assure you, that is a far more interesting place than Palestine."

The others at the table ever so cautiously set aside their concerns or anger and finished their meal while Eichmann told of his non-duty-related adventures in Egypt. Hannah, unable to recover as readily as the adults, remained at the table only long enough to allay any suspicions over her sudden loss of appetite for both the meal and conversation before asking permission to leave the table. When it was given, she dutifully went over to her father and gave him a kiss goodnight on his cheek before heading off to her room. Never once as she was doing so did anyone take their eyes off her, especially Obersturmführer Eichmann.

❈

A very different ordeal awaited Hannah the following week when she was driven to the SS sports arena where she would take her first formal fencing lesson. When Klaus Wendol agreed to take Hannah on as a student, he did so with the understanding she would have to train with the boys since no other girls had parents who would permit their daughters to engage in the sport. To keep Richter from suspecting he was not at all happy either, he used the excuse that some of the parents of his other students might also complain when they found out their sons had to compete with a girl. "They could make trouble, you know," he informed Richter.

Hannah's father replied to the fencing master's remark with the same baleful smile upon which he often relied when dealing with a troublesome subordinate. "What other parents do or think is of no interest to me. Neither should they be of concern to you." Richter's reputation as a man who was not to be trifled with was such that Wendol never again objected to taking Hannah on as a student. Instead, he relied on other, more indirect means of dealing with the issue.

The need to change from her school clothes into her fencing outfit alone came as no surprise to Hannah. She actually preferred to find a quiet corner whenever there was the need to undress in the presence of other girls. Though the efforts of the surgeon Julia Kruger had taken her to in 1935 were more than sufficient to keep her from being seen as anything but female even when undressed, Hannah could never quite forget those changes were merely superficial. This shyness struck her friends as being at odds with a personality all saw as otherwise bold to the point of recklessness. Had she been anyone else, this contradiction would have been a problem. But Hannah was more than the daughter of an SS officer. She was Ernst Richter's daughter, a fact that kept even her greatest detractors from saying anything to her, lest they risk finding out if the similarities between father and daughter were more than physical.

What did cause Hannah to hesitate when she emerged from the changing room and came face to face with her fellow students was their reaction. As she crossed the floor with her fencing mask tucked under her arm to where they were already gathered, they turned toward her as one, causing Hannah's heart to skip a beat. With precious few exceptions, the expressions on the faces of the boys were no different than the one that had greeted her each day at her old school in Munich. That was before the man who had raised her had finally decided to withdraw her after growing tired of seeing his only child return home bloodied and bruised each night. And though the reason for those boys' resentment was so very different than the reason for the unbridled disdain she now faced, the trepidation Hannah felt at that moment wasn't.

Attired in the black of a fencing instructor, Herr Wendol sniffed as he watched Hannah slowly make her way toward him. "If you would be so kind as to join the others, Fräulein Richter, we shall get started."

Having come this far, and not wishing to disappoint her father by backing down out of irrational fear, Hannah did what she always did when faced with a challenge. She drew herself up, gave her hair a slight toss to one side, and forged ahead. Spotting the one face in the crowd not attempting to stare her down, she made her way toward Peter Bauer, Gretchen's older brother.

Peter, not wishing to break with his comrades by openly greeting Hannah as he ordinarily would have, did nothing as she took a seat on the floor next to him.

"Well, now that we are *all* finally here, perhaps we can start," Herr Wendol crisply announced, strutting in front of his students, menacingly whipping his saber from side to side.

Hannah's apprehension ebbed away, replaced by a seething rage as she realized what was going on. They were attempting to rid themselves of her, she told herself, just as the boys in Munich had done. Though their methods of making this clear to her were different, none of them, not even Peter, wanted her among them, spoiling the purity of their little band. Three years ago, the boys and their society had succeeded. They had accomplished what they had set out to do. But not here, Hannah told herself. The smug sons of SS officers seated around her would not cause her to buckle as the man who she had once thought of as a father had.

To that end, she channeled her roiling rage into cold, uncompromising determination. She would stand her ground. She would meet whatever was thrown at her and show them all she was not afraid, for she was the daughter of Sturmbannführer Ernst Richter in every way that mattered to her.

Stopping when he reached the end of the piste, the mat on which bouts were held, Herr Wendol spun about and took to scanning the upturned faces of his student. "Herr Meiner, perhaps you would care to see what our newest student is capable of."

Jumping to his feet like a puppet jerked to life by its master, Theodor Meiner snapped to attention. "As you wish, Herr Wendol."

Casting his eyes in her direction, the fencing instructor gave

Hannah a mirthless smile. "Fräulein Richter, when you are ready, please be so kind as to take your position."

Ignoring Herr Wendol's mockingly sweet tone as she disregarded her father's taunts when they were practicing, Hannah took up her mask and saber. Meiner was three years older than her and a good twenty centimeters taller and, Hannah knew from Peter's talk about his fencing lessons, Meiner was the best in his class. None of this, of course, bothered her. After all, up to now, her opponent had been a full-grown man who not only towered over her and held several regional titles, he had learned his trade fighting communists in the streets of Munich.

With an expression that betrayed nothing, she ignored Meiner's arrogant smirk. The two saluted their instructor, the other students, then each other before pulling their masks over their heads and assuming the First Position. In doing so, Hannah gave her ponytail a quick flick from side to side as she always did when facing off against her father, causing her blond mane to flutter briefly over her shoulders. It was her way of reinforcing complacency in her opponent, lulling him into a false sense of superiority so he would discount her abilities simply because she was a girl. While her father was wise to all her little tricks, Hannah suspected this one might give her the edge she would need here. After all, she told herself, these boys were just that, boys.

Hannah expected Meiner to be aggressive right off the mark in an effort to humble and embarrass her in front of his comrades. She was not disappointed. When given the signal to commence, he brought his lead foot forward, stomped down on the Piste as hard as he could, and bellowed a cry he intended to be bellicose and intimidating while lunging at her. His technique was one she loved to use herself whenever she could, though her father parried such attacks with ease.

Having hoped Meiner would do something along these lines, Hannah was more than ready, both to counter his assault and risk all with a bold move of her own. Rather than parrying, she ducked under his blade, which was easy given their disparity in height and a nimbleness that took the boy by surprise. Dropping her left hand and knee onto the mat, she thrust her sword arm forward to its full extent. With the same unerring accuracy with which she did everything, the tip of her blade stuck the armpit of Meiner's overextended sword arm.

An audible muttering punctuated by gasps rose up from the other students, a reaction to which she paid no heed to. She quickly went over to the attack, striking Meiner once more before he had a chance to retreat and recover from the shock of being so easily bested by a girl. Enraged, the boy didn't bother to take the time he should have to reassess his opponent. Instead, he drew back but a single step before bringing his saber up and renewing his attack with more vigor than skill. Realizing she had succeeded in turning his smugness into rage, Hannah allowed a smirk to dance across her lips behind her mask as she parried his clumsy thrust with ease before delivering another telling counterblow.

And so it went. Herr Wendol had hoped the boy would humiliate the pretentious female to the point where she would beg him to quit. Instead, Meiner gave into his anger and the threat of disgrace before his instructor and fellow students. By doing so, he lost his ability to draw upon his superior skill and experience, handing Hannah an easy victory on the piste and revenge for the wrongs perpetrated against a boy who was no more.

CHAPTER EIGHT

MOTHERS AND DAUGHTERS

More upset with herself than humiliated, Hannah eased her way across the back seat of the Mercedes and stepped out onto the ground, cringing as her wet socks squished with each step she took, causing water and mud to ooze between her toes. When she saw the driver coming around from his side of the car, Hannah looked up at the SS man sheepishly. "I am so sorry, Albrecht. I've made a mess of the seat."

Though he tried not to, Rottenführer Albrecht Pranger could not keep from smirking. "It's no problem, Fräulein Richter. I dare say I'll have an easier time cleaning it off the seat than you will explaining how you managed to turn a nice, peaceful day hiking in the forest into a mud fight."

Tucking her head in and grimacing, Hannah moaned. At the time giving the rope bridge a group of HJs had thrown up across a creek a good shaking while Eva Wenders was crossing it seemed like such a marvelous way of annoying her. Hannah hadn't meant to cause her to fall off it. Nor had she expected the ordinarily prissy little prat to climb out of the creek, latch onto her ankle as she stood there laughing, and drag her down the muddy embankment and into the creek. There, the two had wrestled, ignoring Fräulein Diehl, who remained on dry land imploring them to stop, while Sophie led other girls to cheer them on.

Any hope of concocting a marvelous story to explain all of that away to her parents as nothing more than an accident was dashed by the note Fräulein Diehl had ordered her to hand over to them. Taking her sodden bread bag and canteen from the amused driver, Hannah sheepishly bid him goodbye and made her way to the front door. Trying to slip in through the kitchen unseen was pointless. Fräu Sander would be even more brutal in her admonishments than her mother if she saw her like this.

As bad as that would be, it was her father's parents that caused Hannah the greatest concern. A visit by them was always an especially stressful time for the entire family, particularly Lena Richter. Despite her best efforts to make them feel at home, accommodating their every whim, nothing Lena did seemed to please them. Ernst's mother, the daughter of a noted architect, tended to be downright cruel in criticizing her daughter-in-law. Chief among the crimes Lena stood guilty of in Maria Richter's eyes was her failure to produce more than one grandchild, a point she never failed to bring up whenever she had the opportunity.

Hannah, of course, did not count. In Maria Richter's eyes, the girl was not a true Richter. No matter how much Ernst praised her, or how hard Hannah tried to be the perfect child whenever the woman was about, Fräu Richter saw her as nothing more than a stray her son had taken in for some inexplicable reason. Were it not for a desire to keep from adding to her mother's concerns, Hannah would have gone out of her way to ensure it was clear to all the enmity Ernst's mother had for her was mutual. And while Hannah did all she could to keep from exasperating the situation at home, she felt no need to hold her tongue when discussing the matter with Sophie and Gretchen, referring to Fräu Richter as *the Gray Witch* whenever the subject came up. So letting the old woman see her like this would have added another black mark against her name and given the woman one more thing to grouse about when criticizing her mother.

Being as quiet as she could, Hannah slipped into the house in hope of making it to her room and changing without running into

Fräu Richter. She had made it across the foyer on her squishy tippy toes and reach the stairs when Wolfgang screamed out her name. "Hannah!"

Tucking her head between her shoulders, Hannah winced as she turned around to greet her brother who came barreling out of the parlor toward her. Stopping just short of his sister, the precocious four-year-old boy who had learned he could do no wrong when his Oma and Opa were visiting took to laughing. "You look funny!" he squealed.

Hannah's efforts to shush her brother were for naught. Looking up, Hannah could not help but notice Fräu Richter standing in the archway of the parlor with her arms crossed, looking down the bridge of her nose at her. It was a sight that caused Hannah's heart to sink.

Delighted to see his sister had done something that would have earned him a spanking, Wolfgang twirled about on his heels and took off running back to the parlor, gaily yelling at the top of his lungs. "Mutti! Mutti! Come look. Hannah's all muddy."

When Lena did appear in the archway next to her mother-in-law, there was no missing the disappointment in her eyes. After heaving a great sigh, the woman slipped past Fräu Richter and over to where Hannah was standing with bowed head. "I'm so sorry, Mama," Hannah whispered when Lena was close enough to where only she could hear her.

Reaching out, Lena used the index finger of her right hand to gently tilt Hannah's head back until their eyes met. When they did, she gave the girl a sad little smile. "It'll be all right, " Lena whispered. "Come, let's get you out of those clothes and into a nice warm bath."

With a look of disappointment, Wolfgang stood next to his grandmother as he watched his mother drape her arm about his sister's shoulders and accompany the girl upstairs. "Oma, is Mutti going to spank Hannah in her room?"

Fräu Richter sniffed. "That girl is lucky she even has a room." Then, with a shake of her head, she graced her only grandchild with a smile. "Come, Wolfgang. I have not yet finished reading to you."

❋

Lena took Hannah straight into the bathroom, where the girl tossed her bread bag and canteen in a corner while Lena went to the bathtub and began running water. Straightening up, she turned around and took a moment to study the dejected girl standing before her with her head bowed, waiting patiently to be admonished. Feeling sorry for the child before her, Lena once more sighed. "Go ahead and start undressing. I'll be right back."

Surprised, and not at all sure what to make of this response, Hannah looked up at Lena. Lena knew what was going through the girl's mind. "Go ahead, sweetie. It's okay," Lena murmured reassuringly as she ducked out of the bathroom, leaving Hannah wondering what the woman she now called mother was up to. From the very first day she had taken Hannah in, Lena had gone out of her way to make sure she was not in the same room when the girl was dressing or undressing. Even when Hannah needed to try on a new dress, or have one taken in, Lena had gone to extremes to ensure the girl was not visible to her when naked or even partially undressed. With that thought in mind, Hannah took the precaution of leaving her panties and tee shirt on.

When Lena did return carrying some bottles and found the girl thus attired, a reassuring little smile danced across her lips. "Go on, finish undressing unless you intend to wash your underthings as well as yourself."

Slowly, hesitantly, Hannah removed the last of her clothing, keeping one eye on her mother as she did so as if waiting for the woman to change her mind and order her to stop. Lena didn't. Instead, she set the bottles she'd carried into the bathroom next to the tub, placed a folded towel on the tile floor, and knelt onto it. After testing the water's temperature and finding it satisfactory, Lena took up one of the bottles, opened it, and began to pour some of its contents into the tub before swishing it about in the water with her hand.

"When I'm feeling down, I always find a nice warm bubble bath is just the thing," Lena murmured without bothering to look back at Hannah. "Though your problems are still out there on the other side of the door, a few stolen moments pampering yourself always seems to make them so much easier to deal with."

Suddenly it dawned on Hannah what her mother was doing: something she had never done before. She was treating her like a daughter in the most intimate, loving manner she knew how.

When Lena turned her head and saw Hannah standing there with her hands modestly covering herself, staring at her in utter amazement, she knew what was going through the girl's mind. But rather than explain herself or dwell on the significance of the moment, she smiled. "Well come on, hop in. That head of yours is going to need at least two good scrubbings if we're going to get all that mud out of it and make you presentable for your father as well as not giving the Gray Witch another reason to ridicule you."

As surprising as her mother's behavior up to this point had been, hearing her refer to Fräu Richter using the nickname she'd given that woman caused Hannah's eyes to fly open and mouth drop. Laughing, Lena tiled her head to one side and gave her daughter a wink. "You didn't think you and your friends were the only ones who gossiped about other people, did you?"

"But . . ."

"Gretchen's mother let it slip when I was talking to her yesterday. After sharing with her how that woman carries on about you, we both agreed it was a good name for her. Now, in the tub with you, young lady, before you catch your death of cold."

❁

Right off, Ernst Richter noticed Lena and Hannah's strange behavior when he returned home that evening, conduct that continued throughout dinner that night. Every chance he could, when he suspected they wouldn't catch him doing so, he would glance back and forth between the two, marveling at the way each shared a secret little grin with the other, despite the presence of his mother at the table and the incident Hannah had been involved in earlier, which Wolfgang had informed Ernst of the second he had walked through the door. He set aside the temptation to ask what they were up to. No doubt, Richter concluded, this was strictly a mother-daughter matter, one best left untouched by him.

Instead, he settled in to enjoy his meal and relish the simple pleasure of being there with his family as he listened to his father drone on about things that were of no importance to him. Ernst tolerated men such as his father who pontificated about what should be done or how the government needed to go about dealing with the great issues of the day even though they had no earthly idea what was really going on in Berlin and across Germany. It was best they didn't, Richter always concluded whenever he gave the matter any thought. He had taken on the burdens of righting the wrongs the Western Allies had imposed upon Germany at Versailles and reversing the cultural rot that had followed in the wake of the last war. He was determined to do everything in his power to ensure the Germany his children inherited was one free of the political strife, post-war deprivations, fear, and the uncertainty his generation had endured when he was a young man. Breaking a chunk of bread off before popping it in his mouth, he looked over at his son, then his daughter. No matter what he needed to do, no matter how high the price he would have to pay, he would leave them a Germany that was strong, united, and proud. That he was sure of.

❋

On the following Sunday, Ernst Richter's father insisted on taking his son and daughter-in-law into Berlin to enjoy an opulent dinner at one of the city's finest restaurants. It was decided to allow both Clara and Fräu Sander the day off. "I can look after Wolfie," Hannah announced as cheerily as she could after being informed she wasn't invited along. Lena had no need to explain why she couldn't go. Fräu Richter never missed the opportunity to remind her son in Hannah's presence that he hadn't been permitted to eat with adults until he was old enough to wear long trousers, which in his case didn't occur until he had reached his fourteenth birthday. Far from being offended by this, Hannah always found it difficult to keep from laughing to herself at the image of her father dressed in knickers.

With no adults about, Hannah took advantage of this opportunity to try things in the kitchen she had seen Fräu Sander make she would never have been allowed to attempt had the cook been present. Wolfgang watched everything his sister did, as much so he could recount every detail of her crimes to his grandmother if things turned out badly as to learn how to make what his sister was when he had a chance.

"Wolfie, no!" Hannah snapped, stopping the eggbeater she was using to mix the batter lest the finger her brother insisted on dipping into the bowl get stuck in its whirling blades.

"But I want to taste it."

"I told you, not until it's completely beaten and I've poured the batter into the form. Only then can you lick the bowl."

Settling back onto the chair on which he was kneeling, Wolfgang pouted. "I'll bet if Oma were here, she would let me have some batter."

Hannah couldn't stifle a cynical snicker as she went back to furiously cranking the handle of the eggbeater. "If your grandmother was here, we wouldn't be doing this." Making this statement, of course, was a mistake, one Wolfgang's ever attentive little ears picked up on.

Having done everything exactly the way she had seen Fräu Sander do when baking a cake, and satisfied with the results thus far based on her own sampling of the unbaked batter, Hannah ever so carefully poured it into the cake form, never once suspecting she'd missed a critical step, that of greasing and flouring the forms. Oblivious to this fatal flaw, and pleased with her efforts thus far, Hannah slid the cake into the oven, checked the time, and cleaned up the mess she and her brother had made before going into their father's study. There she settled into reading, leaving Wolfgang free to crawl about the floor pushing the toy U-boat he had coaxed his grandfather into buying him.

Hannah was thoroughly engrossed in the chapter on the Russian siege of Kolberg during the Seven Years War when the sharp rapping of the brass doorknocker startled her. Looking up from her the book in her lap, she panicked when she saw the time. Setting the book aside, she slipped out of her father's favorite chair and dashed for the kitchen, just barely avoiding tripping over her brother who had fallen asleep on the floor. She was in the foyer when the sound of the door knocker presented her with a dilemma. She stopped in mid-stride, her eyes darting between the kitchen and the front door. A third, more insistent tapping on the front door decided the issue for her. Flying to the door, she flung it open without bothering to look and see who was there before racing off to the kitchen.

Amused by the antics of his superior's daughter, Horst Fisher watched as Hannah disappeared into the kitchen. When he saw no one else about, he tentatively stepped into the foyer, removed his cap, and stood about, waiting for someone to come and greet him. When no one did, he began to suspect that the girl was the only one there at the moment. To see if that were the case, he set both his cap and the pouch with Richter's travel orders aside and wandered into the kitchen.

There he found a very dejected girl standing at the table, frowning as she stared at a warm cake form. "Why so sad?" he declared as he approached the table. "It smells wonderful."

"It's ruined," Hannah sighed.

Stepping up behind the young girl, Fischer peeked at the cake over her shoulder. "It doesn't look like it's ruined."

"It is," Hannah whimpered, looking back over her shoulder at Fischer for the first time. "I forgot to grease the form."

The sight of Hannah's sad, blue eyes filling with tears tore at the heart of the young SS officer. "Perhaps we can save this," he offered to keep the girl from crying.

"How?"

"Do you have a long, thin-bladed knife?"

"Yes."

"Well then, fetch it and a plate we can place this on, and I shall show you what we can do," Fischer declared cheerily.

Though she was convinced all was lost, Hannah went over to the drawer where Fräu Sander kept her best knives and selected one she felt would do. She lifted it and carried it over to her father's adjutant before going to the cabinet for the plate.

When he was ready, and Hannah had taken a seat at the table across from him, the SS officer began to cut into the stuck cake. "One must never give up when faced with adversity," he mused as he was doing so. "Often it is adversity that shows us just what kind of people we are here, inside," he declared pausing a moment to look over at Hannah while tapping his chest with the butt handle of the knife before continuing with his efforts.

Hannah did not answer as she gazed up into Fischer's eyes, appreciating what he was saying with greater clarity than she suspected he could give her credit for. Yes, she knew about adversity and what it could reveal about a person. She knew painfully well. If anything did surprise Hannah, it was a man her father often groused about as little better than a bumbling halfwit understood this.

The rapt attention the girl was paying to what he was saying brought a smile to Frischer's face. That and her dry eyes told him he had succeeded in keeping her from tumbling headlong into total despair, a feeling with which he was all too familiar. "Now, Fräulein Richter, let us see what we can do. Slide the plate over here," he commanded as he set aside the knife and took the plate, placing it over cake form.

"That's not how Fräu Sander does it," Hannah informed the SS officer.

Pausing, Fischer made a great show of looking about the kitchen, even peeking under the table as if searching for the cook before turning his attention back at Hannah, raising an eyebrow as he did so. "As I do not see Fräu Sander here, you shall have to settle for the way we in the SS do it."

Amused by the officer's antics, Hannah could not help but laugh.

"Now comes the real challenge," Fischer announced dramatically as he lifted the cake form and plate, spreading his fingers out to hold the two together. "Do me the service of counting down from three to one."

Grinning, Hannah did so. When she reached one, he flipped the plate and cake form over, then set it down. With a careful twisting of the form, he managed to break the portion that was still stuck to the bottom of it free before lifting the form away.

Upon seeing the cake had a hopelessly damaged top, Hannah made a face. "It's still ruined."

"Patience, Fräulein, patience. I'm not finished."

"My name is Hannah."

"To me, you are Fräulein Richter, daughter of my superior officer," he retorted as he took up the knife and began carefully to slice off the top of the cake.

After glancing about the kitchen in the same manner he had, Hannah looked over at Fischer. "I do not see my Father here, so it is Hannah, if you please."

Glancing up at her from what he was doing, Fischer grinned. "Then Hannah it will be. Now," he announced with a flourish as he lifted the top of the cake off using a hand and the knife's blade, "you have a cake that will be fit to serve to royalty once you have covered it with icing."

Hannah took a moment to study the remains of the cake before concluding that though it was different, it was definitely salvageable. With that, she set about gathering up all she would need to make icing while Fischer washed his hands before settling down at the table to watch the girl and enjoy the glass of milk she offered him.

While she was whipping up the icing and he was enjoying the remains of the cake he had cut off by dipping chunks of it in his milk as he had often done as a child, he asked Hannah if she was looking forward to her trip to Linz. Not having heard mention of such a trip, Hannah stopped what she was doing and took to staring at Fischer. "What trip?"

Both the girl's question and the look on her face told Fischer he had blundered. "Oh, I see you have not been told."

"Told what?"

"Perhaps I should not say any more," Fischer muttered.

"Oh please, tell me," Hannah pleaded.

Unable to resist the girl's penetrating blue eyes, so like her father's, yet so very different in the ways she used hers, Fischer relented. "Your father is off to Linz to oversee the establishment of a new facility near there at a place called Mauthausen. In making the arrangements for his travel and accommodations he instructed me to purchase tickets for you, your mother, and your brother as well."

"We're going to Linz?" Hannah squealed in delight. "When?"

"Next week."

A frown suddenly wiped away Hannah's smile. "But that means I shall miss going to camp with my friends."

"Would you rather go with your friends and sleep in a tent, or stay at the Hotel Wolfinger with your family?"

Pouting, Hannah looked down into the bowl of icing she was beating. "Why must we always be forced to make choices?" she grumbled.

"Life is all too often like that, Hannah," Fischer offered in a tone of voice more somber than he had intended. He found himself dwelling on the choices he had found himself having to make. "The challenges that confront us, and the choices we make in overcoming them determine what kind of people we shall become."

"I know," Hannah muttered as she went back to whipping up the icing. Fischer did not know how well she knew. Nor, for that matter, did Hannah appreciate how familiar Fischer was with having to decide between two very different paths to follow, neither of which he would have chosen had he possessed the courage to live his life as he had wished, and not as others expected.

❋

It came as no surprise Fräu Richter didn't waste the opportunity to criticize Hannah's efforts. Not that this was all that difficult. The cake Hannah presented to them later that evening was as square as one of Wolfgang's blocks. The reason she gave her father for the cake's unique design was just as fanciful as it was. "I was inspired by the Führer, who proclaimed that architecture is the word in stone, something I am sure your mother would agree with. After all, her father was an architect who designed many fine buildings we all should be proud of using building blocks that looked like this cake."

Where as Ernst was able to keep his laughter in check, Lena could not help but guffaw in a most unladylike manner as Fräu Richter drew back, regarding Hannah as if she were sucking on a lemon. Any chance of anyone finding out the real reason the cake was shaped as it was was nil, for Hannah had made Fischer promise not to tell a soul just how badly she had messed up in exchange for a pledge from her that she would not let on he had spoiled her father's surprise about the trip to Linz. So, after they had all enjoyed a piece of Hannah's cake with coffee for the adults and milk for the children, and Ernst Richter made his big announcement, Hannah responded with appropriate degrees of surprise and joy.

Wolfgang wasted no time in running over to his grandfather and taking him by the hand, imploring the old man to show him where Linz was on the globe in his father's study. The boy's excitement was diminished somewhat when he discovered Linz was a city and not a strange foreign country in Africa or Asia. Lena, left in the parlor with Hannah and her mother-in-law, turned to her daughter. "Well, it seems as if the two of us have some serious shopping to do, young lady, one that demands we pay a visit to the Kurfürstendamm."

Lena had made the suggestion that she and Hannah shop there for no other reason than to irritating her mother-in-law, knowing full well Fräu Richter considered any money spent on the girl to be a foolish expenditure. The fact that it was also where Julia Kruger had taken Hannah to have her problem resolved, and an appreciation that returning there might upset Hannah never occurred to her. Though Hannah had no regret at having gone through that horrendous ordeal, the suffering she had endured in its immediate aftermath still caused her to wake up in the middle of the night from time to time in a cold sweat. Such was the cost a child like her needed to bear to overcome the sins of her father, Hannah told herself on such nights as she struggled to go back to sleep, sins she could never allowed herself to forget, sins for which she might one day need to atone.

CHAPTER NINE

PERFECTION

ORANIENBURG, DECEMBER 1938

Seated upon the bottom step of the staircase, Hannah and Wolfgang watched as their father paced to and fro from one side of the foyer to the other, stopping every time he passed in front of them. From there he would cast his gaze over their heads and toward the head of the stairs a moment. When he saw no sign of his wife, he would check his watch and grunt before setting off on another circuit of the foyer.

Before being adopted by the Richters, Hannah had never had the opportunity to enjoy Christmas. Not only had the man who she no longer thought of as her father been a Jew, her mother, her biological mother, had never been a practicing Christian. Whether she was a communist or one of the countless Germans whom the Great War had left disillusioned with the traditions of the past was something Hannah was never able to determine.

Not that the reason why they hadn't celebrated the holidays as other families mattered. All that had been important to her back then was her family in Munich made no effort, no effort at all, to mark a time of year when all about them people set aside their troubles and honored the spirit of hope and light in the midst of a season of darkness.

So she was just as anxious as her father and brother were to be off to the Yule party at the assembly hall, the site of all the events held for the families of officers assigned to the Totenkopfverbände's headquarters. Not only would all of her friends be there, but she and Gretchen were part of a trio picked by Anna Diehl to sing while the candles on the Yule tree were being lit. It didn't matter to Hannah that the other girl in the trio was Eva Wenders. Gretchen would be in the center since she was taller than the other two, so Hannah felt safe from any threat of retaliation for the mud fight that had become legendary within the ranks of the local HJ and BDM. Besides, physical violence wasn't Eva's style. She and her friends preferred to extract retribution on those they disliked by campaigns of character assassination.

Unable to wait any longer, Hannah came to her feet and cleared her throat. Upon hearing her, Richter glanced over to where she was standing. "I shall go and see what it is that is keeping Mama," she announced.

After looking down at his watch, then casting his eyes back at the head of the stairs, Richter nodded. "I would very much appreciate that, Mausi," he muttered, doing his best to keep his irritation from shining through, but failing miserably.

On reaching her parents' bedroom, Hannah found the door partially open. Quietly, she poked her head around the door until she was able to see her mother. Lena was seated at her vanity, staring pensively at her reflection in the mirror. Even from across the room, Hannah noticed the sadness in her mother's eyes. Struck by the oddness of this, given where they were about to go, the girl was tempted to call out and ask what was bothering her mother but didn't. Instead, she simply stood there, watching, waiting, wondering.

In time, Lena took notice of her daughter looking at her from across the room. Realizing she'd allowed herself to become lost in her own concerns over the news she had been keeping to herself, Lena gave her head a quick shake. She smiled as her eyes met Hannah's in the mirror's reflection. "I expect your father sent you up to see what was keeping me."

Crossing the room to where her mother was, Hannah nodded. "He is wearing out his new boots pacing back and forth."

Turning about on the vanity's bench, Lena snickered. "He can be rather impatient at times. I remember when we first met. It was on a crowded tram. Ever the gentleman, he gave me his seat," she murmured. As she spoke, her eyes took on a faraway look, a look that told Hannah her mother was replaying a long past scene in her head.

"The whole way, he said nothing. He simply stood there, staring down at me with those wonderful blue eyes of his. Naturally, I pretended I wasn't taking any notice. When I got off, he did as well and followed me home. My mother became quite concerned when she saw him pacing back and forth out on the sidewalk in front of our house, mustering up the nerve he needed to come up the door and knock. 'There's an SS man outside,' Mama gasped."

Looking back at Hannah, Lena smiled. "I knew why he was there. And as much as I wanted to calm my mother's concerns by quickly going out to him, I wished to see just how long the devilishly handsome officer with enchanting blue eyes was willing to wait, either to come to me, or to see if I would come to him."

"Who did go to the other?" Hannah asked, fascinated.

Lena laughed and gave Hannah a wink. "As it turned out, we both did. He was reaching for the doorknocker when I opened the door. The two of us stood there for the longest time without saying a word, looking into each other's eyes, realizing at that very moment we were meant to be together, forever."

Caught up in her mother's story, Hannah forgot all about her reason for coming to her. Instead, she savored the intimacy her mother so freely shared with her, wondering if she would ever be able to experience a moment such as the one that had brought her adopted parents together.

Ever so slowly, the memory of that long ago day drifted away, replaced by the image of a girl Lena had grudgingly grown to love, a girl she would need to rely upon more and more in the coming months. Drawing in a deep breath, Lena reached up and gently placed her hand on her daughter's cheek. "Would you like to have your hair braided, sweetie?"

Hannah was about to remind her mother her father was waiting, but checked herself. She wanted this special moment to last. "Yes, I would love that very much, Mama."

"Good!" Lena chirped as she scooted over on the bench, patted the cushion with her hand, and instructed Hannah to sit.

✺

Unlike his sister, Wolfgang stormed into the room with a stern, no-nonsense expression like his father wore when he was in no mood to mess about. "Papa wants to know what is keeping you," he demanded with as much authority as his squeaky little voice would permit.

Without bothering to look away from the white ribbon she was tying at the end of one of Hannah's braided pigtails, Lena harrumphed. "Go back downstairs, young man, and inform your father it takes time to improve upon perfection."

The temptation to say something was checked by the boy's realization he had just been issued an order. With that thought in mind, Wolfgang dutifully pivoted about and marched back out of the room.

Looking up in her mother's eyes, Hannah was tempted to remind her she wasn't perfect. She didn't need to. Lena saw the doubt in the girl's eyes. Reaching up, the woman gave her daughter a playful tap on the nose with the tip of her index finger. "In my eyes and those of your father's you *are* perfect, sweetie, as perfect as any girl in all of Germany. Now," she continued, "let's see what else we can do to improve upon that."

✺

The second Sophie saw her friend, her eyes flew open and her jaw dropped. "Oh—my—God! You're wearing makeup!"

Still glowing from the way her mother had gently taken her in hand and lavished a very special kind of attention upon her, Hannah did her best to play down her good fortune. "It's nothing, really. Just a little powder, a hint of rouge and a touch of lipstick Mama put on me."

"You are so lucky," Sophie whimpered as she studied every detail of Lena's efforts. "My mother wouldn't even think of allowing me to wear makeup, let alone make me up. She still thinks we're back in East Frisia, where the cows are prettier than most of the women." Then, remembering the retort Hannah was so fond of using, Sophie raised an index finger. "And don't you go trying to tell me you aren't lucky. As far as I'm concerned, you're the luckiest girl in all of Brandenburg."

On this night, Hannah made no effort to deny her friend's claim, choosing instead to beam. "Well, I guess I have had some good fortune come my way."

Sophie moaned. "You cow. Come on," she muttered while grabbing one of Hannah's hands. "Let's go find Gretchen so you can see if she'll fall for that shy little innocent act you're so fond of."

Gretchen's response when she saw Hannah was not all that different from Sophie's. "I shall never be able to wear makeup, at least not until I leave home," the tall, gangly girl sighed. "Mother thinks cosmetics are for girls who are insecure, hopelessly ugly, or tramps. She says I don't need them."

Upon hearing this, Sophie couldn't help herself. Cocking an eyebrow, she took to looking Gretchen up and down. "Perhaps your mother is the one who needs the spectacles."

This earned the outspoken girl a quick slap on the arm from Hannah. "Sophie! That's mean. Apologize to Gretchen."

Feigning contrition, Sophie looked up at her friend through her lashes. "Gretchen, I'm sorry your mother needs spectacles."

Rolling her eyes and shaking her head, Hannah stepped between her two friends, took each by the arm, and briskly stepped off. "Come on you two. Let's go see if there's any chocolate on the table."

"Of course there's chocolate," Sophie snipped dismissively at the very idea things could be otherwise. "It wouldn't be Christmas without chocolate."

"Yuletide," Hannah corrected.

"Christmas, Yuletide, winter solstice, what's the difference?" Sophie replied dismissively. "So long as there's chocolate and gifts, I'm happy."

❋

The highlight of the evening's festivities came when the wives of the SS officers and their older daughters lit the Yule tree in the darkened assembly hall as Hannah, Gretchen, and Eve Wenders sang a modified version of "Silent Night," one carefully purged of all religious references. This was followed by the sudden appearance of a man on a white horse carefully ducking through the low double doors of the hall. Dressed as Odin and carrying a sack full of gifts, he was greeted with squeals of delight from the children and a round of applause by the adults. Despite the mounted figure's false white beard and slouched hat, Hannah could tell "Odin" was actually Albrecht, the driver who catered to the families of SS officers assigned to Oranienburg and Sachsenhausen.

Even before he could dismount and wait for his horse to be led away by an assistant dressed as a Nordic warrior, Albrecht was mobbed by children eager to see what he had in his sack for them. The older children like Hannah, Sophie, and Gretchen were just as excited, though they hung back, waiting until the press of their younger brothers and sisters had dispersed.

"What is it you're hoping for this year?" Gretchen asked as she watched Albrecht make a great show of fishing in his sack for the gifts marked with the names of the children gathered about him.

"I know it would be a waste of breath if I asked for makeup," Sophie grumbled, shooting a glance over at Hannah who stuck her tongue out at her friend in return.

Ignore their antics, Gretchen asked Hannah what she wished for.

"I honestly can't think of anything," Hannah replied wistfully. "I mean, for the first time in history, all Germans, the Sudeten Germans, the Austrian Germans, and the greater Germans are united as one people, free to enjoy a peace the Führer and the English Prime Minister secured for our time and always."

Unable to help herself, Sophie bent over, sticking her finger in her mouth as she did so while making a retching noise. "Oh, please! This is Christmas," she groused after straightening up again and looking at Hannah incredulously. "Save that drivel for our next meeting with the Blond Cow. What do you really want?"

This time Hannah took a moment to ponder the question. In doing so, she realized she really did have all she could wish for. She had a caring family who loved her, a home where she was snug and safe, friends like Sophie and Gretchen, and the respect of her peers. Having experienced life without these, Hannah could not think of anything better. As hard as she tried to come up with something to appease her friends, the only thing she found herself wishing for was to live out her life surrounded by the loving family who had taken her in and friends like Sophie and Gretchen. So as she stood there in the warmth of the assembly hall festooned with holiday decorations mixed in with the symbols of the new German Reich, Hannah silently hoped this world, her world, would last just as it was for a thousand years and beyond.

※

Across the hall, Ernst Richter had been watching the pandemonium swirling about Albrecht and trying his best to catch sight of Wolfgang. Eventually, he took his hand away from his wife's waist before reaching into the pocket of his trousers. Pulling out a small box, he turned to Lena and presented it to her. "It would be such a shame to let the children have all the fun tonight," he murmured as Lena lovingly accepted his gift.

As she opened the velvet box, Lena's eyes sparkled as brightly as the pair of diamond earrings it contained. Speechless, she tossed aside all thought of decorum, threw her arms about her husband's neck, and rewarded him with a heartfelt, passionate kiss. Pulling her face away from Ernst's without taking her arms from about his neck, Lena smiled. "I have a gift for you as well, Sturmbannführer Richter," she murmured seductively.

"What possibly could you bless me with that you haven't already?" he grinned.

"Another son."

CHAPTER TEN

THE PRICE OF DUTY

ORANIENBURG, AUGUST 1939

S itting at her father's desk with the telephone's receiver to her ear, Hannah was doing her best to pay attention to what Gretchen was saying, but failing. The focus of her attention at the moment was on the base of the stairs which she could see out through the open door of the study. "No, Gretchen, even with Father's adjutant staying with us at night I won't be able to make the outing this weekend," Hannah informed her friend. "Horst can't be here all the time. During the day, there's no one here Mama can depend on until Fräu Sander arrives, save me. She certainly can't trust Clara. I know I wouldn't," Hannah added in disgust.

"No, she keeps insisting she won't," Hannah responded to Gretchen's next question. "Mama hates hospitals. Besides, I've heard they're clearing them of all but the most serious cases." A pause. "Yes, I hope it's just another one of those unnecessary precautions like the one they scared us with last year." Pause. "Even with the treaty, the Russians can't be trusted. Father is always saying they're worse liars than the Poles."

The sight of Dr. Dorfmann, the physician who had been tending to Lena Richter during her troubled pregnancy descending the stairs caused Hannah to sit up. "Listen Gretchen, I have to go. Tell Sophie I said hi." With that, she hung up the phone, hopped out of her father's chair, and made her way out into the foyer where Dr. Dorfmann was waiting for her. "How is my Mother doing?"

"She's feeling better," Wolfgang chimed in before Dorfmann could respond. Turning, Hannah watched as her brother came trooping down the stairs wearing a self-satisfied smile. "Mama said we are not to worry about her."

Glancing back at the physician, Hannah saw a look that led her to believe he wished to speak with her alone. Turning her attention back to Wolfgang, she suggested he run out into the kitchen and inform Fräu Sander she said he was to help her. Hannah had no doubt the cook would know why her brother was there and keep the him occupied. Only when he was gone did Hannah once more face Dorfmann, looking up at him expectantly.

"I wish your mother would allow me to place her in the hospital where we could better monitor her around the clock," the physician stated in an even tone.

"Is she in danger?" Hannah asked, doing her best to keep the concern she had over her mother's condition in check.

Dorfmann discarded the temptation to lie to her and downplay the risks her mother would soon be facing. Besides feeling she had a right to know, Dorfmann, like anyone who was familiar with the Richters, knew the girl before him was one of those children who possessed wisdom and maturity far exceeding her given age. "There are always risks associated with childbirth, Hannah. In the case of your mother, they are more pronounced. I would much prefer it if she allowed me to perform what is called a Caesarean section." Pausing, he asked Hannah if she knew what that was.

"You would operate and take the baby," she answered slowly as she averted her gaze, struggling as she did so to keep memories of her own experiences at the hands of a surgeon from clouding her judgment.

"Yes, the sooner we did so the better," the physician concluded. "The baby is full term, so there would be little risk to it."

"And Mama?" Hannah asked as she once more looked up into the physician's eyes.

This time it was he who looked away before going over to a side table and taking up his uniform cap. "As I said, the sooner the baby is delivered, the better."

After a long pause, Hannah drew herself up. "Then I shall speak to my mother now and see if perhaps I can convince her to do as you advise."

With a sad little smile, Dorfmann nodded. "Good, good," he muttered distractedly as he toyed with his cap. "I shall return tomorrow morning and see if your mother has changed her mind." With that, he pulled his peaked uniform cap bearing the distinctive death's head symbol of the SS on and left, leaving Hannah to slowly mount the stairs, taking them one step at a time, peering up as she did so with a dread she had not felt in a very long time.

❀

The girl found her mother propped up in her bed, gazing out a window. The doleful expression she wore was one Hannah had seen often over the past few weeks as the date for the baby's arrival drew ever closer. Ordinarily, she took great pains to do whatever she could to dispel her mother's despondency, a kindness Lena very much appreciated. On this day, however, the matter Hannah needed to discuss with her demanded she set aside such efforts for the moment. Crawling up onto the bed, the girl nestled herself in the crock of her mother's waiting arm before gently laying her head on Lena's chest with her face turned away from Lena's so she wouldn't see the tears welling up in her eyes.

As was her habit at times like this, Lena took to stroking Hannah's hair. "Herr Dorfmann spoke to you, didn't he?" Lena asked as she looked at the child in her arms.

Hannah, unable to keep her voice from betraying the fear that gripped her, replied with little more than a nod Lena felt as well as saw.

"I imagine he wants you to talk to me about agreeing to go to the hospital, doesn't he?"

Again, the girl in her arms simply nodded.

"I would rather not, Hannah. Hospitals are so cold and lonely." What Lena didn't tell the girl snuggled up against her was the fear she felt of such places, having witnessed the death of her own mother in a ward set aside for the terminally ill.

Propping herself up, Hannah turned to face her mother. "But you would be safe there, Mama, you and the baby. It's what Father would want, and it's what . . ." Without finishing, Hannah once more settled into Lena's loving embrace, turning her head away as her tears began to flow freely down her cheeks.

"You wish it as well, don't you?" Lena asked.

A nod.

"Well, it seems I have no choice," Lena murmured as she took to staring out the window at the top of the trees just outside while resuming the gentle stroking of her daughter's hair. "I shall have Horst call Herr Dorfmann and ask if he can make the necessary arrangements for tomorrow. Will that be satisfactory?"

A nod.

With that settled, Hannah was able to choke back her sobs and relax. Closing her eyes, she allowed herself to savor the warmth of her mother, lulled into a gentle slumber by the rhythmic rise and fall with each breath Lena took. Tomorrow all would be well, Hannah thought. Tomorrow.

❋

"HANNAH!"

Lena's pitiful cry shattered the stillness of the pre-dawn darkness, instantly awaking Hannah and sending her scrambling out of her bed. Without bothering with her robe, she raced from her room and down the hall to her mother's even as Lena once more cried out in even greater desperation. *"HANNAH!"*

With a single quick bound, Hannah was up onto her mother's bed. "I'm here, Mama. I'm here."

"The baby, it's coming," Lena panted as she gasped for breath.

"I'll wake Horst, Mama. Stay here. I'll be right back."

That Lena would still be in her bed when Hannah returned was a given. But such was the dread Hannah felt that all reason and logic were wiped away by near panic.

Racing down the hall, she ran into her father's adjutant who had also been awakened by Lena's cry but had prudently taken the time to pull on a pair of trousers. "Horst! You must come quick," Hannah pleaded, grabbing the SS officer's hand and doing all she could to drag the man along. "Mama needs the doctor!"

Fischer was in better command of his senses. Stopping, he looked up over Hannah's head toward the master bedroom door she had left wide open, then back down at the girl. "Go to your mother," he commanded. "I shall call the doctor."

The physician had no need to ask who was calling him at this hour of the morning or why Fischer was doing so. He did take a moment to reassure the excited young officer all would be well, that he needed to calm down. "Everyone there needs you to set the example, obersturmführer," Dorfmann admonished. "Remember who you are. I will be there with help in no time."

Hannah took little comfort in Fischer's reassurance that all would be well, but like him, she bravely fought through her fear as best she could and instead, turned her attention to easing her mother's suffering the only way she knew how. "The doctor is coming, Mama," Hannah blurted out breathlessly as she once more climbed onto her parents' bed and grasped her mother's hand just as a fresh contraction wracked Lena's body and made her go rigid.

"Mama, please," Hannah pleaded. She subconsciously tightened her grip on her mother's hand as if by doing so she could keep from losing the woman who had come to mean so much to her. "The doctor is coming. Please wait, Mama. Please."

Time did not stand still. Nor did it slow. Yet for Hannah, the agony of waiting for someone to arrive who could help her mother was a nightmare, one she became lost in, one that knew no end. Eventually, a pair of hands grasped her shoulders from behind and eased her away from Lena, a familiar voice cooing in her ear. "The doctor is here, Hannah, come with me."

Looking over her shoulder without letting go of her mother's hand, Hannah looked up into Horst Fischer's eyes. "I want to stay with Mama."

Upon hearing this Dorfmann, who was on the other side of the bed across from Hannah trying hard to listen to Lena's heart with his stethoscope, looked up. "The best thing you can do to help your mother is to go with Herr Fischer."

How that would help didn't make sense to Hannah. Her mother needed her to be there, holding her hand just as Hannah recalled Julia Kruger had sat by her bed some four years prior, helping her fight through the pain. "Mama, I want to stay."

Forcing herself to smile, Lena brushed her daughter's unruly hair away from the girl's eyes. "You must do what the doctor asks, sweetie. I'll be all right. I need you to see to your brother. I am depending on you to be there for him, to help him be as brave and as strong as you. Can you do that for me, sweetie?"

Swallowing hard while doing her best to keep her lips from quivering, Hannah brushed away the tears streaming down her cheeks with her free hand. "Yes, Mama. I'll be brave. For you and Father, I'll be brave." With that, she leaned forward and kissed her mother on her cheek before reluctantly letting go of Lena's hand as Fischer eased her off the bed and out of the room.

✻

Surprised to find his father's adjutant seated on the floor just outside his mother's bedroom door with his sister leaning against him sound asleep, Wolfgang marched up to them. "Is my Mama all right?" he asked Fischer, who had been on the verge of dozing off.

Snapping his head up, Fischer took a moment to collect his thoughts. "Hmm, right," he muttered. "Your mother, she's having the baby."

Wolfgang looked away and over at the closed bedroom door. "Can I see it?"

The sound of voices and shifting of the body she had been leaning against caused Hannah to stir. Disoriented, she blinked as she looked about before realizing why she was there on the floor next to Fischer.

Fully awake now, Hannah scrambled to her feet. "Mama! The baby!"

Just as befuddled by his own slumber, Fischer also rose up off the floor. Reaching out, he managed to arrest the girl's rush toward the bedroom door. "Hannah, wait here," he commanded before quietly opening the door and ducking into the room. When he didn't return soon enough for her, Hannah crept up to the partially opened door of her mother's room. She was just about to begin pushing it aside when Fischer reappeared.

Stopping before her, the SS officer looked down at Hannah but said nothing. Behind him, she could see the doctor and a nurse off to one side bending over a bassinette, tending to something in it. Cocking her head to one side, Hannah attempted to look past Fischer at her mother's bed.

"Hannah, please," Fischer murmured as he placed his hand gently on the side of Hannah's head to keep her from doing so, even as he struggled to keep his own emotions in check.

"NO!"

With her own hand, Hannah slapped Fischer's aside and bolted past him.

Looking over his shoulder, Dorfmann caught sight of Hannah rushing to her mother's bedside. For the briefest of moments, he was tempted to call out to stop her, but didn't. Instead, he glanced over at Fischer who was wondering what he should do. With nothing more than a shake of his head, the physician waved the SS officer off before returning to tending to the newborn infant in the bassinette. Not wishing to stay and bear witness to Hannah's grief, Fischer sighed and left the room, taking Wolfgang by the hand before slowly making his way down the hallway and toward the stairs.

For the longest time, Hannah simply stood at the side of the bed staring at the peaceful expression on the face of the woman she had come to know as Mother. With her eyes closed and what Hannah thought of as a smile, it looked as if she were asleep. But she wasn't. Hannah knew this. As much as she wished otherwise, she knew this. Still, the girl crawled up onto the bed and curled up next to her mother, resting her head on Lena's still chest as tears washed away the world around her.

The hushed exchange between doctor and nurse and the soft sobbing of an inconsolable child were eventually joined by a new sound, the sound of a little boy shouting out at the top of his lungs as he came thundering up the stairs to share with his sister the news he'd just heard on the radio.

"War, Hannah! We're at war!"

PART THREE

1940

DEUTSCHLAND ÜBER ALLES

CHAPTER ELEVEN

ABOUT A BOY

BERLIN, APRIL 1940

"I'm cold."

Ignoring Sophie, Hannah gave the collection box she was holding a quick shake as a smartly dressed man who had been surreptitiously eyeing her drew near.

When he realized the fetching young girl with piercing blue eyes had caught him in the act of admiring her, the businessman returned Hannah's smile even as he was reaching for his billfold. Removing a twenty-mark note, he slowed his pace, then stopped before Hannah, pretending to fumble about as he clumsily stuffed the folded note into the slot of the collection box. Hannah was holding the box up at arm's length between them, as much to keep him from getting any closer as to receive his donation. When he was finished tapping the note down, she smiled. "We thank you, sir," Hannah murmured sweetly while batting her eyes.

The businessman broke out into a broad, toothy grin as he doffed his hat. "It is I who should be thanking you."

To ask what he meant by that never entered Hannah's mind. She knew better. Instead, she continued to smile brightly until he had turned and walked away. "Dirty old man," Hannah muttered through clenched teeth when he was far enough away that he wouldn't hear her.

"A war profiteer, no doubt," Sophie grumbled before giving her friend a withering glare. "And you! You've become quite the shameless hussy."

Tilting her head back while staring down the bridge of her nose at her friend just as Anna Diehl tended to do, Hannah replied with the haughty tone their BDM leader often employed when dealing with her young charges. "It's all for a good cause, Fräulein Fromm, one we all must work together to achieve. Remember, one people, one Reich, one Führer."

"Oh, please," Sophie moaned. "Just because you've caught up to Gretchen in height, you routinely best every boy in your fencing class, people think you've grown to be even prettier than Eve, and you've earned just about every academic achievement award there is, don't assume for one minute you're any better than me."

Giving her head a toss, Hannah sniffed. "Well, that's because there's no need to assume."

Sophie was about to call her dearest friend a choice name when she spied another man in a well-tailored suit approaching. Jumping out in front of Hannah, she warned her to stay back. "This one is mine."

When the businessman was close enough, Sophie all but thrust her collection box in the man's face. "We're collecting for orphans relief," she blurted.

Seeing no graceful away of getting around the aggressive BDM girl who was blocking the sidewalk without making a contribution, the businessman dug in the pocket of his trousers for change. As he did, he noticed Hannah standing off to one side, doing her best to remain inconspicuous. When she saw the way he was looking at her, Hannah dropped her chin a smidge and stuck out her lower lip as if dejected over having missed collecting a donation. Taken in by her little act, after dropping a one-Mark coin in Sophie's collection box, he stuck his hand back into his pocket. "All I've have left is a five-Mark piece," he opined when he withdrew his hand and looked at the coin he was holding.

Hannah didn't miss a beat. Sticking her arm out past Sophie, she beamed. "The orphans and the widows of the sailors lost on the *Blücher* will be most appreciative of your generosity, kind sir," Hannah declared in the same sweet little voice she always used when solicit donations.

Eager to escape from the ambush he'd blundered into, the businessman dropped the five-Mark piece into Hannah's collection box before all but fleeing, leaving Sophie free to spin about and glare at her friend. "You cow! That wasn't fair."

Hannah snickered. "As Father is so fond of saying, only a fool engages in a fair fight."

"And what happened to that claptrap of yours about working together?"

With a wave of her hand, Hannah dismissed Sophie's indignation. "Oh, stop whining. You know at the end of the day we always pool whatever we collect and divide it evenly before turning our collection boxes over to the Blond Cow to count."

"And she knows we do that," Sophie countered.

"What difference does it make? All the people she reports our sums to see is that when we're together, we collect the most," Hannah pointed out. "So stop with your complaining."

Knowing her friend was right, Sophie didn't stop complaining but did shift topics, crossing her arms tightly across her chest. "I'm cold."

"You should have worn something under your uniform jacket." Hannah was about to add *"like I did,"* but didn't for fear of starting another round of bickering. While such exchanges were almost always good-natured, she didn't wish to run the risk of alienating Sophie or any of her other friends, girls she had come to rely on for emotional support in the wake of her mother's death. She needed them now more than ever, for there was a terrible hole in her life that nothing she did seemed to fill, no matter how hard she tried.

It was more than a sense of loss she could not shake. A cold, stilted stillness had settled over the home Lena Richter had dedicated herself to making warm and inviting to all who entered it. Unable to put her loss behind her, Hannah had done all she could to fill her waking hours lest she slide back into a grim darkness she found all too familiar. So while Sophie, Gretchen, and the others could never replace Lena, they and her many activities were all Hannah had at the moment.

With this thought in mind, when she spied a prosperous-looking man approaching, Hannah tilted her head toward him while looking over at Sophie. "Perhaps it would help you forget about being cold if you set aside your complaining and saw how much you could milk that one for."

With a gleam in her eye, Sophie took a moment to muster up what she hoped passed as a piteous expression before setting off to accost her next target, using the same techniques that always seemed to work for Hannah.

❋

After returning to Oranienburg and handing over the monies they had collected for what they thought was the benefit of children orphaned by the war in Norway, the girls of Fräulein Diehl's group dispersed. To Hannah's bemusement and Sophie's delight, instead of finding Albrecht waiting to drive her home, Peter Bauer was there, sitting astride the BMW motorcycle with sidecar he had been assigned as part of the HJ motorcycle corps. "Rottenführer Albrecht Pranger was not available, Hannah, so I volunteered to see you were taken care of," he proudly declared as Hannah, Sophie, and Gretchen drew near.

Unable to miss such a wonderful opportunity, Sophie snickered. "And exactly how do you plan on 'taking care' of Hannah?"

While Gretchen took to admonishing Sophie for being so crass, Hannah blushed. Like his sister, Peter Bauer was tall, only more so. The sixteen-year-old youth, attired in the coveralls worn by members of the HJ motorcycle corps was not only two years older than Hannah, he was half a head taller than her. Height was the one feature she was able to exploit from time to time when crossing sabers with a boy who had eyes as blue as hers. At the moment those eyes were practically glued on her, which only caused Hannah's cheeks to glow even brighter.

"What are you waiting for, Hannah darling?" Sophie murmured in a husky, seductive voice while exaggerating the word *"darling"* as she had seen Marlene Dietrich do often before her movies had been banned. "Your knight awaits you."

Twisting her head about, Hannah stuck her tongue out at her friend before looking back at Peter and ever so slowly advancing to where he was waiting. He was sporting a very self-satisfied grin, one that made Hannah feel uncomfortable and yet, at the same time, strangely pleased. It wasn't because all her friends confessed to being jealous of the attention a boy like Peter Bauer showered upon her on those rare occasions when she allowed him to do so. Rather, it was very reassuring to a girl who could never let herself forget, despite what her late mother had so very often told her, that she would never be the perfect German daughter.

❋

Climbing out of the motorcycle sidecar, Hannah crossed her arms tightly across her chest as she thanked Peter for bringing her home even as she was slowly backpedaling away from him to put as much distance between herself and a boy all her friends considered to be quite handsome. "Thank you, Peter. I ah . . . I appreciated the ride. I really did."

Not wishing to lose this opportunity to spend time with a girl who had more than captured his fancy, Peter scrambled for some excuse to engage her in a conversation. "Hannah, before I go, do you think I could borrow the book you were telling Theodor about the other day at fencing practice?" he blurted.

Unable to help herself, Hannah stopped. "You mean von Moltke's book on the 1866 campaign?"

"Yes, the very one," Peter beamed, pleased more about having managed to arrest Hannah's retreat than the idea she recalled the volume he had little interest in.

As much as she wished to be rid of Peter, Hannah found herself unable to treat him, or any other person for that matter, as unfeelingly as she had once been treated. Well, Hannah reminded herself, almost no one. Like Sophie, she took great delight in sniping at Eva Wenders whenever the opportunity to do so came her way. Besides, Peter was staring at her with those puppy dog eyes of his, a weapon he used on her with greater skill than his saber. Hannah had come to rely on using a person's eyes to determine if they were trustworthy or speaking truly. This was becoming more and more important at a time when the words people used often did not accurately express what they meant. Even her father did not escape such scrutiny from Hannah.

"Well?" Peter asked, doing his best to keep his smile in check.

"Hmm, yes. I expect Father won't mind if I lend the book to you, provided, of course, you promise not to ruin it."

"Oh, you have my word," the boy with puppy dog eyes responded. A toothy grin lit up his face, causing Hannah to spin about and silently admonish herself for being so easily drawn in by such an obvious ploy.

❋

The cheeky grin on Peter's face disappeared in the twinkling of an eye when Hannah, whom he had been following, stopped short upon entering the study. "Father! You're home already," Hannah exclaimed in surprise.

Looking up from the report he had been reading on conditions at the Soldau transit camp in East Prussia, Ernst Richter smirked at the surprise, then acute embarrassment, on his daughter's face and the worried expression that replaced the Bauer boy's cocky grin. In need of a bit of a diversion and seeing an opportunity to find out more about a boy he noticed had taken an interest in his daughter, Richter set aside his report and came to his feet. "Well, what a pleasant surprise. Peter, isn't it?"

Snapping to attention, Peter replied as if reporting to his HJ superior. "Yes, sir. Peter Bauer."

Coming around his desk, Richter examined the boy from head to toe with the same discerning eye he used when inspecting members of the Totenkopfverbände. "Hannah mentions you from time to time," he revealed in an even tone, causing Hannah to cringe and try to make herself as small and inconspicuous as possible. "She tells me you're quite good, with a saber that is."

Not knowing how to respond, Peter's eyes darted back and forth between Hannah, who was intently studying an invisible spot on the floor to hide her glowing red cheeks, and the SS officer who had come to a halt before him. "I do my best, sir."

"I would like to see for myself if all she tells me about you is true," Richter ventured smoothly in a manner that allowed Peter to read much more into his comment than Hannah cared for. "I've all you need here, young man, and I am in desperate need to some practice myself."

"As much as I would enjoy accepting your invitation, Herr Sturmbannführer, I have my duty to perform, dispatches to be delivered and such."

"Oh, I wouldn't worry about those," Richter replied dismissively. "I'm sure a phone call from me to your commanding officer is all that's needed to square things up, don't you think?"

Peter, of course, knew a request by Hannah's father was all that was needed to accomplish just about anything, at least within the ranks of the Totenkopfverbände. Swallowing hard, Peter nodded as he surrendered to the inevitable. "It would be my privilege to cross sabers with you, Herr Sturmbannführer."

Looking like a hunter who'd just run his prey to ground, Richter gave Peter what passed as a friendly pat on his shoulder. "Good, good." Without taking his eyes off Peter, he addressed Hannah. "Mausi, be a dear and see to it our guest has all he needs before going into the parlor for your lessons. Herr Lübke is already waiting for you there."

At the moment Hannah was unable to decide who she was more furious with, her father for behaving as he was, Peter for capitulating so easily, or herself for having set this whole farce in motion just because the boy's antics and those puppy dog eyes of his had taken her in. "Come with me," she grumbled as she stormed passed Peter and out of the study.

From where he stood in the open doorway of the study with his hands jammed deep into the pockets of his trousers, Ernst Richter watched them go, chuckling over his daughter's behavior. Fathers, he concluded, often found the strangest ways to enjoy their children.

※

"Fräulein Richter, you're not paying attention to what you are doing," Herr Lübke sniffed. "I *know* you can do better than *that*. Again."

It took all of Hannah's willpower to keep from telling off the little queer seated on the piano bench next to her. At the moment, she found herself wishing he was securely locked away with all the other homosexuals instead of beside her, berating her efforts. Of course, if she could be honest with herself, she would have agreed with her instructor. She wasn't doing anywhere near her best. How could she? At the moment, she could not keep from worrying about what her father and Peter were doing rather than focusing on the piece she was supposed to be learning.

"Any time you've a mind to begin again, Fräulein Richter," Herr Lübke sighed impatiently in the high-pitched voice he knew annoyed Hannah.

In an effort to keep the pathetic excuse of a man seated next to her quiet, Hannah set aside her concerns over what was going on in the fencing room and resumed playing the classical concerto. She would be expected to perform it at a gathering of SS officers and their families during a celebration of the Führer's fifty-first birthday. She had just about managed to make it to the end of the piece when she heard her father's voice. Without a word, she slipped off the piano bench and all but took off at a run toward the foyer, ignoring Herr Lübke's protests that they were not yet finished with the day's lesson.

The sight of her father and Peter standing at the front door sharing a good laugh over something caused Hannah's heart to sink. "Dear God, Father likes him," she muttered under her breath. That could only mean trouble for her, as Peter would now become even bolder in his efforts to express his interest in her. Furious with the both of them, Hannah spun about and marched back to the piano, where she took out her indignation on the keys.

CHAPTER TWELVE

THE ADJUTANT

ORANIENBURG, MAY 1940

Horst Fischer needed something to keep his mind off the desperate struggle in the west that was entering a critical phase. He waited until there was something of a lull in their busy day and Richter was in what passed as an amiable mood for him, to asked if he could take the afternoon off.

"I've already missed one Sunday ride with Hannah," he ventured, knowing full well his commanding officer could not find it in himself to refuse his daughter anything. "It would be a shame to do so again this week, particularly with the fine weather we've been enjoying."

Looking up from the latest intelligence summary he'd been studying, one which outlined the scope of the task they would soon need to deal with in France as well as the Low Countries, Richter nodded. "Yes, of course, Horst. I would very much appreciate it if you did. Hannah is in desperate need of an opportunity to get out and about, just as I imagine you are."

Fischer was tempted to remind Richter he could do with one himself but didn't bother. Since his wife's death, only the need to spend time with Hannah and his sons was able to pry him away from his duties. Even sleep, Fischer imagined, was something he avoided as evidenced by the dark circles under his superior's eyes. Instead, he asked if there was something he wished him to pass onto his daughter.

Easing back, Richter spun his chair about and stared out the window as he pondered the question. "Yes, Horst," he finally answered without looking back. "Tell Hannah she's not to hold dinner for me. I will be late again."

Both men knew she would, at least for her and her father. After seeing to it Wolfgang and Siegfried were fed and tended to at an appropriate time, Hannah would wait, no matter how late it became, to serve whatever Fräu Sander had prepared for dinner and share a meal with her father when he finally returned home. Neither suspected doing so was just as important to her as it was to Richter. Having lost one family to circumstances not of her making, Hannah was determined not to lose another. She had no control over the events outside her home, but a desperate need to cling onto some sense of normalcy drove her to hold the Richter family together. It was a goal that often left her having to make sacrifices and choices none of her friends had to face, which was why she found herself in need of someone could talk to, someone who was mature and could be trusted.

That someone turned out to be Horst Fischer, a man Hannah took to be intelligent and gentle and with whom she discussed concerns she didn't feel comfortable sharing with her friends or bothering her father with, whether it concerned news of the day that piqued her curiosity, or, more and more, nothing of any real consequence, topics that simply struck her fancy at the moment. For his part, Fischer always listened attentively to Hannah, never passing judgment on her or dismissing her concerns as childish or irrelevant as other adults tended to do. When asked for an opinion, he would weigh his response rather than blurt out something that sounded recycled from the Reich Ministry of Public Enlightenment and Propaganda or lifted from the pages of *The German Girl* Magazine as Fräulein Diehl tended to do. Though Hannah had never had an older brother, she imagined the relationship she and Fischer shared was as close to that as she would ever get.

This was why she so cherished her rides with him, for by becoming a confidant, he also filled the gaping hole in Hannah's life Lena Richter's death had left as no one else could.

❧

Right off Horst could tell Hannah had something on her mind that was troubling her when she arrived at the stables. It was more than the pensive expression she wore, or the way she went about saddling her beloved horse, a tall strawberry roan mare that stood seventeen hands high. At first, Horst had attempted to dissuade her from using the roan. "She's far too tall for you. Coco would be a better match."

Hannah chose to ignore his advice, and with good reason. In a way that defied any logical explanation, she and the lively young mare she had taken to calling Pixie had formed a bond from the first day the two laid eyes on each other. "You can keep your Coco," she would tell Horst whenever he brought the subject up. "You have your Thunder and I, I have my little Pixie." Though *little* was the last word Horst would have used to describe Pixie, he could not deny the two were a perfect match in temperament and spirit.

Sensing the girl was not quite ready to discuss whatever was troubling her on this day, Horst allowed Hannah to take the lead when it came time to leave the paddock and head off along one of the many forest trails and unpaved roads they used as bridle paths during their Sunday afternoon rides. Pixie also seemed aware her rider was in no mood to go galloping about. With little guidance, the horse settled into a leisurely gait that allowed Hannah to mull over the thoughts and concerns she was struggling to process.

Following at a respectable distance as they ambled along, Horst used the opportunity to study the tall girl with a boyish figure from behind. There was no one thing that set her apart from other girls her age, he surmised. She was not the prettiest girl, at least not in the conventional sense. Nor did she have a figure one could even remotely consider voluptuous or alluring. "She's a late bloomer," Ernst Richter would declare whenever fellow officers assigned to the headquarters found the time to discuss their families. "Not that I mind. As far as I am concerned, it's something of a blessing," he would joke, pointing out it kept lecherous old men like his peers and the young bucks now filling the ranks of the Totenkopfverbände from showing any interest in her.

Yet despite Hannah's less than remarkable presentation and who her father was, more than a few young officers assigned to both the headquarters and the camp at Sachsenhausen did express an interest in the Sturmbannführer's daughter. In addition to being well above average in intelligence and driven to excel in all she did, Hannah was a prize any ambitious young SS officer would be thrilled to secure. With a father considered indispensable to the commanding officer of an ever-expanding branch of the SS, the girl with flaxen hair and piercing blue eyes all but guaranteed who ever won her hand would become a part of the inner circle of a powerful clique within the Reich. The only things that kept the ambitions of such men in check were Hannah's age, her father's less than subtle warnings issued when any Totenkopfverbände officer overstepped his bounds, and Horst Fischer, a man Sophie had nicknamed Leibstandarte Hannah.

The qualities that caused Horst Fischer to spend as much time with Hannah as he did were no different than those Sturmbannführer Richter had come to appreciate in the young officer. Horst's unassuming demeanor, at odds with what had become expected of an SS officer, made him the perfect choice to serve as Richter's adjutant. Whereas Richter was uncompromising and demanding, Fischer was approachable, a reasonable fellow to whom people very often went first before going to Richter with a problem or a request. This allowed Fischer to filter out many of the trivial matters timid subordinates afraid to deal with on their own tended to pass up the chain of command, a foolish practice that hobbled many of Richter's peers. It also provided Richter with a set of eyes and ears he could use to ferret out information Fischer's peers in other directorates freely shared with him, gossip, rumors, and news not yet generally known they would never have discussed openly if Richter were around.

Above all else, Horst Fischer had proven himself dedicated, loyal, and trustworthy. Over time, Ernst Richter had come to appreciate he could use Fischer to tend to those dirty little jobs he was responsible for looking after but had no wish to involve himself in personally. Some were demeaning. Others involved risks Richter did not wish to be associated with if they did not turn out well. While the time Fischer spent with Hannah was not among those less than choice assignments, his trustworthiness allowed Richter to use him as a stand-in when his duties and other activities prevented Richter from being there for her. There was no need to caution Fischer what would happen to him if he overstepped the bounds of his charter. Richter had no need to. Hardly a day passed when Fischer did not see for himself what happened within the confines of the camp at

Sachsenhausen to those who fell afoul of the Reich or the men who enforced its laws and policies. Besides, as attractive as Hannah was to many of his peers, Horst Fischer found himself unaffected by the girl's charms or the unique appeal that captivated so many, a quirk upon which Richter could capitalize.

❋

It was close to an hour before Hannah finally reined in her mount and began waiting off to one side of the path they had been following for Horst to catch up. Gently sidling up next to her, he paused until Hannah gave Pixie a slight nudge with her heels and once more took up a leisurely pace. "Father's latest request to be transferred to the Waffen SS has been refused, hasn't it?" Hannah asked quietly without looking over at Horst.

Casting his gaze off in the opposite direction, Horst sighed. "Yes, it has been."

"He's not at all happy about being denied the opportunity to serve in a frontline combat unit," Hannah stated quietly. "He hasn't told me as much, but I can tell."

"No, he's not," Horst replied, doing his best to keep from chuckling. When the refusal had come, Horst had not found the matter funny at all. Richter had behaved like a caged bear, muttering vile oaths under his breath and snapping at anyone foolish enough to approach him. This had been his third request to be assigned to the second regiment for the SS Totenkopf Division, formed from personnel drawn from SS units in and around Sachsenhausen and Oranienburg.

After a few moments of silence, Hannah continued. "He was a soldier once, you know. He fought with the freikorps against the Communists in 1919. Whenever he speaks of it, there's a gleam in his eye, the kind a person has when discussing something they are proud of."

"Your father should be proud of his service during those dark days. It was men like him who saved Germany from the evils of communism."

Hannah ignored the way Horst used party-approved rhetoric to describe the revolutionaries who had attempted to turn Bavaria into a Soviet republic. Instead, she rode along in silence for several long minutes before picking up the thread she had been tugging at. "He's not particularly proud of what he's doing at the moment, is he?"

At a loss as to how best to answer such a question, Horst took his time, wondering if he should even try as he looked about while they rode on. Realizing she'd put him on the spot, Hannah broke the uncomfortable silence. "You don't need to answer that. I know he isn't, and I suspect you feel the same." Then, she peeked over at her riding partner. "Do you? Do you feel the same way about, well, about what you're doing?"

The girl's penetrating gaze and question cut through to his very soul. Unable to stand it, Horst looked away. When he finally did answer, he chose his words carefully, deliberately. "We all have duties, obligations, and responsibilities we must shoulder, even those some might consider unpleasant. Just as you have taken on many of the tasks once handled by your mother, as a soldier, I am required to carry out my orders and assignments without question, whatever they may be."

For the first time that day, something of a grin tugged at the corner of Hannah's lips. "Horst, you're not answering my question."

Glancing over at the fetching young girl riding astride a tall horse that, save for her clothing, must have been what the storytellers of old had in mind when describing the Valkyrie, Horst chuckled. "I know."

"Well?"

"Well, what?"

Rolling her eyes, Hannah sighed. "Are you proud of what you're doing?"

Drawing himself up, Horst gazed out ahead. When he spoke, he did so with an affected, officious tone of voice. "I am proud to serve the Führer, Adolph Hitler, and the German folk. It is an obligation I take on gladly and without reservation."

"Oh, please, don't do that to me," Hannah whined. "Listening to such talk from Peter is bad enough. I've no wish to hear it from you as well."

Seeing an opportunity to change the subject of their conversation, Horst asked Hannah about Peter. "Your father seems to like the boy."

Hannah responded with a grunt. "Tell me something I don't know. All Peter talks about these days is the war."

"Everyone is talking about the war these days," Horst countered.

"You don't."

"If you like, I could."

"If you do, you'll find yourself riding alone," Hannah threatened.

"Oh, really?"

"Yes, really," Hannah replied mischievously even as she was digging her heels into Pixie's flanks, spurring the horse into a gallop. Glad to see his young companion and friend had managed to set aside her troubles, Horst grinned as he took off after her in hot pursuit.

❃

The two rode hard for as long as they dare before slowing their pace. "We should walk them a bit, let them cool down," Horst advised, a suggestion to which Hannah readily agreed, for she had something else on he mind she wished to discuss with him.

After several minutes, during which they enjoyed the stillness of the forest in their own ways, Hannah glanced over at Horst out of the corner of her eye. She mulled whether she should even bring up a matter that had been bothering her for weeks.

Unable to help but notice her behavior, Horst looked over at the girl. "Go ahead, ask whatever it is you're wondering about."

Looking down at the path just ahead in a vain effort to hide her glowing red cheeks from Horst, Hannah kept weighing the wisdom of bringing this particular subject up.

"Hannah, you know there isn't anything outside of my duties or those of your father that you are not free to ask me about."

Once more Hannah glanced over at the young SS officer for a second before bowing her head. "Do you ever visit the women from the camp, those who have been set aside for the guards?" she asked slowly.

Not sure if he had heard right, Horst gave his head a quick shake. "Excuse me?"

Wincing, Hannah debated if she should drop the subject, one she was now sorry she'd broached, or repeat her question. Deciding she did need to know, she looked over at Horst who was regarding her in near disbelief. "Well, do you?" she asked.

"Do I what?"

"Do you visit the women who have been picked to cater to the needs of the guards at Sachsenhausen?"

The temptation to ask Hannah how she knew about the whorehouse set aside for SS personnel was dismissed out of hand. She was, after all, fourteen years old, a young girl on the cusp of womanhood. Horst had no doubt some of the less than discreet guards bragged about that particular benefit which, in turn, led to word of what went on at the camp to spread, even among the families.

He looked away from Hannah as he spoke. "I'm not going to answer that question. First off, you have no need to know. Such things are personal, matters men and women should not discuss, especially when the female is underage. But even more important," he continued, looking over at Hannah and waiting until she returned his stare, "I am not at liberty to discuss with you what it is that goes on in Sachsenhausen or any of the camps we are responsible for, both out of respect to your father's wishes and for professional reasons."

Realizing it had been a mistake to bring this subject up, Hannah averted her gaze. "I'm sorry, Horst. It's just that . . ."

Though he knew it was probably best if he simply dropped the matter, Horst had an insatiable curiosity of his own. "What led you to ask me?" he ventured tentatively.

A long silence followed before Hannah replied in a low, almost mournful tone. "Father does. I can tell. I can't help but notice the lingering scent of the cheap perfume the women use. It clings to his uniform."

Having no idea what to say, or even if he should say anything, Horst remained silent.

"The only reason I asked was I was wondering what kind of women they were," Hannah muttered without bothering to look over at him. "I mean, are they political prisoners, or Romani or . . .?"

She knew they were not Jews. Whereas her father considered political malcontents as misguided fools and Romani as a degenerate people, in his eyes Jews were no better than vile vermin, loathsome creatures apart from the human race. The idea he would associate with a Jew, much less have sex with one, was unimaginable to Hannah.

Coming to a halt, Horst turned to face Hannah, who did likewise. "While I will not lie to you, I must once more request that you do not ask me, or anyone else for that matter, about the camps or what goes on in them, not now, not ever. Do you understand?"

Horst's expression struck Hannah as very much like the one her father assumed when he wished to make it clear to her she had overstepped her bounds. Dropping her gaze, she nodded. "Yes. I understand perfectly."

CHAPTER THIRTEEN

TO THE VICTORS

ORANIENBURG, JULY 1940

At her wit's end, and unable to stand the pounding of the drum Wolfgang had been beating on incessantly for well over an hour, Hannah clamped her hands over her ears without bothering to scrape the bread dough off of them. "I don't know who I want to shoot first," she muttered angrily through clenched teeth. "My father for giving him that damned thing or the miscreants who made it."

From across the table, Fräu Sander rapped her wooden spoon on the side of the bowl she had been stirring. "Hannah! Language."

Cringing, Hannah peeked up at the cook as she pulled her hands away from her ears, ignoring the way stray strands of hair now stuck fast to her doughy fingers. "Sorry, Fräu Sander. It's just that he hasn't stopped beating that, that thing since Father gave it to him."

"And where do you think I have been all afternoon? Hiding in the woodshed with cotton stuffed in my ears?" the older woman countered.

"How do you tolerate the noise?" Hannah asked as she began to gingerly pull her fingers away from the hair they were stuck to.

With a sigh, the cook set aside her spoon, came around the table, and gave Hannah's hands a light tap. "Here, let me help you." With that, Fräu Sander gingerly began to separate Hannah's hair, strand by strand, from her sticky fingers. "In time you will learn to tolerate such annoyances. It is something women must do if they hope to maintain harmony and peace within their homes."

"Am I expected to learn to like that?" Hannah countered.

"I didn't say *like*," Fräu Sander replied as she continued the tedious task of cleaning the dough off of Hannah's hair one strand at a time. "I said *tolerate*. I expect you are already coming to discover the need to do so."

Fräu Sander had no need to say any more. Like Hannah, she was not blind to the way Ernst Richter had been behaving since the death of his wife. It was why she tried to be there for a girl who, in her eyes, had already suffered enough in life. And while Fräu Sander understood her place within the Richter household, she was a mother and, as such, found herself unable to turn away when she saw a child such as Hannah in desperate need of guidance, a warm smile, and, from time to time, a shoulder to cry on.

"How do you know?" Hannah asked after a long silence.

"How do you know what?"

"How do you know when you need to tolerate something and when you need to confront a problem?"

Before answering, Fräu Sander took a moment to recall all the times she had turned a blind eye to things happening around her, choosing to stand by in silence and do nothing for no better reason than to avoid causing trouble or becoming involved in something she didn't think concerned her. "Sometimes you don't," she finally muttered regretfully.

The sound of an infant squawking preceded the appearance of Maria Riese, who burst into the kitchen cradling young Siegfried Richter in her arms. "That infernal pounding woke poor Siggy from his nap," the flustered nanny stated as she made her way over to the highchair and struggled to slip an uncooperative and very cranky child into it.

With a twinkle in her eye, Hannah held her right hand up, pointing the index finger on it toward the ceiling. "Ah! I've just answered my own question."

Not having been privy to their previous conversation, and not needing to ask how Hannah had managed to get the dough in her hair, Maria looked over at the cook. "What question would that be?"

Fräu Sander responded without bothering to look away from what she was doing. "I am guessing Wolfgang is about to lose his drum."

"There's no need to guess," Hannah chuckled fiendishly as she went to stand up before Fräu Sander was finished.

"Hold still, girl," the cook harrumphed, tugging the handful of hair she was holding to reel in a young girl awkwardly straddling the line between childhood and adulthood.

❊

At dinner that night, Wolfgang wasted little time in appealing to his father over the grave injustice that had befallen him earlier in the day. For the longest time, Ernst Richter said nothing, listening to his son complain bitterly about how mean the women in the house had been to him that afternoon.

"After Hannah took my drum and put it up where I can't reach it, she said I couldn't have it back until I learned to be responsible and respect others in the house," Wolfgang groused, glaring at his sister as he was doing so. "When I ordered Fräu Sander and Maria to take it down, they refused, Papa. Fräu Sander even wagged her finger at me as she laughed."

Barely able to keep from laughing himself, as much from his son's beet-red expression as from the story he was telling, Ernst Richter set his spoon aside, folded his hands on the table before him, and stared over where his son was seated. At the far end of the table, Hannah continued to enjoy her soup, pretending her father and brother weren't even there.

"First off, young man, how many times must I remind you, when I am not here, Hannah is in charge." Richter used his eyes to pin Wolfgang to his seat. "You may be my son, but you haven't yet earned the right to issue orders as if you were the commandant of this home."

Wolfgang let his head droop as he stuck his lower lip out in a last desperate bid to elicit a modicum of sympathy from his father.

As much as this little act amused both Hannah and her father, they managed to maintain their composure as Richter continued. "I expect there was a good reason your sister felt compelled to confiscate your drum."

Had Hannah not been there, Wolfgang would have played innocent, spinning one of the marvelous little tales he so often used to beguile his father into believing he had done nothing wrong. But he knew better than to try, not with *her* listening to every word he said, ready to correct the record. Father always believed what she said, Wolfgang sadly concluded as he glanced at his sister out of the corner of his eyes. Not only was it unfair, but it was also embarrassing to the boy of seven to be dominated so by women. All of that would change, of course, when he was finally old enough to join the Hitler Youth. They didn't have to listen to their sisters. They only needed to obey the Führer.

❋

After seeing to it that Wolfgang was tucked away and Maria had little Siggy all settled in for the night, Hannah joined her father in his study, as she always did on those evenings when he returned home at a reasonable hour. Upon entering the room, she noticed he was seated in his favorite chair, holding a brandy sniff in one hand and a cigar in the other as he stared vacantly into a darkened fireplace devoid of light or warmth. "Shall I play for you, Father?" she asked as she stood in the center of the room.

Before answering, Richter gave his head a quick shake as if banishing an unwelcome thought. With the hand in which he held his cigar, he pointed to a chair across from him. "Please, take a seat. I have something I need to discuss with you."

Having no idea what he was going to say, Hannah prepared herself as she slowly made her way to the chair and demurely settled in, just as Lena had taught her to do at times like this.

"I've been ordered to Paris," Richter announced while staring at the fireless hearth.

Hannah's heart sank. Despite Horst's best efforts to keep her company in the evenings when her father was away, she hated being alone at night. As much as she tried to purge all memories of her childhood in Munich, she could not help but recall how she'd often been left alone by the man she'd once thought of as a father when he was called away in the middle of the night to tend to one of his patients. She had never felt safe there, not after her mother had left them and the Brownshirts had begun paying visits to the house, taunting her and throwing rocks against the side of the house even as policemen amused themselves by merely standing back and watching.

Suspecting he knew why his daughter was wearing such a long face, Richter chuckled. "There's no need to be so glum, Mausi."

"I can't help it, Father. I miss you when you are gone."

"Well, I suspect you shall not miss me this time," Richter mused as something of a smile lit up his face.

"I always do. Why should this time be any different?" Hannah shot back without realizing she was being played.

"I do not see how that is possible, since you will be with me."

Not sure if she was hearing him right, Hannah blinked. "Excuse me?"

Unable to keep his little game going any longer, Ernst Richter grinned. "You will be going with Horst and me to Paris, provided of course that is agreeable to you."

When what her father was saying finally sank in, Hannah leaped from her seat, bounded over to where he was, and threw herself at him, wrapping her arms about his neck in a fierce hug. Not even the reek of cheap perfume was able to dampen the joy Hannah felt as she buried her face into the shoulder of Richter's uniform.

❀

Hearing the door of the rail carriage's compartment slide open, Horst Fischer looked up from the book he had been reading. When he saw Richter was alone, he cocked an eyebrow. "Are the girls not with you, sir?"

In a playful mood, Richter made a great show of looking behind him before answering. "Apparently not. I seem to have lost them somewhere between here and the dining car."

"Is it wise to leave them on their own like this?" Horst asked, astonished that his commanding officer would allow three young girls to wander about on their own.

"How much trouble can they possibly get into on a train?" Richter asked.

Realizing Richter was in a playful mood, something rare as of late, Horst snickered. "If they were ordinary girls, I would have to agree.

But those three, God in Heaven! Together they are capable of wreaking more havoc on the poor French than Fast Heinz and his panzers."

Pretending to give his adjutant's comment careful consideration, Richter nodded. "You have a point, Horst. Perhaps it was a mistake to give in to my daughter's pleas to allow her to bring her friends along with us."

"Perhaps?"

Richter shook his head as he laughed. "You know as well as I do no man can stand up to my Hannah when she's set her mind to something. Besides," Richter added as his voice took on a more serious note. "We've much to do in Paris. Unlike Austria, Czechoslovakia, and Poland, we can't simply march in and demand local authorities cooperate with us. We're going to have to convince the French it's in their best interest to acquiesce to our requests for information concerning their Jews as well as assess what arrangements can be made to handle them and other people of interest."

Unable to help himself, Horst chuckled. "Oh, I don't think we'll have any trouble with the French, not if what they say about Pétain's national revolution proves to be true."

"Pétain is a wily old fox," Richter countered. "Neither he or any of the French we'll be dealing with are to be trusted. We are going to have to let them know who is in charge and the cost of ignoring our demands . . ."

"Requests, sir," Horst corrected his superior. "We're making requests."

Richter sighed. "Yes, yes. Requests, for now at least."

The opening of the door and the sudden appearance of three giggling girls piling into the compartment cut Richter's and Horst's conversation short. Turning to his daughter, Richter scowled. "And what have you been up to?"

Throwing herself in the seat next to Horst, Hannah did her best to play innocent. "Nothing, Father, nothing at all."

Those words no sooner had left her mouth when Sophie, who had been tarrying at the door of the compartment, pulled her head in and slammed the door shut. "He's coming this way!"

Before Richter could ask who "he" was, Sophie took a seat next to him, reached across him, and grabbed a book Gretchen had taken up to make it look as if she had been sitting there peacefully reading the whole time. Pressing the book up to her face, Sophie took to pretending she was intently studying it even though she was holding it upside down.

Amused by the girl's behavior, the two men took to exchanging glances with each other before Richter, seeing Horst's eyes look away, turned to see what was distracting him.

In an instant, he realized what his daughter and her friends had been up to. Standing outside the compartment looking through the glass was a German soldier. When he and Richter locked eyes, the blood in the soldier's face all but drained away as his smug expression took on one Hannah's father was very familiar with, that of sheer terror.

Paris, August 1940

As Gretchen stood next to Horst, doing her best to pretend she was actually interested in what he was telling her about the painting they were standing in front of, Sophie latched onto Hannah's arm and dragged her aside. "When are we going to go off on our own and have some fun?" she whispered when they were far enough away to where Horst couldn't hear them.

"You heard what my father said," Hannah countered, peeking over Sophie's shoulder as Gretchen glanced in her direction, rolling her eyes by way of indicating she too had had her fill of culture for the day.

"Oh, he won't mind," Sophie continued. "And even if he does, what's he going to do, turn us all over on his knee and give us a good spanking?"

A devilish grin lit up Hannah's face. "Oh, you'd like that, won't you?"

Scandalized, Sophie's eyes flew open as she gave her friend a quick slap on the arm, one loud enough to reverberate off the walls of the gallery. Horst glanced over his shoulder to where they were standing. Though he knew what they were up to, he went back to pointing out the unique quality of Monet's thin, yet visible brushstrokes.

"Listen, you," Sophie hissed. "Either you find a way to rid us of Leibstandarte Hannah for the afternoon, or Gretchen and I will take off on our own."

Wishing to experience some of the city's many delights without the burden of an SS officer monitoring their every step and causing people to avoid them as if they were lepers, Hannah decided to appeal to Horst rather than attempt to slip away from him. To that end, she eased up to him as they continued along the gallery, signaling Gretchen with nothing more than her eyes to go over to where Sophie was.

When they were alone, Horst surprised Hannah by turning to face her. "Okay, what are you three planning now?"

Rather than deny what she was up to, Hannah took to pleading with Horst. "We've been good so far," she pointed out. "We've followed all the rules Father laid down for us and have done everything you asked us to do. But . . ."

"But you wish to rid yourselves of a millstone like me and have some fun on your own," Horst concluded when Hannah didn't bother finishing her thought.

"Well, yes," she responded with a well-measured coyness by clasping her hands behind her back as she dropped her chin a smidge, all the while maintaining eye contact with Horst.

"You know I am immune to your charms, Fräulein Richter."

"Yes, I know, which is why I am appealing to your kind and understanding nature."

No longer able to keep from smirking, Horst closed his eyes, tilted his head back, and shook it. "No wonder your father finds himself unable to say no to you."

"Then you will let us go?" Hannah beamed.

"Only if you promise to be back at the hotel well before dinner time and assure me Herr Sturmbannführer never, ever finds out just how lax I was in my duties."

Squealing, Hannah threw her arms about Horst's necks, causing him to look about nervously. It wouldn't do, he told himself, for Frenchmen to see how easily an SS officer could be embarrassed by a mere girl.

❋

Though they had already strolled down des Champs-Élysées, the three girls had been in the company of Hannah's father and his adjutant. The experience this time was entirely different, that is until people passing by heard them speaking German. Yet even then, most were able to shrug off whatever animus they felt for their conquers and go about their business without another thought. Some of the men who felt there were more important things in life than dwelling on politics even gave the stylishly dressed young girls a second look.

The German soldiers they ran into were an entirely different matter, but one the girls were able to handle with ease when they wished to rid themselves of those who behaved loutishly. All Gretchen or Sophie had to do was to look at their wristwatches, turn to Hannah, and remind her they needed to hurry if they were to be on time to meet up with her father, the Sturmbannführer. If the soldier they were trying to shake didn't buy their story, Hannah would turn on the man and stare him down with her piercing blue eyes while demanding to know his name, the name of his commanding officer, and his unit. That approach never failed, leaving Sophie to muse that Hannah had the makings of a wonderful interrogator.

Well versed in Parisian culture thanks to all the pre-war movies they had been raised on, the girls couldn't resist enjoying coffee and pastries at one of the many street cafés. While watching the hustle and bustle of the people of Europe's most famous city pass them by as if there had never been a war, they discussed what they'd do next.

"Shopping," Gretchen suggested. "I would like to go in some of the shops we passed yesterday, the ones *your* father wouldn't let us go in," she added in an accusatory fashion while glancing over at Hannah.

"Don't be silly," Sophie replied. "We can't purchase anything. I know I haven't near enough to afford anything here."

"Gretchen didn't mention anything about buying something," Hannah pointed out. "It costs nothing to try things on."

"Yes," Gretchen added. "It would be so much fun."

"Hmm, I suppose," Sophie grumbled as she caught a pair of Luftwaffe officers who had been walking by slow down when they heard the girls chatting away in German. "Maybe we can find a lacy brassiere with the padding Hannah needs to make up for her, ah, rather sad showing," Sophie quipped. She sat up straight to display her own blooming bosom, as much to give the Luftwaffe officers a show as to poke fun at her friend.

"Show-off," Hannah grumbled.

"Yes, I am," Sophie sniffed proudly. "Finally, I have an advantage over our very own Little Miss Perfect."

Not wanting to see their afternoon spoiled by her friends' tit-for-tat, Gretchen stood up before Hannah could respond. "If you children are finished, I suggest we be on our way."

As one, both Hannah and Sophie turned toward their bespectacled friend and stuck their tongues out at her.

❋

The three girls enjoyed themselves as they wandered down the avenue, going into shops that featured clothing none of them could afford and trying on everything they could before exasperated clerks and shop owners realized their little game and chased them out. They were about to enter another when Hannah stopped short. Having been looking the other way and not paying attention to where they were going, Sophie was about to ask what the problem was but didn't. She had no need to the second she saw what a pair of Gestapo men were doing.

For the longest time, Hannah simply stood there watching a familiar scene play out. The message on the placard they were posting was one that haunted her no matter where she went. The word "Juden" in bold black letters identified the shop as one that German soldiers were discouraged from patronizing. Even more disturbing to Hannah was the way a pair of French gendarmes stood by, watching with expressions of approval. It shouldn't have bothered her as it did, she told herself. She was no longer a Jew. She never had been, not in her heart.

And yet it did. Long after they had turned their backs on the scene as they had been taught to do and headed off to the next shop, despite her best efforts, Hannah was unable to forget she wasn't perfect. Even more devastating was an appreciation that no matter what she did or how hard she tried, she never would be, not in the eyes of the people who mattered to her.

PART FOUR

1942

SONDERBEHANDLUNG
(Special Treatment)

CHAPTER FOURTEEN

THE CONFERENCE

Having completed his examination, the physician jammed his hands into his lab coat pockets. He stepped back to study the overall appearance of the patient stripped bare of all clothing standing before him. He ignored the way she held her head bowed, staring intently at her toes to avoid his steady, unflinching gaze. Nor did he pay any attention to the ruddiness of her cheeks, aflame with embarrassment, the twitching of her hands as she fought the urge to cover her exposed groin, or the way the cold, tile floor of the sterile room that caused her to quiver like a leaf whipped about by a gust of wintery wind. It was the girl's breast and her figure as a whole that held his interest. He had never had an opportunity to study a subject such as this, much less try the drugs he'd only read about in professional journals on one. If for no other reason than professional curiosity, coupled with a touch of pride for what he had been able to do for her, the physician continued to stare at Hannah, unable to see her as anything other than what she was attempting to present herself as, a young girl on the cusp of womanhood.

A sudden, violent shiver shook the girl's entire body and brought an end to the physician's musings. "You are free to dress now, Fräulein Sander." He turned his back on the girl and headed over to his desk to record his observations in the medical journal he was keeping. It didn't matter to him that the name the girl had given him was as false as her gender. All the physician was concerned with was the knowledge he had gained from treating her. Expanding the boundaries of science, after all, far outweighed the price those who did so had to pay.

❀

In desperate need of time to calm herself and sort through the jumble of emotions roiling within her before returning home, Hannah ignored the bitter cold that held the city in its frozen grip like an unseen hand. Lost in her own thoughts, she slowly made her way along near-deserted streets lit only by a pale winter sun bereft of even a hint of warmth.

Rounding the corner, she set off down Unter den Linden. Glancing up, she found herself unable to escape how the wind shook the leafless linden trees, much as the doctor's office had shaken her. While she understood the shedding of leaves every fall was part of the cycle of life, just as her visit to the doctor was proving to be if she were to continue as she had been since arriving in Berlin some seven years prior, she hated the winter as much as she did her trips to the physician.

It was more than the way the doctor treated her as if she were nothing more than a lab rat. It was the reality of the awkward situation she found herself having to deal with that bothered her. Both her visits to him, as well as the synthesized hormones he told her she'd need to take for the rest of her life, served as annoying reminders that no matter how hard she tried, no matter how much she endeavored to put her past behind her, she couldn't. It, like her heritage, was like unseen rocks strewn along the path she wished to follow, just waiting to trip her up.

A gust of wind whipping down the broad avenue brought on a sudden chill. How different things were now, she found herself thinking as she caught sight of the Brandenburg Gate just up ahead. In the summer of 1940, when her father had brought her and Wolfgang here to watch the great victory parade that passed down this very avenue, the crowd had been packed twenty and more deep, all pressed together and cheering wildly over their good fortune. That good fortune, like the cheering crowds, were now gone. So too, Hannah realized, was the hope she'd once had of ever being a perfect German girl. On days like this, especially after the way the physician treated her, Hannah wondered if she would ever be able to think of herself as a real girl. This never failed to lead to the next, even more troubling question, one Hannah was reminded of all too often. Could she ever be a real German, a part of the thousand-year Reich that stretched from France's Atlantic seacoast to the very gates of Moscow?

Drawing the collar of her coat tighter around her neck, Hannah stopped to gaze up at the Quadriga atop the Brandenburg Gate. The peace Frederick II had meant it to symbolize now seemed as far off as the warmth of the summer sun or, for that matter, her dream of putting her past behind her.

❋

Knowing the kitchen was always warm in the afternoon as Fräu Sander went about preparing dinner, and the cook would be anxious to see she had returned from Berlin safely, Hannah ducked into the house through the back door. The warmth of the stove and the cook's smile were all that were needed to banish the dark thoughts and the lingering memory of the treatment she had endured at the hands of the physician earlier in the day.

"So, how did it go?" Fräu Sander asked as she watched Hannah slip off her coat and throw it over the back of a chair as she walked toward the stove.

Holding her hands before it to thaw her numb fingertips, Hannah grunted. "Well enough, I guess."

"You guess? What did the doctor say?"

Before answering, Hannah looked about as she always did when discussing this matter. Fräu Sander had helped her find a doctor willing to discreetly assist Hannah, believing her problem was nothing more than a minor imbalance of female hormones. "As always, he didn't say much. He just prodded, poked, felt around more than I thought he needed to, and looked. He did a lot of that," Hannah added in disgust.

"All doctors do that," the cook ventured. "They need to, in order to know what to do."

Rather than mention that her father, the one in Munich, had never treated his patients as if they were specimens, Hannah drew upon her more recent experience as a Red Cross volunteer with Sophie and Gretchen at a local military hospital. "Not all doctors are as cold and unfeeling as the one I'm seeing in Berlin. Major Strasser is a kind man. He's always smiling and making little jokes with the wounded soldiers while he's treating them."

Looking up from what she'd been doing, Fräu Sander waved the spoon she was holding at Hannah. "Then, he is an exception. All the doctors I've ever known like to lord over you as if you were a schoolchild and they're the headmaster. And they like to look, at least they used to, when I was something to look at," the cook chuckled to herself as she went back to what she had been doing.

After Hannah had rid herself of the chill she'd had since leaving the doctor's office, she fetched a glass from the cabinet, sat down at the table, and began to fill it with milk from the pitcher Fräu Sander had been using. "Take care," the cook warned as she was doing so. "That's all we have until tomorrow."

In a much better mood now that she was warm and safe in her home, Hannah looked over at the cook. "What, have they sent all the cows to Russia as well?" she asked doing her best to make her question sound as if it were a serious one even as she was snatching a fresh-baked biscuit from a plate. After taking a bite from it, she held the biscuit out at arm's length and made a face. "And the sugar? Did the cows take it with them?"

"Do not speak with your mouth full, young lady," Fräu Sander admonished. "And to answer your question, it wouldn't surprise me in the least if they did. Thank God my Gerhardt is in Africa and not Russia."

"I wish I were in Africa," Hannah muttered as she went back to nibbling on the near-tasteless biscuit. "At least I'd be warm."

"I don't think you'd like being in Africa," the cook countered as she continued to beat the dough she would be using to make noodles. "My boy writes that it often becomes far too warm for him and his comrades, and he's not talking about the weather."

"At least he's doing something important rather than sitting about here at home freezing."

Looking up from what she'd been doing, Fräu Sander regarded Hannah with a stern, no-nonsense stare. "You are doing what you are supposed to be doing. You have two brothers to look after and a father who needs you now more than ever. He has much on his mind. The last thing he needs is to come home to a sourpuss of a daughter."

"I'm not being a sourpuss, Fräu Sander. I'm just, well, . . ."

"You are being a sourpuss. Now, fetch the flour and a rolling pin," the cook directed by way of letting Hannah know she was tired of her complaining and wished to hear no more of it. "You can roll out the dough and cut the noodles while I look to the stew."

Hannah didn't mind the way the cook ordered her about or had her tend to some of the kitchen chores. She actually found helping Fräu Sander quite enjoyable and, in a strange way, relaxing. There was no need to think when working in the kitchen, no reason to rationalize what she was doing or why. All she needed to do here was to follow orders, just like everyone else was doing these days. Here she could set aside her concerns and throw herself into the mechanical process of doing what was expected of her. That was the best thing she or anyone else could do during difficult times such as this. It was what Hannah did whenever she could. It's what she wished she could do all the time, just like she wished she could forget her past.

❋

Before long, Fräu Sander and Hannah were joined by Maria hauling a hefty little bundle nestled on her hip. As soon as the boy saw Hannah, he screeched. *"Mutti!"*

Hannah's efforts to discourage little Siegfried from calling her his mother had been for naught. He called all the women in the house *Mutti* since they all catered to him in equal measure. Setting aside her rolling pin, Hannah went over to where Maria was holding the child. Wide-eyed and smiling, she greeted her brother by calling out his nickname in much the same way he had greeted her before leaning forward and rubbing noses with him. "And what has my little Siggy been up to today?" Hannah asked while looking at the boy, though her question was directed at his nanny.

"Making messes," Maria groused as she took to sliding her charge into his highchair. "I can assure you, there's nothing wrong with this child's ability to digest food and pass it on."

Taking a moment away from what she had been doing, Fräu Sander reached over and gave Siegfried a playful tap on the nose.

"He does that because he enjoys eating and wishes to make room for more."

Hannah found it difficult to ignore the cook's comment, for, despite admonishments from the Reich Ministry of Public Enlightenment and Propaganda to obey the stringent rules of rationing and stories her friends shared with her about shortages they had to endure, with few exceptions, the Richter household lacked for nothing. Rather than saying something, Hannah remained silent. Secretly she found herself thanking God she didn't have to suffer the same way others did. Besides, she reasoned, she'd already suffered enough for one person. Her suffering was as unique as it was personal, and it would not end, not even when the war was finally over.

With Maria needing to tend to Siegfried, who was clamoring for food by pounding on the tray of his highchair, and Fräu Sander going back to her cooking, neither noticed the sudden change in Hannah's demeanor as she went about sprinkling flour on the dough she'd been rolling out, struggling to lose herself by tending in the simple, mindless task at hand.

❄

Hannah was cutting into noodles with speed and precision that impressed even an old hand in the kitchen such as Fräu Sander when she looked up at the sound of a motorcycle pulling around the front of the house. Was Peter was stopping by to visit her? Unlikely, Hannah told herself. He was lucky whenever she gave the boy a thought or Gretchen brought his name up in passing. He had been able to achieve his most cherished goal, enlisting in the Waffen SS as soon as he had come of age. Neither Hannah nor Peter's sister expected him to remain a common soldier for very long. In time he would find his way to officer training at Bad Tölz. And while it wasn't quite the same tumultuous and haphazard route her father had taken, Hannah had little doubt that in time, Peter would become an important man within the SS, a person destined to leave his mark on the Reich, just as her father was doing each and every day.

With her hands coated with flower, Hannah resisted the temptation to stop what she was doing and go out to see who it was.

By the time she washed up, took off her apron, and made herself presentable, Wolfgang or Clara would have answered the door, provided of course the housekeeper, a woman her Father refused to let go, was in the mood to do what she was being paid to do. Besides, Hannah expected it was of little concern to her. More than likely, it was a courier delivering dispatches her father would need to look over after dinner. She hated it when his commanding officer or some self-important bureaucrat did that to him. It was bad enough they had him working six days a week, twelve hours a day. To take away what little time he had to spend with his family looking over meaningless reports that could easily have waited until the next day was, in Hannah's mind, asking too much of him. Of course, if she were to be reasonable, she would have found herself having to admit at least her father was able to sleep in his own bed most nights. That was more than could be said for all the men serving at the front, whether it be Russia, Africa, or standing watch in far-flung garrisons throughout occupied territories that spread across the width and the breadth of Europe.

Hannah had just settled back into the smooth rhythm of slicing strips of dough from the flattened ball, separating them, and setting them aside when Wolfgang came barging into the kitchen. "It was Hauptsturmführer Fischer," he proclaimed louder than was necessary.

"Well, where is he?" Hannah asked, looking over at her brother who was wearing an aviator's leather helmet Horst had given him, though it was several sizes too large for him.

"Here I am," her father's adjutant smoothly replied as he entered the kitchen just behind the boy. Stopping, he took a moment to look around. "So, this is where all the lovely ladies of the Richter household are hiding."

"Hiding? No," Fräu Sander corrected him. "We are doing what is expected of us."

"Yes," Hannah proclaimed with a mock severity as she straightened up to greet Fischer. "We are at our posts, working for the greater glory of the Reich. Why aren't you back at the office doing likewise, manning those paper parapets you and Father retreat behind every morning when the time comes to do serious work around the house?"

Rather than rising to Hannah's challenge as he often did and engaging her in a lighthearted joust of wits, Horst grunted. "Your father called me from the conference he's been attending, one presided over by Heydrich himself, and ordered me to meet him here," Horst explained in an even tone that betrayed nothing. It did not need to. Upon hearing the name of the man who had convened the meeting, all knew that no matter the topic, it had implications no one dared take lightly. This was especially true of Hannah.

Though her father never said an unkind word about the man whom Horst called the Hangman when it was just the two of them, every time his name came up, his expression clouded over. From that, Hannah could tell there was an underlying tension between them. Whether it was a personal matter or a professional disagreement did not matter. Her father didn't much care for Heydrich, and therefore she didn't. That his own son didn't share this attitude annoyed Ernst Richter to no end. Like so many young boys in Germany, Wolfgang had become a fan of the Deputy Reich Protector of the Protectorate of Bohemia and Moravia because of his well-publicized exploits as a fighter pilot on the Russian front the previous summer.

"Will you be staying for dinner?" Fräu Sander asked.

Horst shrugged. "I don't know. That all depends upon the Sturmbannführer."

"You're staying for dinner," the cook stated flatly, making it clear even if the Führer himself walked into her kitchen and ordered otherwise, Horst would not be at liberty to leave until he had eaten. "Now sit, young man, and enjoy a biscuit and some milk."

Both Hannah and Horst shared a knowing glance as he complied. "You can try them, but don't get your hopes up," Hannah warned. "The cows took all our sugar with them when they left for Russia."

Not privy to Hannah's previous exchange with the cook, Maria and Horst exchanged searching glances before they shrugged and settled in. Horst then enjoyed a most welcome late afternoon snack that reminded him of a home he had not seen in months while Maria shoveled food into Siegfried's mouth as fast as she could, but not fast enough for the ravenous young boy.

❃

The easygoing, lighthearted mood of the kitchen came to an abrupt halt the second Ernst Richter entered it. Without bothering to acknowledge the greetings that welcomed him, he gruffly ordered Horst to come with him. When Hannah asked when he wished to have dinner served, his response was curt. "Not now, Hannah."

"But, Father, I was just wondering—"

"I said, not now," Richter snapped.

Startled by the sharpness of her father's retort and the anger in his eyes, Hannah visibly withered as she took a step back. If Ernst Richter took note of the bewilderment on his daughter's face, or felt any remorse over barking at her as he had, he did not show it as he stormed out of the kitchen with Horst close on his heels. In his wake he left a stunned silence punctuated only by the sound of an innocent child pounding the tray of his highchair with his tiny fists, clamoring for his next mouthful of food.

❀

When one hour had passed and began to stretch into a second without her father or Horst emerging from the study, Hannah concluded the time had come for her to screw up her courage and try once more to find out what to do about dinner. Tiptoeing up to the study door as if she were approaching a wolf's lair, Hannah put her ear to the door and listened for a moment. When she heard nothing, she softly tapped on the door with her knuckles. After waiting a minute, maybe two, she once more put her ear to the door. After a second, slightly louder knock with her ear still pressed against the door went unanswered, Hannah stepped back slightly, drew herself up, and took hold of the door handle.

Ever so slowly, she gave it a turn and eased the door open, listening as she did so, ready to pull back and slam it the instant her father barked out for her to go away. But there was no sound from the room other than the crackling of a fire. When the door was open wide enough for her to stick her head through, Hannah took a deep breath and did so, again prepared to draw back if either of the two men objected to her intrusion.

They didn't. Eventually, Hannah managed to catch sight of both her father and Horst in the room's semi-darkness slouched in a pair of chairs set before the fireplace. As best she could tell, they were doing little more than silently watching the flames as they consumed the logs neatly stacked one upon the other, seemingly oblivious to the other's presence as well as hers. Each of them held a brandy sniff off to one side at arm's length.

The temptation to call out from the doorway was checked by her curiosity, leading Hannah to steal into the room with all the subtleness of a cat creeping up on an unwary mouse. The sudden motion of her father's hand, the one holding the brandy sniff, caused her to stop. After taking a sip, she heard her father grunt in disgust. "Evacuation," he snorted. "The lot of them sat about the table discussing the matter as if they were the board of directors of Deutsche Bank haggling over a business deal."

There followed a long pause during which each of the men enjoyed long, lingering sips of brandy. "Do they really think they can do this?" Horst asked incredulously.

"*We*," Hannah's father intoned. "Not only does Heydrich think *we* can do this, he left no doubt *we* will."

After a long pause, Hannah heard Horst muse out loud as if to himself. "Eleven million people collected, transported, and processed. That's going to take some doing."

"Yes, it will," Ernst Richter agreed. "We have got our work cut out for us."

Hannah was not at all certain she understood what they were saying. Not that she needed to. Her father's affairs were of no concern to her. All she needed to concern herself with was ensuring she did what was expected of her, just as her mother, Lena Richter, had dutifully done right up to the very end. With that thought in mind, Hannah eased her way out of the room, taking great care she did not disturb her father's conversation with Horst. After quietly closing the door, she took a moment to give her head a quick shake as if trying to set aside the gloomy scene she had just witnessed before returning to the warmth and safety of the kitchen.

CHAPTER FIFTEEN

ADIEU

ORANIENBURG, JUNE 1942

For the longest time, none of the girls spoke. They simply sat together as they often did in a shady, secluded spot on the shore of the Lehnitzsee they had come to think of as their own, a place untouched by the troubles of the outside world. There, on the edge of the placid lake, Hannah, Sophie, and Gretchen often gathered to chat amongst themselves, touching on subjects they didn't dare discuss within earshot of their parents, teachers, or irksome siblings who didn't appreciate young girls needed to spend time with their most trusted friends. Whether it was to ferret out the many mysteries and problems that bedeviled all girls on the cusp of womanhood, or to enjoy time away from ever-increasing demands that pressed down upon them like a millstone, the trio took solace in a companionship each had come to cherish.

At the moment the three of them were looking off in different directions, the stillness of the late spring day disturbed only by the lake's water rhythmically lapping upon the shore and an occasional sniffle that could not be stifled. All were hopelessly lost in their own thoughts as they struggled to absorb Hannah's news. In time, it was Gretchen who found she could not keep from whining plaintively without looking over to where her dearest friend sat with her arms tightly wrapped about legs and drawn up against her chest. "Poland? Why Poland?"

Barely able to keep her own emotions in check, Hannah sniffled as she gazed vacantly out over the lake's ruffled surface. "Well, because that's where the camp is, or will be, once they've finished building it."

"Why can't they simply build another one here?" Sophie snapped bitterly. "God knows, according to what I hear there are camps all over Germany. I don't see how one more here in Brandenburg, one they could give your father to command would make a difference."

"I don't think that's the way they do things," Gretchen explained patiently. "Besides, I for one wouldn't wish to see all those Poles and Russians transported back to Germany. Do you?"

"If it would mean keeping Hannah here, yes," Sophia snipped.

"You're not being logical," Gretchen countered as she leaned forward a bit and looked past Hannah, who was nestled in between them. "Think of all the trains that would tie up doing something as silly as that. I mean, who in their right mind would shuffle people all over the place when there's no need to?"

Already on the verge of breaking down again as she had when she had shared the news she would soon be leaving Oranienburg, and having no desire to listen to them bicker, Hannah jumped up, turned, and walked away. This caused Sophie to furrow her brow as she glared over to where Gretchen was sitting. "Now see what you've done. You made her cry again."

"I'm not crying," Hannah called out from where she was standing with her back to her friends, even as she was wiping away the tears streaming down her cheeks with the back of her hand.

Feeling guilty, Gretchen came to her feet, went over to where Hannah was, wrapped her arms about her friend, and joined her in weeping.

Unable to hold off any longer herself, Sophie joined them. "I'm going to miss you," she whimpered as she began to sob uncontrollably.

For the three girls, time came to a halt as they stood there, the silence of the warm, peaceful spring day disturbed only by the sound of water lapping upon the shore and their shared sorrow.

❁

The somber notes of Beethoven's Moonlight Sonata drifting softly, mournfully from the parlor told Ernst Richter all he needed to know. Hannah was still upset over the news he had given her the previous evening. Deciding it might be best if he fortified himself before confronting her once again, Richter made his way into his study where he poured himself a schnapps, a very tall one.

The footfall of boots on the floor behind her alerted Hannah that her father had entered the room. But rather than stopping and greet him as she did on most days, she chose to ignore him just as she had that morning. She was well aware it was childish of her to behave in this way. After all, it wasn't his fault he had been assigned to command a new cluster of camps being built in Poland. Her father was a soldier, and as such, he was expected to obey the orders of his superiors, no matter how unpleasant they might be to him or inconvenient to his family. All Germans needed to do what was expected of them, especially her. That was the way of things.

Still, Hannah found herself unable to set aside her feelings.

"You are only human, child," Fräu Sander had taken great pains to remind her as the cook did her best to console her earlier in the day. "As much as we sometimes wish we could set our feelings aside, stoically accepting whatever life hands us dry-eyed and unmoved, to do so would make us little better than the beasts of the forest."

Learning to live with sorrow was something Fräu Sander knew painfully well. Her husband had been taken from her during the previous war, one of countless souls lost without a trace on the Somme where the British had ground the once-mighty German Army down in the mud of Flanders, bit by bit by bit. More recently, she had received word her only son, her precious Gerhardt, had been posted missing at Bir Hakeim, a place that was nothing more to most Germans than an obscure dot on a map on the front page of their morning newspaper. In her grief, the cook had been unable to perform her duties for more than a week, leaving it to Hannah to prepare her family's meals as the woman sat at the kitchen table, lost in the memories of happier times when her whole world revolved around a bright-eyed child who was no more.

Taking a seat across the room from where his daughter sat playing the piano in a manner so reminiscent of the way his beloved Lena often had whenever she felt the need to lose herself in her music, Ernst Richter said nothing for the longest time. Closing his eyes, he allowed the music to wash over him, purging him of his cares, if only for a while.

Upon reaching the end of the piece she'd been playing, Hannah paused, letting her hands fall into her lap as she stared down at the piano's keys, wondering what she should play next, if anything. From behind, she heard her father's voice.

"Something more joyous, if you would."

His request was not an order. It sounded more like a plea, an appeal made by someone who, like her, was in desperate need of a diversion, an escape from his troubles. For a moment, Hannah was tempted to ignore his request by playing Chopin's Raindrop Prelude. But she didn't. She couldn't. She had sulked like a spoiled child long enough. The time had come to get on with life.

"What would you like to hear?" she asked quietly without looking back at her father.

A hint of a smile brightened Richter's face. "Rachmaninov, I think. Your mother loved Rachmaninov."

"Yes, she did," Hannah whispered before settling to play Rhapsody On a Theme By Paganini.

For the next few minutes, the world outside that room did not exist for the father and daughter as each set aside all their concerns and gave themselves over to the music, their memories, and the feeling one enjoys when they are with someone they love and care for. Only when she was finished did Hannah slowly turn around on the piano bench and face Richter. "When we go, I should like to take Fräu Sander along with us," Hannah declared with quiet firmness. "With her daughter serving as a domestic in Dresden and her son now listed as missing, she has no one here, no one other than us."

Having been occupied wrapping up all his duties at headquarters and preparing himself for the momentous task ahead, Richter had devoted little attention to the needs of his family other than telling them they would be going with him to Poland. Never having had to trouble himself with the domestic affairs of his family, he had not given any thought to the details that would need to be tended either in preparing to leave Oranienburg or settling in once they had reached Borkow. "Well, I expect that should not be a problem, provided she's agreeable to going with us," he replied.

"She is," Hannah announced. "I have already discussed the matter with her."

Though he knew he should not have been, Richter found himself pleasantly surprised his daughter had seized the initiative in dealing with matters that rightfully were the purview of the mistress of the house. "And Clara?"

"No, not her," Hannah declared sharply. "She is worse than useless. I should not like to see her go with us."

Upon hearing this, Richter cringed. He knew the housekeeper was far from perfect. He had received many complaints about the girl, first from his wife, then when she was gone from Fräu Sander. That he kept her on as a favor to a high-ranking party member to whom he was indebted was something he had never shared with either of them. "We shall have to discuss that, Hannah."

"There is no need to discuss anything in regards to her, Father. I refuse to allow that woman to go with us."

Taken aback, Richter cocked a brow. "You refuse?"

"Yes, Father. I refuse."

For the longest time, the two stared at each other, Hannah with her arms now folded tightly across her chest and Richter wondering if he should be angry or amused. It seemed, he realized for the first time, his little Hannah was no longer so little. She was taking on a woman's role, at least in matters concerning his household. Coming to his feet, Richter made his way over to where his daughter was seated, watching his every move.

Leaning forward, he kissed her on the top of her head. "Fine, fine," he finally muttered. "We shall find a new housekeeper in Poland."

Determined to avoid being saddled with another Clara, Hannah also came to her feet. "And I must insist on having a say in this matter when it comes time to pick her."

Again Richter drew back, this time he couldn't help but smirk. "You insist?"

"Yes, Father, I insist," Hannah sniffed before giving her head an all too familiar flick that caused her hair to flutter about, an annoying habit of hers she always employed to irritate an opponent before crossing swords with them.

"I see. Tell me, *Fräulein Richter*, what else have you decided?"

Ignoring her father's mocking tone, Hannah drew herself up

much as she had often seen Lena do when addressing important matters. "I think it would be best if we discussed them later, after we have all enjoyed a peaceful family dinner together. Now, if you would excuse me, Father, I must see if Fräu Sander needs a hand with that."

"By all means," Richter declared as he bowed slightly at the waist in a manner that was neither mocking or demeaning. "Do not let me stop you."

Though the thought of leaving this house and her friends saddened her, Hannah was pleased that at least in Poland she would have a greater say in how the Richter household would be run. Even more importantly, it seemed as if her father was finally waking up to the realization she was no longer a child. Though she was far from being his equal, he was at least willing to see her as more than a pleasant diversion from his duties. In Poland, she would take on the responsibilities that had once belonged to her mother, responsibilities Hannah was only now beginning to realize Lena Richter had been preparing her for. Whether this was what the woman had had in mind when she first brought her to this house did not matter. What happened on the other side of the wire that separated her world from her father's was of no importance to her. Seeing to it he had a warm, comfortable home to return to each night after he had laid aside his burdens for the day was all that concerned Hannah.

❋

"*HANNAH!*"

"Wolfgang! There is no need to yell," Fräu Sander snapped.

Turning from where he stood at the base of the stairs, Wolfgang looked over at the cook who was standing next to Maria and a very startled three-year-old. "If Hannah doesn't hurry, we'll miss the train."

Knowing the boy was right, Fräu Sander decided she had given the young girl all the time she could afford to. With that in mind, the woman made her way across the foyer, past Wolfgang, and up the stairs. It was time to move on.

The cook found Hannah where she had expected to find her, standing in the open doorway of her parents' bedroom. With one hand resting on the doorframe, she was staring at the bed, now stripped bare and covered with dust cloths. Coming up behind the girl, Fräu Sander placed her hands gently on Hannah's shoulders.

With her free hand, Hannah reached up and put it over one of the cook's. "I had thought this house would always be my home," she whispered mournfully. "I suppose that was silly of me," she added. "I, of all people, should have known just how capricious life can be when it comes to such thing."

Fräu Sander could never have appreciated what lay behind Hannah's lament. It was anguish she could never share with anyone. The cook was, however, able to commiserate with her despair, for she had also come to see the mansion on the quiet lake as a home.

Giving Hannah's shoulders a slight squeeze, Fräu Sander spoke as she had to her own daughter when it had come time for her to leave home. "It is difficult to turn your back on your childhood home, to accept the time has come to part with your past and begin a new life, one that will be so very different than everything you have known up till then."

Unable to help herself, Hannah sighed as memories of another time once more leaped to the fore. "Yes, I know," she whispered. She was about to add, "*but that was different.*" but didn't. To have done so was pointless. The cook would never have understood. Not that it mattered. The life she had turned her back on in Munich had been a sad existence, one that held only the promise of isolation, degradation, and suffering. Leaving it had not been a loss. For Hannah, it had been liberation.

Leaving here was different. She had known only love and adoration here. Even more, it was here, in the empty bed before her, where she had suffered the greatest loss she had ever endured in her entire life. For unlike her natural mother, who had turned her back on her simply because she had become inconvenient, the woman who had died in the bed had come to love her despite everything she knew about her past. Lena Richter had taken Hannah into her heart as if she had been her own, and Hannah had, in turn, learned what true love and the willingness to risk all for the life of another truly meant.

"Come, child. We must go," Fräu Sander finally stated as she gave the shoulders her hands were resting on a slight tug. "It is time to close this chapter in your life and begin a new one."

Yes, Hannah told herself as she allowed Fräu Sander to lead her away, it was time to move on to a new and better day. And though she had no idea what she would find in Poland, in a way, Hannah knew it would be for the best if she did turn her back on this place. It had far too many memories that haunted her. Her new home in Poland would only know her as Hannah Richter. There would be no traces, no memories of the nine-year-old mischling who had been wanted by no one, not even the boy himself.

※

Fräu Sander waited until after the train had left the station and Hannah had recovered from a last tearful farewell with her friends before suggesting Maria take the boys to the dining car for an afternoon snack. Only when they were alone did the cook broach a subject she had felt she needed to cover with Hannah. "When we arrive in Poland, you understand things will be different."

After taking a moment to wipe away the last of her tears, Hannah looked across to where the cook sat, staring at her with familiar intensity, one that told Hannah the matter she was about to cover was to be taken seriously. "Yes, I appreciate that, Fräu Sander."

"What I am trying to say, what I need to say, Hannah, is that you will find yourself in a role you have been avoiding," the cook explained patiently, doing her best to keep from being accusatory or shaming a girl she had come to love as dearly as her own daughter. "At sixteen, many will view you as little more than a child and attempt to treat you as such, some because they do not know you as I do, and others because they wish to lord over you. In Oranienburg you were free to continue behaving as if you were still a young girl without a care in the world. But in Poland things will be different, they must be different."

Suspecting she knew where the cook was going with this, Hannah nodded. "Go on."

"With your mother gone, God rest her soul, and your father the commandant of an important facility, you must take on new responsibilities, assuming a role normally held by the wife of a man such as your father."

Swallowing hard, Hannah again nodded. "I know," she whispered.

"Our relationship and that of all the household staff must also change," Fräu Sander continued. "You are a dear, sweet child, but you cannot allow yourself to be seen as a child. You have responsibilities now, and part of them include representing your father by behaving in a manner that brings credit to him. Even when dealing with other women, the wives of other officers there, you must not allow yourself to be bullied or dismissed simply because you are so young. Remember, you are the camp commandant's daughter and the head of his household. If it is not given, you must command the respect and obedience that position will demand."

"I shall do my best, Fräu Sander."

For the first time, the cook allowed her familiar smile to shine through. "I know you will. It is what is expected of us and what we must do if men like your father are to be free to carry out their duty without the need to worry about his home and his family. I expect he will have more than enough on his mind in Poland."

"Yes," Hannah replied. "I expect he will."

CHAPTER SIXTEEN

"WELCOME TO BORKOW"

BERLIN-WARSAW-BORKOW, JULY 1942

The journey to his new home was a great adventure for Wolfgang. His boundless enthusiasm served as both a counterpoint to the grief Hannah felt over parting with her friends and a distraction that left her little time to indulge in it. Unlike previous trips the boy had taken with his family, their passage from Berlin to Warsaw was aboard a train crammed with military personnel, a smattering of government bureaucrats, and German businessmen who owned or operated companies they had acquired following the conquest of Poland. Hannah and her brothers, accompanied by Fräu Sander and Maria, were traveling in the first-class rail carriage reserved for senior officers and Party officials. But when Wolfgang didn't have his nose pressed against the window of their plush compartment, he spent every second he could wandering through the carriages filled to capacity with soldiers returning to their units either from ordinary leave or a stay in hospital. Naturally one of the women needed to go along with him. Feeling responsible for the boy, Hannah was almost always the one who took on the chore.

The reaction to each was predictable. In need of a diversion and unconstrained by any artificial social restraints, the soldiers behaved as men frequently did when an attractive young female foolishly wandered into their midst. Those who wished to engage Hannah in a conversation, if only to feast their eyes on her for a while, took advantage of Wolfgang's desire to chat with real soldiers by telling him stories of their "heroic" deeds. This placed Hannah in a very awkward position. Not wishing to be rude, she did her best to ignore most of the comments the soldiers made freely within her presence, or the way some leered at her as she stood next to Wolfgang, holding him in check as he listened to their tall tales. Only when one of the more loutish landsers crossed some invisible line did an NCO within earshot intervene, reining in the miscreant with little more than a cough, a withering glance or, if need, be, a sharp rebuke.

Eventually one of the older sergeants had had enough of the way his fellow soldiers were behaving. But rather than trying to rein them in, he made his way along the narrow aisle until he was behind Hannah. Leaning over, he whispered in her ear, informing her this was not a proper place for either her or the boy. This bit of advice was followed by a strongly worded suggestion that she and the boy should go back to their carriage. It was advice Hannah gladly heeded. The problem arose when she informed Wolfgang they needed to go. Having no intention of doing so, the boy turned on her and snapped. "No. I am not ready to."

Already on edge and well aware every eye in the carriage was on her, Hannah was in no mood to argue. "You will go, and you will go now," she hissed as quietly as she could even as her eyes were darting from side to side, taking in the amused grins and smirks the bored soldiers were sporting.

Wolfgang decided this was an excellent time to make a stand and show his overbearing sister he had no intention of kowtowing to her. He assumed the soldiers would take up his case if he showed a bit of backbone. So he folded his arms across his chest and glared at Hannah down the bridge of his nose. "I shall go when I am ready," he declared haughtily.

"You shall go and go now," Hannah countered as she returned the boy's defiant gaze.

All around them soldiers, seeing an opportunity for a little entertainment, began to shout encouragement to the defiant little boy. "You've no need to listen to her, boy. Stand your ground," one whispered in his ear.

Another, who had turned around in his seat and was watching from afar, sneered. "What kind of soldier are you going to make if you allow yourself to be ordered about by a girl?"

"Show that stuck-up cow who's wearin' the trousers," a third shouted out.

Seeing an opportunity to put his sister in her place for once with what he thought was a supportive group of men, Wolfgang grinned. "I am going to stay here as long as I wish."

Hannah was finding it harder and harder to ignore the shouts and jeers of the soldiers as long-dormant fears and memories of the way brown-shirted thugs had treated her when she had been no older than Wolfgang began to merge with the scene playing out around her. The howling pack was beginning to press in upon her. Eager to be away from them, she became frantic. "You will come with me, and you will come now," she commanded even as she was reaching out to take her brother by the arm.

Emboldened, Wolfgang smacked Hannah's hand away. "No!"

In astonishment, Hannah's eyes flew open. Never before had Wolfgang dare raise his hand to her. She knew why he was doing so, just as she knew why she had to do what she did next if she were to have any hope of controlling him in the future. Without hesitation, she used the same hand Wolfgang had brushed aside to deliver a loud, telling slap across the boy's face.

Stunned speechless, Wolfgang could do little more than stand there before her sister, more startled than hurt. Before he had an opportunity to recover from his shock, Hannah grabbed him by the arm and dragged him out of the carriage to a cacophony of cheers, hoots, and laughter.

Upon returning to their own compartment, no one save little Siggy needed to ask what had happened. Hannah, more furious over what she had been forced to do than her brother's behavior, threw herself into her seat, crossed her arms, and sulked. Wolfgang, enraged and embarrassed in equal measure, resumed his seat next to the window and gazed out it at a long eastbound train that had been pulled off onto a siding to let their train pass. He paid little attention to the countless hands clinging to the bars of the small windows of the other train's cattle cars or the wretched expressions of people pulling themselves up to the opening to catch a lungful of fresh air uncorrupted by the stench from the press of people behind them.

The strange people he was looking at were of no concern to him. He didn't even give them a second thought. He had other, more important things to deal with, chief among them was how he could put his sister in her place. The idea that he, a boy who would soon be a member of the Hitler Youth, could be bossed about by a girl who wasn't even related to him by blood was galling. Such foolishness would have to come to an end, he told himself. The sooner the better.

❋

Long before the train had come to a complete stop, Wolfgang was out of the compartment, pushing his way past other passengers in the narrow corridor toward the end of the carriage. Maria, who had tried to catch him, apologized to Hannah.

Hannah told the harried nanny not to worry. "He's off to find his father and complain about his mean sister."

"But what if he should get lost?" Maria asked as she was hurriedly gathering up her things and those of her little charge.

"The worst that could happen is a band of Polish partisans capture him, tire of his behavior, and return him to us."

"That's your brother you're speaking of," Fräu Sander admonished.

Hannah made a face. "Why must you always remind me of that? And why did you insist I change into this outfit?" she continued as she gave the hem of her tailored jacket a tug. "It makes me look like a frumpy old maid."

"It makes you look like you should, a responsible, level headed young woman," the cook replied dryly as she gave her young charge a last minute inspection from head to toe. "Now, if you could, please do try to behave like one, at least when you're in public. Otherwise . . ."

"Yes, yes, I know," Hannah muttered. "Wooden spoons have other uses."

Amid good-natured laughter, the two women and Hannah, with little Siegfried in tow, made their way out of the compartment and toward an uncertain future.

Borkow

Unlike Wolfgang, Hannah wasn't bothered in the least her father wasn't there to greet them. It was, after all, midmorning. She expected he was where he was supposed to be, at the camp's administrative building tending to his duties. Besides, upon seeing Horst Fischer standing on the station's platform listening to her brother, Hannah decided it was better he was there waiting for them. The young man her father had insisted on taking with him to Poland would provide her with more insight into the dos and don'ts she'd have to abide by. Moreover, she would be able to wean from him just how well her father was settling into an assignment he'd fought to avoid.

Hannah could tell Wolfgang didn't seem to share her joy at seeing Horst. For his part, Horst was ignoring the boy. Instead, the man Hannah had come to rely on as both a companion and a confidant was eagerly searching the faces of the disembarking passengers. When he finally did catch sight of her stepping down from the rail carriage, Horst turned away from Wolfgang and came to attention. When she was near enough for her to hear, Horst bowed ever so slightly before straightening up and greeting her. "Fräulein Richter, welcome to Borkow."

Both his deadpan expression and crisp, formal greeting puzzled Hannah until a woman in her late thirties or early forties, whom Hannah had thought had been waiting for someone else, stepped forward and offered her a bouquet. "Fräulein Richter, we have so been looking forward to finally meeting you," the woman proclaimed in a tone that struck Hannah as being a wee bit pretentious. "Your father talks of nothing else," she continued after stepping back and taking a moment to inspect her with a single, well-measured glance. "You are not at all what I expected."

Hannah checked the temptation to ask the woman what she had been expecting. She had no need to. Fräu Sander, it seemed, had been right. Of course, Hannah was hard pressed to remember a time when the cook hadn't been. This woman's overly affected manner and a smile that was as warm and welcoming as a mid-January dawn, coupled with Horst's stiff and very formal behavior, served as warnings to Hannah. The woman was there to win her over to whatever local feminine faction she represented, the sort Hannah recalled Lena Richter had gone out of her way to avoid. Or if not that, she wanted to make it clear to the camp commandant's daughter she was the queen bee of this little German enclave. In either case, Hannah took an instant dislike to the stout matron who introduced herself as Fräu Klopf, wife to the commander of the camp's guards. It was a position that, according to her at least, made him the second in command. Latching onto Hannah's arm and without giving Fräu Sander, Maria, or Horst a thought, Fräu Klopf proceeded to escort her over the edge of the station platform to where a pair of autos were waiting.

❋

Being an intelligent man, Horst sat in the front next to the driver, leaving Hannah alone in the backseat with Fräu Klopf. Klopf took full advantage of this opportunity to fill Hannah in on the nature of what she called "our own very special piece of the Fatherland," which it seemed was several kilometers from the camp Ernst Richter now commanded. "You will find the wives of our little community here to be a rather tight-knit group, dedicated to providing our husbands with a caring home environment to which they can return to in the evening after they have laid aside their burdensome duties," Fräu Klopf informed Hannah as they drove from the station, through the small provincial town, and into a thick coniferous forest heavy with the distinctive scent of pine sap.

The two autos were escorted by a Krupp Kfz 70 lorry carrying half a dozen well-armed and very attentive SS men. This small convoy covered a distance of no more than five kilometers from the station to an enclosed compound where the families of the senior SS officers and civilian managers who oversaw the running of the various factories in the area lived. The trip had only taken a few minutes.

That was long enough, however, for Hannah to grow tired of Fräu Klopf's patronizing manner. Having no desire to spend any more time with the woman until she could speak with Horst in private, Hannah all but leaped out of the auto the second it pulled up in front of an impressive Ninetieth Century manor. Quickly pivoting about, she slammed the auto's door and stepped back.

"I thank you for the flowers and greeting me at the station," she called out through the open window. "I look forward to hearing more of what you have to say as well as meeting the other women. Unfortunately, I have to see to my brothers and settle in if I'm going to have things ready for my father by the time he returns tonight." With that, she spun about and marched calmly into the house.

There she was quickly joined inside by Horst who dropped all formality. "That was not at all nice of you, Hannah. What would your father say if he saw you treating the wife of one of his officers like that?"

"He would say tut-tut, then go about his business," Hannah replied as she slowly made her way through the foyer, peeking into the rooms that opened out into it as they went.

"A word of advice, if I may?" Horst intoned as he followed her.

"Do I have a choice?" she asked without looking back at him as she wandered into the paneled study already filled with her father's books and personal mementos.

"It would not do well to get on the wrong side of Fräu Klopf."

"I expect you're going to tell me why."

"Her husband was supposed to command this camp," Horst informed Hannah as he stood in the doorway of the study watching as she slowly made her way around the room, lightly running her fingertips over the rows of books all lined up neatly on shelves that covered an entire wall. "Unfortunately for him, as well as your father, the man has no administrative or managerial skills. He was making a complete hash of things here."

Stopping when she was behind her father's desk, Hannah leafed through an open file sitting in the middle of it. The schedule of trains arriving at Borkow over the next few days listed down the left-hand side of the page and the columns of figures meant nothing to Hannah. What Horst was telling her did. "So instead of honoring Father's request to be assigned to a combat unit, they sent him here."

"Himmler himself recommended your father for this position."

When she heard the name of a man her father didn't think much of, Hannah looked up at Horst. "Oh?"

Knowing what Hannah was thinking, Horst explained. "It would seem your father has some kind of deal with the Reichsführer."

"Let me guess," Hannah interrupted as she came around from behind the desk, marched over to where Horst was standing, and stopped before him. "If Father can sort things out here, our gentle

Heinrich will reward him by seeing to it he gets his wish and is transferred to the Waffen SS, where he will be free to run off and play hero by getting himself shot by some ignorant Russian peasant."

Looking down at the floor between them, Horst nodded. "That would seem to be what was agreed to."

"And you?" Hannah asked, barely able to check her mounting anger. "Are you going to march off to war as well, arm in arm with Father, gustily singing the Horst Wessel?"

In an effort to defuse the situation, Horst looked up and met Hannah's eyes. "I would have thought you knew me better than that. I am no soldier."

Taking a moment to look up and down at his uniform, Hannah sniffed. "You could have fooled me." With that, she walked past him and made her way to the kitchen.

❋

Already on the verge of giving herself over to her anger, Hannah burst into the kitchen and found herself confronted by an SS oberschütze. She came to a stop, drew herself up, and snapped. "Who in the hell are you?"

Before the startled SS enlisted man could respond, from off to one side where she had been going through the cabinets, Fräu Sander growled. "Language, young lady."

Ignoring the cook's familiar admonishment, Hannah continued to glare at the befuddled enlisted man who was standing before her, all but quaking in his boots. "Well?"

Not knowing what else to do, he snapped to a rigid position of attention and reported as if Hannah were the camp commandant himself. "Oberschütze Riese, orderly to Obersturmbannführer Richter."

"Orderly?" Hannah snapped. "What's is my father's orderly doing in Fräu Sander's kitchen?"

"I . . . I . . . I . . ."

"It seems he was doing the cooking," Fräu Sander responded as she continued to open cabinets and inspect their content. "Although for the life of me I have no idea *what* he was cooking," she snorted in disgust. "Hopefully the pantry is better stocked. Come, you," the cook ordered with a no-nonsense brusqueness that left no doubt in the orderly's mind he was expected to obey. "Show me your stores and be quick about. I've work to do."

When they were gone, Hannah pulled a chair out from the small kitchen table and sat down. For the longest time, she did nothing but stare at the bare tabletop. It was so unfair, she told herself. Unfair and cruel of her father to make the sort of deal he had without even thinking to discuss the matter with her. She knew he had no need to. She was, after all, his daughter. But to go and make a bargain such as that, one that could very well take him away from her, was selfish on his part. While it was true as a soldier he had his duty to the Reich and the Führer, he also had his duty to her and the boys. The mere thought she could lose another parent, one she loved with all her heart, was simply too much for Hannah to stand. Folding her arms on the table before her, she lay her head on them and began to sob.

❋

Despite her best efforts, Hannah was unable to fool Fräu Sander when she returned from inspecting the pathetic content of the pantry her father's orderly had been responsible for stocking. Puffy red eyes and a forlorn expression told the cook all she needed to know. Her young mistress was feeling terribly lost and overwhelmed. Not that she could blame her. By the time a child all had come to know as Hannah had arrived in Oranienburg at the age of nine, she had already endured a lifetime's worth of suffering. Of course, like everyone associated with the Richter household save Lena Richter, Fräu Sander had always assumed the source of the girl's grief was the fire her parents had supposedly perished in.

Not that the true reason for Hannah's current doldrums mattered, at least not to Fräu Sander. What was important was finding a way of banishing the gloom that had a hold on the girl and setting her on a new path, one the cook hoped would lead to a better place than where she had come from and where she was at the moment. "We have much to do if we are to make this sad, cold house a home worthy of your father," Fräu Sander declared.

Drawing herself up, Hannah turned her face away in a vain effort to keep the cook from seeing her wipe off the last of her tears. Only when she was sufficiently in control of her emotions did she come to her feet and once more face Fräu Sander. "Yes," she muttered as she looked about a kitchen bereft of the little touches only a woman would think of adding to make it a place of warmth and comfort, the true living heart of a home and the family that occupied it. "We have much to do. If you would, could you put something together for the boys' lunch while I go and help Maria settle them in?"

"Yes, of course, Fräulein Richter," the cook replied giving Hannah a knowing wink. In response, Hannah gave her hair a quick toss to one side before setting off to meet a new challenge, one she had not asked for but, as with so much in her life, she found herself having to confront.

CHAPTER SEVENTEEN

SELECTION

BORKOW, JULY 1942

At the sound of an auto pulling up to the house and stopping, Hannah set aside the clothing she had been unpacking and made her way over to the window of her room to see who it was. She watched as Wolfgang, who had been in the yard exploring his new realm, came charging around the side of the house to greet his father as he stepped out of the auto. She considered rushing down to see him as well, but thought better of it. Her brother, no doubt, would dominate their father's full attention for some time, just as she had when she had been Wolfgang's age, informing him of every little thing he'd done since the two had last seen each other.

Well, Hannah snickered as she turned away from the window and went back to finish unpacking, most of it, anyway. She seriously doubted Wolfgang would mention the incident on the train, knowing full well their father would interrogate him until he'd learned why his sister had found it necessary to slap him. By now, both she and Wolfgang had come to understand incidents such as that were the kind of thing siblings kept to themselves. Instead of relying on their father to abitrate their disputes, they more often than not found a way of resolving them amicably after enough time had passed to allow bruised feelings to heal or, if the transgression demanded it, devise a devious and underhanded revenge.

It was close to half an hour before there was a knock on the door, followed by her brother's voice. "Papa wishes to see you, now."

Having no idea what her father had on his mind, Hannah took a moment to run a brush through her hair and slip on the tailored jacket of her suit, though she chose not to button it. Her adult attire, as well as its intentionally disheveled workaday appearance, would make a statement Hannah expected her father would not miss. She was right.

Upon entering the study, Ernst Richter found he needed to take in the image of his daughter as she stood there before him, head held high and hands clasped before her. "You wished to see me, Father?"

It was Richter's turn to give his head a shake, as he remembered the girl before him was no longer a child. "Hmm, yes. Please, take a seat," he muttered as he motioned to a chair with his hand. When he followed suit, taking one across from her, Hannah found it difficult to suppress a smirk. Had his invitation been the prelude to a lecture, he would have remained standing before her or paced back and forth as he delivered whatever sermon he'd pieced together in his head beforehand. This, Hannah concluded, was to be a serious discussion delivered to her as if she were an adult.

"I trust you are settling in and all is satisfactory."

Rather than addressing personal issues, Hannah told her father how the boys were situated, the needs Fräu Sander had identified in the way of foodstuffs, items required to make the kitchen fully functional, and what she thought should be done to liven up the various rooms, intentionally leaving out her own. "While all is quite nice and comfortable, this house is far from being a home," she pointed out tactfully. "What I need from you, Father, is a clear idea of what I will be permitted to do by way of decorating and procuring items for the house as well as what the household budget will be, provided you're going to allow me to have a say in managing it."

It took all of Ernst Richter's willpower to keep from snickering, something he'd not been able to do since he had arrived in Borkow. In the same manner with which she dealt with him each time they faced off on the piste when fencing, straight off the mark his daughter was being aggressive and bold, pressing home a perceived advantage. Easing back in his seat, he regarded her for the longest time, but not to consider what he would say. He had already decided that. Rather, he used this opportunity to admire the young woman across from him, for she was all a father could wish for and, at the moment, exactly what he needed.

"Well, it seems as if you have arrived, young lady," he declared as he brought his hands together before him and finally allowed a reassuring smile to shine through. "Might I suggest you give me a bit of time to think over the particulars as well as an opportunity to relax some before dinner?"

Realizing she had won him over, Hannah returned her father's smile as she came to her feet. "Of course, Father. And speaking of dinner, I should check on Fräu Sander and see how she is proceeding with it."

Without waiting for permission to do so, Hannah left the room, allowing Richter to rise off the chair, go over to his desk, and take a seat there. Opening the file a courier had left in the middle of it earlier in the day, he began to review the schedule of transports arriving from the west. While his daughter was seeing to his dinner, he needed to determine just how many of the people from each of those transports would have to be selected as workers for the factories that were part of the camp complex he oversaw and how many the sonderkommando charged with the special handling of excess personnel would need to dispose of.

As he did, Richter decided it might not be a bad idea if he had Klopf, his deputy in charge of the selection, pull some promising candidates out of a train due in from Holland the following day. It would be better, Richter concluded, if Hannah picked the housekeeper she needed from women who had not yet been processed rather than from those who had already experienced life in the camp. There'd be fewer questions that way, both from Hannah and the boys, and less of a chance of that housekeeper filling their head with stories of what was going on in the camp. Though there was always the chance Hannah might come to appreciate the true nature of the camp, there was no need to increase the likelihood of that.

Preserving his daughter's innocence, keeping one thing in his life pure and untouched by the brutal reality of the world he had known since he was Hannah's age was becoming more and more important to Ernst Richter with each passing day. That was what his Lena would have wanted. That was what he needed. Like most officers assigned to the Totenkopfverbände, he saw his home as a sanctuary, a place apart from the camp on the other side of the twin electrified barbed wire fences, fences that separated his family from people deemed enemies of the state. Hannah had long ago ceased being only a daughter. Although she did not know it, she had become the caretaker of his humanity. As such, she allowed him to do what was necessary to create the brave new world order their Führer envisioned and he longed for.

※

"They're here!" Wolfgang shouted as he ran into the kitchen where Hannah and Fräu Sander were seated at the table, going over the list of things they would need to order.

Coming to her feet, Hannah took a moment to prepare herself for her first major decision, one she herself had insisted on. Having seen the impact a slovenly housekeeper could have on the entire household, she knew it would be a crucial choice they all would have to live with. "Are you sure you wouldn't like to come with me?" she asked Fräu Sander.

"What do you imagine the girl you select would think if she saw you turning to me for my approval? She will think I am the one running the house, not you," Fräu Sander both asked and answered before Hannah had a chance to respond. "By having you make the selection on your own, the girl will know she is answerable to you and no one else. That is the way it must be."

"As always, Fräu Sander, you are right," Hannah admitted.

With a sad little smile Hannah quite didn't understand, the cook placed a gentle hand on Hannah's cheek. "Not right, child. Just old enough to know." Then, stepping back, Fräu Sander drew in a deep breath. "Now go while I finish this list."

※

Doing her best to present a calm, no-nonsense appearance despite the butterflies roiling her stomach, Hannah sallied forth through the front door and into the bright, mid-morning sunshine over to where an SS NCO had lined up a dozen young women, all facing into the sun. Off to one side, across a broad stretch of lawn that separated the manor house that was now her home and a cluster of other, more humble dwellings, Hannah could not help but notice a gaggle of women had gathered around the only one she recognized, Fräu Klopf. They were watching her, just as the SS NCO waiting for her was. All wanted to see just what kind of woman the new commandant's daughter was. The only people who weren't were the group of women from whom she would have to select her housekeeper. They were staring intently at the ground, as much to keep the sun out of their eyes as in submission.

With the same precision he used when reporting to his commanding officer, the SS NCO snapped to attention. "Unterscharführer Esler at your service, Fräulein Richter."

Hannah returned the NCO's salutation with nothing more than a nod and a polite smile as she walked up to the line of young women.

"They are all Dutch," Esler informed Hannah as he fell in beside her. "Just arrived from Amersfoort. This lot is mostly from Limburg and, from what little I've been told, all can understand German well enough."

Never having done anything like this, Hannah suddenly realized she had no idea how to determine what kind of woman she was looking for, or even what questions to ask. Slowly making her way down the line, she looked into the face of each young woman, trying hard to see if there was something that would recommend one of them for the position. As she did, Hannah did her best to ignore the pungent stench of urine and unwashed bodies that caused her nose to twitch, leading her to wonder how she could rely upon any woman as a maid who was unwilling to tend to her personal hygiene. Once more Hannah found herself regretting her decision to insist on replacing Clara, and once more she forced herself to set aside her misgivings. As with so many other decisions she had made in her life, she now had little choice but to live with it.

It was while she was inspecting the young women paraded before her that Hannah became acutely aware of three things. The first was that while all of them were older than she was, none looked as if they were any more than twenty. The second was that they were, in truth, no different in appearance than the girls she had gone to school with back in Oranienburg, girls who had been her friends. The third was that all but two were Jews. It was then, there in front of a grand old manor house that was to be her home, that Hannah realized something. Had it not been for a simple twist of fate, she would be in a line not very different than the one they were in, unable to do anything more than wait for a stranger to decide her fate.

As if to drive this point home, she stopped in front of a Dutch girl with blond hair and blue eyes wearing a yellow star of David sewn to her dress. Hannah decided she could not ask the girl her name for the same reason she could never select her, or any other Jew, to be her housekeeper. To do so would be beyond foolish. It would be downright dangerous to have a Jew in the house, especially one with hair and eyes that matched hers.

Doing her best to tamp down her growing anxieties, Hannah continued down the line until she came to a young woman with brunette hair and a red triangle affixed to the short, cropped jacket she was wearing. "Are you a communist?" Hannah asked.

When the Dutch girl looked up and met her gaze, Hannah noticed a spark of defiance in her eyes. "A communist? No," she replied as if Hannah had asked her a silly question. "Of course not. I am a member of the Social Democratic Workers' Party."

Though the name of the party the girl was proud of sounded as if it were a communist organization, Hannah decided to have a political malcontent in her home was far safer for her than a Jew. "Have you ever worked as a domestic?" she asked, doing her best to keep the nervousness she felt from showing through.

"Never. I was a student attending university," she replied with a smugness that reminded Hannah of Sophie. "I was studying to be a professor of literature."

Hannah was about to ask if the woman wished to be a housekeeper, but quickly caught herself. To have done so would have put the decision into the woman's hands. This defiant Dutch woman could very well have refused merely to embarrass the daughter of the camp commandant in front of an SS NCO and the gaggle of women who were watching them from afar. Instead, Hannah asked the girl her name and age. "Tessa van Roon," she replied. "I am nineteen."

Stepping back, Hannah took a moment to study the Dutch girl before looking over at the other non-Jew. Since the black triangle on her dress marked her as being either asocial or work-shy, Hannah saw she had little choice, not if she was going to avoid the risk of bringing a Jew into her house.

Heaving a sigh, Hannah turned to the SS NCO while pointing at Tessa van Roon. "She'll do."

"Very good," Esler declared before ordering the van Roon girl to take up her suitcase and step out of line. "The rest of you, onto the truck. Quickly," he barked. "We haven't all day."

As they were doing so, Hannah asked what would become of them. "Oh, I expect if there's another trainload going through selection later today they'll get thrown in with them. Otherwise, the sonderkommando will be left to deal with them."

Hannah quashed the impulse to ask what the sonderkommando would do with the girls. One did not ask a question if one did not wish to know the answer. Ignorance, especially of matters related to the SS and what her father did, was more than prudent, it was safe. Besides, she had a new housekeeper who needed to be trained in her responsibilities and the rules she would be expected to follow, rules Hannah suddenly realized she had given no thought.

❊

"Do you think it wise to allow that girl to wander about the house unsupervised?" Maria asked Hannah quietly as the two were tiptoeing out of Siegfried's room after laying him down for a nap.

Having been asked the same question by Fräu Sander, Hannah gave Maria the same answer once they were out of the boy's room and the door was closed. "Don't you think it would be rather pointless to have a housemaid who required constant supervision? There are other, more important things I need to tend to other than following the Dutch girl about, making sure she doesn't pinch the silverware. Besides, what would she do with it?" Hannah asked as she and Maria made their way toward the stairs.

Maria was about to quip, "*Use it to slit our throats in our sleep,*" but didn't. Besides being anything but a joke, the nanny knew it was not her place to contradict the mistress of the house, a role the young girl next to her had previously shied away from but now seemed determined to assume. Instead, Maria excused herself, informing Hannah she needed to see what sort of mischief Wolfgang was getting into now. "I dread to think what he will be like once he is accepted by the HJ," Maria groused. "He's already insufferable as it is without having his head filled with the rubbish they feed the young boys these days."

Unable to find fault with anything the nanny was saying, Hannah regretfully agreed. "It is the way of things," she muttered sadly, having long ago concluded the sweet little child she had once known as Wolfie was no more. In his place was a boy no different than the ones who had tormented her when she had been but a child. Her efforts to rein in his smugness, to teach him some degree of humility, and instill a sense of humanity had been overwhelmed by what he was learning in school, the demands peer pressure placed upon him to conform that she herself was familiar with, and the deluge of propaganda he was exposed to day in, day out. Like Maria, Hannah appreciated the best they could do now was to keep Wolfgang's behavior from becoming too extreme while waiting for her father to take a greater hand in raising the boy properly.

That Ernst Richter thought he was already doing just that never crossed Hannah's mind. If anything, her father was beginning to fear his son was being coddled by her and the other women who made up his household. In his eyes, his son was in serious need of a toughening up, the sort the Hitler Youth movement excelled at.

❋

"I thought I would find you here," Horst announced as he breezed into the kitchen, snatching a fresh-baked biscuit off a plate set in the center of the table as he did so.

"Those are for the boys," Fräu Sander called out from where she stood at the stove, slowly stirring the content of a pot.

"Am I not one of your boys?" Horst asked playfully.

"Yes," the cook muttered. "The most annoying one. Now, take a seat while Hannah fetches you some milk to go with your snack."

"I am afraid neither Hannah or I have the time for that. We must be off."

Having been fetching milk for Horst from the icebox, Hannah glanced over at him quizzically. "Off? Off to where?"

"It's a secret," he replied while giving his commanding officer's daughter a wink.

"Well, am I dressed appropriately?" Hannah asked, trying to ferret out what Horst had in store for her.

Making a show of wandering over to where she was standing, the young SS officer inspected Hannah as he slowly circled her. "You might wish to change your shoes, Fräulein Richter," he finally declared.

"And what kind of shoes would the Hauptsturmführer recommend?" Hannah asked coyly.

"Hiking shoes, if you have them."

Unable to help herself, Hannah guffawed. "Oh, please, you do remember who you're talking to, my dear sweet Horst. I am a product of Fräulein Diehl's proud little command. I trust you remember Fräulein Diehl. According to Sophie, she remembers you."

Rolling his eyes, Horst grunted. "Please, you've no need to remind me of that. She already does so in every letter she sends me, letters, for your information, I do not bother responding to." After sharing a good laugh over this, Horst drew himself up, clicked his heels together, and bowed. "Now off with you and fetch your shoes. Your carriage awaits you, Fräulein Richter."

❊

"*PIXIE!*" Hannah screamed as she rushed over to the strawberry roan held by an older man out into the center of the stable's paddock. Recognizing her voice, the mare threw back her head and tugged at the lead rope her handler was holding.

Ignoring the way both German guards and Polish laborers were watching her, Hannah wrapped her arms about the horse's neck and hugged it before stepping back, grasping the bridle and gently pressing her forehead against the animal's muzzle. "Did you miss me?" she asked quietly. "I know I missed you."

As if in response, the animal pulled its head away and bobbed it up and down, much to Hannah's amusement.

From where he was leaning over the gate watching her, Horst was enjoying the moment almost as much as Hannah. "I told your father you would be pleased."

"Pleased?" Hannah quipped. "I am thrilled. And Thunder? Did you think of bringing that brute of an animal along as well?"

"I had no choice," Horst replied as he entered the paddock and came up next to Hannah. "When he heard Pixie was leaving, Thunder insisted on going as well."

After sharing a good laugh over this, Horst took to introducing Hannah to the groom who'd been standing off to one side holding her horse's lead rope. "This is Jozef Cybulski, a local Pole who knows about horses and, when needed, serves as a handyman in the civilian compound. He and his son Jan will be looking after Pixie for you if you've no objections."

Turning to the Pole, Hannah smiled. "I shall appreciate it if you did care for her. She is like family to me."

Rather than answering her, the Pole turned to Horst wearing a puzzled expression. "Please?"

Pausing a moment to find the right words, Horst haltingly translated Hannah's remarks into Polish as best he could. When he finally understood what the young girl had said, the Pole turned to face Hannah again, smiled, and bowed his head. "I care like mine," he stuttered in badly fractured German. "My boy and me, we good with horses."

"Good, good. Thank you," Hannah replied returning the Pole's smile.

"Come, Fräulein Richter," Horst announced as he took Hannah by the arm and led her back to the auto. "You and I have another stop we need to make."

"What? Does Father have another surprise for me, Herr Hauptsturmführer?" Hannah asked playfully.

With a deadpan expression, Horst grunted. "Not quite."

❀

Looking about after stepping out of the auto, Hannah made a face. The small arms range was little more than a clearing with a covered area at the end where she was standing, a row of dugout positions lined with sandbags a few meters away, and at the far end, a berm fronted by targets. On the other side of the berm was a forest and beyond it, off in the distance and to one side were a pair of chimneys spewing thick clouds of black smoke she assumed were part of the camp. "And what, may I ask, are we doing here?"

Coming up beside her, Horst informed Hannah her father felt it might not be a bad idea if she learned how to use a weapon, adding he felt the same. "There are any number of reasons you might find it necessary to use this," he stated calmly as he came around in front of her and held up a small pistol between them. Having once wished she had been free to defend herself with just such a weapon, Hannah now found herself curiously fascinated by the pistol Horst placed in her hand. "It is a Walther PPK, a double action, magazine feed, 7.65 mm pistol."

"Is it loaded?" Hannah asked as she held the weapon up and studied it.

"No, not yet."

"Show me how to load it," she commanded, making no effort to conceal her excitement.

"First I need to show you how to handle it safely," Horst replied, taking the pistol from her before heading over to a small table behind the firing line. There he went over the basics, pointing out the various parts of the weapon, explaining how it functioned, how to engage and disengage the safety, and what to be careful of when firing. After handing the weapon back to Hannah, he listened attentively as she repeated back to him everything he had told her. Only when he was satisfied she had a grasp of the basics did he proceed to the next step by demonstrating how to load rounds into the magazine and, in turn, how to insert the magazine into the weapon. "Each magazine holds eight rounds. Most officers and guards armed with pistols carry one round in the chamber, but I would not recommend doing so in your case, not with a boy like Wolfgang in the house."

"He's not to know I have this," Hannah blurted.

"I for one have no intention of telling him, and I suspect your father will not either," Horst replied dryly. "I suggest you also take particular care to conceal it from your maid."

The idea the girl she'd brought into their house could be a deadly threat to them suddenly caused Hannah to shiver, making her wonder if Clara, for all her faults, would not have been a better choice. Well, Hannah told herself, there was no going back on that decision. To change her mind on something about which she had been so adamant would be seen as a sign of weakness to her father, a trait he detested. "Yes, of course. I shall not even tell Fräu Sander," she finally muttered as if to herself. "The fewer people who know of this, the better."

With the preliminaries out of the way, Horst took Hannah up to the firing line where he proceeded to demonstrate a stance he thought would be best for her to hold the PPK when firing it. "This is not like fencing. Do not try to be fancy or clever should the need to use this ever arise. And do not hesitate. If you do find yourself having to use this pistol, make sure you intend to follow through. Don't mess about, don't threaten. Just aim for the center mass of your target and fire."

With that, Horst took up a proper stance, brought the weapon up, and began to take careful aim. "There will be a recoil with every shot," he stated calmly. "So take your time between shots to recover and aim." With that, he opened fire, pausing briefly after each round to bring the weapon down and correct his aim before loosing the next round, as much to impress Hannah with his own proficiency as to show her how to do it.

"Have you ever shot someone, Horst?" Hannah asked after he'd emptied a full magazine and relaxed his posture.

He did not answer her. He had no wish to. Such things were of no concern of hers, a message his silence more than conveyed. Instead, he smoothly ejected the empty magazine from the pistol and handed it to her along with a fresh magazine. "Here, now you try it. Just remember what I told you about the slide. If you do not hold the pistol correctly, it will bite your hand during the recoil."

Rather than being apprehensive or intimidated by the weapon, Hannah found herself curiously excited at the opportunity to fire it. Like so many other things in her life, she did not bother to dwell upon why she felt as she did. All she knew was fate was once more handing her an opportunity to do something she never would have had if fortune had not smiled upon her. As much as Hannah denied it every time Sophie had made mention of it, she knew she was lucky. The chain of events that had started with the death of her natural father had saved her from whatever fate awaited the Jewish girls she'd turned away earlier in the day. Like the smokestacks off in the distance, the camp her father ran, even the war itself, were of no concern of hers. All of that was part of another world, one she had no interest in, one that did not touch her.

PART FIVE

1943

ARBEIT MACHT FREI

CHAPTER EIGHTEEN

FRÄULEIN RICHTER

Having spurred Pixie into a full gallop without giving Horst the slightest bit of warning, Hannah managed to reach the fork in the forest trail well before he did. There she stopped, but not because she wanted to provide Horst an opportunity to catch up to her. Rather, she wasn't sure which path she wished to follow. To the left was the one that led back to the stables and home where Fräu Sander, Maria, and the Dutch girl were busily preparing for that evening's dinner party. It was the one she knew she should take, the one her duty demanded she take. It was one, however, she was finding increasingly difficult to follow.

Tugging the reins to the right, she peered down the other trail as far as she could see. It wasn't much of a trail, grown over for lack of use. When she had asked the Polish boy who looked after Pixie where it led to, he had informed her that before the war it had been used by woodcutters who ventured deep into the heart of the forest to harvest the sturdy, old growth trees found there. She had often pleaded with Horst to allow her to follow it when they were out riding together, if only to break the monotonous routine into which her life had fallen. It was a request he steadfastly refused to honor. "These are difficult times, Hannah," he would admonish by way of response. "Those who consider themselves wise know their place and keep to it."

The opportunity to be free of the rules and restrictions she and her friends had once thought oppressive, to mingle with adults and be treated as one, was not turning out to be quite the paradise Hannah had imagined. If anything, she found herself wondering more and more if the life she was now leading was the way things would always be for her. As there was no chance of her ever being able to lead a normal life, at least one as prescribed for women by the Party, Hannah found rather than seeing her horizons expand with the coming of age, with each passing year her prospects for the future were diminishing. She had little to look forward to other than losing herself in the day-to-day mindless, repetitive chores and routines as Fräu Sander did through her cooking, or even the Dutch girl who filled her days cleaning the same rooms. Hannah found this disappointing and, every so often, a little frightening. Perhaps, she wondered, that was why women like Fräu Klopf were so bitter. They were not angry with anyone in particular. It was life, or rather the one they were leading, that robbed them of the ability to enjoy the good fortune their status and position afforded them.

Lost in these thoughts, it wasn't until Horst asked her why she was so pensive that she realized he had eased his mount next to her and Pixie. "If I didn't know any better, I'd say you were on the verge of crying," he intoned half-jokingly.

After giving her head a quick shake in a vain effort to dispel her gloom, Hannah straightened up in the saddle before turning her gaze away from the forest trail and over at Horst. "No, not crying," she muttered. "Just thinking."

"Dare I ask what you were thinking?" he asked tentatively.

"No," she replied sadly as she tugged her reins to the left, gently nudged her heels into Pixie's flanks, and reluctantly took the path she was expected to follow.

❋

By the time she and Horst reached the stables, her gloom was beginning to melt away. What little remained disappeared completely upon seeing Jan Cybulski awaiting her return at the gate of the paddock. Like his father Jozef, young Jan loved horses, an endearing quality Hannah shared with the two Poles. Whereas the father's German was spotty at best, the boy was becoming quite good conversing in what was, for him, a foreign tongue even though this part of Poland was now official as much a part of the Greater German Reich as Brandenburg. This allowed Hannah to converse with Jan freely as they tended to Pixie. Jan was forever eager to learn all he could about the people who were now his masters. She, in turn, was more than willing to feed a young and attentive mind yet to be molded into a useful and well-ordered instrument of the state as well as listen to the little stories of his adventures he freely shared.

The two of them, the daughter of an SS officer and the son of a Polish peasant, were chatting amicably as they stood on opposite sides of Pixie when Horst came up to her, tapped her on the shoulder to get her attention, then made a show of tapping his wristwatch.

In a much better mood now, Hannah looked at Horst's watch. "Ah, I see you have a new watch. Very nice, and very expensive-looking. Since when have you been able to afford such luxuries, Herr Hauptsturmführer?"

"Very funny, Hannah," Horst replied dryly, regarding the Polish boy listening in on this exchange with an expression that betrayed the contempt the SS officer felt for him and all Poles. "I've got to get back to the office at a reasonable hour if I'm going to make my way to the bottom of the stack of papers your father is in the habit of dumping on my desk," he concluded as he once more turned his full attention back to Hannah.

"While you're at it, do me a favor, stop by the house, and clear away the files and reports sitting on the desk in his study as well," Hannah quipped. "It would be nice if he had some free time at night so he could enjoy his family instead of having to bury himself in bureaucratic minutia his adjutant should be tending to."

Stepping back, Horst threw his hands up in mock surrender. "I swear, I do my best to save your father from himself," he declared. "But you know him far better than I and, I dare say, you can be far more persuasive. Me, I'm just a humble servant of the Reich, a simple soldier who follows orders."

Hannah snorted as she dropped the currycomb in a bucket at her feet. "Simple is right." After turning to Jan and asking if he'd see to it Pixie was fed, watered, and safely tucked away in her stall, Hannah pulled on her jacket and followed Horst out of the stable.

As he watched them go, the Polish boy found himself hoping the German officer didn't do as the commandant's daughter asked him to and clear away the reports from her father's desk. He had no idea what value the information gleaned from them was to the Polish Home Army or the British to whom they forwarded the information. Like his father, Jan Cybulski wished only to play a role in the liberation of his country, even if that role was as little more than a courier for the partisans his father commanded, passing on copies of those reports. Besides giving meaning to his young life, playing at being a courier was both exciting and, for a nine-year-old boy, quite fun.

✳

Noticing the door to her father's study ajar as she entered the house, Hannah paused. Drawing herself up, she prepared to lay into Wolfgang for going in there without her permission or in the company of her father. So she had to mentally regroup when instead she saw the Dutch girl busily dusting the bookshelf with a feather duster. Standing in the doorway of the study, Hannah took a moment to assume an appropriately severe expression before calling out the Dutch girl's name. "Tessa!"

Spinning about, the Dutch girl greeted Hannah with a surprised expression, an act Hannah did not buy for one second. "You know very well you are not to come in here unless Fräu Sander or I am with you," Hannah stated evenly, making her way over to a shelf where she noticed a gap between two books. Canting her head to one side to read the titles of the books on either side of the missing volume, Hannah smirked when she recognized it as being one of the few works of literature her father had in his collection. Coming about, she studied the Dutch girl who was standing across the room from her with her head bowed. "In the future, Tessa, when you borrow a book, you might wish to shift the other books on either side of it, so the gap isn't as noticeable."

A slight nod was all the girl gave in reply.

Doing her best to suppress a smirk, Hannah left the study and headed to check up on her brothers before going to the kitchen to see if Fräu Sander needed a hand with dinner.

When she was gone, the Dutch girl heaved a great sigh of relief, satisfied the German girl had not noticed the open file sitting in the middle of the desk she had been copying.

❊

As expected at this time of day, Hannah found Wolfgang with the man her father had hired as a tutor in the small room she had had converted into a classroom for them. At the moment they were going over the day's lessons. She did not go in or say a word. She merely cracked the door open wide enough to peek in, see what was going on, and allow Herr Langer, the tutor, to see she was checking up on him.

Hannah neither liked the man nor cared for the way he was teaching her brother. A veteran of the last war, Herr Langer had an annoying knack of couching everything he taught in a way that somehow always related to the National Socialist movement. From science to literature, Langer used examples and teaching points that made Hannah cringe. Even worse in Hannah's eyes was the way he was distorting history. When she confronted him about this shortly after his arrival, the portly old veteran took great umbrage at her temerity. "Fräulein Richter, I would never think of venturing into your kitchen and telling you how to run your household. So be so kind as to stay out of my classroom and leave the teaching to me, a man who has both the credentials and experience for that task."

An effort to make her case to her father met with an equally strident rebuff. "The education of your brothers is of no concern of yours. Herr Langer is eminently qualified to prepare Wolfgang and, in time, his brother for attendance at a suitable National Political Institute. I suggest you tend to running the household and leave training the boys to me." It was more than the tone Richter took with Hannah or his use of the word "train" when referring to the boy's education that shocked her. Rather, it was the sudden realization she was now to assume what amounted to a subordinate role within the household, one not all that different than Fräu Sander's or, for that matter, the Dutch girl's.

From the private classroom where Herr Langer tutored Wolfgang, Hannah made her way to the kitchen. There she found the cook humming to herself as she went about preparing dinner and

Oberschütze Riese, her father's orderly, seated at the table. He was enjoying a cup of coffee, real coffee and not the ersatz coffee most German households had to settle for. When Riese saw Hannah, he leaped to his feet, explaining he was just passing through on his way to the laundry without Hannah needing to do anything more than frown while glancing in his direction. How it was her father allowed such a worm of a man to be his orderly was a question that always intrigued her but, like so many other questions she had, she didn't bother to ask it. Instead, she watched as the man took up his sack of dirty laundry and headed out the kitchen to the mudroom where all laundry was left to be collected and taken to the camp where the prisoners cleaned it.

When he was gone, Fräu Sander chuckled. "You terrify him, you know."

In response, Hannah grunted as she wandered over to see what the cook was preparing for dinner. "If that is so, he is the only one in this household I have that effect on. Not even the Dutch girl seems to be intimidated by me anymore."

"Do you wish people to be afraid of you?" Fräu Sander asked, cocking her eyebrow as she glanced over at Hannah.

Crossing her arms tightly against her chest, Hannah shrugged. "I don't know," she muttered. "I'm not sure what I want. I mean, when I was younger, I always dreamed of growing up and doing something, something important."

"You are doing something important, child. You are looking after your brothers and providing your father with a warm, safe home to which he can return to each night after tending to his duties."

"Is that all there is to my life now?" Hannah asked making no effort to rein in the desperation she felt at times such as this.

Setting aside what she had been doing, the cook came over to Hannah, took her face between her hands, and smiled. "No, of course not. In time you will find a good man, perhaps someone like Horst, and marry him. Together you will start your own family. Only then will you appreciate the real meaning of your life."

The cook's words, meant to comfort the troubled girl, did no such thing. Rather, they had quite the opposite effect.

❀

Hannah was not the only member of the Richter household buckling under the stress of life at Borkow. Whether it was the responsibilities Ernst Richter faced every day at the camp, the denial of his request to be transferred to a combat unit, or events taking place further afield didn't much matter to Hannah. What was important to her were the unmistakable changes in his personality and how he dealt with his family, changes she could not help but notice. When he did set aside his duties at the camp to spend time with them, it was painfully clear to Hannah he could not separate himself as neatly or effectively from those duties as he had once been able to.

This inability was most obvious whenever he crossed sabers with her. Unlike the way he had previously approached a sport both he and Hannah had once enjoyed, he now treated fencing as little more than a brief respite from his troubles, in the same way Hannah used riding with Horst, the time she spent in the kitchen with Fräu Sander, or moments alone at the piano lost in the music. All that had once mattered so much to her had receded to little more than a way to escape the mind-numbing sameness that now dominated her life.

On those days when he did return home early in the evening and ask her to change into her fencing outfit, it was obvious to Hannah by the manner with which her father behaved he was not really engaging in a pleasurable pursuit. Gone was the well-honed finesse with which he had used to counter her impetuous thrusts and aggressive lunges. Both his lack of technique and the fierce, almost reckless manner with which he pressed his attacks told Hannah he had come to rely on these matches as a way of working off his anger. If truth be known, Hannah welcomed the opportunity to cross sabers with her father when he was in a bloody frame of mind, for it also meant she could physically work off some of the simmering rage she harbored over her current circumstances. Thus, when the two went at each other, neither held anything back, each fighting something entirely different than the actual person across from them, a person who hid behind a mask that concealed more than their face.

There was one positive aspect of these bloodless combats. On most days they purged Ernst Richter of his duty-related concerns, even if only for a while, allowing him to discuss family matters with Hannah that were troubling him or other, broader concerns much as he had in the past. On this day, at the conclusion of their last bout, as he stood before her looking down at the gauntlets he was removing, he asked offhandedly if she would join him in the study. "There are things I wish to discuss with you, things for your ears only."

Despite the need to check on Fräu Sander and the Dutch girl, ensuring all was set to receive the guests they would be having for dinner later that evening, Hannah nodded without hesitation. "Of course, Father. As you wish."

After setting aside their sabers, masks, and gauntlets, Ernst Richter led his daughter to his study where they settled in before a fire his orderly had set while they had been fencing. Opening a chilled bottle of Rhein wine left for them on a side table, Richter poured a glass for himself and one for Hannah. Though this was most unusual, Hannah behaved as if it were an everyday occurrence.

There followed several minutes of silence during which Hannah surreptitiously watched her father out of the corner of her eye as she sipped her wine, preparing herself for what she suspected was to be a discussion of some importance. She was not mistaken.

Drawing in a deep breath after a long, lingering sip of wine, Ernst Richter spoke as he peered intently into a fire that could do little to banish the chill the subject he was about to address left in its wake whenever it was brought up.

"I expect you appreciate the war is not going well," he began, speaking in a low, somber tone. "The debacle at Stalingrad has been nothing short of catastrophic. In North Africa, Rommel has run out of tricks. His efforts to turn back the Americans and the British have failed. I expect it won't be too long before his vaunted Afrika Korps, like the Sixth Army, is no more." Pausing, Richter took a sip of his wine. "Bombing raids on the Fatherland are increasing. The Americans have begun to bomb during the day while the British raids at night are growing in intensity and effectiveness. And now there's reliable word that Mussolini's hold on Italy is slipping, which could very well mean they might go over to the Allies, not that we would miss the Italians. Still . . ."

In the silence that followed, Hannah sipped more of her wine in a vain effort to steady herself. She was no fool. She was well aware things were not going well. Still, to hear her father admit as much was something of a shock. Had anyone else done so, she would have discounted their talk as unduly pessimistic, even defeatist. Ernst Richter, however, was not a man who gave himself over to idle speculation or rumors. When it came to facing cold, hard facts, he was no different than Hannah, a realist who did not allow emotions or wishful thinking to cloud his judgment.

After what seemed like an interminable pause, Richter leaned forward in his chair, set his wine glass aside and looked over at his daughter. "Though we must all continue to work toward our final victory, there are those of us who feel it would be prudent to prepare for the worst. Having lived through the chaos Germany fell into after the last war and the depression that followed, I do not wish to see you and the boys suffer as I did."

For the first time in her life, Hannah heard what could only be described as desperation in her father's voice. Also setting aside her glass, she shifted in her seat uncomfortably. "What is it you wish me to do, Father?"

For the briefest of moments, Ernst Richter hesitated as he stared into his daughter's eyes. No doubt, Hannah told herself, he was wondering if he should continue. Was his wavering due to doubts about her loyalty to him or other, more unspoken fears? Hannah found herself speculating over that as the two sat there, staring into each other's eyes with only the sound of the fire crackling and spitting as it consumed the pine logs. Spreading defeatist rumors, even if they were true, was in of itself a crime against the State.

Deciding he had no choice but to put his faith in Hannah, Richter eased back in his seat, took up his glass of wine, and looked down into it as he swirled it about. "I wish you to travel to Switzerland, where you will open a numbered bank account. You will deposit funds with which I shall supply you as well as proceeds from items of value you are to sell in Switzerland into this account. Those funds are to be used by you should it become necessary for you to look after the boys."

There was no need to ask where the funds and items of value her father was speaking of would be coming from. That much was obvious even to someone as ignorant of what was going on around her as she was. And though she suspected she already knew the answer, Hannah could not keep from asking an even more pertinent question. "Why Switzerland, Father? Why not the bank you have always used?"

Richter didn't look up at his daughter, choosing instead to continue staring down at the content of his wine glass. "Because, Mausi, we may lose this war. And if we do, I expect the money we have now will be just as worthless as it was in the aftermath of the last war. By converting the money and other items I give you to Swiss Francs and keeping them in an account in that country no one can trace back to me, you and the boys will avoid being left destitute if things go badly."

With that, Richter emptied his glass. Coming to his feet, he stared down at Hannah. "Will you do this for me? For the boys?"

Without hesitation, Hannah also stood up. "Yes, of course, Father. I will be more than happy to."

Relieved, Ernst Richter allowed himself something of a smile before placing a hand on her shoulder, leaning forward, and kissing his daughter on her forehead. "Good, good. Now," he muttered by way of moving onto other, more immediate concerns. "We must clean up and change. We have guests arriving in a little while and, I am happy to say, something of a surprise for you."

Realizing the surprise he was speaking of now would bear no resemblance to the one she had just received, Hannah allowed herself to behave as if she were once more the wide-eyed child who had been able to look upon the man before her in awe and admiration. "What kind of surprise?" she asked excitedly.

"One you and I will be able to enjoy."

The prospect of something special they alone could share would be most welcome, for any chance to recapture the joy she had once shared with her father was truly a treat to be cherished.

CHAPTER NINETEEN

MADAME DELOME

Having enjoyed attending a concert performed by Madam Margarette Delome, an acclaimed pianist at the Salle Pleyel in Paris in the summer of 1940, the very idea of meeting her there, in her own home in of itself exciting. But to have the world-famous musician as an instructor was beyond thrilling, and more than a little intimidating.

Just how her father had managed to arrange this most wondrous gift was something Hannah did not bother to trouble herself with. Over the years, she had come to appreciate men who belonged to the SS could work wonders, as evidenced by the performance of the Waffen SS units in the recently concluded battle for the Russian city of Kharkov. There the SS Panzer Corps had all but singlehandedly stopped the Russians, not only saving the Wehrmacht troops caught in the Caucasus but throwing the Red Army back. For men who could do that, arranging for a piano teacher, even one as renowned as Margarette Delome was, in Hannah's mind, trivial. Besides, she had more important things to tend to during the run-up to what would amount to a master class, the kind only a handful of gifted musicians ever had an opportunity to enjoy, than waste her time speculating on how this wondrous gift had been arranged.

Though no one who knew her would ever be able to accuse Hannah of frivolity or vanity, she found herself agonizing over what she should wear during her initial meeting with Madam Delome. She knew she wanted to present herself as a serious student, someone not only mature and refined, but deserving of this singular honor. That the woman was not only French, but a lifelong resident of Paris, the center of the fashion world, made Hannah's choice of attire all the more difficult. Women, she had learned long ago, could be cruelly judgmental and quite catty when it came to such things.

The memory of the elegant black gown accented with a simple strand of pearls Madam Delome had worn when she had seen her in concert made Hannah's choices all the more difficult. She knew the woman wouldn't be wearing a gown. That would be silly. Added to the need to decide on her attire was the question of how to fix her hair. Braids were definitely out of the question. While Hannah still enjoyed wearing them, she feared they would make her look not only childish, but a tad too Teutonic. The last thing she wished was to appear as if she were auditioning to be a character in a Wagnerian opera. In the end, after trying on half a dozen outfits and dresses, and messing with her hair until she felt like pulling it out by the roots, Hannah finally settled on a mid-calf black skirt and a white silk blouse with full drop-shouldered sleeves gathered at the wrists by wide, buttoned cuffs. As for her long, flowing hair, she decided it would be best if she wore if pulled back using a simple black velvet headband. That would keep it out of her way as she played as well as adding a touch of sophistication.

The sound of the Dutch girl softly knocking on the bedroom door and informing her Madam Delome was in the foyer waiting for her caught Hannah standing before the full-length mirror admiring her choices. Yes, she thought as she placed her hand over her stomach as if to quiet the butterflies madly flapping about in it, this was perfect. Now came the real challenge, to see how well she could play under the attentive and discerning eye of a world-acclaimed master.

❁

The adage that expectations never live up to reality was a truism of which Hannah was painfully aware. It was something she had learned in the most brutal manner imaginable when she had been a young child. She was not much older than six when she came to appreciate just what it meant to be a Jew. But that had been in 1932, before the ascent of the National Socialist Party. Only fate had saved her from becoming just another victim of a program set in motion by the 1933 Reichstag Decree and the Nuremberg Laws. The death of her natural father, the assumption of an identity so at odds with the one she had been condemned to at birth, and her eventual adoption by the Richters had allowed her to step away from her heritage by burying what she was beneath layer upon layer of lies, deceptions, and subterfuge. In the splendid isolation Ernst Richter sought to maintain around his family, Hannah had almost been able to forget her past, an effort she contributed to by avoiding anything or anyone Jewish. By doing so, she had been able to adopt the same view many Germans had concerning the Jews, that they had been relegated to the past, an extinct culture with no more relevance than the ancient Assyrians or Hittites. Which was why when Hannah descended the stairs and entered the foyer, her introduction to Madam Margarette Delome came as a shock.

Hannah started at the sight of Unterscharführer Esler standing in the foyer next to a wretchedly pathetic creature shorn of hair, attired in the simple striped smock dress bearing a yellow star of David and reeking of disinfectant. Stopping at the base of the stairs, she looked over at Esler. "Is there something you wish, Unterscharführer?"

Snapping to attention, he reported to Hannah with a smartness she had come to expect of those subordinate to her father. "I was ordered to see to it this Jew was cleaned up and brought to you, Fräulein."

Now thoroughly mystified, Hannah looked over at the frail woman who stood shivering next to the SS guard, her head bowed and eyes lowered in abject submission. "Who ordered this and why?" Hannah asked as she remained apart from the pair.

"I was informed the orders came down from your father himself. It seems this prisoner is supposed to give you piano lessons," Esler replied, making little effort to mask his incredulity over such a preposterous supposition.

It took the longest time for Esler's revelation to sink in. When it did, Hannah was dumbstruck. Slowly tearing her gaze away from the

SS guard and shifting it to the wretch at his side, Hannah addressed the woman for the first time. "You are Madam Delome?"

Without lifting her gaze, the woman merely nodded. It was a response Esler found unsatisfactory. Glancing over at the woman, he screamed in her ear. "You were asked a question," he barked "Answer the woman properly."

Mechanically, Madam Delome's head snapped up. "Yes! I am she," Madam Delome replied in broken German.

Reeling under the realization the refined, talented woman she remembered had been reduced to such a pitiable state, it took all of Hannah's willpower to keep from breaking down into tears. To have done so in front of one of her father's NCOs, however, would have been a grievous error. Not only was she was the daughter of the camp commandant, expected by men like Esler to be unmoved by such sights, to be seen to be openly sympathetic by the plight of a Jew would be dangerous. With that in mind, she drew upon all her strength to remain as calm and in control of her emotions as she could.

Only when she was sure she could do so with the expected degree of authority and composure her station demanded, Hannah spoke. "I thank you for bringing the woman here, Unterscharführer. You are free to go until it is time to return for her."

Not sure if the girl understood, Esler regarded Hannah quizzically. Realizing what was going through the SS guard's mind, she resorted to an act she had found most effective in cutting short any discussions or debate when dealing with people at Borkow. She played the imperious daughter of the camp commandant. "Is there a problem?" she sniffed haughtily as she threw her head back and took to regarding the SS man down the bridge of her nose.

"Fräulein, I do not think you understand," Esler cautiously replied. "I am to remain here with the prisoner. She is . . ."

"When she is in my house, she is my responsibility," Hannah snapped before the man could finish. "Is that clear, Unterscharführer?"

Having no desire to become involved in a tiff with the commandant's daughter, Esler clicked his heels together as he came to attention. "I shall return in one hour." With that, he pivoted about and marched out of the house.

Ever so slowly, Hannah approached Madam Delome who had taken to warily eyeing her every move. Stopping when she was within arm's reach, Hannah could not help but notice how the woman shivered. "Are you cold?" she asked haltingly using what little French she had learned at school in Oranienburg.

Not at all sure what to make of the German girl before her, Madam Delome nodded.

Without thinking, Hannah placed an arm about the woman's shoulders. "Come, it is always warm in the kitchen."

At first Madam Delome did not move, choosing instead to stare into the girl's eyes as if shocked by this sudden turn of events. Understanding what was going through the woman's mind, Hannah managed to muster up something of a smile. "It's all right. You are safe here."

Those words, uttered by a German, brought no comfort to Madam Delome. She had heard Germans tell her and her fellow countrymen so many lies so often, the idea that there was one among them who could be trusted was unimaginable. Still, seeing she had no choice, she obeyed, just as countless thousands who had been selected at the railhead to proceed to where they were told they would be taking showers had while she and other musicians had played Mozart.

❋

The sudden appearance of Hannah and Madam Delome in her kitchen left Fräu Sander in something of a quandary as to how to respond to this most unwelcome visitor. Ignoring the cook's behavior, Hannah ushered the Frenchwoman to the chair nearest the stove and sat her down.

Like a lost child, Madam Delome stared wide-eyed at the two Germans in turn, wondering what to think. She refused to allow herself to believe somehow she had come upon a tiny patch of good fortune, that instead of beating or abusing her the two Germans towering over her were going to treat her with something she had not known in months, kindness. And yet, little by little, almost reluctantly at first, each did so. The young girl she should have been giving piano lessons to went off to an adjoining mudroom where she fetched a sweater and draped it over her shoulders. Upon seeing this, the cook placed a plate before her and served up warm, fresh-baked bread, several slices of cold ham, and butter, real butter. Fear turned to confusion, then gratitude as Madam Delome looked up from the bounty that had been placed before her at Fräu Sander, then at Hannah as tears filled her eyes.

Unable to maintain the act with which she had assumed in the foyer, Hannah found she had to look away as her eyes also began to fill with tears. The only difference was that hers were brought on by shame.

✾

There was no music lesson that day. Instead, Hannah, then Fräu Sander, took a seat at the kitchen table across from Madam Delome and did something Hannah knew she should not have done, something no German in their right mind did. They asked the Frenchwoman questions as she ate whatever the cook placed in front of her and then enjoyed a cup of coffee, the first she had had in over eight months.

It started innocently enough, with Hannah asking Madam Delome how it came to be she had been reduced to such a pitiful state. "It began in October of 1940 with the Vichy government passing statutes governing us," Madam Delome replied.

"Frenchmen?" Hannah asked tentatively.

"No, Jews. French Jews. At first, I didn't pay much attention to what was going on. I did not need to worry. I was Margarette Delome, a renowned pianist living in a city known the world over for its love of artists such as I. That all changed when I was banned from public performances. The last one I gave was in July of that year at the Salle Pleyel."

Hannah was about to say she had been there, but didn't. Nor did she need to ask Madam Delome to describe the other limitations that had been placed upon her. She had little doubt they were no different than those she had become familiar with as a child living in Munich.

"Little by little, things became more difficult for Jews throughout the occupied zone until July of last year," Madam Delome continued tentatively. "That was when we were rounded up."

"The Gestapo, they came for you?" Fräu Sander asked quietly.

"No, not in my case. French police came to my home. They told me I had ten minutes to collect a blanket, a sweater, a pair of shoes and a few pieces of clothing. I took some of my jewelry as well, a pearl necklace, diamond earrings, and the such, but they were taken from me when I arrived here."

There followed a few moments of silence, during which Hannah wondered if the necklace Madam Delome had worn the night she had seen the Frenchwoman in concert was the same one her father had given her on her last birthday. The very thought it could be caused Hannah to shiver.

Eventually, Hannah found herself unable to keep from asking a question she knew she should not. "What is it you do in the camp?"

"I play the piano."

"For whom?" Fräu Sander asked without thinking.

Looking up from the cup of coffee she had been staring into, Madam Delome found herself amazed by such a question. How, she wondered, could these two women not know what was going on in the camp? How could the daughter of the man responsible for what went on there be so naïve? It was then, as she was pondering this most improbable question that something of a smile tugged at her lips. It was a wicked smile, as she realized she had just been handed an opportunity to extract a bit of vengeance on the bastards who had reduced her life to a living hell from which there was no escape, save death.

"I play while they are making the selection," Madam Delome informed the two German women in a voice no longer capable of expressing emotion. "With the other female musicians in the camp, I play as those who are deemed to be fit enough to work are sent to the right and into the camp. The rest, old men unable to work, cripples, mothers clutching small children, and the weak are sent to the left. We play while they are taken before a doctor who makes a show of examining them. We play while they are being led to a building where they are told they will be taking showers. We play as they undress under the watchful eyes of members of the sonderkommando, Jews no different than them, who instruct the new arrivals to hang their clothing on numbered hooks and remember the number before herding them into rooms equipped with showerheads in the ceiling. And," Madam Delome concluded as she took to staring into Hannah's eyes with an unnerving intensity, "we play as they scream while they are being gassed."

CHAPTER TWENTY

THE REPORT

BORKOW, MAY 1943

The typist clerk was tempted to rip the final page of the report from the typewriter's carriage and be done with the damned thing. What kept her from doing so was the fear that if she did, the cheap grayish paper they had been reduced to using would rip, forcing her to redo it. As it was, she frowned as she inspected the page she had just completed, hoping the way the type hammer cut holes in the page every time she had to type small O's wouldn't be noticed. Slowly rotating the platen knob of her typewriter, she ever so carefully removed the page before adding it to the others, praying this tiny imperfection would not cause the commandant to send it back to her to be retyped.

The report, a summary of material collected during the past week from transports arriving from the west as well as various Polish ghettos, had become the bane of her existence. Not once in the past few months had she been able to escape having to do the entire report a second time. To ensure she didn't need to do it again, the typist went over the document's numerous columns and row upon row of tightly packed numbers item by item, checking each and every figure twice. She swore that if she ever found out who the miscreant was that had provided the camp adjutant with erroneous numbers, she'd throttle the bastard. No doubt somewhere along the line, someone responsible for inventorying some of the more precious items like diamonds, jewelry, and foreign currency was double-counting or, more likely, pocketing the items. Either way, the commandant always seemed to catch the discrepancies, for he returned the summary with figures he personally corrected.

The clerk typist didn't much care one way or the other whether someone was pilfering items collected during the processing of the Jews and other undesirables who were arriving at Borkow every day save Sundays. Other than a few trinkets like the fine lady's watch she had been given as a reward for her dedicated service, she'd never see any of it, not one pfennig. What annoyed her about the errors, whether they were simple mistakes or something else, was her need to retype the entire report, from start to finish, ensuring it was accurate and precise, just as the commandant demanded.

Only when she was finally satisfied all was correct did she slip it into a folder and hand-carry it to the adjutant who would review it before passing it on to the commandant, hoping as she did so the mess hall would still be open. Having to retype the report was bad enough. Missing the noon meal to do so only made things worse, for her and for the poor nameless bastard she dreamed so often of throttling.

❋

The sound of a motorcycle pulling up at the front of the house caused Wolfgang to look up from the math problem that had been bedeviling him for the past fifteen minutes. Noticing his tutor was dozing off, as he so often did whenever he was allowed to sit in one place for too long, Wolfgang set aside his pencil, slowly rose up from his seat, and tiptoed out of the room, carefully closing the door behind him.

Seeing if he could slip out of the room without waking his tutor and ambush whoever it was stopping by the house had become a great game Wolfgang enjoyed playing. With precious few children his age in the small German enclave and a domineering sister determined to keep him under her thumb, sneaking about playing spy was one of the few fun things he could do. Today, he managed to catch his father's adjutant as he was emerging from the study. "What important news have you brought me today?" the boy called out briskly as he sallied forth from his hiding place under the stairwell and marched up to Horst Fischer.

Looking down at the boy of nine who was attired in a Deutsches Jungvolk uniform even though he was still several months shy of the minimum age to join, Horst playfully assumed a position of attention. "I have nothing to report, my most esteemed Hitlerjunge."

"Nothing?"

Relaxing his stance, Horst grinned as he reached out and ruffled Wolfgang's hair, knowing full well the boy resented it when people did that to him. "Sorry, I have nothing of any interest to pass on to you today. Just a routine report your father wishes to look over." Then, looking about, he asked Wolfgang where his sister was. An opportunity to see Hannah was the only reason Horst bothered to personally deliver a report as dry and dull as the grey paper it was typed on to his commanding officer's home.

"In the kitchen where she belongs," the boy growled, smarting from the way Horst and the others treated him as if he were still a child. Having Hannah as a sister was bad enough. Listening to the way people praised her was galling to a boy eager to take his place in the ranks of the Hitler Youth and, in time, proudly serve his Führer as a member of the SS, just like his father.

Alerted to Horst's presence by the sound of the dispatch rider's motorcycle as well, Hannah emerged from the kitchen. "Is there something I can help you with, Hauptsturmführer Fischer?" she asked dryly.

Ignoring the cool, detached manner with which she had been behaving around him of late, Horst shook his head. "No, nothing at all," he replied. "I was just dropping off a report your father wished to review before sending it off to Berlin."

Though eager to look at it, Hannah needed to bide her time and behave as if it was no concern of hers. "Well, if that's the case, I shall not keep you from your duties. Good day, Herr Hauptsturmführer."

Disappointed Hannah wasn't going to invite him into the kitchen to enjoy a mid-afternoon snack and some amiable, non-duty related chit-chat, Horst turned to another subject. He hoped it would lighten the mood and provide him another opportunity to discover why Hannah was now treating him as if he were little more than hired help. "Will you be riding this afternoon?"

At first, Hannah was going to dismiss the idea of spending time with Horst, or anyone connected to the camp other than her father, out of hand. Then it struck her just how foolish it would be to deny herself an opportunity to be away from the house doing something she enjoyed. If anything, she was in desperate need of some time alone, time to think things through and perhaps come up with a solution to the awful paradox her newfound knowledge of what was going on in the camp had presented her.

"Yes," Hannah replied crisply. "On your way back to your office, stop by the stable and tell the Polish boy he is to bring Pixie here at the usual time," she ordered in a manner so at odds with the way she had once dealt with her father's adjutant. "Now, if you will excuse me, I have things I need to tend to, as I am sure you do as well." With that, Hannah gave her hair a quick toss.

Realizing he had been dismissed, Horst bade Hannah a good day and left, leaving her free to turn to her brother. "Aren't you supposed to be going over your math with Herr Langer?"

The temptation to lie to his sister and tell her he was on a break was quickly dismissed. He was only allowed a five-minute respite between every subject, once an hour on the hour. Since it was currently at the bottom of the hour, his sister would know he was up to something. Dejected and muttering to himself under his breath, Wolfgang made his way back to the room where Herr Langer was still dozing, blissfully unaware that his sole student had wandered off.

Only when she was sure there was no one about who would interfere with her for a while did Hannah finally make her way to her father's study. Once there, she closed and locked the door before taking a seat at her father's desk.

For the longest time, Hannah sat there staring down at the cheap cardboard file Horst had left in the middle of the desk, just as he always did. Her hesitation wasn't due to apprehension that she had no business going through the report it contained. Rather, it stemmed from a fear of what else she would learn about her father. Within her, a struggle raged between a childish desire to remain blissfully ignorant and a compelling need to face reality. After closing her eyes and taking a deep breath, Hannah opened the file.

Like so much else, in the past Hannah had not bothered herself with the reports her father spent so much time going over in the evenings when everyone else in the house had gone off to bed. She had attached no great significance to the occasional glimpses of the columns and rows of numbers, figures, and calculations all neatly laid out in the documents he labored over late into the night. Like any balance sheet listing net gains and operating costs, those reports were cold and terribly analytical.

But the report before her was no ordinary balance sheet, Hannah reminded herself as she carefully leafed through its grey, lifeless pages. In the wake of what she had learned from Madam Delome, she now knew what all the numbers on the pages represented, that what she was reading was more than simply an accounting of material collected. The figures listed on page after page represented the property and intimate possessions confiscated from the people who had been brought to Borkow, people as real as Madam Delome, people whose only crime had been to be born to Jewish parents.

It was a crime Hannah herself was guilty of as well, making the terrible dilemma she found herself having to deal with all the more awkward. "I was proud to be French," Madam Delome had told her one day after listening to Hannah play Debussy's *Clair de Lune*. "Being Jewish meant nothing to me. I was an artist, an acclaimed concert pianist," she declared with pride. "Like politics and politicians, those who adhered to the strictures of their faith were not part of my world. Foolishly, I thought I wasn't part of theirs," the Frenchwoman admitted ruefully as her gaze fell upon the ivory keys before her. "Only after they came for me, after they took everything from me, did I finally understand what the English poet meant when he wrote that no man is an island."

That conversation, like others Madam Delome shared with Hannah, took place either during brief pauses in her lessons or at the kitchen table where Fräu Sander provided the pianist a meal of soup and bread. Though the cook found Hannah's habit of bringing the Jewish woman into her kitchen at odds with the way she should have been treating her, given the girl's father was the camp commandant, Fräu Sander always gave the Frenchwoman a jar of soup and some bread to take back to the camp for her daughter.

In sharing her stories of what life was like for her and others in the camp, Madam Delome had put a human face on the numbers so carefully laid out and tallied in the reports Horst dutifully delivered week after week after week. Even more disturbing to Hannah, they also told her exactly where the items her father gave her to deposit in a Swiss bank account were coming from.

The more she learned, the more appalled Hannah became by what was going on around her. All Reichmarks, foreign currency, diamonds, precious stones, pearls, gold teeth, and pieces of gold collected from newly arrived prisoners were deposited in Account No. 158/1488 of the SS-Wirtschafts-Verwaltungshauptamt in the Reichsbank. Watches, fountain pens, lead pencils, shaving utensils, penknives, scissors, pocket flashlights, and purses went to the workshops for cleaning and repair, after which they either were offered to SS personnel or put up for sale.

Clothing was dealt with in an equally efficient manner. While some of the articles listed were retained for the use of the prisoners, items of special value were given to the camp guards. The rest was transferred to Hauptamt Volksdeutsche Mittelstelle, the Main Welfare Office for Ethnic Germans. Everything from men's clothing to women's underwear was sold to them, except for pure silk underwear, which was sent directly to the Economic Ministry. What the bureaucrats there did with the silk underwear was something Hannah found odd. But then, the entire process being carried out in the name of the German people made little sense to her. The idea that in the middle of a war so much manpower, railroad rolling stock, and material was being devoted to the collection, transporting, and murder of innocent people, people who could have been employed in a much more efficient manner was, in Hannah's mind, nothing short of insane. That she could very well have been little more than an entry on one of the reports Horst delivered to her father only made what she was reading that much more frightening.

The list on her father's desk was long and detailed. Nothing was missed. Featherbedding—four hundred and six. Wool blankets, (plain)—three thousand and seventy-eight. Umbrellas—nine hundred and forty-three. Baby carriages—one hundred and thirteen. Handbags—one thousand, eight hundred and one. Leather belts, baskets, pipes, sunglasses, mirrors, briefcases, towels, tablecloths, and on and on and on.

As disturbing as all this was, it was the disposition of such intimate items as eyeglasses that stood out. Those, according to the documents, were to be forwarded for the use of the Medical Authority, except of course for glasses with gold frames. After the removal of the lenses, gold frames were stored with the other precious metals along with all reclaimed gold teeth and fillings.

Of all the things addressed by the report, the mentioning of gold teeth and fillings was, to Hannah, the most appalling. The entry, in of itself, was no different than any of the others. The small "O" in *gold teeth* cut through the cheap grey paper as it did elsewhere in the report. It was the imagery that this entry evoked, and the symbolic gap the missing "O" left on the page that was especially troubling to her. The very idea there were people who her father held domain over who spent their days opening the mouths of corpses and yanking teeth from them sent a chill down Hannah's spine.

The connection between her recent trip to Switzerland and these reports had become patently clear one day when she had reviewed a document after her father had gone over it. He had crossed out numbers and substituted other, lesser sums in certain columns, such as the number of diamonds or foreign currency collected. The difference between the amended sums matched exactly what she had been given to take to Switzerland. Hannah realized she was no different from the Jews Madam Delome told her of, men she despised who worked in the gas chambers assisting in the extermination of their own people.

A knock on the study door startled Hannah. Having lost track of time, she quickly closed the file she had been leafing through and jumped to her feet. After taking a moment to look about to make sure she had returned everything on her father's desk just as she had found it, Hannah asked what the person knocking on the door needed.

"Fräulein Richter, the boy from the stable is here with your horse," the Dutch girl called out.

After pausing once more to look about the room, Hannah went over to the door, unlocked it, and left the study, taking care to close the door behind her. Turning to the Dutch girl, she thanked her perfunctorily before going over to the side table where she took up her riding crop and gloves.

Just as Hannah had bided her time as she had watched Horst go before quietly slipping into the study, Tessa van Roon waited patiently for the German girl to leave. Only when she was sure there was no one about would she move into the study where she would use the camp commandant's own stationery to copy pertinent information from the report his adjutant always left in the center of his desk. It did not matter to her what the Polish partisans or the Allies did with the information she passed onto them. All that was important to Tessa was that the report provided her with an opportunity to strike back at the Nazis. Extracting a modicum of vengeance, even if it was nothing more than passing on cold, lifeless facts and figures copied from a report, was all that mattered.

❋

On most days the sight of nine-year-old Jan Cybulski and her Pixie brought a smile to Hannah's face. Whether it was the boy's infectious grin that seemed to be a permanent feature, or the way Pixie threw her head back whenever she saw her didn't matter to Hannah. The pair had become inseparable in her mind, a combination that seldom failed to ease her concerns and enjoy spending time with each of them. But not today, not after what she had read.

Still, she couldn't ask the Polish boy to return Pixie to the stable. She desperately needed a diversion, an escape. She needed something innocent and pure to take her mind off the disturbing thoughts racing through her head. Anything that would allow her to forget about the world she had now become an integral part of would do, even if it was only for a while.

"Where's the adjutant?" Hannah asked as she approached the Polish boy.

"He is with your father's orderly," he replied. "They were just taking Grzmiec out of his stall when I was leaving."

Jan's refusal to use the German word for *Thunder* never failed to put a smile on Hannah's face, primarily since it so annoyed Horst. Horst took great pains to explain to Jan that the horse's name was Thunder, not Grzmiec. Hannah knew the boy was having some innocent fun with her father's adjutant, that Jan's German was now almost good as her Polish had become. Her French was improving as well, thanks to her lessons with Madam Delome, though her reason for conversing in that woman's native tongue was worlds apart from why she wished to learn Polish. Since no one else in the Richter household spoke French, the two women were able to freely discuss issues that were forbidden topics in the camp commandant's home, topics Hannah wished she had remained blissfully unaware of, but now that she knew, found herself needing to know more.

In learning about the camp and the entire program her father was a key part of, Hannah found herself becoming more and more conflicted with each passing day. That was the great paradox she found herself struggling with, a cruel contradiction she could not reconcile. She truly loved her father, her German father, which was how she thought of Ernst Richter. He was the kindest, most amiable man she knew. He had never denied her anything of any real importance. Even more important, he had opened up a world to her she would never have known had she not left Munich with Lena Richter and assumed an identity so at odds with her true nature.

But the cost of being part of that world was proving to be high. Like so many Germans, Hannah had chosen to willfully ignore that which had always been there for all to see. The idea that her father participating in the systematic extermination of an entire race of people was almost too monstrous to believe. He was a German, an educated man who could lay claim to a cultural heritage second to none.

And yet . . . And yet it was true, Hannah found herself having to admit. Together with the men he reported to and those he commanded, Ernst Richter was dedicated to the slaughter of Europe's Jews. People like her natural father. People like Madam Delome. People like her.

Eager to be away from everyone, if only for a while, Hannah took Pixie's reins from the Polish boy, thanked him, and pulled herself up into the saddle. "Go find the Dutch girl," she told Jan. "She'll take you around to the kitchen, where I am sure Fräu Sander will give you a treat."

Without waiting for the boy to respond, Hannah gave the reins a quick jerk, tugging the mare's head away from the house. Digging her heels sharply into Pixie's flanks, she spurred the animal into a gallop, riding hard as if trying to put as much distance as possible between her and the report sitting on her father's desk. She rode as if doing so would allow her to escape what she had just read. Unfortunately, there was no escaping from it and what Madam Delome had told her. The old saying *"the truth shall set you free"* sprung bitterly to mind.

In reality, the truth was a quagmire, a dark bottomless morass she found herself stuck in with no means of escape. Just as it had been for Madam Delome, a world she had thought she had nothing to do with had collided with the one she had once found so safe, so secure.

※

Jan Cybulski stood there watching the German girl ride off until she was no longer in sight. Only then did he go up to the front door and enter the house without bothering to knock. Tiptoeing up to the study, he used his fingernails to scratch on the door as a cat would. After a few seconds, the Dutch girl opened the door, saying nothing as she shooed him past her and into the room.

Once there the nine-year-old boy looked about at all the books the camp commandant possessed while the Dutch girl resumed her seat at the desk where she went back to madly scribbled away. Playing courier for the Polish Home Army was turning out to be even more fun than Jan had thought it would be. Like the others in his father's partisan unit, he had wanted to shoulder a rifle or learn how to use explosives. Unfortunately, the weight of the weapons they had, not to mention the kick they delivered when fired, made that impossible, at least for now. Until he was old enough to handle a rifle, Jan would have to be content running messages, a task that allowed him to at least pretend he was an important part of the effort to rid his homeland of the Fascists.

※

From his hiding place under the stairs, Wolfgang waited for the Dutch girl and Polish boy to reappear. He wondered if it would be best if he marched right up to them and demanded to know what they had been doing in his father's study or to wait and see if he could catch one of them with some incriminating evidence on them. Deciding no one would take him seriously, not even the Dutch girl if he attempted to confront her on his own, Wolfgang decided to wait until he had all the proof he needed to put an end to whatever it was they were doing. Until that opportunity came his way, until he was able to prove to his father he was even more deserving of his admiration and praise than his obnoxious sister, Wolfgang was happy to play this very real game of hide-and-seek he was finding thrilling and most enjoyable.

❋

In time, Pixie started to blow, unable to maintain the breakneck speed with which Hannah had set out. Slowing to a walk, she allowed the mare to catch her wind while she once more tried to reconcile her life to the reality of her father's world, one in which she was equally complicit. All of them were, she admitted to herself. Fräu Sander, who cooked her father's meals, provided him with substance. Horst, her father's administrative assistant, oversaw the preparing of the reports she read, reports that reduced what they were doing to nice neat columns of facts and figures bereft of any trace of the humanity. Maria looked after the boys and allowed their father the freedom to carry out his grisly work by day and tinker with the accounts by night. Even by doing nothing more than cleaning up after them the Dutch girl was, in Hannah's eyes, just as guilty as she was, for all of them provided various services to Ernst Richter. By turning a blind eye to what he had been doing, they allowed him to carry on with his work unchallenged and without interference. If the truth be known, Hannah reasoned, all Germans were playing a role in what was going on in the camp, even if they were unaware.

Without having to give the matter any serious thought, she knew it was no longer possible to pretend what her father was doing was right or even justifiable. Unconfirmed rumors, wild speculations, and idle gossip could be ignored. The wretched state of a renowned and talented woman such as Madam Delome could not.

Understanding what was going on was one thing. Doing something about it was a very different matter. With so much she needed to hide, the idea of taking a principled stance, of directly confronting her father and demanding he explain how he could engage in such a barbaric policy was ruled out. Hannah knew it was a pathetically naïve notion that would accomplish nothing. The time to do that had long since passed. No, she sadly concluded, she needed to find a way of doing more than simply feeding one of her father's victims twice a week.

It was then, as she was thinking of Madam Delome, that an idea popped into Hannah's head. Listed among the items on the report she had just read was a pearl necklace. She had no idea what it looked like, and knew it couldn't possibly be the same one that had been taken from Madam Delome when she had arrived at Borkow. Still, Hannah thought if she could save it, if she could return just one thing that had been taken from a woman so gifted and damned at birth, just maybe she could do something to atone for her own sins.

Ever so slowly this idea led to another, an even more ambitious plan. If she could do it for one person, maybe she could do it for others, she found herself thinking as she and Pixie ambled along. While there was no chance she could give something back to everyone who might survive the camp when the war was over, at least she would be able to compensate some of them for what her father had taken from them.

It would be stunningly simple to do so, Hannah reasoned, since her father, a man who was an able administrator and soldier didn't have a clue when it came to appraising the jewelry he gave her to sell in Switzerland. That was something Hannah had to take care of when she visited Basel. Her first two stops there were always to a diamond testing laboratory and an appraiser. The latter was always very impressed by the quality of the loose diamonds she brought to him, quoting a price far above that which her father had thought they would bring. If the same thing happened the next time she went, Hannah reasoned, no one would be the wiser if she opened another account, an account separate from the one she had opened for her father using the assumed name and Swiss passport he had somehow managed to procure for her.

That there would be risks was without doubt. But then, every day of her life since she had left Munich eight years before had been filled with risks. The only thing separating her from sharing Madam Delome's fate, or even that of her natural father, was luck and a legion of lies. Adding a few more lies that would benefit others would not matter one bit. Perhaps they might even prove the key to her salvation.

The sound of a horse coming up behind her at a gallop caused Hannah to set aside her thoughts on what she would do the next time she went to Switzerland. Instead, she turned in the saddle and watched as Horst and Thunder came on fast.

"Why didn't you wait for me?" he called out when he was near enough for her to hear after reining in his mount. "You know you shouldn't be out here alone in the woods. How many times have I told you you're not to leave the compound without an escort?"

To Horst's surprise, Hannah smiled. "You worry too much. Besides, what fun would life be if we never took chances?"

Pleased to see the girl was in a better mood than she had been earlier in the day, Horst never thought to give what she was saying a second thought. Instead, he came up beside her and returned her smile. "The Polish boy told me you took off at a gallop. No doubt you've worn yourself and Pixie out already."

Grinning, Hannah gave her hair a quick toss. "Oh, but you're wrong, my dear Hauptsturmführer. There's so much more to us than I think you or anyone else give us credit for." With that, Hannah once more dug her heels into her mare's flanks and took off, laughing to herself.

❉

That evening, after giving his daughter a perfunctory kiss on her forehead as she was preparing to head up to her room for the night, Ernst Richter made his way to the study. There he locked the door before pouring himself a tall schnapps and settling down at his desk. Upon opening the file Horst had left for him, Richter made a face, annoyed by the little holes the typewriter made in the page whenever the small letter "O" appeared. Only the need to forward the damned thing before someone in Berlin became suspicious kept him from sending it back to be retyped.

CHAPTER TWENTY-ONE

THE POLISH BOY

BORKOW, OCTOBER 1943

Upon returning from her ride, Hannah decided it might not be a bad idea to look in on her brother and see how his lessons were going before heading off to see if Fräu Sander needed any help with dinner. If truth be known, she was more interested in checking on Herr Langer. That man's habit for falling asleep in the middle of the day was becoming an annoying habit. She was coming to believe that he either had a serious medical problem or was like the former housekeeper in Oranienburg her father had refused to let go, an otherwise unemployable relative of a high-ranking party official he was trying to curry favor with.

Not that the reason Ernst Richter steadfastly refused to do anything about Wolfgang's tutor mattered. What annoyed Hannah even more about the man than his sloth was the way he was filling Wolfgang's head with the most absurd notions of everything, from natural science to history. That, and his penchant for allowing Wolfgang to sneak about the house during the day when he should have been studying, never failed to wind Hannah up. This day proved no different.

Even as she was opening the door to the small classroom set up and fitted out to Herr Langer's demanding specifications, Hannah could hear the pathetic old sod snoring. Without bothering to enter the room, she stood in the doorway, debating whether she should rouse Herr Langer and ask him what had become of her brother or head off on her own in the hope of finding him herself.

Sighing, Hannah concluded waking the old man would accomplish nothing. Quite the contrary, once he was fully awake, he would assume a most indignant manner and admonish her, informing her she had no authority when it came to the way he taught her brother. It was a sentiment she would be treated to again later in the evening by her father who would, inevitably, be informed by Herr Langer of her impertinence. After closing the door, Hannah headed off to the kitchen, drawn there by the smell of fresh-baked biscuits.

There she found everyone save Wolfgang and the Dutch girl. From his seat at the table, Siegfried called out her name, causing Fräu Sander to look behind her. The cook could tell by the expression on her young mistress' face she was in a foul mood, a most unusual state for her at the conclusion of a ride with the dashing young SS officer she imagined Hannah would marry once she came of age. "I see your brother's esteemed tutor has allowed him to slip the leash again," Fräu Sander stated, trying her best to make her comment come across as lighthearted.

Miffed by both Herr Langer's conduct and her own inability to do anything to curb her brother's behavior, Hannah marched over the table, jerked a chair out, and took a seat. "If Wolfgang is behaving like this now, what am I going to do when he does join the HJ?" she muttered as she was reaching out to snatch a biscuit from the plate.

Maria, who had remained silent up until then, nodded her head in agreement. "Young boys can be quite headstrong and wild at this age. Now is when they need a father's firm hand," she pointed out, something Fräu Sander readily agreed with.

"When my Gerhardt reached the age of 14, he knew everything," the cook informed Hannah as she returned to what she had been doing. "We had some serious rows whenever he got it into his head I was being unreasonably harsh or cruel."

"How did you manage to rein him in?" Hannah asked as she got up from her seat, went over to the icebox, and took out a pitcher of fresh milk.

"While a good thumping with a wooden spoon every now and then did help curb some of his more outrageous behavior, only time and an appreciation he really didn't know everything finally caused him to settle down," the cook informed her.

Hannah replied with nothing more than a grunt as she took up a glass from the dish rack and returned to her seat where she filled it with milk. There was no need for her to point out her father was doing nothing to check his son's aggressive behavior. If anything, he was encouraging it. Whenever she made mention of Wolfgang's transgressions to their father, he informed Hannah when it came to the boys, he knew what he was doing. "The Reich will need bold leaders, men unafraid to face the challenges they must master, just as my generation did. You do not produce such men by swaddling them in cotton," he would proclaim with an air of confidence intended to forestall any thought of argument from his daughter. "You must trust me on this. After all, I was a boy once myself."

The temptation to mention that when she had been nine she hadn't been sneaky and headstrong was discounted out of hand. Besides, Hannah was beginning to suspect the boy wasn't measuring up to their father's expectations. So instead of disciplining Wolfgang whenever he stepped out of line, he always seemed to find a way of seeing the boy's defiance of authority or misconduct as a sign he was becoming more assertive and bolder. Undercut by this attitude, Hannah's ability to control her oldest brother was steadily diminishing.

Neither Fräu Sander nor Maria said anything as Hannah sat there, absentmindedly munching on a biscuit between sips of milk as she mulled over how best to deal with her brother. Though they both wished there was something they could do to help, if only by offering suggestions, each had long ago come to the same conclusion Hannah was now waking up to. Wolfgang Richter was no longer theirs to control and mold. And if Ernst Richter had been more attuned to what was happening in his own household, he would have realized that he too had little to say when it came to his son. As the man to whom he had dedicated his adult life and in whose name he carried out his duties had proudly declared when speaking of Germany's youth, "Your child belongs to us already . . . What are you?"

※

Having tamped down some of her ire over how Wolfgang's tutor and his father were handling him, Hannah was preparing to leave the kitchen and continue her search for her brother when a loud pounding on the front door, quickly followed by the sound of a man barking orders, sent her flying out of the kitchen. The scene that greeted Hannah when she reached the foyer caused her to stop short. There, standing before Unterscharführer Esler, was the Dutch girl who had answered the door. At the moment she was being firmly held by two SS men, one on either side of her. After catching her breath, Hannah marched out up to Esler who snapped to attention upon seeing her. "I beg your indulgence for causing such a ruckus, Fräulein Richter."

"What is the meaning of this?" Hannah demanded.

"This girl is under arrest, Fräulein."

"Arrest? For what?"

"I do not know, Fräulein," Esler replied. "I was only ordered to arrest her. I wasn't given a reason."

Though Hannah was tempted to ask the SS NCO if he was in the habit of doing things without knowing why, she knew that was not only an exercise in futility, it was a silly question to ask. From the very first day she had joined the BDM, it had been drilled into her and all her friends they were expected to follow orders no matter how unpleasant they might be. In the new Germany, one she had once been so eager to be a part of, young and old, men and women, soldiers and civilians were expected to obey without question. It was a lesson her own father used every opportunity that came his way to reinforce in her and her brothers. "Obedience and unquestioning loyalty is the cornerstone of the Third Reich," he told them. "Our final victory depends upon every German doing their duty without hesitation, without question." Like she did every day in the very house they were standing in, Esler was merely doing what was expected of him.

Instead of wasting her time dealing with Esler, Hannah went over to the cupboard, took out her jacket, and headed out the door. She expected Horst not only knew what this was all about, but had also known of the Dutch girl's pending arrest beforehand. He had to. Which led to the question of why he hadn't warned her something like this was going to happen, a question that only served to ratchet up her already considerable anger to a fever pitch.

❋

Hannah didn't find Horst in his office. Nor had he returned to his quarters to clean up after their ride, according to an orderly she found on duty there. As unconscionable as such a thing could be to Hannah given what was going on, she could only conclude he was still at the stable tending to his precious Thunder. If that proved to be true, and it turned out he had known about the pending arrest of her housekeeper, Hannah decided she would find some way of making him pay for whatever role he had played in this violation of her trust. That she was the last person in the world who could claim to be truthful in all things never entered her mind.

Save for the horses, the stable was deserted, which came as no surprise to Hannah for this time of day. When she found Thunder in his stall, lazily munching on a fresh bucket of oats, Hannah took a moment to figure out how she could have missed bumping into Horst as she was making her way first to the admin building, then to his quarters, and finally to the stable.

She was still mulling this question when she heard what sounded like grunting coming from the tack room. At first, she thought whoever was there was in distress or doing something physically demanding. Both of those assumptions were quickly dismissed when she noticed they were not the sort of sounds a person engaged in a laborious task made. Rather, there was a soft, rhythmic quality to them.

Hannah may have once been willfully ignorant of what was going on in the world around her, but she was not naïve. When it came to her curiosity concerning sex between a man and woman, she was no different than any of her friends had been back in Oranienburg. It was a topic they had often discussed among themselves in hushed tones when they were sure there were no adults about. Sophie, in particular, enjoyed scandalizing poor Gretchen by telling her how she would sometimes slip out of bed at night and stand outside her parents' room, listening at the door when they were making love. *"Sometimes it sounds just awful,"* Sophie declared before mimicking the sounds her mother made.

The idea Horst would choose to engage in sex in a place like this, if it was him, struck Hannah as odd. He had his own private quarters as well as a brothel run specifically to tend to the physical needs of the camp's male personnel. If it was Horst, Hannah realized she had just been handed the perfect opportunity to embarrass him as a means of extracting a modicum of revenge for his failure to warn her of the Dutch girl's arrest. With that in mind, she slowly made her way toward the door of the tack room, taking care to be as quiet as possible. Only when she was ready did she throw open the door.

The shock on the faces of the two men mirrored that which Hannah felt. For the longest time all three did nothing but stared at each other, wide-eyed and mouths agape. Horst was the first to break the silence, calling out her name. "Hannah!"

That was enough to shake Hannah from her stupor, allowing her to turn and flee from the barn before either Horst or her father's orderly had an opportunity to do up their trousers and chase after her.

❊

The temptation to ignore the sound of her brother pounding on the door of her bedroom while informing her their father wished to see her in his study straight off was overpowering. Hannah did not wish to see or talk to anyone, not until she had managed to reconcile the events of the day and calm herself. Remaining in her room and hiding, however, was a childish notion. She was no longer a child. If truth be known, she hadn't been one for a very long time. Just when she had lost the serene safety of childhood was something Hannah was unable to put her finger on. Had it been when the woman who had given her life walked out on her without so much as a goodbye? Or was it the day her natural father had died and she had allowed herself to be taken in hand by a stranger who had led her step by step into a life so at odds with what she was? Were the troubled girl to be completely honest with herself, she would have concluded her childhood had come to an end when she had learned that no matter how hard she tried, or what she did, as a Jew she could never truly be a part of the New Germany she had once been captivated by.

"HANNAH!"

Pushing herself up off the bed, she went to the door of her room and opened it. Before her stood a very smug little boy. "Father demands that you report to him in the study immediately."

Rather than rushing out of the room and down the stairs, Hannah drew herself up. "Tell Father I shall be along in a moment." With that, she closed her door and went over to her dresser where she took the time to run a brush her hair and straighten out her skirt and blouse. Only when *she* was ready did Hannah make her way to what she expected would be a trying confrontation with a man whom she had once thought the very ideal of what a father should be.

※

She found Ernst Richter standing at the window of his study with his back to the door and his hands tightly clasped behind his back. Without looking to where she was standing just inside the room, he ordered Hannah to close the door. Only after he had heard it snap shut did he slowly turn around and make his way over to her, picking up a several folded pieces of paper from his desk as he was doing so. When he reached her, he waved the pages in her face. "Can you possibly tell me how it is a Polish stable boy came to have copies of a report on him, a report that had been left on my desk here?"

In the twinkling of an eye, Hannah was able to grasp what was going on, that the arrest of the Dutch girl and the documents her father claimed had been found on Jan Cybulski were connected. She also realized that in all likelihood her brother had played a role in this affair. For the second time in as many hours, she found herself shocked into speechlessness. Unfortunately, unlike the incident at the stable, there was no running away from this. For better or worse, this was her home, and the man before her was now her father. By her acquiescence, she had accepted this life and her role within the Richter household. With no place to go and no one to turn to, Hannah knew she would have to stand there and take whatever punishment her father had in mind for her.

Both his daughter's stunned silence and the expression on her face told Ernst Richter all he needed to know. She was just as staggered by what his son had managed to discover as he had been. He was still sorely tempted to admonish Hannah for selecting a maid who had played a role in this betrayal of his trust as well as her failure to properly supervise the Dutch girl. But Richter knew none of this would have come to pass if he had merely taken the precaution of locking the door to his study.

Still, allowing Hannah to go with nothing more than a severe reprimand in the privacy of his study was not possible. Too many people were aware of what had happened. People would want to know how such a thing could have occurred, particularly an ambitious bastard like Klopf, a man who had never forgotten how Richter had replaced him as the camp's commandant. Richter needed to find someone to lay the blame on for this breach of security and see to it they were punished. By placing responsibility for the incident on Hannah's shoulders, he could show his superiors he was as ruthless as they, while at the same time moderating Hannah's punishment. It was a solution that was just as cynical as it was useful to him. He appreciated no one would expect him to physically punish his own daughter for what could be passed off as nothing more than an error in judgment on her part. She was, after all a female, little more than a girl. And while there was no denying she was intelligent, women could sometimes be forgiven for lacking common sense when it came to dealing with important matters such as security.

With all of this in mind, Ernst Richter concluded he could make an example of his daughter in a very public way while serving notice to her she was no longer a child, that she was accountable for her actions.

After making his way around his desk, he took a seat at it, leaned back in his chair, and knitted his fingers together before him as he took a moment to stare into his daughter's eyes. "Here is what is going to happen, Hannah," he declared in the same cold and uncompromising tone of voice he used day in, day out while running a camp dedicated to executing what was euphemistically referred to as the final solution.

❋

Once they were in the car, Hannah again pleaded with her father to spare her from what he had deemed an appropriate punishment. Ernst Richter pretended to be unmoved by her plea. Turning his face away from his daughter, he looked out the window as he once more explained the reason for his decision. "You brought both of those people into the house, *my house*," he growled bitterly. "You were entrusted with the responsibility of ensuring it was a safe place for my sons. You failed, Hannah. You failed in every way possible. So now you must pay the price for that failure."

"I can't," Hannah pleaded as tears once more began to flow freely down her cheeks. "I can't do what you ask of me."

Mechanically, Ernst Richter turned to face her. "I am not asking you," he stated calmly. "I am ordering you."

It was at that moment that Hannah finally came to appreciate the man she had loved for so many years as if he was her natural father was capable of doing everything Madam Delome claimed the men he commanded did in the camp. She saw in his eyes the same heartlessness she remembered seeing in the eyes of classmates who had tormented her in Munich. It wasn't hatred. Nor did she see anything that would hint at mindless rage. What she saw was worse, much worse. What she saw were the eyes of a man who had no doubt that what he was doing was more than right, it was righteous.

❋

The site selected for the execution was the village of Borkow itself, purposely chosen so the Poles could see what awaited them if they raised a hand against their masters. Across from the Poles was a contingent of off-duty guards and administrative personnel from the camp, all drawn up in neat ranks, marched there to witness the manner with which their commandant dealt with those guilty of transgressions against the Reich. Between these two very different groups was a makeshift gallows from which two nooses were hung, one from a short rope and the second a longer piece.

With great ceremony, the auto bearing Ernst Richter and his two children pulled up to where Horst Fischer was waiting. When he opened the door, Horst did his best to keep from making eye contact with Hannah. For her part, she avoided looking at anything but the ground before her. As much as she wished she were someplace else, that she could run away, Hannah knew there was no escaping this.

With nothing more than a nod when he was ready, Ernst Richter signaled his deputy camp commander to have the condemned prisoners brought forth. Neither had been cleaned up after the beatings each had endured during their interrogations. Yet as bruised and bloody as they were, Tessa van Roon and nine-year-old Jan Cybulski held their heads high.

Once they had reached the gallows, the two were hoisted up onto a pair of wobbly stools and held in place until an SS NCO had slipped the noose over their heads. When all was ready, the NCO and escort stepped away.

For the briefest of moments, there was silence. Then, as if inspired by the significance of the occasion, the Polish boy with an infectious smile that shone through even now began to sing the Polish national anthem.

> *Poland has not yet succumbed.*
> *As long as we remain,*
> *What the foe by force has seized,*
> *Sword in hand we'll gain.*

Not wishing to turn this exercise into a rallying cry for the Armia Krajowa, Richter took Hannah by the upper arm, leaned over, and whispered in her ear. "You know what you must do. Now go."

Blinded by the tears filling her eyes, Hannah once more begged with him to spare her. In no mood to relent, he gave her a shove.

Stumbling forward, Hannah slowly approached the Polish boy. When he saw her coming, Jan looked down at her from his precarious perch. Dry-eyed, he smiled and nodded as if he were giving her permission to carry out the duty her father had assigned her. That did it for Hannah. Unable to take another step, she dropped down onto her hands and knees and began to vomit violently, weeping uncontrollably between heaves.

When Wolfgang realized his sister was going to fail in the duties their father had assigned her, he left Richter's side. Without hesitation, he marched up to where Jan Cybulski was waiting. There he took a moment to look up into the boy's eyes before kicking the stool out from under him. Fascinated, Wolfgang stepped back and watched as the Polish boy kicked and struggled. Wolfgang watched as the Polish boy's face became engorged and distorted when his tongue took to protruding from his gaping mouth and his eyes all but popped out of their sockets. Forcing himself to ignore the stench created by the loose bowels running down the boy's legs, the eldest son of Ernst Richter trooped over to where the Dutch girl stood with her eyes screwed shut. To fight through her fear, she followed the Polish boy's example by belting out the "*International*" in her native tongue for all she was worth. Not waiting for her to finish the verse she was singing, Wolfgang kicked her stool out from under her as well.

Though annoyed by his daughter's failure to carry out the orders he had given her and her pathetic display of weakness, Ernst Richter found he could not help but take pride in the way his son had stepped forward without hesitation. In time he would grow to be the kind of man Germany would need to finish what he had started, Richter told himself. His son was a true child of the Reich.

PART SIX

1945

GÖTTERDÄMMERUNG
(Twilight of the Gods)

CHAPTER TWENTY-TWO

SETTLING ACCOUNTS

ZURICH, SWITZERLAND, JANUARY 1945

Having finished settling the young woman's bill, the hotel clerk looked up at her sad, careworn expression and smiled, hoping as he did so his cheerfulness would dispel her gloom. "It's always such a pleasure to have you as a guest, Mademoiselle. I do hope you enjoyed your stay with us."

The hint of a smile momentarily lit up Hannah's face for the briefest of moments as she glanced up from the bill she had been going over. "Hmmm, yes, very much," she muttered distractedly in French before once more averting her eyes.

"Will you be returning anytime soon?" the clerk asked in the language she insisted on using during her stays at the hotel, even though he suspected it, like the passport she presented whenever she stayed with them, was not hers by right of birth.

Before responding, Hannah gave the clerk's question some thought. There would be no more deposits to be made in either of the accounts she had opened at the National Bank of Switzerland. It had been almost two months since the last transport had arrived at Borkow, drying up the stream of income from which her father had been skimming. No, Hannah sadly concluded, her next trip here would not be for quite a while, if at all.

There was no need for the clerk to guess what was going through the young woman's mind. He knew Nazi Germany would not last out the year. With the British and Americans closing up on the Rhein from the west, and the Russians poised on the Vistula, it was no longer a question of if, but when Germany would be forced to sue for peace. When that day came, he expected Germany, as a nation, would cease to exist. To allow it to once more rise from the ashes, to again amass the economic and military wherewithal to threaten its neighbors, was unthinkable. No, the clerk sadly concluded as he watched Hannah take up her suitcase and leave without another word, it would be a long time before he or anyone else here saw the fetching young German woman again.

❋

In no great hurry to reach the Hauptbahnhof, Hannah walked rather than catch the tram. Besides needing time to think, she relished the freedom she was able to enjoy whenever she visited Zurich. It was more than being able to come and go as she pleased, where she pleased, and when she pleased. As the daughter of a man who was now a Standartenführer, she was virtually free to go just about anywhere in Germany and at Borkow. She had even taken up the habit of riding off on her own despite her father's warnings and Horst's pleas, venturing along trails that took her to the heart of the forest. Ernst Richter thought she was merely doing so to spite him and not for the real reason she avoided spending any time with Horst. The freedom Hannah had come to relish more than anything else whenever she had the opportunity to travel to Zurich was far more precious. Here she was free of the fear that gripped her native land and its people.

There was more to that fear than the destruction wrought by Allied bombers. They could be avoided by taking refuge in an air raid shelter or fleeing the cities, as all who could had already done. What no one could escape these days was the fear created by the Gestapo and their legions of informers. No one could be trusted as friends, neighbors, even one's own children eagerly reported every transgression against the state, real and imagined. In her own home, Hannah was not free of such vigilance. When she was not being watched by her own brother, the housekeeper her father had brought in from Germany all but stalked her. Even when she traveled to Switzerland on her father's behalf, she found herself wondering if he had someone follow her. That, of course, would have been a foolish thing for him to do, Hannah always concluded whenever she found herself looking over her shoulder or wondering if the man staring at her from across the lobby was Gestapo. After all, what would keep that person from informing on him, since her father was the one who was actually stealing from the Reich?

Upon reaching the intersection of Bahnhofstrasse and Börsenstrasse, Hannah paused to look over at the building belonging to the Swiss National Bank, a place where she had two numbered accounts, one her father knew about, and a second only she was aware of. Both now contained substantial amounts. The account she had initially opened at the behest of her father was more than enough to ensure she and her brothers would be able to live comfortably after the war, no matter what happened in Germany.

It was the second account Hannah found herself reflecting upon as she stood there on the corner, ignoring the coming and going of people who didn't need to worry about being bombed out of their homes or dragged from them in the middle of the night because someone overheard them saying something the Party disapproved of. When she had started siphoning off funds from the diamonds, jewelry, and currency her father gave her to take to Switzerland and sell, Hannah's only purpose had been to provide a way of ensuring she would be able to compensate Madam Delome for what had been taken from her by men like her father. Hannah had since come to appreciate just how naïve she had been back then, thinking that simply giving the woman a tidy sum would offset the physical and psychological abuse she had suffered at the hands of the SS. The Frenchwoman would want more, much more. She would want revenge. So too would Jan Cybulski's father and the family of the Dutch girl. All who had been oppressed and brutally exploited would be seeking some way of exacting vengeance upon the German people. Even Hannah found herself thinking of ways of repaying Ernst Richter for taking the things she had thought she had found when she had become a part of his household, a safe haven and two loving parents. While her loss of innocence was trivial in comparison to what he had done to people like Madam Delome, to

Hannah the way he had stripped her of her last shred of decency was just as devastating. It had killed her ability to believe that one day she would be free to live a happy, normal life.

It was then, without needing to give the matter a second thought, that Hannah knew what she needed to do. Drawing herself up, she put off heading off to the train station. Instead, she crossed the street and entered the bank, for she had realized you didn't need to use a knife to extract a pound of flesh from those who had wronged you.

Borkow

The absence of her brothers made the house Hannah returned to all that much colder and lonelier. The greeting she received from Fräu Joest, the new housekeeper her father had hired, only served to accentuate those feelings. Even before Hannah had an opportunity to remove her coat, the woman was right there as if she had been waiting in ambush. "I trust you had a pleasant journey?" the woman asked in a most perfunctory manner as she was taking Hannah's coat and suitcase.

Hannah was tempted to say it was as satisfactory as one could expect after being delayed three times along the way due to the need to repair rail lines and bridges damaged by air raids and once when the train's engineer thought it prudent to hide in a tunnel when he spotted a flight of American fighter-bombers on the prowl. But she simply nodded and asked if Fräu Sander was in the kitchen.

The housekeeper replied with an equally indifferent manner, "Of course, Fräulein Richter."

With that, Hannah retreated to the one place in the house where she was sure to find both warmth and a friendly smile.

✻

"It is not the same without you or your little brother about," Fräu Sander sighed after accepting the package Hannah had for her which contained chocolate for both baking and eating.

Hannah knew the cook meant Siegfried. Since the hanging, her older brother had been all but intolerable, lording over everyone he could. That and the way he spied on them both had caused Hannah and Fräu Sander to all but celebrate when Ernst Richter announced he was sending them back to Germany to stay with his parents. "I never thought the day would come when I said this, but I am glad they are away from here," Hannah muttered as she took a seat at the table and enjoyed the first cup of real coffee she'd enjoyed since leaving Switzerland. "At least in Munich, they will be safe from the Russians." Then, looking up over the edge of her cup, Hannah took to staring at Fräu Sander. "You should go as well."

"Go? Go where?"

"To Dresden where your daughter is. I understand they've not bombed that city."

The cook furrowed her brow. "No, not yet," she intoned before making the sign of the cross while uttering a silent prayer. When she had finished with that, she took a seat across from Hannah, folding her hands on the table before her and staring down at them. "You have become my family," the woman confessed. "I don't know what I would do if I ever left you."

Setting her cup aside, Hannah reached out and placed her hands on those of the cook. "You know I feel the same about you, Fräu Sander. From the very first day I wandered into your kitchen, you have been like a mother to me, which is why I want you to go. I don't know what I would do if I lost you as well."

The two women were sitting there, on the verge of crying when Fräu Joest entered the kitchen. Without waiting for either Hannah or Fräu Sander to collect themselves, she announced Hauptsturmführer Fischer was in the foyer.

The mere mention of Horst's name was enough to cause Hannah to pull herself together in double-quick time. With a quick swipe of her hands to brush away the tears that had been gathering in her eyes, Hannah drew herself up as she turned to the housekeeper. "What does he want?" she demanded curtly.

"He wishes to see you, Fräulein. He says it is important."

"Well, tell the Hauptsturmführer I do not wish to see him."

"He told me to inform you he had no intention of leaving until he has had an opportunity to speak to you."

Fräu Sander gave Hannah a nudge by informing her she promised to think about what Hannah had just said while she went off to see what it was her father's adjutant wished to say. Deciding not doing so was childish on her part, Hannah sighed. "Oh, very well. But I intend to hold you to your promise, Fräu Sander."

Reaching across the table, the cook tenderly placed a hand on Hannah's cheek. "Now go, child. See what he wants."

✾

Spending time with the commandant's daughter since the incident at the stable had been just as awkward for Horst as it had been for Hannah. Attempting to justify what she had witnessed there, or ask her to overlook his failings both as a man and an SS officer were dismissed out of hand. In his eyes and those who truly knew her, Hannah Richter was more than the camp commandant's daughter. Not only was she the ideal Aryan woman, the kind idolized by both the party and State propaganda apparatus, Horst imagined had his inclination been otherwise, she would have been a perfect match for him. Only his undying respect for Hannah and the knowledge he could never be the kind of man a woman like her could love and admire kept him from taking her as a wife, something every SS officer was expected to have, whether he wanted one or not.

Doing her best to keep her emotions in check, Hannah announced her presence by clearing her throat. When Horst looked over his shoulder to where she was standing, the two locked eyes, each lost in their very own private thoughts neither wished nor dared to share with the other. It was Hannah who broke this awkward silence. "You wished to see me?"

Before uttering a single word, Horst took a moment to quickly glance about as if trying to see if someone was listening to them. There was, of course. Like Hannah, he suspected the housekeeper Ernst Richter had brought in to replace the Dutch girl was there to do more than tend to domestic chores. With that in mind, he crossed the foyer to where she was standing, took Hannah by the arm, and led her into the parlor, where he closed the double doors before speaking.

Horst's behavior stifled Hannah's impulse to ask him what this was all about in the most imperious tone she could muster. Something was going on, something Hannah imagined she wasn't going to like. With that in mind, she said nothing as Horst came up to her and placed his hands on her shoulders. "Why did you come back?" he asked incredulously.

Hannah stared into his eyes for several seconds before giving him the only answer she could think of, one he would believe and not the real reason she had. "This is my home."

"Not for long," Horst replied crisply. "The camp is being evacuated."

Having come to understand what evacuation meant in SS phraseology, Hannah's eyes flew open. Realizing she misunderstood his meaning, Horst hastened to explain. "Those prisoners who can be will be marched back to Germany starting tomorrow."

"Why?"

"Because the Russians have unleashed their winter offensive," Horst explained, thinking she was seeking an explanation as to why the camp needed to be abandoned. "They'll be here in a matter of days."

"No, the prisoners. Why are they being marched back to Germany?"

Now it was Horst's turn to be confused. "The Reich needs them as laborers, in the factories and coal mines."

Stepping back and out of Horst's grasp, Hannah stared at him as if he were mad, which in her mind he and whoever had issued the order to empty the camp was. "Setting aside the fact the war is lost and nothing anyone can do will prevent that, you know as well as I do most of the people in the camp are in no condition to march all the way to Germany, not in the middle of winter."

Setting aside his curiosity as to just how she knew what kind of condition the prisoners were in, Horst closed the gap she had opened between them. "It's not for me to decide such things. We have our orders."

"Orders?" Hannah scoffed as she once more stepped away from Horst. "Like that uniform you hide behind, you use your precious orders to justify what you are doing as if that makes everything right and proper. Well, it doesn't, Herr Hauptsturmführer. Nothing can justify what men like you and my father are doing or have done. Nothing."

Unable to find fault with what she was saying, for in his heart he knew it to be true, all of it, Horst took a moment to collect himself. When he spoke, his voice was mournful, almost apologetic. "Hannah, I didn't come here to argue with you or debate what is right. I came here in the hope I could talk you into saving yourself."

"Save me?" Hannah sneered. "You think you can save me?" No longer able to hold back the rage that had been welling up within her for weeks, Hannah marched up to Horst. Drawing herself up to her full height, she glared at him. "There is no salvation for a pathetic wretch like me. The best I can hope for is to do something, just one thing that will allow me to atone for the sins I am guilty of."

Horst, of course, had no idea why a person he admired and, in his way, loved was saying what she was. Nor did he feel there was any point in trying to find out. Averting his eyes, he allowed his head to droop. After standing there for a minute without Hannah saying anything more by way of explanation, he left.

When he was gone, Hannah took to pacing, trying to gather her thoughts and decide what to do. She could not simply ask Madam Delome be brought around at once and then flee. The same logic she had hit Horst with concerning the ability of the prisoners in the camp to survive an arduous trek to Germany in the dead of winter applied to the Frenchwoman as well. To have any chance of succeeding, Hannah could not act on the spur of the moment as she had in Zurich. She needed to think things through and make a few common-sense preparations. With that in mind, she left the parlor, heading off to her father's study where she could telephone the camp's admin office and arrange to have someone bring Madam Delome and her daughter by the next day. If what Horst said was true, to wait any longer was a risk Hannah was unwilling to take. Only now did she realize she had already waited far too long.

❈

Unterscharführer Esler showed up the next day as expected, but only had Madam Delome with him. Hannah wasted little time demanding to know why he had failed to bring the woman's daughter along as she had ordered. Both the SS NCO and Hannah ignored the way the Frenchwoman avoided looking at either of them as Esler attempted to explain he had no idea what Hannah was talking about. Though she was annoyed, and more than a little concerned as to how she could go about rectifying the situation, Hannah decided it would be best if she proceeded with her plan for now, hoping that somewhere along the line she could come up with some way of freeing Madam Delome's daughter. With that in mind, she dismissed Esler.

But rather than leaving as he always had, the SS NCO informed Hannah he was to remain with the woman. "I have orders to take her directly from here to where the rest will be taken."

"Taken? Taken to where?" Hannah demanded. "And who are these other people, Unterscharführer?"

Esler hesitated before replying, glancing over at the French Jew, then back at Hannah. When he did answer, Esler did so not because he saw no harm in telling her the truth. Rather, he wished to add to the Jew's mental anguish. "She is to be evacuated with the sonderkommando."

Though she did not fully understand what the sonderkommando was, since any discussion of what they did in the camp was something even Madam Delome had always avoided, Hannah appreciated the significance of what he was saying. Doing her best to tamp down the mounting fears she had for the Frenchwoman's safety as well as her ability to pull off what she had in mind, Hannah assumed what she hoped was an appropriately indignant demeanor. "I won't be able to concentrate on my lesson with you standing about," she sniffed. "You are to go back to whoever is in charge of that detail and inform him we are not to be disturbed for one hour."

Setting aside the astonishment he felt over the realization the camp commandant's daughter was still behaving as if the Russians were a thousand kilometers away and not bearing down on them, Esler did his best to stand his ground. "Fräulein Richter, Hauptsturmführer Fischer himself gave me my orders."

"And I am giving you new orders," Hannah growled. "Now go."

Seeing no harm in doing so, and having other things he needed to tend to himself, Esler nodded to Hannah before regarding Madam Delome with what could only be described as a sardonic grin.

Only when he was gone did Hannah take the Frenchwoman by the arm and attempt to lead her off to the kitchen where she had all she hoped the two of them would need.

Madam Delome didn't follow, however. Instead, she sheepishly looked up at Hannah. "Fräulein Richter, I must tell you something."

Anxious to be away as quickly as possible, Hannah brushed aside the Frenchwoman's hesitation. "Later. You can tell me later, after we're gone."

"No, now," Madam Delome insisted as she drew herself up as best she could.

Despite the urge to argue, Hannah realized there was something the women felt was even more important than escaping. "What is it, Madam?"

"I have been lying to you, Fräulein. I have no daughter." Dropping her gaze, the Frenchwoman crossed her arms tightly against her chest. "I shared the food you gave me to take back for a daughter I do not have with the others."

"What others? The other prisoners?"

"The others in the women's orchestra," she replied looking up into Hannah's eyes. "I am sorry I lied, but I had no choice."

Reaching up, Hannah placed a gentle hand on the Frenchwoman's cheek. "Madam, though you may find this difficult to believe, I understand perfectly what one sometimes must do to survive. Perhaps in that regard, you and I are alike."

Though the idea that she and the daughter of the camp commandant could be alike in any way was absurd, Madam Delome nodded. "Perhaps."

With that, Hannah once more urged her on. "We do not have much time, Madam. Can you ride a horse?"

Indignant at being asked such a silly question, the woman of culture sniffed. "But of course!"

"Good. Now come."

❅

Fräu Sander was waiting for Hannah and the Frenchwoman. Though she had been leery of what her young mistress was planning, the cook had come to love Hannah as her own daughter. And so she had done all she could to see to it the girl had the best possible chance of succeeding in her mad venture. While Hannah was rummaging about in the mudroom adjoining the kitchen, Fräu Sander called out to her, doing her best to fill her in on what she had prepared for them. "If you are careful, you should have enough food for four or five days. There is plenty of bread, some wurst that should keep in this weather for several days, and all the canned goods I could find. I've even included a little brandy to keep you warm at night."

Emerging from the mudroom carrying a pair of boots, a pair of trousers, a shirt, a wool jumper, and a military greatcoat belonging to her father's orderly, Hannah handed them to Madam Delome, who had been warily watching the two Germans. "There are two pairs of socks in the boots," Hannah told her. "They should help some if your feet are too small for them."

Taking a seat, the Frenchwoman picked the socks out of the boots and held them up, taking a moment to admire them. When Hannah looked at her with a quizzical expression as if wondering why she was doing so, Madam Delome pointed to the clogs she was wearing. "I have not worn proper shoes or stockings since Paris," she explained.

Understanding, Hannah smiled. "When we reach Paris, you shall have all the stockings a woman could ever want."

In the blink of an eye, Madam Delome's expression darkened. "I shall never go back to Paris. Never!"

Though she was tempted to ask her why she was so strident about not wishing to return to her homeland, Hannah knew time was pressing. Instead, she gave Madam Delome the greatcoat. "After you put on the trousers and boots, slip this on as well as the cap in the right pocket. When we leave here, walk behind me with your head bowed. Don't look anyone in the eye."

"And if we're stopped?" she asked as she was slipping the socks on.

"No one will stop me," Hannah declared.

Having seen the way the SS NCO who always brought her here behaved whenever the German girl put on what she thought of as her snooty little Nazi bitch routine, Madam Delome found herself unable to keep from chuckling. "No, I do not think anyone can stand up to a girl like you," she declared.

"That's because there has never been a girl like me," Hannah answered, smiling for reasons Madam Delome could never have imagined. Then, turning serious once more, she urged the woman to hurry. "Now we must be quick. We do not have a great deal of time." With that, Hannah changed into the warmest clothing she could, for the forest where she planned to take the Frenchwoman was a cold and desolate place.

CHAPTER TWENTY-THREE

THE FOREST

BORKOW, JANUARY 1945

It was not until the moment had come to leave that Hannah realized she had done everything she could think of to prepare for her flight but brace herself for the trauma of saying goodbye to a woman who had come to mean so much to her. For the third time in her young life, she was losing a mother. Though the circumstances in each case were so very different, the anguish was no less harrowing. If anything, this time it would be worse, for she had to find the strength to walk away from Fräu Sander, knowing there would be no turning back once she had. For the first time in her life, she would be on her own in every way imaginable. The cook must have understood this as well, for the two clung to each other, the silence broken only by the sound of their sobs.

From where she stood, Madam Delome looked on incredulously, wondering if the German women were part of a vicious hoax, a final effort by her tormentors to once more wave a glimmer of hope in front of her eyes before dashing it. Having suffered cruelly at their hands for more than two years, enduring unspeakable mental and physical abuse, the Frenchwoman could not allow herself to believe this was happening. Why should she, of all people, be spared by a God she had never paid homage to? What had she done that entitled her to be blessed by such a miracle when she had made the horrors of countless thousands destined for the gas chamber worse by playing music that had once brought such joy to her? Try as hard as she could, Madam Delome could not find it in herself to accept she had been chosen over so many others who were more deserving. What made her any different than the woman who clutched her innocent baby to her breast as she was being hurried along toward their death by other Jews? How could the God of her ancestors allow her to live while not showing a whit of mercy to an old man holding the hands of his grandchildren, imploring them to be brave as they waited their turn to be murdered? All of this, and so much more, made the idea that the commandant's own daughter would cast aside everything to save her, a Jew, simply too fantastic a notion to accept. So when the German cook pushed the girl away and out the door, Madam Delome braced herself for the final act of sadistic barbarism this malicious ruse was leading up to.

※

It took every bit of willpower Hannah could muster to set aside the anguish her parting from Fräu Sander had evoked and collect herself. She needed a clear head and dry eyes if she was going to be able to see her way through the coming ordeal. To keep from dwelling on what was behind her, Hannah turned her attention instead what lay ahead.

Her plan was rather simple, ridiculously so. Using both Pixie and Thunder, she planned on leading Madam Delome deep into the forest to an abandoned woodcutter's hut nestled in a small clearing at the end of the little-used trail she had taken to exploring whenever she was out riding on her own. There, with the cache of food Fräu Sander had prepared for them, she and Madam Delome would wait for the Russians. Though she didn't know exactly how she would be able to make her way back to Switzerland, Hannah did not doubt that once there, her troubles would be over. With the funds she had transferred from her father's account into one she had opened for herself, she would be able to recompense the Frenchwoman, at least monetarily, before setting off on her own in search of someplace where she could find the freedom to live her life as she saw fit in peace.

※

In the beginning, fortune seemed to favor them. Save for the horses and a lone guard, the stables were deserted. The guard didn't give Hannah or Madam Delome a second thought as he nervously paced back and forth at his post. Hannah could tell by the way he kept glancing off in the direction of the camp that he was hoping in all the haste and confusion he wasn't forgotten by his sergeant when it came time to abandon it.

Once in the sable, Hannah dropped the rucksack, canteen, and sack of food next to Pixie's stall on her way to the tack room. There, as she was handing the Frenchwoman a saddle, bridle, reins, and a horse blanket, Hannah warned her she would need to be firm with Thunder. "He can be rather headstrong and unruly. Horst is always having to rein him in."

Her comment brought something of a smile to Madam Delome's face. "One must know how to handle a male," she murmured. "A kind word, a pat on the head, and a little treat every so often when they've been good is all it takes to satisfy both a horse and a man." With that, she headed over to the stall Hannah had pointed out to her and began to saddle Thunder. Though she still believed what they were doing was all part of an insidious ploy to lull her into a false sense of safety, Madam Delome was determined to relish the sense of normality it was allowing her to enjoy for as long as she could.

And enjoy it she did. Once they were mounted and away from the stables, galloping through the snow-filled forest, the Frenchwoman found herself recalling how she and her brothers would ride for all they were worth whenever their father allowed them to join him and follow the hounds during *"La Chasse."* For the briefest of moments, she could forget the unspeakable horrors that lay in her wake and what the future held in store for her. All that mattered was that in this moment, she was free.

The Forest of Borkow

Upon reaching the fork in the forest trail where they needed to go right to reach the woodcutter's hut, Hannah reined Pixie in. Caught off guard by the German girl's sudden stop, Madam Delome needed to use all her strength to bring the big stallion she was riding to a halt. Only after she had regained control of the beast was she able to cautiously ease her mount up next to Hannah's. "What is it?" she asked, staring off in the direction Hannah was.

"Trucks have been by here," Hannah muttered as she peered down along the narrow track as far as she could see.

"Is that a problem?"

"Perhaps," Hannah replied, unsure what this meant to her plan.

"Maybe we should go another way?" Madam Delome suggested.

Hannah bowed her head as if embarrassed before looking over at the Frenchwoman out of the corner of her eye. "I do not know another way. The place I was taking you to where we could hole up and wait for the Russians is at the end of this trail."

"Well, maybe the trucks are gone," Madam Delome offered cautiously.

Looking over her shoulder, Hannah thought about backtracking some before seeking an alternate route. To do so, however, would be dangerous. In addition to all the westbound military traffic and German refugees clogging every road they would need to cross, she expected her flight had been discovered by now, if not by her father's housekeeper whom Fräu Sander had sent off on a fool's errand, then by Esler when he returned to fetch Madam Delome. Deciding it would be unwise to go bumbling about in search of a new refuge, Hannah decided to press forward, though she did so cautiously.

Before reaching the clearing, Hannah once again came to an abrupt halt. Bringing Pixie about, she instructed Madam Delome to leave the trail and hide while she went ahead to see if the trucks that had recently used it were up ahead.

Once more, Madam Delome found herself wondering if this was all part of a cruel joke the German girl might not be aware she was part of. Not that it mattered. The idea she would be spared the fate she expected her father and brothers had suffered long ago had been a foolish one. If anything, she found herself thinking the worst that could happen would be if she somehow did manage to survive when so many others hadn't. Death, whether it be quick or brutal, just might be the kindest thing the German girl could lead her to. With that thought in mind, she shook her head. "We shall go forward together."

Ever so slowly, the two women made their way along the trail. In time they heard voices, Germans shouting orders. Once more

Hannah reined in Pixie and told Madam Delome to hang back. And once more the Frenchwoman refused to leave her side.

After taking a moment to gather up her courage, Hannah lightly tapped Pixie's flanks with the heels of her boots and pressed on down the center of the snow-covered trail. In time, as she drew near the clearing, she could see the trucks that had cut deep ruts in the snow parked near the woodcutter's hut. Around them were soldiers, guards from the camp as best she could tell, milling about as if waiting for something. Across the clearing from them, huddled together in a mass before a long, freshly dug trench were prisoners, male and female.

Pausing, Hannah was taking in the scene before her, trying to make sense of what was going on, when Madam Delome came up beside her. "Dear God no!" she exclaimed under her breath.

Looking over at her, Hannah asked if she knew who those people were.

"The women, they are all part of the orchestra," she replied as tears began to well up in her eyes.

"And the men?"

This time Hannah could not help but notice the bitterness in the Frenchwoman's voice as she answered. "Sonderkommandos."

Without needing to hear more, Hannah spurred Pixie on, riding out into the center of the clearing between the two groups, frantically searching the stunned expressions of the German guards for someone who looked as if they were in charge as she tugged wildly on Pixie's reins, causing the horse to rear up and wildly dance about. She stopped doing so when her eyes fell upon Horst. Loosening the reins, once Pixie had settled down Hannah slipped out of the saddle and marched up to him.

"You can't do this," she declared brusquely before Horst was able to recover from the shock of seeing her there. Instinctively he reached out to grab her by the arms.

Hannah drew back, away from him before repeating her plea as she clutched her fists at her side. "You can't do this, Horst. You can't let this happen."

Seeing he wasn't going to have any luck taking her in hand and moving her out of the line of fire, Horst stopped. "Hannah, are you mad?" he muttered in a low voice.

"Am I mad?" she shrieked. "You're about to murder those people for no other reason than they are different and you ask me if I am mad?"

"Hannah, please," Horst uttered in exasperation. "I have no choice. I have my—"

"*DON'T YOU DARE,*" she growled even as she was closing the distance between herself and Horst until she was all but in his face. "Don't you dare try to justify what you're doing by hiding behind your precious orders."

Having reached the end of his patience, and wishing to be done with this and away from Borkow before the Russians arrived, Horst drew himself up. "If I must, I will have you carried away from here, Hannah. Now go."

Realizing the man she had once thought of as a kind and gentle soul was not going to be swayed by her pleas, Hannah slowly began to backpedal away from him. "I can't, Horst. I can't leave here, and you can't allow me to. If you shoot them, you must shoot me as well."

"You know I can't do that."

"But you must, Herr Hauptsturmführer," Hannah spat. "It is your sacred duty as an officer in the SS to purge the Reich of the poisonous influence of the Jews and their infectious culture. If you are to be true to your orders, your oath, and all you profess to believe in, you must shoot me as well."

"Hannah, stop this foolishness and leave at once."

As she continued to move away from Horst, Hannah's anger ever so slowly gave way to the realization she was not at all like the people she had once aspired to be a part of. She never had been and never could be. For beneath the veneer of righteous honor Horst wore like his uniform was a loathsome, contemptible creature who, like her, had hidden his true nature for no other purpose than to survive. In doing so, he had willingly turned a blind eye to the crimes Ernst Richter, a man she had called Father, and countless others like him had been committing in the name of a state-sponsored philosophy that was as flawed as it was evil. Stopping, Hannah stood alone between the prisoners and Horst, gazing into his eyes. "I cannot leave, Horst. And you cannot allow me to go," she finally announced in a calm voice. "You see, I am a Jew, an enemy of the state. I belong with them. And so do you." With that, she turned her back on Horst and made her way to the far side of the field where the prisoners had been watching.

Stopping just short of them, Hannah took a moment to scan their gaunt faces. They, in turn, looked upon her in uncertainty. Like Madam Delome, they did not know what to make of the strange German girl putting her own life at risk for them. Not having heard what had passed between her and the German officer, let alone been privy to how an orphaned nine-year-old child from Munich had come to find herself standing in a snow-covered clearing in Poland, they could not have possibly understood. They didn't need to, Hannah concluded. She did, and that, as well as the reason she was there, was all that mattered.

When she could no longer stand the way the wary prisoners were watching her as if waiting to see what she would do next, Hannah bowed her head and took to staring at the ground before her.

Not even during her darkest days in Munich had she ever felt so alone, so lost and hopeless as she did at that moment. It was this sudden onset of utter despair, and not the fear of what was about to happen that caused Hannah to shudder as she forced herself to block out what was going on around her and prepare to meet her end. Never having uttered a word in prayer, all she could do was wait for it to come. Closing her eyes to the world around her, a world she no longer wished to see, Hannah could only hope death would be both swift and final.

From the edge of the clearing where she sat astride the big stallion, Madam Delome watched as the scene between the German girl and the camp adjutant played out. Like Hannah, she waited for the Germans to fire, realizing as she did so the girl who had brought her here was just as naïve and innocent as she had once been. Deciding she could not leave the German girl to meet her end alone, the Frenchwoman climbed down out of the saddle and made her way over to where Hannah stood, ignoring the way the Germans were watching her tromp through the snow in boots two sizes too large for her. Coming up behind Hannah, she placed her hands upon the girl's shoulders and drew her into her.

For several long minutes no one moved, no one spoke as the leaden grey clouds hovering over the strange gathering began to shed snowflakes. In time Horst concluded he could not give the order to fire. For any number of reasons, none of which he could admit even to himself, he would never be able to issue the final order to the men who were standing behind him, waiting with a mixture of amusement and curiosity to see what he would do.

Coming about, Horst made his way over to where his senior NCO had been overseeing the setting up of a machinegun. "Break down the machineguns and have the men fall in on the trucks," he muttered as he was making his way past the NCO and over toward a motorcycle and sidecar.

Though he had heard the adjutant correctly, the SS NCO was confused. Slowly turning to continue to face Horst as he was trudging by, the NCO drew himself up. "But sir? Our orders?"

In no mood to argue or explain, not that he could, Horst spun about and stormed up to the NCO until he was in the man's face. "I gave you an order, oberscharführer. Now be quick about it."

Snapping to attention, the SS NCO gave Horst a crisp, *"yes, sir,"* before turning away from the adjutant and barking out orders to his section. "Everyone, to the trucks. *NOW!*"

Like Madam Delome had earlier in the day, the prisoners standing with their back to the ditch they had all expected would be their final resting place were incredulous as they watched the Germans scrambled about, climb into their trucks, and prepare to leave. All imagined this was part of an elaborate joke, a cruel trick no different than those the SS guards had enjoyed playing on them back in the camp for no other reason than to amuse themselves.

Only when she saw the last of the German trucks fall into line and head down the trail did Madam Delome realize that perhaps she and the women of the orchestra she so loved would live to see a new day, a day that would belong to them. Without thinking, she gave Hannah's shoulders a gentle squeeze. "They are gone, child."

That was all it took. Having used up every bit of self-control she could draw on, Hannah's nerve finally gave way. Pivoting, she wrapped her arms about Madam Delome, buried her face in the coarse wool greatcoat the Frenchwoman was wearing, and began to sob uncontrollably.

At first, Madam Delome did not know what to do, or more correctly, she did not feel she could do. And yet the woman who had been stripped of everything she had, including her very soul, found herself reaching out and wrapping her arms about the weeping child clinging to her. It did not matter that she was the daughter of the man who had been the author of her torment. Like her, the German girl was now just another lost soul in need of a shoulder to cry on and someone to hold onto. To deny the girl that would have made her no different than the people she had come to hate, something Madam Delome refused to allow.

Among the sonderkommando, a man tore his eyes from the sobbing German girl in the orchestra woman's arms to watch as the last of the German trucks vanish from sight. Only when he was sure they were gone did he take to staring about the clearing in bewilderment as if he were lost. He was, of course. Like Hannah, he was lost in every way imaginable. Having denied everything in his quest to survive long enough to bear witness to the suffering of his people, Rabbi Asher raised his eyes toward the heavens for the first time in years, realizing that his God, the God of his people, had not forgotten them. For that, he owed Him thanks.

Hesitantly, he broke the deathly silence that had fallen upon the clearing after the sound of lumbering truck engines had faded in the distance. His words of thanksgiving, familiar words he had often uttered in the past without giving thought to their true meaning were hoarse and uncertain after years of neglect. Only now, here in the wilderness, far from his native home, was he able to truly appreciate what the words of Psalm 100 meant as he uttered them.

From among the men behind him, another voice joined his. Asher looked round to see a man he knew only as Gavi, one of the men who had scraped the ashes and bones from the still hot ovens standing there, singing with his head bowed, staring down at the dark Polish mud they had churned up while digging what they had thought would be their grave. Like Asher, despite all he had seen and all he had done, he felt the need to give thanks.

One by one the other men of the sonderkommando, men who had served the devil himself, joined Asher and Gavi. Deciding what to do and trying to figure out what the morrow would bring could wait. Paying homage to the God that had delivered them from the hands of those who had enslaved and persecuted them was all that mattered.

As she held the weeping girl tightly, only Madam Delome appreciated that whatever role God had played in saving them, He could not have done it alone, not without the help of a most unusual savior. It was not important to her why the girl in her arms had risked all to save her and the others. In her eyes, all that mattered was she had. For that, she gave thanks to the one most deserving it in the only way she knew how. Ever so slowly, the Frenchwoman began humming an old lullaby she had often sung to her little brother when he had been in need of comforting. If anyone deserved to be comforted, it was the young woman she held, a girl who was little more than a child but had, on this day, possessed the courage of Ruth.

CHAPTER TWENTY-FOUR

RABBI ASHE

THE FOREST OF BORKOW, JANUARY 1945

With night fast approaching, the prisoners found they needed to decide what to do. This was not at all as easy as it should have been, for many assumed just as Madam Delome had earlier in the day what they had just witnessed was part of a cruel joke. Like her, they could not allow themselves to believe they had been spared the fate countless others had suffered, that this seemingly miraculous reprieve was anything more than a sadistic trick on the part of their former tormentors to raise their hopes one last time before utterly dashing them by returning and finishing what they had started.

Their distrust was not limited to the Germans. From where she watched, apart from the former prisoners, Hannah noticed how the two groups drew away from each other as soon as they had recovered from the sudden shock of being spared. The division was between the women who had been in the camp's female orchestra and men who belonged to something called the sonderkommando, a term that meant nothing more to Hannah than *special unit*. It seemed so very strange to her that people who had survived such a shared ordeal weren't embracing each other.

This inexplicable rift between the two groups became all the more contentious as they debated over whether it would be best if they stayed where they were or hide in woods least the SS guards come back. The women turned to Madam Delome, whom they saw as the true author of their salvation. Among the men, a gaunt figure who impressed Hannah as once having been a person of authority took on the mantle of leadership for them.

For the longest time they squabbled among themselves, within each of the two groups and between them. Some argued it would be best if they fled deeper into the woods where they could hide, an idea others bitterly ridiculed by pointing out all the Germans would need to do was to follow the tracks they left in the snow. In the end, only an appreciation no one had any clear idea as to where they were, let alone in which direction to go, put an end to any thought of leaving the clearing. "Not even the German girl knows where we would be safe from the Nazis," Madam Delome pointed out. "To wander around in the forest in the dark would be foolish. I for one intend to stay here and rest, at least for the night. In the morning, when our heads are clear, we can discuss this matter once more." When the man who had taken on the responsibility of speaking for the sonderkommando made it clear he agreed, the two groups separated. The women followed Madam Delome to a spot near the tumbled-down woodcutter's hut and the men remained near the edge of the clearing where, if need be, they could flee into the forest if the Germans suddenly did return.

Feeling very much apart from both groups as this debate was taking place, Hannah busied herself gathering Pixie and Thunder and leading them to the spot where the trail ended. Knowing both her father and Klopf, she could not dismiss the possibility one of them might turn the SS guards Horst had led away around and send them back to carry out their orders or, at the very least, fetch her. Her adopted father would take her role in this affair particularly hard, seeing it as a personal affront to his honor as an SS officer as well as treason of the highest order. If she were taken back to him to account for her actions, Hannah knew it would not at all go well for her. The memory of how he had dealt with the Polish boy and the Dutch girl was still fresh in her mind.

She left both animals saddled after securing them to a tree, taking from the saddles the rucksack containing a blanket, warm clothing, and a few items she would need to survive during her flight to safety, as well as the sack of food Fräu Sander had given her.

As she was preparing to settle in for the night, Hannah looked over to where Madam Delome was organizing the women, sending some off to gather wood for a fire while showing others how to snap off branches from the fir trees and fashion beds on which they could sleep. There wasn't near enough to feed them all, Hannah reasoned as she jiggled the sack of food she was holding as if to gauge its content. When Fräu Sander had filled it, she had been thinking of only two people. Still, to hold back that which she did have seemed wrong. Even if everyone received little more than a mouthful of food, Hannah reasoned it was more than some had seen in days. What they would do on the morrow when there was no more could wait until then.

❋

Madam Delome had come to appreciate she had been wrong about the German girl. When she saw Hannah approaching her with the sack of food in her hands, she knew what the girl was going to do. The other women belonging to the orchestra, however, were still suspicious of a person they had come to bitterly refer to as the German girl in spite of what they had witnessed earlier in the day.

It was just as well, for Hannah was just as uncertain of them, but for entirely different reasons. She had, after all, turned her back on being a Jew, embracing instead the very people who had brought such suffering and misery to them. Overcoming years of conditioning and beliefs people like Fräulein Diehl had so patiently instilled in her and embracing the wretched creatures she had risked so much to save was more than Hannah could do in a single day. She was only human, confused and, though she did not show it, very frightened.

With a hesitancy all could see, and her eyes downcast, Hannah stopped in front of Madam Delome. "It is not much, Madam," she muttered as she handed the sack over to the Frenchwoman. "But it is all I have. If you would, divide it up as best you can with the others."

As she had before, Madam Delome comforted the forlorn girl before her. After taking the sack of food from Hannah with one hand, she gently placed the other on Hannah's cheek. "It will be more than enough. To us, it is like the manna God gave our people to see them through their flight from Egypt."

Ignorant of the stories of a people she had been taught to loathe or the tenets of their faith, Hannah had no idea what the woman was talking about. What she did know, what she was able to feel, was the warmth of a loving hand against her cheek. Closing her eyes, she pressed her face into the Frenchwoman's palm, recalling as she did so all the times Lena Richter and Fräu Sander had sought to ease her anguish by showing their compassion and love in this simple, heartfelt manner.

Not wishing to break down into tears once again where all would be able to see just how weak she was, in time Hannah peeked up at Madam Delome and thanked her for her kind gesture with a sad little smile. Then, she turned away and went back to where she planned on spending the night, alone with her horses and her thoughts.

❄

The crackle and sputtering of wood burning in three separate fires and the muted muttering of voices were the only sounds that filled the clearing that night as light snow fell upon the huddled refugees. Hannah sat alone hunched over her own little fire, staring vacantly into the flames as she tried to sort through the jumble of emotions and thoughts that filled her head. Once more she found herself adrift, suddenly cut loose from the moorings of home and family. The hastily laid plans she had cobbled together to save Madam Delome were in tatters. Only now was she able to appreciate just how naïve she had been to believe she could make a difference, that by saving one life she could undo all the crimes against these people she was guilty of, real and imagined.

Oblivious to all around her save the bitter cold, Hannah was so consumed by the disparaging thoughts swirling around in her head that she did not notice someone was approaching until he was standing just across the small fire from her. With a start, she looked up into the eyes of the intruder.

Realizing he had startled the German girl, Rabbi Asher did his best to put her at ease. "I apologize for frightening you so," he declared in heavily accented German. "But I could not let the night pass without coming over here and thanking you on behalf of the men for the food you gave the Frenchwoman to pass out among us."

"I am afraid it was not much," Hannah muttered as she went back to staring at the flames as they lapped about the pine logs she had found buried under the snow near the head of the trail.

"The amount did not matter," Asher stated. "It was the gesture, one that has given many of us the first thread of hope we have been able to latch onto for in a very long time."

"What hope is that?" Hannah asked bitterly without looking up at him.

Asher ignored the German girl's tone of voice and instead, expressed a heartfelt sentiment so many in his group had expressed to him in the wake of what was, to them, nothing less than a miracle. "The hope we may yet see this terrible ordeal through."

Glancing up, Hannah scoffed. "I am afraid it is a hope that may be ill-founded."

Having borne witness to despair for years without being able to do anything to dispel it, Asher saw an opportunity to do something he had not been able to do for the longest time, something that had once given him a great deal of pride. Without knowing it, the German girl was providing him with a chance to once more be a rabbi. "May I sit with you a while?" he asked in the same manner he had often used when preparing to minister to a member of his congregation in desperate need of guidance but without the strength or courage to seek it.

Not bothering to look up at him, Hannah replied with a shrug.

When the German girl said nothing to him, Asher took the initiative by introducing himself. "Before the war, I was a rabbi," he began. Then, with a shake of his head, he corrected himself. "I am a rabbi, Rabbi Asher Kulish." After waiting for Hannah to reciprocate by giving him her name, something she failed to do, Asher continued. "Even in your darkest hour, you must never give up hope. If anything, that is when you must draw upon every fiber in your body and put your faith in the belief you will see your way through to better times."

"I was taught by my natural father to ignore the way my peers were tormenting me," Hannah explained in a soft, almost mournful tone without looking away from the fire. "He told me the persecution being heaped upon us by our neighbors was but an apparition, that better times were sure to come. My German father taught me to be bold and aggressive, that in order to survive one needed to stand before their foe with a clear head, a sharp eye, and strike swiftly. The woman who commanded my BDM troop taught me we needed to rid ourselves of those who were different, that by doing so we would become a stronger, better race of people." Then, looking up across the fire at Asher, she hesitated for a moment as she stared into his eyes. "So much of what I have been taught, what I was led to believe in has turned out to be lies, nothing but lies. I do not know what to believe in. I don't even know if I can."

A smile tugged at the corner of Asher's lips. "Of course you can, child. But you must have faith."

"Faith in what?" Hannah asked incredulously.

"To start with, faith in God."

"God? What god?" Hannah spat. "The god the Christians bowed their heads in prayer to every Sunday before returning to their homes where they belittled those who did not pray as they did? The god my teachers and BDM leaders taught me to follow and die for? Or would you have me put my trust in your god, the one who allowed his chosen people to be slaughtered like sheep? Tell me, rabbi, where does one go to find faith when everyone and everything they have ever put their faith into has been taken away from them, used against them, or proven a lie?"

Having heard the same argument many times before, Asher could not help but chuckle, a response that caused Hannah to draw back and furrow her brow. She wondered how he could possibly be amused by what she had just said.

"Why did you save the Frenchwoman?" he asked quietly.

Confused, Hannah could not understand what that had to do with their discussion. "I would think that was obvious," she sniffed while giving her hair a toss to one side by flicking her head.

"Answer the question. At a time when so many Germans are doing everything in their power to kill every Jew they can, why did you risk your own life to save one?"

The idea of using her own heritage as a means of justifying her actions was dismissed out of hand. This was neither the time nor place for that. If anything, it would only complicate the issue. Once more gazing down at the flames as they consumed the wood she had fed into the fire, Hannah instead told Asher the truth. "I thought by saving her, by doing one thing right in my life, I could do some good for a person who is as deserving to live as Madam Delome is."

"Do you know what atonement is?" Asher asked quietly after a long pause.

"It is punishment, the payment one makes for their crimes,"

Hannah replied without bothering to give the matter any thought.

"It has other meanings. It can be an admission of guilt. It can also be a plea for forgiveness, a request made by someone who has come to realize they have done wrong and wishes to seek forgiveness. In my faith we turn to God when we find we must atone for our sins, seeking to amend our behavior and ask forgiveness from Him as well as those whom we have sinned against."

Asher waited until Hannah was once more looking up and into his eyes. Only when he was sure she was taking in what he was saying did he continue. "In trying to save the Frenchwoman, you sought to atone for the suffering she had endured at the hands of your father. By my way of thinking, a person who did not believe in something more than what they can see, what they can hear, and what they can feel is not capable of such an act. Your gesture tells me you know there is evil, for you tried to save one person, a single soul, from its grasp. Therefore you must believe in good. And if you believe in that, you have faith in your own ability to do both good and evil. You have faith," he declared with a confidence Hannah did not share. "Perhaps it is not in what I call God, but you have faith in something more important than yourself. That I am sure of."

Once more dropping her gaze, Hannah found she could not deny there was some truth in what the man across from her was saying. There was a question he could not answer for her, the one she needed to give serious thought to now. Having turned her back on her heritage, having come to understand a philosophy she had once embraced was inherently evil, she wondered what she could put her faith into.

Realizing he had done all he could for the German girl for the moment, Asher came to his feet. "I must go back and look after the needs of my people." After waiting for a response from the German girl but receiving none, he asked what her name was.

Without looking up, Hannah wondered how best to answer him. Did she give him the name she had been born with? Or was it more appropriate to continue using the one she had adopted, one she knew the rabbi would find repulsive? With a sigh, she concluded she didn't know the answer to such a simple question. So when she finally did look back up the rabbi, she gave him the only response she was sure of. "Hannah."

CHAPTER TWENTY-FIVE

THE RUSSIANS ARE COMING

THE FOREST OF BORKOW, JANUARY 1945

The sound of rumbling in the distance woke Hannah from a fitful sleep. Pushing herself up off the bed of fir tree branches, she shook the snow off her blanket and took to looking about. Both Pixie and Thunder, still tethered to the tree right where she had left them, were nervously shifting about. Glancing behind her at the clearing, she noticed the two groups had managed to set aside whatever apprehensions they had about each other and were now all gathered as one about the woodcutter's hut. While some were chatting quietly with the person next to them, others were looking off into the distance, wondering as she was if the steady drumbeat of artillery was heralding their liberation, or merely serving as a prelude to a brutal end.

Rising to her feet, she finished brushing herself off before heading over to where Madam Delome and the rabbi were standing side by side. "That's artillery, isn't it?" Hannah asked no one in particular.

"Yes, artillery," the man called Gavi replied in broken German. "Big guns."

"And you know this how?" another man asked sarcastically in Polish.

"I was a soldier," Gavi replied proudly in his native Polish.

"Well then, tell me, whose guns are they?" the cynic asked.

"It does not matter whose they are," Madam Delome muttered in German. "All that matters now is surviving long enough for the Russians to reach us."

"Or we go to them," Asher offered.

Upon hearing this, the Frenchwoman scoffed. "Look about you," she intoned sharply. "Do any of these people look as if they are fit enough to go tromping through the woods or evade any German troops we might come across? No," she snapped, answering her own question. "Though I wish to be away from this place as much as you or anyone else, it is best we stay where we are and let the Russians come to us."

"And until then?" Asher asked.

"We do what we have been doing for all these months. We survive."

From among those who had gathered around them to listen to what they were saying, a woman called out. "On what? There is nothing to eat here."

"Yes, on what?" Asher asked Madam Delome. "It could be days before the Russians find us. With nothing here to eat, the only thing they will liberate is our bones," he pointed out.

Ever so slowly the Frenchwoman turned to Hannah until the girl's eyes met hers. Then, she looked over to where the two horses were tethered. Without having to say a word, Hannah knew what she was thinking. Bowing her head, Hannah ever so slowly nodded her assent, bracing herself even as she was doing so for yet another in what was, for her, a never-ending string of heart-wrenching farewells.

❋

No one was paying a bit of attention to what was going on around them as the former prisoners huddled about several small fires near the woodcutter's hut. They chatted with each other while gorging themselves on strips of horseflesh they had roasted by holding it stuck to the ends of sticks or skewered on spits resting upon "y" shaped braches set on either side of the fires. Hannah, wanting no part of what they were doing, and not wishing to let them see her cry as they slaughtered her beloved Pixie, had retreated to where she had spent the previous night. There she sat between the empty saddles with her back to the others, covering her ears with her hands as she desperately tried to block out the sound of people enjoying themselves. The only solace she had when the time had come to slaughter the horses was one of the men in Rabbi Asher's group had been a butcher. He was able to dispatch Pixie as quickly and painlessly as had been humanly possible, a blessing so many of those who had been delivered into the care of her father had been denied.

❁

The same smell of meat roasting over an open fire that was so distressing to Hannah served to guide a group of soldiers to the clearing. With well-practiced cunning and stealth, they deployed into a skirmish line, advancing through the woods toward the unsuspecting refugees. When they were close enough, each of them eased into a crouched position or dropped to one knee before flicking the safeties off their weapons as they await the order to go forward. Only when he saw all was ready did the platoon commander cautiously ease out from behind his concealed position. Tightly clutching the grip of his pistol with his right hand, he slowly raised his left arm, waved it forward, and began to advance.

A sudden flurry of crisp orders shouted out in German accompanied by a woman's terrified scream caused Hannah to jump to her feet and look around. At first, she thought some of her father's men from the camp had come back for them, just as Asher and a few of the others had feared. Only when she saw the uniforms of the German soldiers, the eclectic nature of their equipment, and the manner in which they were overrunning the primitive encampment did she realize they were combat troops. If they were Wehrmacht, Hannah reasoned as she took off running toward them, they all had a chance. But if they were Waffen SS, there would be no hope, not even for her.

A grizzled veteran wearing a white parka saw Hannah first, causing him to bring his weapon to bear on her. Without needing orders to do so, others followed suit, swinging around and away from the pathetic creatures they had fallen upon and toward what they at first thought was a real threat.

Wide-eyed, Hannah stopped short, thrusting out her right arm with the palm of her hand up. "No! Don't shoot. I am German."

Having learned their trade in the cauldron of battle, none of the soldiers relaxed their stance. They knew Russian and Polish partisans spoke and understood German, a skill they put to good use to lure unwary landsers into an ambush. Only when their platoon commander decided Hannah presented no immediate danger to them did he signal his men to lower their weapons. Still, a few of the NCOs continued to regard the only person there who bore any resemblance to a German with wary eye while keeping their weapons trained on her.

After holstering his pistol, the officer began to approach Hannah. "Who are you? And what in the hell are you doing here with them?"

A sense of relief swept over Hannah when she noticed the insignia on the collar of his tunic worn on the outside his camouflage parka marked him as being an officer in the Wehrmacht. With that in mind, she conjured up a story she hoped he would buy into. Reaching out, she took him by the arm and led him far enough away from the refugees so they could not hear what she was saying. "Herr Leutnant, I cannot tell you how glad I am to see you, though I must admit I am a little disappointed."

Wondering if he had heard the girl correctly, the German officer pulled away ever so slightly. His expression told Hannah he was trying to determine if he had heard her right. Doing her best to muster up a dismissive little smile, Hannah explained. "My father is, or I should say was, the camp commandant at Borkow," she proclaimed calmly. "We were part of a column headed west to Germany. Unfortunately, we became separated from them in the night."

Having seen the confusion and chaos on the roads, which was why he had decided to go through the woods rather than deal with it, the German platoon commander appreciated how such a thing could have happened. Still, he asked her why they were just sitting around rather than continuing their flight and why, in God's name, she had stayed with them.

Flashing him a smile that was as innocent as it was forced, she looked up at the officer who was not that much older than her, regarding him for a moment as if he had just asked her the silliest question she had ever heard. "I have to stay with them until my father returns for us, Herr Leutnant. Were I to do otherwise I would be guilty of neglecting my duty to him and the Reich."

After giving his head a quick shake, the officer frowned. "But you can't stay here. The Russians are right behind us, no more than a few hours from here."

Tilting her head, Hannah brushed aside the officer's concern. "Herr Leutnant, if you were a father, would you leave your only daughter, not to mention all these valuable workers, behind to be taken by the Russians?"

Looking over to where the refugees had huddled together, the officer didn't see a single one among them who looked as if they could do anything of value. Still, he concluded, this wasn't a matter he needed to concern himself with. His orders were to cover the retreat of his battalion, not look after a silly girl and a motley collection of Jews.

As the officer was going over this in his mind, Hannah could not help but notice the way some of his men were staring at the meat the refugees had left roasting over the fires. "Your men, are they hungry?"

The platoon commander grunted. "We've not seen our cooks or mess wagon in days. Knowing them, I expect the worthless louts are already in Berlin."

"Well, would you care to join us? We have plenty of food to spare."

This time, when he looked about and saw the expressions on the faces of his men, he could not help but notice the way they were eyeing the food. "I suppose we could use a rest."

With feigned cheerfulness, Hannah beamed. "Good." With that, she turned to where Madam Delome, who was still wearing the military greatcoat, boots, and forage cap had been watching them. As the two locked eyes for a moment, Hannah did her best to reassure the Frenchwoman using only her eyes before calling out to her in German to have some of the women standing behind her to see to it the soldiers were fed.

Like Hannah, Madam Delome appreciated just how precarious their situation was. She also understood what the girl was doing. With a nodded, she acknowledged both Hannah's order as well as the role she was expected to play. Turning about, she took a moment to lock eyes with several of the women she knew she could count on to obey her without question and without going to pieces before quietly instructing them to feed the German soldiers. Having bowed to their every demand for months, Madam Delome and the women she had selected prepared themselves to endure one last indignity, hoping that by doing so they could manage to survive the next few hours.

From where she watched, it came as no surprise to Hannah the German soldiers were just as uncomfortable being fed by the Jewish women as the Jewish women were. How odd, Hannah found herself thinking, that even when they were in such direr want of the most basic of all requirements a human needed to survive, the soldiers could not set aside the senseless bigotry drilled into their heads. Whether they, like she, would ever be able to do so was something Hannah found herself wondering.

In time, the sound of artillery that continued to reverberate all around them caused the German soldiers to hurriedly wolf down the roasted horseflesh they had been given as people who had all but given up hope of ever seeing another day looked on in silence.

❄

It was late afternoon when the sound of a vehicle's engine once more brought the refugees, now all clustered about the woodcutter's hut, to their feet and away from the fires where they had been struggling to warm themselves. Unlike the Germans, the pair of American-made White Scout cars bearing red stars came crashing out of the woods and into the center of the clearing like rampaging predators. Crouched low behind the thin armor plate of their vehicles, Russian soldiers in the rear of the cars trained their submachineguns on the huddled mass of refugees.

Unlike before, Hannah did not step forward, for she understood all too well what the Russians would do to her if they discovered she was German. It was Asher who took the lead this time, as an officer hopped down from the lead scout car even before it had come to a full stop and looked about, taking in the pathetic scene before him. He had no need to ask who the refugees were. Having heard reports of what the Germans had done to the Jews and seen how they had treated his own people in that area of Russia that had been occupied, the officer knew all too well who they were. Instead, in broken Polish, he asked Asher what he knew about the area and if there were any German troops about.

The temptation to go over and lose herself among the Jews was overpowering for Hannah. She knew she should have done so as soon as she had heard the rumble of the Russian scout cars. It would have been the smart thing to do. Yet she found she was unable to. Although she had finally come to accept she could never truly be the daughter of Ernst Richter, at least not the kind of daughter a man in his position was expected to have, Hannah could not deny he had carefully modeled her in ways that could not easily be undone. Her father, her German father, had taught her to stand tall and face her fear with scorn in her eyes and courage in her heart. For her to suddenly run over to where the Jews were gathered, to seek safety among a people she had turned her back on in every way imaginable would be more than wrong, Hannah sadly concluded. Having denied her heritage for so long, to seek their protection now would be the height of hypocrisy and an act of cowardliness that went against the way she had been raised. So she stood her ground. While it was foolish to do so, she did not have it in her to do otherwise.

It didn't take long for some of the soldiers who had climbed down out of their scout cars to notice Hannah. Right off they saw her for what she was, a German female, someone who was not only fair game, but would provide them with a means of extracting a modicum of revenge for what the Germans had done to their own wives, sisters, and mothers. After discussing the matter among themselves to see who would do the honors, a trio began to make their way over toward Hannah.

Realizing what was about to happen, Madam Delome slipped off the German military greatcoat she had been wearing and ran over to where Hannah was standing stock still, waiting to be taken by the Russians.

The Frenchwoman's screams of protestation and the sudden flurry of activities caused both Asher and the Russian officer to interrupt their parley and rush over to where Madam Delome had interposed herself between the German girl and the three soldiers. As before, the Russian officer had no need to ask what was going on. He only wished to know why the woman was foolishly trying to protect the German girl.

At a loss for how to best explain what was going on, Asher translated the Russian's question into German for Madam Delome. By way of answering, she moved behind Hannah, proudly drawing herself up as she placed her hands upon the girl's shoulders, all the while glaring at the Russian officer as she replied to Ashe's question in German. "Tell him she is my daughter. Tell him that if his men wish to take her, they must go through me."

Asher was still in the midst of translating Madam Delome's response when something happened that Hannah could not believe, much less understand. One of the women who had heard what Madam Delome had told Asher and understood what she was doing left the huddled mass of refugees and went over to join her and Hannah. Then another, and another, and another. Before long some of the men led by Gavi joined them as well. Eventually, as Asher and the Russian officer watched in silence, all of the refugees made their way over to Hannah and circled her.

Befuddled, the Russian officer first looked at Asher, then over at the trio of soldiers who had stopped in their tracks before casting his gaze skyward. Noticing it was growing dark, and having no wish to waste any time here sorting out a trivial matter that had no military significance whatsoever, he turned away from the refugees and ordered his men to mount up.

None of the former prisoners moved until the pair of scout cars had disappeared back into the forest headed west, toward Germany. Hannah was the first to do so. Turning around, she faced Madam Delome. She wished to thank the woman for what she had done. She needed to. Yet words did not seem adequate to express the gratitude she felt for the selfless act she had just witnessed, an act of courage she felt she was undeserving of. So instead of words, Hannah slipped a hand into the pocket of the coat she was wearing and pulled out a strand of pearls she had been waiting for the right time to present to the Frenchwoman.

Taking an end in each hand, Hannah reached up around the Frenchwoman's neck. "I know these are not yours, but they are not mine either, not anymore," she murmured as she fastened the clasp and stepped back.

Without taking her eyes off of Hannah's, Madam Delome reached up and gently ran the tips of her fingers across the strand of pearls resting upon the stripped smock dress adorned with nothing but a number and a yellow Star of David. Though it was an odd sight, it was both fitting and appropriate as two souls who had thought they had lost everything reached out to each other and embraced. Though neither knew what lay ahead, both realized that whatever the future held, they would never again be alone.

CHAPTER TWENTY-SIX

FIFTY-SEVEN DPs

Before heading off to his own office, Lt. Col. George Keating turned to his fellow JAG officer just as he was about to duck into his. "Will you be joining us later tonight? Ted claims to have found a gasthaus where the squareheads serve cold beer."

As much as Lt. Col. David Westerfeld would have loved to, he knew it would be a mistake to take the night off. With the sudden and inexplicable loss of every witness he had been relying on in the case he was putting together against Ernst Richter, he all but needed to go back and start from scratch. While everyone involved in the case told him he already had more than enough to proceed with just the evidence he had covering Richter's activities at Oranienburg, Westerfeld had been counting on the testimony the DPs who had been prisoners at Borkow were to provide to assure Richter would hang for his crimes. Just how the damned Brits had managed to "misplace" fifty-seven full-grown adults and a dozen orphans, displaced Jews who didn't have a pot to piss in, was beyond him. Reluctantly, and with a shake of his head, Westerfeld begged off. "Sorry George, not tonight. Maybe this weekend."

Keating knew better than to argue with his friend. Though Westerfeld's ancestors had left Germany centuries before to settle in York, Pennsylvania when it had been the western frontier of a nation as yet unnamed, the hardnosed Dutchman could be just as dogged and pigheaded as the Nazis they were working to bring to justice. Not that that was a bad thing. After all, who better to have prosecuting the bastards than one of their own? "Sure thing. Just remember, don't let this whole DP thing get you down. We'll nail 'em, every last one of 'em. It's just going to take a little more effort on our part."

With that, the two men parted.

Upon entering his office, the female clerk who doubled as his secretary looked up from the document he had sent back to her to be retyped. "Sir, a Major Burnet from G-2, Office of Military Government in Frankfurt called while you were out."

"Did he leave a message?" Westerfeld asked eagerly.

"No, sir. He did ask that you return his call."

"Be a dear, Carol, and get a hold of him. When you have him on the line, put it through to my office."

Though he had no idea if the call was related to the missing Borkow DPs, Westerfeld was feeling lucky. After hitting stonewall after stonewall as of late, it was time something broke in his favor. Unfortunately, the news Major Keith Burnet had to share with him wasn't it.

A dyed-in-the-wool Texan if ever there was one who spoke with a drawl that flowed from his mouth like the Brazos, Burnet took his sweet time getting around to the point. "Well, Colonel, I have some good news for you and a whole parcel of bad news. It seems we've finally been able to identify the two people who met with the characters you were asking about up in the British DP camp. Well, actually, we didn't. The British did," Burnet corrected himself while chuckling.

"And?" Westerfeld asked impatiently.

"The older of the two is named Delome, a Margarette Delome. She's French. A concert pianist who plays longhair stuff, you know, stuff like Mozart and Beethoven."

"What's her connection with the Borkow DPs?"

"It seems Margarette Delome and the other woman who claimed to be her daughter were at Borkow as well."

Reaching over with his free hand, Westerfeld took up a file containing a list of known survivors of the Borkow concentration camp, flipped it open, and quickly leafed through it until he found Margarette Delome's name. "I don't see any mention of a daughter," he muttered as he ran his finger down the page to make sure he hadn't missed anything. "Does the daughter have a married name she might have been using while at Borkow?"

With a deep, audible sigh, Burnet continued. "No, sir, not that we know of."

"Well then, is she on another list of former prisoners, one more current than the one dated 6 August 1945?"

"Oh, you won't find her name on any lists of former prisoners. You see, Colonel, it just so happens Margarette Delome never had a daughter, at least one the French government knows about."

Tiring of the major's roundabout manner, Westerfeld all but growled. "Well, do we know who this other woman was and what her involvement in this affair is?"

"You sittin' down, Colonel?"

"Yes, Major, I'm sitting down," Westerfeld muttered as he fought to keep his temper in check.

"The Brit officer I spoke to described the other woman as being twenty years old, a blond with striking blue eyes who called herself Hannah Sander."

"I take it that's not her real name."

"No, sir, it's not."

By now Westerfeld was on the verge of losing his patience. "Well, Major, are you going to tell me her real name?"

"It's Richter, Hannah Richter."

Unable to help himself, Westerfeld lurched forward, all but rising out of his seat. "Excuse me?"

"You heard right," Burnet confirmed. "The adopted daughter of Ernst Richter."

Westerfeld didn't bother to ask why she was visiting DPs who had once been prisoners of a camp her father had run. He had no need. The dossier they had on her left no doubt the woman had been a committed Nazi, a true believer who had remained at her adopted father's side until the very end at Borkow. All had assumed she'd died during the flight of German civilians from the east. To suddenly have her show up like this, out of the clear blue, was ominous and more than a little disturbing. Setting aside his concerns as to what this would mean for the fifty-seven missing DPs and the orphans they'd taken with them for the moment, he asked Burnet what the good news was, hoping as he did so it was that the Richter girl was in custody and the Borkow DPs had been found.

"I'm afraid that was the good news, Colonel," Burnet replied.

Groaning, Westerfeld slumped back in his seat as the G-2 major told him how Margarette Delome and Hannah Richter, using Swiss passports, had crossed into the British zone from Holland and visited the DP camp two days before the Borkow DPs and orphans went missing. "The two women met twice with that rabbi you're interested in, the one named Asher, as well as a Pole called Gavi," Burnet explained.

"Do the British know what they discussed?"

"They haven't a clue. The report they forwarded to me on the incident does mention Delome and the German girl were quite well dressed, if that's of any help to you."

It was, but Westerfeld was in no mood to share his suspicions with the G-2 major. Instead, he asked what was being done to track the women and missing DPs down.

"Well, naturally, we've alerted everyone to keep an eye out for them. We've even notified the Russians, though I hardly think the Richter woman would be fool enough to go that way. They and their Polish toadies want to nail Richter almost as bad as you do. As for the DPs and the orphans they took with them, I don't expect they'll be all that hard to find. I mean, where can fifty-seven Polish and Ukrainian Jews dragging twelve kids along with them who don't have a dime to their name go? The women, well that's another story, I'm afraid. According to the Brits, they were throwing money around like it was going out of style."

"Did the British happen to tell you what were they spending it on?"

"Clothes, mostly," Burnet replied. "The Brit I spoke to, a Scotsman with an accent you could cut with a knife, said the Germans up there are like the ones in our zone, willin' to sell just about anything if the price is right, even the shirt of their back."

Annoyed as much by Burnet's manner as what he was saying, Westerfeld took a moment to absorb this latest setback. He had to come up with some way of salvaging a situation that was going downhill at an alarming rate. "Did you think to have someone check with Richter's parents? They are, after all, taking care of his two sons, Siegfried and Wolfgang."

"Oh, you've no need to worry 'bout that, Colonel," Burnet replied with an air that came across as being a little too self-assured, given how everything else connected with this aspect of the case against Richter had been playing out. "Our people in Munich have been watching them like a hawk for months, especially that unrepentant little thug of a boy. He's been running messages for a bunch of local fanatics who haven't quite figured out the war's over and they lost. If Hannah Richter so much as shows her face there or tries to leave Germany, we'll have her before she knows what hit her."

Not at all reassured, Westerfeld asked Burnet to keep him posted before hanging up. That a woman such as Margarette Delome would stand by and watch her fellow prisoners be slaughtered at the behest of Hannah Richter so they would not be able to testify against her father was all but inconceivable to Westerfeld. The very idea sickened him. Had anyone even suggested such a thing as little as a year ago, he would have laughed in their face. Now, however, nothing surprised him. He had learned what had gone on in the camps men like Ernst Richter had run. Report after report recounted how the Nazis had brutalized prisoners until they had literally turned on their own, using Jews to shepherd their fellow Jews right up to the doors of the gas chambers. As to why they had taken the children, well, that was even a greater mystery. Unfortunately, if there was one thing the JAG officer had learned from the time he'd spent putting together cases against the former SS officers who had authored what they had called the Final Solution, it was that people were capable of just about anything.

Leaning forward, Westerfeld clasped his hands together on the desk and took to gazing at the stack after stack of files piled before him. They contained reports of material pilfered from Jews and other prisoners who had been sent to Borkow from all over occupied Europe to be murdered or worked to death. As damning as such evidence was, without a witness who had been there to put a face on it, who had suffered at Richter's hands, he would have a much harder time seeing to it Richter got what he deserved.

Westerfeld's only regret was that he wouldn't be able to personally march the bastard into one of his own gas chambers before stuffing his worthless corpse into an oven, just as he had done to men, women, and children whose only crime had been to be born to the wrong parents. It was a sentiment shared by many of his fellow officers who had been selected to bring captured Nazis to trial for crimes against humanity, crimes he still had difficulty coming to terms with. Well, he thought as he eased back into his seat, perhaps the bastard will find justice in the Hereafter when he comes face to face with all the countless thousands he sent to their deaths, provided, of course, he goes to the same place the Jews have gone.

As quickly as that thought came to mind, the JAG officer dismissed it. If there were a Heaven and Hell, Richter wouldn't be sharing the former with the Jews. They had already seen their Hell. Now it was up to him to see that Richter found his.

Bremerhaven, January 1946

The sound of a horn belonging to a vehicle stopped at the pole barrier just outside the guardshack next to it drew a collective groan from the trio of American MPs on duty. All took to exchanging glances to determine which of them would leave the relative warmth of the guard shack and venture out into the freezing rain that had been lashing their cozy little refuge all night. Jeff Novak, an eighteen-year-old private who had joined the unit just before the end of hostilities, knew without being told he would be the one his sergeant would wind up tagging. He always got the shit details. Always. Still, Novak was determined he wasn't going to go until he was told.

"Well?" Staff Sergeant William Emerson finally growled as he stared at the young private. "What are you waiting for, kid? A personal invitation?"

Knowing it was pointless to argue with the veteran NCO, Novak slowly came to his feet and moved away from the coal-fired stove glowing cherry red and over to a row of hooks next to the door. There he took his time pulling his overcoat on, slipping a flashlight into a pocket of the coat, and slinging his carbine over his shoulder, muttering to himself all the while. Only when he had braced himself to venture into the teeth of the storm whipping in off the North Sea did Novak open the door. Even so, the blast of cold air and freezing rain that hit him full on took his breath away.

"Hey! Do you live in a barn?" Emerson bellowed from across the room. "Close the goddamned door."

With head bowed and shoulders hunched into the wind, Novak made his way to the military sedan parked before the red and white pole barrier. Only when he had reached what he thought was the driver's door did he realized it was a British vehicle and the person rolling down his window was a passenger. With one hand clutching the collar of his overcoat tightly about his throat and the other grasping the sling of his carbine, Novak made no effort to sort out whom he was addressing before he spoke. "It's after midnight, Mac," he whined plaintively. "What do ya want?"

"That would be Captain Mac to you, soldier," a distinctively English voice replied haughtily.

Realizing he was on the verge of really stepping in it, Novak let go of his collar, reached into his coat pocket, and pulled out his flashlight. Flicking it on, he flashed it in the officer's face.

"If you don't mind, I would appreciate it if you wouldn't shine your torch in my eyes."

A glance was all Novak needed to see he really was being addressed by a British Army captain. Knowing the Limeys were sticklers when it came to proper military courtesy, and not wishing to piss off the captain to the point where he insisted on dragging Emerson out to dress him down, Novak came to attention and attempted to salute, forgetting as he was doing so he was holding his flashlight in his right hand.

It took every bit of Captain Lev Harel's willpower to keep from chuckling to himself as the American MP fumbled about after hitting the brim of his own white helmet liner with his torch. Instead, he assumed a suitably impatient tone of voice delivered with the pitch-perfect English accent he used at times like this. "Could we get on with this? We have a very tight schedule to meet."

"Sorry sir," Novak muttered as he struggled to sort himself out. "May I ask what your business is and your destination?"

"We're here to deliver a group of DPs to a ship bound for Italy," Harel stated crisply as he was offering up the forged orders he'd been traveling under for the American's inspection.

It was only then that Novak bothered to look up and saw there was a pair of military buses behind the sedan he was standing next to.

"Oh, yeah. And them?" he asked as he aimed the beam of his flashlight back into the sedan and at the pair of women seated in its backseat.

"They are representatives of the United Nations Relief and Rehabilitation Administration. They are responsible for seeing to it the DPs we're escorting reach their final destination without mishap," Harel replied, once more making it amply clear by his manner he was on the verge of losing his patience.

Novak knew he should have asked to see their papers as well as inspect each of the buses to ensure all the people in them were listed on the travel orders and had proper identification. But he didn't, suspecting he was on the verge of a royal ass chewing, one the British officer would begin and his own sergeant would finish. Besides, he wasn't in the mood to stay out in the pelting, freezing rain any longer than was necessary. Eager to return to his spot next to the stove, the shivering private stepped away from the sedan and made his way over to the pole barrier.

As he waited for the American MP to wave them through, Harel snickered. "Well Mademoiselle, that was far easier than I expected." Though he was always sorely tempted to address the younger of the two women who had masterminded and underwritten this exploit as *Fräulein,* Harel appreciated that no matter what her motivations were, the German girl was a valuable asset. Both he and the other former members of the Jewish Brigade who had more or less taken over the Bricha would need to rely on strange allies like her to succeed in smuggling their fellow Jews out of Europe and into Palestine. Besides, Harel suspected, had he shown her even the slightest disrespect he would have incurred the unbridled wrath of the French woman and the Ukrainian rabbi. They all but fawned over the German girl as if she were their own daughter and not someone who belonged to a race that had been the author of their suffering. So the captain, who had once served King and Country as part of the Jewish Brigade, but now answered to the Haganah, kept his own counsel as he signaled his driver to proceed with nothing but a nod.

In the back seat, Hannah let out a breath she had been holding once they were clear of their last obstacle. Relieved as well, Madam Delome reached across the seat, took the young woman's hand and squeezed it in a manner that reminded Hannah of the day a stranger had taken it at the Berlin Hauptbahnhof and led her away.

EPILOGUE

Still reeling from the shock of another failed assault on the Latrun police fort, Yanni Ben-Heim was slowly making his way back to the village schoolhouse that served as the headquarters of the brigade his ad hoc unit had been assigned to when he was waylaid by the young woman who served as his adjutant. "I know this is not a good time, Yanni," she stated quietly, "but I need you to identify some of the dead whose names I am unsure of before we bury them."

Though sorely tempted to pass the task off to someone else, Yanni had no wish to saddle another with such a grim chore. After wiping the sweat from his brow with a filthy rag, he followed the fair-haired, blue-eyed girl to where all the dead who had been recovered from the wheat field where their last attack had faltered were neatly laid out in the late afternoon sun. Ever so slowly, the Haganah officer made his way along the line of lifeless men and women who had come to the land of their ancestors in the hope they would find a home they could call their own, a place free of the persecution that had pushed their people to the brink of extinction. Though disappointed they would have to fight for the peace they so craved, all had taken up the rifle without complaint or reservation. Well, Yanni thought as he called off the names of those who had willingly followed him into battle, *at least some of them have at last found peace, if only in death.*

He was nearing the end of this grim task when he found himself looking down at a face curiously peaceful and unmarked. Odd as it was, it was only then that he realized he only knew the German girl's first name despite her being one of his best fighters, a young woman who tended to be aggressive to the point of being reckless. Many a time, he had found himself having to hold her back, checking her desire to press home the attack. No more, Yanni thought. Eyes that had so often flashed like brilliant sapphires as the battle was joined now stared back dully under a fine coating of yellow dust. Looking up at the faces of those who had come by to pay their last respects to their fallen comrades, he pointed to the girl before him and asked if anyone knew her full name.

"Hannah," muttered a gaunt-faced Polish Jew named Gavi whose time at Borkow had aged him well beyond his years. "Those of us she brought out of Europe knew her only as Hannah."

"We all did," added a dark-eyed sabra who made no effort to hold back her tears. "Even old Rabbi Asher who she looked after never called her anything but Hannah. That's all she ever went by."

Looking back down at the girl, Yanni found himself having to tamp down his emotions. The German girl would not have wanted that. In the short time he had known her, she had never asked for or taken anything for herself, freely sharing whatever she had until she had nothing. Nothing, that is, save the tattered clothes on her back, the rifle she carried, and a cold, uncompromising resolve to fight for the homeland all Jews could call their own, a resolve not even he could match.

Drawing himself up, Yanni forced himself to set aside his grief. He was a commander. He needed to be strong, even at a time such as this. "On her marker, put down . . ."

Once more he paused, struggling as he did so to stifle his emotions. "Put down *Hannah, Daughter of Israel.*"

With that taken care of, he drew himself up and looked over at the hodgepodge collection of men and women he commanded who felt no need to hold back their tears. "*This* year," he croaked as the grief he felt for those who would never stand before the Temple's West Wall threatened to overwhelm his best efforts to keep it in check. "This year in Jerusalem," he muttered once more under his breath as if to rededicate himself to the grim task that lay ahead.

With that, Yanni turned and walked away. There was much to be done if Hannah's sacrifice was to have meaning and the peace she had struggled to find was to be won, if not for her, then for her people.

Israel, June 1949

For the longest time, no one spoke as the gathered mourners stood quietly before the shrouded marker, each lost in their memories. Some thought of loved ones who would never have a monument such as the one before them they would be able to visit. Others recalled the long, horrific ordeal they had endured, a living nightmare that had viciously ripped mothers and fathers, sisters and brothers, other loved ones, and even their humanity from them. All included a prayer of thanks in their solemn musings, not only to the God who had delivered them from their tormentors, but to the agent of their salvation as well, the one to whom the monument before them was dedicated.

Though she wished things could have been otherwise, Margarette Delome took comfort in the words from *Leviticus* Rabbi Asher had had inscribed beneath the simple name the Haganah had interned her under.

> *"I have given it to you upon the altar to make*
> *an atonement for your souls,*
> *for it is the blood that maketh an atonement for the soul."*

The idea that through her death Hannah had atoned for her sins brought peace to the Israeli concert pianist. Those who had known Hannah as well as she did had come to accept it could not have been otherwise.

The young teenager selected by Rabbi Asher to remove the shroud from the monument did not understand the sentiment expressed by the inscription chiseled beneath the name. As she stood gazing down upon it, the girl found it difficult to relate the message it conveyed or the dry, cold stone in which it was etched to the young woman with a smile so at odds with the sadness in her eyes who had taken her by the hand when she had been only nine and led her away from the horrors of her old life. Both seemed too cold, too lifeless, and utterly inadequate. At least, the girl reasoned, the woman who had adopted her had let her set aside her birth name and take the name of the author of her salvation, a woman who had given everything to her people until she had nothing more to give but her life, something, the young girl expected, her savior had done without hesitation, without regret.

Perhaps, Hannah Delome thought as she rejoined the woman whom she now called Mother, she would one day have the opportunity to follow in the footsteps of her namesake by rising above her fears and petty concerns to make a difference in the lives of the people who had taken her in when no one else would have her. In doing so, she hoped she would be able to repay the debt she owed to a girl who was so very different, and yet no different than her.

SS RANKS AND
THEIR US / UK EQUIVALENT

Oberschütze................................ Private 1st Class

Rottenführer .... Corporal

Unterscharführer .... Sergeant

Oberscharführer .... Sergeant First Class

Untersturmführer .... 2nd Lieutenant

Obersturmführer .... 1st Lieutenant

Hauptsturmführer .... Captain

Sturmbannführer ....Major

Obersturmbannführer................... Lieutenant Colonel

Standartenführer .... Colonel

Oberführer .... No US or UK equivalent. An SS rank
between colonel and brigadier

Gruppenführer .... Major General

Reichsführer ....No US or UK equivalent.
A rank just below Hitler

GLOSSARY

Afrika Korps—Units of the Wehrmacht sent to Africa in 1941

Alamanni, Hermunduri, Marcomanni, Quadi, and Suebi—Ancient Germanic tribes

Anschluss—The annexation of Austria into Germany, conducted on 12 March 1938.

Appel—In fencing, stamping the front foot to the ground to produce a sound to distract or startle the opponent.

Arbeit Macht Frei—*"Work sets you free,"* the motto on or over the gates of most German concentration camps

Armia Krajowa—Polish Home Army

Aryan—In the context of Nazi Germany, the Northwestern or European branch of the Indo-European peoples.

Bad Tölz—A town in southern Bavaria, the location of the SS Officer Candidate School.

Bairisch—The Austro-Bavarian branch of the German language.

BDM—Bund Deutscher Madel or League of German Girls, the female component of the German youth movement collectively known as the Hitler Youth movement for girls ten and up. Technically there was no limit to the age a female could remain in the BDM so long as the girl remained unmarried and did not have children.

Beer Hall Putsch—Hitler's failed coup against the Weimar Republic inspired by Mussolini's March on Rome, launched on 8 March 1923 in Munich.

Bir Hakeim—A remote oasis in the Libyan desert where the Afrika Korps fought elements of the 1st Free French Division between 26 May to 11 June 1942 as part of the Battle of Gazala. In Paris, it is the name of the Metro station nearest the Eiffel Tower.

Blood and Honor—This refers to the 1935 anti-Semitic Nuremberg Laws entitled *"The Law for the Protection of German Blood and German Honor."*

Borkow, Poland—A fictional concentration camp patterned after Auschwitz.

Brownshirts—Members of the SA, Sturmabteilung or storm battalions. A paramilitary organization within the Nazi movement. In the early days, it was used to protect Nazi party gatherings as well as disrupt the meetings and gatherings of opposing political parties, particularly the Communists. When the SA became a threat to Hitler's primacy in the Party, on June 29, 1934, its leadership was rounded up by the SS in what was called the Night of the Long Knives. Between 150 and 200 of the SA's senior leaders were killed on that night or shortly after that, effectively eviscerating the SA.

Cimbri—An ancient Germanic or Celtic tribe that fought the Romans in 101 BC

Croissard—A groin strap designed to keep a fencing jacket from riding up during a bout.

Dachau—The first full-scale concentration camp, located sixteen kilometers northwest of Munich, in operation from March 1933 until April 1945. Two hundred thousand prisoners passed through it. Thirty-two thousand died there.

Deutsches Jungvolk—A subdivision of the Hitler Youth for boys ten to fourteen.

Deutschland Über Alles—Germany above all. Originally meant as a call for all German princes and minor kings to put greater priority on a united Germany. During the Nazi era, it came to have sinister connotations, with good reason.

Fast Heinz—The nickname given to Heinz Guderian, father of the German Panzer force and architect of what became known as Blitzkrieg, the modern concept of combined arms tactics centered around the tank, or in German the Panzekampftwagen.

First Position—The initial stance taken by fencers before a bout.

Freikorps—Independently raised military units. In the aftermath of World War I when the German Army was demobilized by the Allies friekorps units, composed of former soldiers and supported by the Weimar Republic, fought Communist uprisings and efforts of the new Polish state to claim more German territory.

Frisian—Of Frisia, the portion of German bordering the North Sea.

Fräu / Fräulein—Mrs / Miss

Führer—German for leader.

G-2—The G stands for general staff; the 2 is the military intelligence section of the staff.

"The German Girl"—A magazine published for the BDM, or League of German Girls.

Gestapo—Short for **Ge**heime **Sta**atspo**l**izei, Nazi Germany's secret state police and the most feared branch of the SS.

Götterdämmerung—Literary *"Twilight of the Gods."* It is the name of one of Richard Wagner's operas that tells of the end of the world.

Grzmiec—Polish for thunder

Haganah—A paramilitary organization formed by the Jews of Palestine during the period of the British Mandate from 1920 to 1948. It later became the core of the Israeli Defense Force.

Hauptbahnhof—Chief or main train station

Hermann, son of Segimerus—The German name for Arminius, the German tribal leader who organized and led the Germans during the Battle of Teutoburg Forest in 9 AD that destroyed three Roman legions and ended Rome's eastward expansion beyond the Rhein River.

HJ—Short for Hitler Youth, the Nazi Party's youth movement for children from age ten to eighteen.

Juden—German for Jew

Kolberg—Once part of Brandenburg, it is now known as Kołobrzeg, a city in the Polish province of West Pomerania.

Kristallnacht—Night of Broken Glass, a nationwide attack on Jews, their property, and synagogues that took place on the night of November 9–10, 1938 in the wake of the murder of the German diplomat Ernst vom Rath by Herschel Grynszpan, a German-born Polish Jew in Paris, France.

Krupp Kfz 70 lorry—A six-wheeled German military lorry, commonly known as the Krupp Protze.

Kurfürstendamm—The most famous and most fashionable avenue in Berlin, the German equivalent of the Avenue des Champs-Élysées.

"La Chasse"—French for the hunt, usually referring to fox hunting.

Landser—A term used when referring to the common German soldier, the equivalent to the American *G.I.*, the British *"Tommy,"* and the French *"Poilu."*

Lehnitzsee—A lake north of Berlin in Brandenburg. Oranienburg is located on its western shores.

Leibstandarte—Body standard or bodyguard. The Leibstandarte was Adolf Hitler's personal bodyguard. It grew into a regiment, then the 1ˢᵗ SS Panzer Division.

Lorelei Rock—A rock on the eastern bank of the Rhein River near St. Goarshausen, which marks the narrowest part of the Rhein. Because a number of boats had accidents there, a legend grew up of how an enchanting female's singing lured men to their deaths on the rocks. It was made famous by Heinrich Heine in his poem, *Die Lore-Ley.*

Mark—Short for Deutschmark, the primary German monetary unit until replaced by the Euro. In 1938 there were 2.5 DMs to the 1938 U.S. dollars and 12.4 DMs to the 1938 Pound Sterling.

Mauthausen—A concentration camp twenty kilometers from Linz, Austria in operation from August 1938 to May 1945. Approximately 195,000 prisoners passed through it. An estimated 95,000 died there.

Mausi—Little mouse, a term of endearment.

Mercedes-Benz 770—A luxury automobile built between 1930 and 1943. It was known as the Grosser Mercedes.

Mischling—Crossbreed in German. The term was used during the Third Reich to denote persons deemed to have only partial Aryan ancestry. According to the Nuremberg Law of 1935, people who had two Jewish grandparents were classified Mischling of the first degree. Someone with only one Jewish grandparent was Mischling of the second degree.

Munich Soviet Republic—Also known as the Bavarian Soviet Republic. It was proclaimed independent of the newly formed Weimar Republic on 6 April 1919 and brought down by 3 May by the German Army and friekorps units.

Mutti—Short for mutter, or mother

National Socialists—The Nazi Party. Its full title was National Socialist German Workers' Party and abbreviated NSDAP.

NCO—Non-commissioned officer, lance corporal to sergeant major.

Odin—A chief god in the Norse pantheon of gods. The Nazis used Odin to replace St. Nicholas (Santa) during the Yule Holidays (Christmas).

Oma—German slang for grandmother

Opa—German slang for grandfather

Oranienburg—A town 35 kilometers north of Berlin in Brandenburg. In addition to being where Sachsenhausen concentration camp was located, Oranienburg was the center of Germany's nuclear energy project. The Soviets believed the American March 1945 bombing of the facility involved in this work was aimed at denying it to them.

Ostmark—The name given to Austria after the Anschluss. It means "the Eastern Province."

Panzer—German for armor, a term used for all tanks.

Passata-sotto—An evasive action in fencing which is initiated by dropping a hand to the floor and lowering the body under the opponent's oncoming blade. Often accompanied by a straightening of the sword arm to attempt a hit on the opposing combatant.

Piste—The fencing area, roughly 14 meters by 2 meters, where bouts are conducted.

Platen knob—On a manual typewriter, it rotates the platen or the roller around which the paper rests during typing.

Polish Home Army—In Polish, the Armia Krajowa. It was the dominant resistant movement in Poland during World War II. Its largest operation was Operation Tempest, the 1944 Warsaw uprising.

Psalm 100—Part of the Jewish daily prayer service, recited as part of the Songs of Thanksgiving.

Quadriga—A chariot drawn by four horses driven by Victoria, the Roman goddess of victory that sits upon the Brandenburg Gate in Berlin

Reich—A term applied to Germany during various periods of history, with the First Reich being the Holy Roman Empire, the Second Reich the German Empire founded in 1871 and the Third Reich being Nazi Germany.

Reichsbank—The central bank of Germany from 1876 to 1945.

Reich Ministry of Public Enlightenment and Propaganda—The ministry run by Dr. Joseph Goebbels. It was responsible for controlling the press and regulating the German culture.

Romani—A people who trace their origins to the Indian subcontinent.

Sabra—A term used to describe a Jew born in Israeli territory.

Sachsenhausen—A suburb of Oranienburg where the Sachsenhausen (House of Saxons) Concentration Camp was located. In operation from July 1936 until April 1945. Approximately 200,000 prisoners passed through it. One hundred thousand died there. Sachsenhausen became a training center for the Totenkopfverbände. It was also where the SS recruited 142 inmates for *"Operation Barnard,"* the counterfeiting of British bank notes, an effort meant to bring down the British economy. (The 1981 BBC comedy-drama miniseries *Private Schulz* is centered on this effort). During the Soviet era, it was renamed NKVD Special Camp No. 7, then Special Camp No. 1 and was operated by them from August 1945 to 1950. An additional 12,000 people died in the camp under Soviet control due to starvation and disease.

Salle Pleyel—Concert hall in Paris opened in 1839.

Schnecke—Snail, a term of endearment.

"Selection"—The process of sorting prisoners arriving at a concentration camp into those who could be used as slave labor and those who would be immediately sent off to be murdered. The method I describe in this story was used at Auschwitz.

Siegfried legend—Derived from the Sigurd Nordic legends and the centerpiece of Richard Wagner's operas *Siegfried* and *Götterdämmerung*

Social Democratic Workers' Party—A Dutch socialist party.

Sonderbehandlung—Special treatment or special handling, a Nazi euphuism for extermination.

Sonderkommando—Literally "special unit." In the Nazi lexicon, it was a unit made up almost entirely of Jews who assisted in processing those selected to be murdered and the disposal of their bodies.

SS—Schutzstaffel, which translates to protection squadron or defense corps. There were several branches of the SS to include the Totenkopfverbände, the Waffen SS, and the Gestapo.

Stuka—The JU-87 dive bomber

Sudeten Germans –Ethnic Germans living in the border region of Czechoslovakia.

Swastika—An equilateral cross with its arms bent at right angles that dates back to the ancient civilizations of the Indus Valley.

Teutonic—A word derived from the tribe of the Teutons that has come to refer to all Germanic people, their culture, or behavior.

Totenkopf Division—The 3ʳᵈ SS Division of the Waffen SS. Its original complement of personnel was drawn from the ranks of the Totenkopfverbände, hence the name.

Totenkopfverbände—Death's-Head Units, the organization within the SS responsible for administering the concentration camps. Its abbreviation is SS-TV.

United Nations Relief and Rehabilitation Administration (UNRRA)—An international relief agency founded in 1943. The UNRRA planned, coordinated, and administered measures for the relief of victims of World War II. It was the forerunner of the International Refugee Organization.

Unter den Linden—An east-west boulevard in the Mitte District of Berlin, named for the linden trees that line it. The Brandenburg Gate is located on it.

von Moltke—Here, it refers to Helmuth von Moltke the Elder, the Chief of the German General Staff during the German Wars of Unification, (1864–1871).

Wachverband—The original name of the Totenkopfverbände.

Waffen SS—The military branch of the SS. By 1945, it had expanded to over 38 divisions and included foreign units, such as the 5ᵗʰ SS Viking Division, drawn from Scandinavian countries, and even a Muslim Bosniak division, the 13ᵗʰ SS Mountain.

Walther PPK—The 7.65-mm/.32-cal PPK was released in 1931 and immediately became popular with European police and civilians for being reliable and concealable. During World War II they were issued to the German military, police, and the SS. It was the weapon Hitler used to kill himself in 1945. It is also famous as fictional secret agent James Bond's signature gun.

Wehrmacht—Though it means defense forces, which was inclusive of the Army (Heers), the Air Force (Luftwaffe), and Navy (Kriegsmarine), in World War II it came to be used when referring to the German Army.

White Scout cars—An all-wheel-drive 4x4 armored car also known as the M3 Scout Car built by the White Motor Company. Many were sent to the Soviet Union under lend-lease where they were used by reconnaissance units.

Western Front—In Germany, the front in France and Belgium during World War I.

Wirtschafts-Verwaltungshauptamt—Main SS Economic and Administrative Department, responsible for managing the finances, logistics, and business concerns of the SS.

Yuletide—Originally a Germanic pagan celebration held during the winter solstice. During the Nazi era, it replaced the Christmas celebrations using many of the Christmas traditions and songs de-Christianized. For example, instead of placing a star on top of the "Yule" tree, a sun cross was used.

HISTORICAL NOTES

In writing *The Other Side of the Wire,* I have remained true to the events touched upon and stayed within the realm of what was possible and reasonable, especially in relation to Hannah's gender. Hannah and the Richters are fictional. Their experiences and actions are based on the lives of those who perpetrated the Holocaust and the people, organizations, and places they were associated with as well as the historical figures they came in contact with. A brief summary of the historical elements I drew upon or referred to in writing this story not addressed in the text follows.

CHAPTER 1

<u>Nuremberg Laws (*Nürnberger Gesetze*) of 1935:</u>

The Laws for the Protection of German Blood and German Honor

(September 15, 1935) Moved by the understanding that the purity of German blood is essential to the further existence of the German people, and inspired by the uncompromising determination to safeguard the future of the German nation, the Reichstag has unanimously resolved upon the following law, which is promulgated herewith:

SECTION 1

1. Marriages between Jews and citizens (German: *Staatsangehörige*) of German or kindred blood are forbidden. Marriages concluded in defiance of this law are void, even if, to evade this law, they were concluded abroad.

2. Proceedings for annulment may be initiated only by the Public Prosecutor.

SECTION 2

Extramarital sexual intercourse between Jews and subjects of the state of Germany or related blood is forbidden.

- *(Supplementary decrees set Nazi definitions of racial Germans, Jews, and half-breeds or Mischlinge. Jews could not vote or hold public office under the parallel "citizenship" law.)*

SECTION 3

Jews will not be permitted to employ female citizens under the age of 45, of German or kindred blood, as domestic workers.

SECTION 4

1. Jews are forbidden to display the Reich and national flag or the national colors.
2. On the other hand, they are permitted to display the Jewish colors. The exercise of this right is protected by the State.

SECTION 5

1. A person who acts contrary to the prohibition of Section 1 will be punished with hard labor.
2. A person who acts contrary to the prohibition of Section 2 will be punished with imprisonment or hard labor.
3. A person who acts contrary to the provisions of Sections 3 or 4 will be punished with imprisonment up to a year and with a fine, or with one of these penalties.

SECTION 6

The Reich Minister of the Interior in agreement with the Deputy Führer and the Reich Minister of Justice will issue the legal and administrative regulations required for the enforcement and supplementing of this law.

SECTION 7

The law will become effective on the day after its promulgation; Section 3, however, not until January 1, 1936.

CONCENTRATION CAMPS

When they were established in the 1930s, their primary purpose was to house political opponents, those opposed to Nazi rule such as clergymen, and social malcontents, including homosexuals and Romani. The idea of using these prisoners as forced (slave) labor came later. The wholesale imprisonment of Jews began after Kristallnacht and the invasion of Poland, with the ghettos being the first ad hoc concentration camps for them.

There were several types of camps. Some, like Auschwitz, had sub-camps of more than one type. Auschwitz I and III were labor camps, and Auschwitz II (Birkenau) was an extermination camp.

Labor camps: The prisoners were used as slave labor. Death here resulted from malnourishment, disease, overwork, and individual executions as punishment or entertainment. Dachau and Sachsenhausen were classified as labor camps.

Transit camps: Collection points where prisoners were held until they were sent onto other camps. Mechelen in Belgium, Westerbork in the Netherlands (where Anne Frank was held for a month), Bolzano in Italy, and Drancy in France were transit camps.

Extermination camps: These were established after the Wannsee Conference of January 20, 1942, as part of *Operation Reinhard* for the expressed purpose of eliminating the Jewish population of Europe. Only a small handful of prisoners were kept alive upon arrival to serve in the sonderkommando. Treblinka is a prime example of such a camp. Though it covered only some 33 acres and was in operation for less than 15 months, 875,000 prisoners were murdered there. Only 67 who were taken there are known to have survived it.

POW camps: Soviet prisoners of war were treated differently than Western Allied POWs since they were Slavs or untermenchen. Between 3.3 and 3.5 million Soviet POWs, 60% of all taken died in prison camps. The death rate for British POWs held by the Germans, by comparison, was 3.5%.

CHAPTER 4

Soviet Republic of Munich: In April 1919, the socialists who had declared Bavaria a free state the previous November established a Soviet Republic under a left-wing radical playwright by the name of Ernst Toller. Toller's regime collapsed within six days, to be replaced by a communist government led by Eugen Leviné, who immediately began to implement Soviet-style reforms to include expropriating homes from the wealthiest citizens and giving them to the homeless. His government lasted less than a month. In the suppression of the Republic, approximately 1,000 people were killed during the fighting with friekorps units arresting and executing an additional 700.

Friekorps units: While many were small, some such as Marinebrigade Ehrhardt and the Iron Brigade grew to brigade size. A number of leaders of the Nazi party served in freikorps units to include Ernst Röhm, Heinrich Himmler, and Rudolf Hoss, the future commandant of Auschwitz.

SS Wachverband: On 26 June 1933 Himmler appointed Theodor Eiche as the commandant of Dachau. Eiche requested that he be permitted to form an SS guard unit. It was initially called the Wachverband, or guard unit. The name was changed when the SS-Totenkopfverbände (SS-TV) was formally established in 1936.

Theodor Eiche: He was the son of a station master and youngest of eleven children, serving in the 23rd Bavarian Infantry Regiment and winning the Iron Cross, 2nd Class in 1914. After the war, he served as a policeman, a career which ended in 1923 due to his political activities. In August 1930, he joined the SS. When he was arrested for building bombs for use against political opponents, he fled to Italy until the Nazis came to power. In June 1933, he was appointed the commandant of Dachau. It was Eiche, together with his adjutant, who shot Ernst Röhm, leader of the SA at Dachau, after the Night of the Long Knives. Heydrich's failed attempt to take over the running of the camps from Eiche resulted in hostility between the two. Eiche went on to command the SS Totenkopf Division, dying in Russia when his Fiesler Storch was shot down on 26 February 1943.

Reinhard Heydrich: Too young to serve in World War I, he joined the Navy in 1922 as a cadet. In 1926 he was promoted to the rank of ensign. He was dismissed in 1931 due to his dalliances with the daughters of important men. In 1931, Himmler hired Heydrich to organize a counterintelligence division of the SS, which became the Geheime Staatspolizei or Gestapo. He went on to become the governor of Moravia and earned the nickname "The Hangman." On May 27, 1942, four months after he had chaired the Wannsee Conference, he was wounded in an attack in Prague staged by Czechs trained by the British SOE. Heydrich died on June 4, 1942, due to septicemia. In retaliation for his death, Himmler ordered all males over the age of 16 in the village of Lidice killed and the town burned and leveled.

National Socialist German Workers' Party: Founded on January 5, 1919, by Anton Drexler as the German Worker's Party. In July 1919, Adolf Hitler was ordered to join the party by the German Army to spy on it, becoming its 55th member. By July 1921, he had managed to become its undisputed leader. On 24 February 1920, the party was renamed the Nationalsozialistische Deutsche Arbeiterpartei (National Socialist German Workers' Party) or NSDAP, which was shortened by the party's opponents to Nazi and used as a derogatory term.

"Tomorrow Belongs to Me" is a song written by John Kander and Fred Ebb for the 1966 Broadway musical *Cabaret.* Though it is not historical, I used it because it is both powerful and conveys the sense of hope so many young Germans had while the Nazi party was in its ascendency.

CHAPTER 5

Hirschfeld: Magnus Hirschfeld was a German physician and sexologist. He is sometimes called the first advocate for homosexual and trans rights. He founded and ran the Institute for Sexual Research in Berlin from 1919 until 1933 when the Nazis closed it. It was at this institute where Ludwig Levy-Lenz, M.D pioneered gender reassignment surgery.

Ludwig Levy-Lenz: The gynecologist Levy-Lenz worked at Magnus Hirschfeld's Institute for Sexology. During this time, he was one of the first physicians to perform gender reassignment surgery. He also wrote educational materials for the general public, for example about the prevention of STDs. In 1933 he fled to Paris, where he acquired new skills as a cosmetic surgeon. He returned to Berlin in 1935, taking advantage of a sudden climate of tolerance before the 1936 Olympic Games, and opened a surgical practice on the fashionable Kurfürstendamm. He fled Nazi persecution again in late 1936, this time going to Egypt, where he had a very successful career (his first patient was the great singer Om Kalthoum). After WWII, while maintaining his residence in Cairo, he regularly returned to Germany, teaching cosmetic surgery at various hospitals and writing one of the first German textbooks on the subject. His *Memoirs of a Sexologist* contain, among other things, descriptions of his work at Hirschfeld's Institute for Sexology.

CHAPTER 7

Albert Sauer: The first commandant of Mauthausen. He was replaced as commandant by Franz Xaver Ziereis in February 1939.

Adolf Eichmann: One of the primary architects of the Final Solution, he served as the recording secretary at the Wannsee Conference. In 1937, he did travel to the British Mandate of Palestine with his superior Herbert Hagen to assess the possibilities of massive Jewish emigration from Germany to Palestine. They landed in Haifa but could obtain only a transit visa, so they went on to Cairo. There they met Feival Polkes, an agent of the Haganah who discussed with them the plans of the Zionists and tried to enlist their assistance in facilitating Jewish emigration from Europe. Eichmann escaped to Argentina after the war and lived there until captured by the Mossad and taken to Israel for trial. In 1962, he became the only person to be executed by the modern state of Israel.

CHAPTER 11

The Blücher: A German heavy cruiser sunk on April 9, 1940 by Norwegian coastal defenses guarding the approaches to Oslo, Norway. Between 600 and 1,000 sailors and soldiers tasked with seizing Oslo and the Norwegian King in a coup de main perished aboard the Blücher. Its sinking was depicted in the 2016 film *The King's Choice* filmed using the fortifications and guns that sank her.

Marlene Dietrich: She began her film career in Germany, but made her name in Hollywood, sought out by Paramount Pictures as a foil to MGM's Greta Garbo. The Nazi Party approached Dietrich urging her to return to Germany and work. A staunch anti-Nazi with outspoken political views, she became an American citizen in 1937. After Pearl Harbor, she became one of the first Hollywood stars to campaign for the War Bond drive. She conducted tours for troops as well as bond drives during the war. In 1947, she was awarded the Medal of Freedom.

Soldau Concentration Camp: Established in Działdowo, Poland, (German: Soldau), which after the occupation of Poland was part of East Prussia. With the approval of Reinhard Heydrich, Otto Rasch founded the camp in the winter of 1939/40 as a Durchgangslager (Dulag), or transit camp, where political prisoners could be secretly executed. In accordance with Action T4, (euthanasia program), mental patients at sanatoria in East Prussia and Regierungsbezirk Zichenau were taken to the Soldau camp. There 1,558 patients were murdered by the Lange Commando in a gas van from May 21 to June 8, 1940. During the summer of 1941, the Soldau camp was reorganized as an Arbeitserziehungslager (literally "work education camp"). The labor camp's prisoners, divided into separate camps based on gender, engaged in forced agricultural labor. This camp was closed in January 1945. In all, 13,000 out of 30,000 prisoners were murdered at Soldau.

Homosexuals: In 1933, all gay organizations were banned, as were books on the subject. Between 1933 and 1945, an estimated 100,000 men were arrested as homosexuals. Fifty thousand were officially sentenced. An estimated 5,000 to 15,000 of those sentenced were incarcerated in concentration camps.

CHAPTER 12

Totenkopf Division: The 3rd SS Division of the Waffen SS. Its original complement of personnel was drawn from the ranks of the Totenkopfverbände, hence the name.

CHAPTER 13

Pétain:Philippe Pétain. In World War I, he was the French general who won the Battle of Verdun, eventually becoming a Marshal of France. Between the wars, he served in a number of governments. During World War II, he was the Chief of State for the Vichy government, urging his fellow countrymen to collaborate with the Germans. For this, he was branded a traitor, tried after the war, and found guilty. Though he was found guilty and sentenced to be executed, the sentence was commuted to imprisonment for life. He died in 1951.

CHAPTER 14

Synthesized hormones: In 1929, Adolf Butenandt and Edward Adelbert Doisy independently isolated and determined the structure of estrogen. After that, the market for hormonal drug research opened up.

The first effective oral estrogen was Emmenin, derived from the late-pregnancy urine of Canadian women. It was introduced in 1930 by Collip and Ayerst Laboratories. At the same time, a German pharmaceutical company formulated a similar product known as Emmenin that was introduced to German women to treat menopausal symptoms.

Wannsee Conference: Mass killings of about one million Jews had occurred before the conference, but it was only with the decision to eradicate the entire Jewish population that the extermination camps were built and the industrialized mass slaughter of Jews began in earnest. The Wannsee Conference took place in Berlin in the Wannsee Villa on January 20, 1942. The conference was chaired by Reinhard Heydrich acting under the authority given to him by Reichsmarschall Göring. A surviving copy of the minutes of this meeting was found by the Allies in 1947, too late to serve as evidence during the first Nuremberg Trials. Today the Wannsee Villa is a memorial and museum.

In 2001 the BBC/HBO film *Conspiracy* was scripted according to the exact timeframe and minutes of the original meeting.

CHAPTER 16

Borkow Konzentrationslager (concentration camp) is fictional. Descriptions of it in this story are based on accounts of life at several different camps, Auschwitz in particular.

The Horst Wessel Lied or song, also known as "Die Fahne hoch," was the official song of the Nazi party, named after the "martyrdom" of an SA member named Horst Wessel who was shot in the face by an unknown assassin when Wessel answered the door of the apartment belonging to Erna Jänicke, an 18-year-old Berlin prostitute he was living with. The local communist leader was arrested and eventually was executed for the crime. Today the lyrics and tune are illegal in Germany and Austria except for educational purposes. In early 2011, this resulted in an investigation against Amazon and Apple for selling the song to German users.

CHAPTER 17

Transport Trains: Transport trains consisted almost exclusively of freight or cattle cars packed, according to SS regulations, with 50, but sometimes up to 150 occupants. No food or water was provided during the journey, while the freight cars were only equipped with a bucket latrine. A small barred window provided irregular ventilation, which sometimes resulted in deaths from either suffocation or exposure to the elements. Sometimes the Germans did not have enough cars to make it worth their while to make a major shipment of Jews to the camps, so the victims were stuck in a switching yard, sometimes for days. At other times, the trains had to wait for more important military trains to pass. An average transport took about four and a half days. Due to cramped conditions, many deportees died in transit. The longest transport of the war, originating in Greece, took 18 days. When the train arrived at the camp and the doors were opened, everyone was already dead. On August 18, 1940, a Waffen SS officer wrote that he had witnessed at Belzec the arrival of "45 wagons with 6,700 people of whom 1,450 were already dead on arrival." To avoid contamination between loads at times the floor of the freight cars had a layer of quicklime which burned the feet of the human cargo.

Westerbork: A transit camp in the Netherlands. In the period from 1942 to 1945, a total of 107,000 people passed through Westerbork on 93 outgoing trains. These trains left almost every Tuesday for the following concentration camps;

- Auschwitz-Birkenau—65 trains containing 60,330 people, most of whom were gassed on arrival.
- Sobibór- 19 train of 34,313 people, all of whom were killed on arrival.
- Bergen-Belsen and Theresienstadt—9 train of 4,894 people of which 2,000 survived the war.

Only 5,200 of all prisoners who were interned at Westerbork survived, most of them in Theresienstadt, Bergen-Belsen, or liberated when the Western Allies overran the camp. In the summer of 1944, a fifteen-year-old girl by the name of Anne Frank passed through this camp before being put on the first of the three final trains leaving Westerbork on September 3, 1944, for Auschwitz, arriving there three days later.

Yellow Star of David: In the camps, a system of patches worn on clothing, usually triangles, was used to identify the nature of a prisoner. Below are the most common colors and their meaning.

Double yellow: A Jew, although it could be combined with other colors such as one yellow triangle and a red one to identify a Jew who was also a political prisoner.

Red: Political Prisoners

Green: Professional criminals

Blue: Foreign forced labor

Pink: Sexual offenders, mostly homosexuals but also rapists and pedophiles

Purple: Religious, such as Jehovah witnesses as well as Catholic clergy and nuns who broke with official church policy and spoke out against the Nazis. (Note: Of the 2700 ministers who were ultimately imprisoned at Dachau during World War II, over 2600 were Roman Catholic priests, 2000 of whom were ultimately put to death for their efforts to protest against the Nazis.)

Black: Asocial or work shy to include alcoholics, vagrants, pacifists, prostitutes, draft evaders and, oddly enough, lesbians

Brown: Roma

CHAPTER 18

Swiss Banks, the Third Reich, and Corruption in the SS: In the course of World War II, both Allied nations and Germany did business with the Swiss, though being surrounded by Fascist countries, especially after the German occupation of Vichy France in late 1942, cut off all direct Allied contact with Switzerland. People who were trying to protect assets from the Nazis, particularly Jews, opened a number of accounts in Switzerland. Later in the war, when the tides turned against them, many individual Germans did the same.

Corruption in the SS was not unknown. Odds are, it was quite common. Karl Koch, the first commandant of Buchenwald, was shameless when it came to skimming from monies and valuables pilfered from prisoners. His downfall came because of his sudden lavish spending habits and the amount of money he deposited in the Reichsbank. For the crime of stealing from the SS who were stealing from the Jews, Koch was imprisoned. He was tried and executed at

Buchenwald in April 1945. His remains were cremated in the same ovens he oversaw being built. His case, however, was the exception.

CHAPTER 20

The disposition of items collected from incoming prisoners: Money, valuables, and personal items collected from Jews arriving at the camps as described in this chapter was drawn directly from what is called the "Frank Memorandum." Dated September 26, 1942, August Frank of the SS Main Economic Administration Office issued a top-secret memorandum entitled *"Utilization of property on the occasion of settlement and evacuation of Jews"* to the chief administrator of Auschwitz and the SS Garrison commander of Lublin, instructing them on how to deal with material collected.

CHAPTER 22

Women's orchestra: The orchestra mentioned in this chapter was modeled after that which was organized at Auschwitz in June 1943. The character "Madam Delome" is inspired in part by Fania Fénelon, a French pianist, composer, and cabaret singer who was part of the Auschwitz Women's orchestra.

CHAPTER 24

The psychological and emotional trauma experienced by many Germans at the end of World War II, especially their inability to put their trust in anyone or anything such as religion, is adeptly described by Maria Anne Hirschmann in her autobiography, *Hansi, The Girl Who Loved the Swastika.* As a young Sudeten German, she embraced Hitler's new Germany, only to find much of what she was taught to believe in as a member of the Bund Deutscher Madel was a lie.

CHAPTER 26

Nuremberg Military Tribunals: The trial mentioned in this chapter would have been the Pohl Trial, in which eighteen SS officers who participated in administering or overseeing the Final Solution were tried. One of the defendants was August Frank, author of the memorandum used as a reference in writing Chapter 20. While four of the eighteen were condemned to be executed, only Oswald Pohl was. Two were acquitted, and seven were released in 1951 as part of what was known as the 1951 Amnesty. None of the remainder served more than twenty years for their role in the Holocaust.

Displaced Persons: In the immediate aftermath of World War II, there were approximately 11,000,000 displaced persons throughout Europe. Most were former prisoners, forced labor, and refugees. Of these, some 1,500,000 refused to be repatriated. In early 1947, there were still 667,000 DPs in the British, American, and French zones of Germany, many of whom were Jews and Poles.

An organization named Bricha, Hebrew for "escape" or "flight," had been formed in Poland in late 1944 to assist Jews wishing to escape anti-Semitism in Eastern Europe. At the conclusion of hostilities, officers of the British Army's Jewish Brigade took control of Bricha and, together with Hagana, worked to smuggle Jews out of Europe and into Palestine. Incidents such as the 1946 murder of 40 Jews by their neighbors in Kielce, Poland based on nothing more than a false rumor accelerated the flight of Jews from the east. By 1948, Bricha had succeeded in moving 250,000 Jews out of Poland, Romania, Hungry, Czechoslavakia, and Yugoslavia into Germany and Austria. From there, they smuggled as many displaced persons as possible into Palestine through Italy using funds provided by The American Jewish Joint Distribution Committee.

As aptly depicted in the 1947 novel *Gentleman's Agreement* by Laura Z. Hobson and the movie starring Gregory Peck based on it, anti-Semitism did not die with the Third Reich.

EPILOGUE

Latrun police fort: The Battle for Latrun was part of the fight for Jerusalem during the Israeli War of Independence. The fort was built by the British during their mandate in Palestine. Its commanding position allowed it to control the road to Jerusalem. Despite five assaults between May and July 1948 that cost 240 dead and 327 wounded, Israeli forces were unable to wrestle control of the fort from the Arab Legion. In a last desperate bid to break the siege of Jerusalem, a road named the Burma Road was cut through the hills around the fort. The fort did not fall into Israeli hands until 1967 during the Six-Day War. The 1966 movie *Cast a Giant Shadow* featured Kirk Douglas as the American Colonel Mickey Marcus, recruited by David Ben-Gurion to advise the Haganah. It depicts the effort to take the fort as well as the effort to work around it.

Matzevah (monument): In the Hebrew faith, the headstone is known as a matzevah. Although there is no Halakhic obligation to hold an unveiling ceremony, the ritual became popular in many communities toward the end of the 19th century. There are varying customs about when it should be placed on the grave. Most communities have an unveiling ceremony a year after the death. Some communities have it earlier, even a week after the burial. In Israel, it is done after the shloshim, the first thirty days of mourning. There is no restriction about the timing, other than the unveiling cannot be held during certain periods such as Passover or Chol Ha'Moed. At the end of the ceremony, a cloth or shroud covering the headstone is removed, customarily by close family members. Services include reading of several psalms (1, 23, 24, 103), Mourner's Kaddish (if a minyan is available), and the prayer "El Malei Rachamim." The service may include a brief eulogy for the deceased.

Even when visiting Jewish graves of someone that the visitor never knew, it is customary to place a small stone on the grave using the left hand. This shows that someone visited the gravesite, and is also a way of participating in the mitzvah of burial. Leaving flowers is not a traditional Jewish practice. Another reason for leaving stones is to tend the grave. In Biblical times, gravestones were not used; graves were marked with mounds of stones (a kind of cairn), so by placing (or replacing) them, one perpetuated the existence of the site.

ACKNOWLEDGMENTS

I would be remiss if I did not acknowledge the assistance Jennifer K. Ellis, a dear friend and writer in her own right, rendered while I was writing *The Other Side of the Wire.* Her comments, suggestions, and editing of the first very rough drafts of this work, not to mention the emotional support she provided while I was dealing with this subject, were, as they say, priceless.

Thanks, Jenny.